CITY

OF

BROKEN

MAGIC

CITY

OF

BROKEN

MAGIC

❧

MIRAH BOLENDER

A TOM DOHERTY ASSOCIATES BOOK TOR NEW YORK

CITY OF BROKEN MAGIC

Copyright © 2018 by Mirah Bolender

A Tor Book
Published by Tom Doherty Associates
175 Fifth Avenue
New York, NY 10010

www.tor-forge.com

Tor® is a registered trademark of Macmillan Publishing Group, LLC.

The Library of Congress Cataloging-in-Publication Data is available upon request.

ISBN 978-1-250-16927-3 (trade paperback)
ISBN 978-1-250-16926-6 (ebook)

Our books may be purchased in bulk for promotional, educational, or business use. Please contact your local bookseller or the Macmillan Corporate and Premium Sales Department at 1-800-221-7945, extension 5442, or by email at MacmillanSpecialMarkets@macmillan.com.

First Edition: November 2018

Printed in the United States of America

0   9   8   7   6   5   4   3   2   1

DEDICATED TO MY FATHER,

WHO ONCE DESCRIBED HIMSELF AS:

"the sagest person she knows, the inspiration of her life, and the source of all things creative."

ACKNOWLEDGMENTS

The first draft of every book is challenging, so I have many people to thank for helping to whip this story into shape: Firstly, to my family, who I bombarded with what seemed every question under the sun to the point where they groan every time I say "So, about the story . . ." Secondly, to the members of Coe College's manuscript workshop, who witnessed the first-first draft and pointed out the worst of the plot holes. Thirdly, to my agent, Peter Rubie, who saw potential in my writing and worked with me literally for years to help it grow into a proper work. Fourthly, to my editor, Jen Gunnels, whose insight in edits took the story to fantastic new heights, and whose passion and enthusiasm made her an absolute joy to work with.

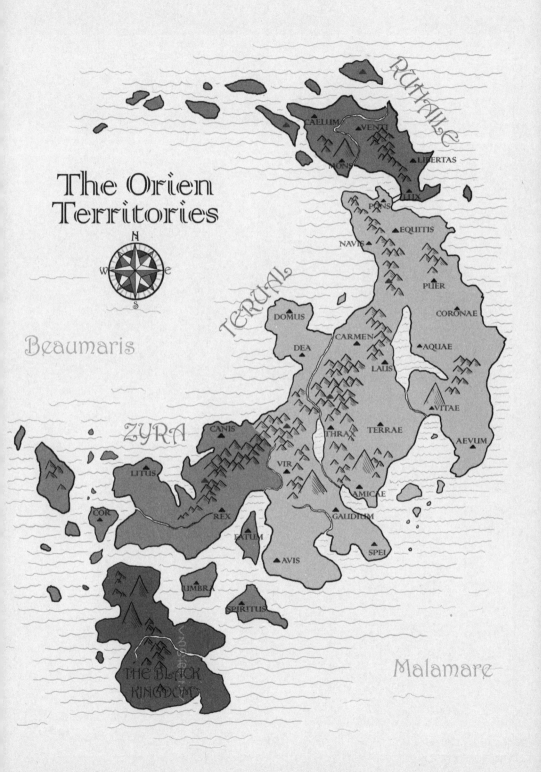

CITY

OF

BROKEN

MAGIC

The first sound was arguing.

Indistinct, deep voices, angry in tone but meaningless in words. They garbled up from below, just loud enough for *it* to take notice.

It stirred slowly, waking from a long sleep in a similar way to your regular human: Shift, roll, stretch, pause for effect. Wait for consciousness to surface properly. This took longer than usual. Hibernation slowed everything, after all. The voices rose, and it grew irritated. Must they really disturb it so soon?

Suitably awake now, it reached out with dark, slimy hands. It met resistance and pondered it before the definition came, unbidden. *Door. That is a door.* And doors had handles, it recalled, stretching one arm to feel at the rest of the surface. The door swung open. The creature seeped out onto the carpet. There was nothing interesting here—the voices were below. Stop the voices for more sleep, more peace. The next door was taller, but easier. The creature branched out to seep and squirm up the vertical surface, tangled itself about the knob, and twisted. Another one down. It kept its weight on the door so the way was cleared and came down to the floor again with a heavy, wet smack. The voices skipped a beat, but it didn't care. It slithered across the ground, forming small arms to propel itself faster. The stairs came up quickly and it slid down them with a more watery movement of its tar-black body.

Light at the bottom of the stairs. It recoiled, milled there in hate and fright. Light, of course humans had light. This didn't burn the same way as the sun, but was still unappreciated. The voices were so close.

It quivered in frustration before lashing out. It spread arms across the hallway, hauling its bulk up at the light fixture. The glow caused its slimy surface to hiss and dry out, but it reached its destination before more damage could be done. The glass smashed under it, and it pressed flat against the ceiling to muffle the sound. The hallway had gone dark. It stayed there, absorbing broken pieces into its body before moving again.

The humans had paused again, their anger colored by unease.

It swarmed across the ceiling, circled its way through the top of the doorway and into the last lit room. Here they were, the humans: three adults and a child. Two argued while the third adult kept the child hidden behind her skirts. The light of the room came from a dull lamp, so *it* felt unrushed now. It coiled, picking out the first target. The louder man. That would be good. With him gone there would be blessed silence. That decided, it peeled another arm out of its bulk and swung. It caught the man at the elbow and mutated, wrapping around his arm before wrenching up. The man barely had time to shout before he was sucked into the creature's body. The other humans gawked in stupefied fear. It took a moment for one to realize what was going on and scream. The other rushed for the door.

If they escape, bad things come. They will bring Sweepers, and there will be no peace.

Startled and angry at the thought, the creature swelled. Its body expanded all along its laid trail, enough to fill and block the doorway. The woman skidded to a stop before it and shrieked. Viscous black hands grew out of the creature, snatching her by the arms and dress to pull her in too. She sank in with one last wail, thrashing in vain. Inside the room, the creature had grown big enough to envelop the whole ceiling. It sent feelers down the walls, breaking the lamp on its way. The last human had lifted his child and made a break for the window, but now the creature's many limbs curled over it. He backpedaled, searching desperately for an escape as the child remained petrified in his arms. The creature took its time closing in, relishing in the amount of emotion they gave off. How easy to detect. How easy to eat. This would be a good snack, and afterward it would have peace again.

Peace until the Sweepers, whispered a thought too coherent to be its own.

1

AUGUST 1233

Is he going to know?

Laura gripped the handles of her bike harder and squinted, taking in the building before her. No, she decided, no one was visible through the windows. Perfect. All she had to do was sneak in, sit down, pretend she'd been there the entire time. Late? Ha, of course not, what are you talking about? All that stood between her and impunity was that damn squeaky door; though its noise was usually unnoticeable, in the quiet of 8:30 A.M. she was sure it would reach anyone in a mile radius. She glared at it while climbing the few stairs, lugging her bike up alongside. She grabbed the handle, pushed lightly inward . . . and the hinges groaned.

"Shit!" she hissed. An answering sound came from inside, and she grimaced.

"Someone's running late," a voice drawled.

She kicked the door open with no more attempt at subtlety. No bell jingled by the door, but a cheap set of wind chimes clinked as a breeze filtered in. Apart from that chime, there wasn't much decoration to be had. The place looked like it had once been a candy shop, with a long counter along three sides of the room, wood on top but glass below to display shelves there. All these shelves and the majority of the countertop were cluttered with glass bottles, tubes, and flasks. Some were held by wiry frames, others suspended above open flame, still others connected by a myriad of tubes, the entire contraption being called "the Kin system." Throughout the maze of glass, golden liquid simmered and frothed. Odds and ends were strewn about in the clear spaces, lingering close enough to the Kin to blacken, or spread amid the glass-encased shelves: papers, a stray fountain pen, small clips and fasteners. Behind the glass sat a large metallic briefcase, long lengths of wire, tools, and a mess of mismatched objects and papers. Four rickety stools were scattered about in the open space between door and counter; on the right wall hung black drapes, and in the back wall was a closed door. It was warm in the room, the bottles and flasks hissing and steaming around her and making the heat even worse than it was outside.

Her boss sat on a stool just behind the Kin machine. He looked at her through the steam, partially obscured and in a position to block the drapes, as was his wont. No wonder Laura hadn't seen him through the windows. Clae Sinclair was fairly young to be running his own business. Laura didn't know his exact age, but he couldn't be any older than thirty. His face was arranged in a look of nigh-permanent bored tranquillity, though when he was angry, it showed in his eyes. He bore three small scars on his face: two on the rise of his left cheekbone, one above his eyebrow; other scars marred his hands and lurked out of sight under his sleeves. Otherwise he was fairly attractive, shorter than the average man, with dark hair curled loosely to frame his face and hanging about halfway down his neck. His eyes were nearly as dark. On the job Laura had heard some other women twittering loudly about his looks, but for her he held all the appeal of a flowering cactus.

While he practically teemed with quirks, there was one so intertwined with his existence that it seemed just as ingrained as all his scars: the black drapes he sat in front of. No one was permitted to venture beyond them or even catch a glimpse of whatever was there. He guarded these drapes with a zeal hard to detect but terrifying to witness the scarce times it hit full force, and this had garnered the attention of some neighbors (who of course talked, and the whole thing was distorted and spread). When people weren't talking about his attitude or latest stunts, they muttered about black curtains. What could he be hiding? A treasure, a monster, an heirloom? Nothing at all? Could it be the cause of his madness? It was rumored that he killed someone who tried to get behind those drapes. The one time someone had mentioned it to his face he'd smiled—actually smiled—and snapped his pocket watch closed with the most menacing *click* Laura had ever heard. This was the only "proof," so it remained only jeering hearsay. These simple scraps of fabric were the eternal conundrum of the neighborhood. Laura didn't know what was there, and was somewhat obsessed with the mystery herself.

Laura took her sweet time leaning her bike against the only open wall and taking a seat.

"Good morning," she muttered.

Clae didn't reply, just looked at her with that same blank expression. The flasks and tubes continued to spit, and smoke wreathed around him to make a halo above his head.

"I'm not going to make excuses."

"I wouldn't listen to them anyway."

Of course not. "Sorry."

"Don't let it happen again. This job is time-sensitive. There's a reason we have hours."

Laura knew time was important, and the implication that she didn't made her fist her hands in her lap. She tried not to make any other sign of anger, though. She hoped one day she'd master the same serenity Clae had, so when she was angry it carried that much more weight.

"Right. What are we doing today?"

"There's an infestation in the Second Quarter," he replied, finally taking his eyes off her to look at the pseudo chemistry lab around them. "Judging by the description in the report, it's been working away for nearly two months now."

"Two months?" Laura felt her face pale. She'd never encountered a monster that strong.

"It seems to have taken root in a house, eaten the insides."

"And the people inside?"

"I did just say it ate the insides."

Laura felt nauseous. "How big is it, exactly?"

"It's overtaken the entire house, and Second Quarter houses are usually much larger than the Third ones."

"Damn," she breathed.

Clae slid off his stool and pulled the briefcase from under the counter, setting it on his vacated seat. He stalked around the room, picking up little glass and metal containers, tipping some golden mixture from the Kin into them. These he snapped into corresponding slots in the briefcase. As he did this he spoke, and Laura paid rapt attention.

"All entrances to the building will probably be sealed off, so the creature can hide from the light. It took advantage of the early morning to bulk up its defenses."

She remembered another time with only a month's growth, where tables were pressed to the windows and couldn't be moved.

"We'll have to attack through an entrance it hasn't noticed. We may not be able to use bombs or anything highly destructive though, as that may damage the root amulet and make the situation worse."

He pulled out one of the long lengths of wire and unraveled the end. He squinted at it, as if to be sure the silvery material was undamaged, before coiling it up to store in one of the many bags on his belt.

"How do we find one of those entrances?" questioned Laura, slipping off her own stool. "It wasn't exactly hard for you to find one last time." But last time was in June; Laura hadn't been at all knowledgeable at the time. No other high-level incidents had happened since. "What's the secret?"

"It varies. We'll have to investigate the house itself, figure out which is the most opportune place, and once we know that we can come up with a plan of attack." He plucked a small gun from somewhere in the mess of Kin. "Once that's settled, it's fairly straightforward."

"Can we keep a distance?"

"As usual, all that stands between us is the walls of the house."

In Laura's cheap Third Quarter apartment, the walls were thin enough that she could hear people in other rooms and outside talking. It seemed like little protection.

"Second Quarter houses are better, right?"

"Of course. They're only a step down from First, after all. But if we seriously piss this thing off, a few more inches won't stop it."

If Laura thought about it too much, she'd psych herself out and end up getting herself killed. She had to do something, occupy her hands and her mind. She rolled up her sleeves, took a glance at the briefcase, and asked, "Okay, what else do we need in there?"

Nearly an hour later, their cable car arrived in the Second Quarter. When their cab reached the platform it stuttered to a halt. Everyone else stood slowly, but Laura hopped off the cable car as fast as she could to avoid getting caught by the door. Clae followed more sedately. She could hear his boots on the thin metal grating while she wandered toward the edge.

The cable car station was mostly an open-air platform. Jutting out from the main wall, a metal structure reached up and out to better accommodate the slant of the cable car's ascent. This particular station was only a two-stopper, not a main continuous line throughout the city, so had fewer decorations. The metal was painted rusty red with subtle accents, the platform, ticket booth, and covered seating area lackluster compared to those on the main line. A structure behind the platform housed the machinery used to raise and lower the cars, enclosed and locked to keep away saboteurs. While the main line's platform might have been fancier, the smaller ones had less to get in the way of the view, so Laura could lean on the railing to peer down at the other Quarters.

The city of Amicae rose from the flatlands like a massive tiered cake, First Quarter on top, sitting on the wider Second, which lay above the bigger Third, and so on, all the way down to Sixth Quarter. Job and status determined which Quarter a person lived in: First Quarter the richest, with the best buildings, best shops, best food, best people; Second a step down, still clean and decent; Third Quarter almost a standard of mediocrity; Fourth miserable; Fifth *abysmal.* Sixth Quarter was the army central, to more easily protect the city and keep the disorderly Fifth in line. From the Second Quarter platform Laura could see clearly how, with each terrace, it grew darker and dirtier. The cable cars rattled up and down their lines all over, shining bronze beetles on wire.

"Laura, this way," Clae called.

Laura jumped and ran after him, making a loud clatter on the metal grate.

Clae led her to a trolley. It was much cleaner than the ones Laura was used to, and much emptier than the cable car. Many seats remained open, with only a middle-aged couple sitting near the back. The man slept, but the woman, in her fancy lilac dress, eyed them like a hawk. Clae stayed standing, gripping one of the rails on the ceiling in one hand, briefcase in the other. Laura didn't know why, but chalked it up to some sort of etiquette of the upper Quarters. She couldn't reach the bar so hesitantly gripped the elbow of Clae's sleeve as the trolley moved off. The woman in the back relaxed, and Laura wondered if she thought they'd soil the seats by sitting down. She also wondered how Clae could possibly wear this big jacket in the sweltering heat.

The ride went by quietly, and Clae directed her off at a corner with a statue of two large birds. The trolley trundled off behind them.

There was a crowd down the street, in front of the row of trendy houses. The black uniforms and silver badges of the police stood out amid the brighter fashions of the residents. The sight made Laura nervous again. As usual, Clae's face betrayed nothing. One of the policemen spotted them and jogged over.

"You're the Sweepers?" he asked hopefully.

A thin scar twisted across the bridge of his nose, skewing to trail under his right eye. He was bald, but between his hat and dark uniform the August heat was making him sweat up a storm. Laura caught a whiff and fell behind Clae, happy to let him take charge.

"We are," Clae answered. "Any change in the situation?"

"Another death. There was a relative. She seemed calm, but the moment we turned our backs . . . She got into the house before we could catch her." The policeman mopped his face with a handkerchief. "Got in through the cellar. We tried to pull her out, but the door shut and we couldn't get it open again."

Clae opened his mouth to reply, but a voice cut him off. "Is that the Sweeper?"

A policewoman approached, a gold badge on her uniform instead of silver. She glared at them through thick glasses that magnified her brown eyes, and gestured at the house.

"Get him to work! I've had enough of this crap!"

The policeman looked highly embarrassed. "Please don't mind the chief," he muttered. "We've had a number of calls today and she's a little stressed."

"Pleasant as always, Chief Albright!" Clae called.

He gave a slight, mocking bow, holding his briefcase out to the side. The chief's eyes narrowed further. The little nameplate under her badge did, indeed, wink H. ALBRIGHT, just as the policeman's read W. BAXTER.

"I'm not willing to deal with your sass today, Sinclair," she retorted. "Just take care of this and get the hell out."

"Of course."

As Clae strode toward the building, Laura asked, "You know her?"

"Police of a certain rank have to deal with Sweepers, so they're required to do patrol with us," Clae explained. "She and a group tagged along with me last year, before she was promoted."

"She's only been police chief about as long as I've been apprentice, right? Three months?"

"Sounds right. I'd say she's got more experience than you, but it isn't by much."

Laura pursed her lips as she watched Albright moving more police into position, quelling any arguments as the onlookers were shuffled away. "She seems to have settled into it already."

"They've debriefed her on the situation, so she knows how to carry it out."

Ah, the situation. The situation was laughable.

Laura turned her gaze on the building as well. The house in question appeared nearly identical to all the others on this row. They were tall and thin, like dominoes stacked side to side, and their gently sloping roofs came within inches of brushing their neighbors'. Every roof had dark shingles, but homeowners added their unique flair in the color of siding and trim, this one being pale blue. Three ornate windows lined the front, all of them blocked. A dresser was pushed up against one with drawers facing out, a table's surface was against another with a fabric table runner stuck between, and the last had curtains drawn but something pressed up behind it. The cellar door was in a dip next to the stairs, seemingly harmless.

"What do we do with Mr. Two-Months?" Laura asked, pleased when her nervousness didn't show in her tone.

"We can't break in through the cellar. One person already got through, so it's probably most wary of that. Front door is too obvious. They've learned about front doors. Back doors, too. Not that this district even *has* back doors. Design flaw, really. It's 1233, you'd think they'd have done something about that."

"The Collective knows about the doors, you mean?"

"Collective, hive, whatever." He looked sideways at her, apparently judging now to be an opportune quiz time. "Considering the hive mind. What to remember?"

"It's not particularly smart, but it picks up on routines," Laura recited. "If Sweepers use the same tactics enough times in a row, it learns to expect that. Since the hive mind shares its knowledge with its offspring, *all* the monsters will start operating on that information. The further south you get the smarter they are, because they're closer to the hive mind and it's easier to communicate. Being in southern Terual, Amicae is close enough to the source for the creature to be more dangerous, but not so much the intelligent breed of the far south, Zyra."

"You sound like a textbook."

"It's right, isn't it?"

"Correct." His voice fell flat and bored. "This creature was created by the indigenous kingdom," he prompted.

"Created as an anti-magic defense against invading kingdoms during the high age of magic. They lost control of it, and the monsters destroyed the creators and spread northward."

"Textbook," he repeated. "I'm not teaching you for a test. Parroting a book at me isn't going to help you fight these things."

"So long as I can act on the information, what do you care?" Laura challenged, crossing her arms.

"Hettie was book smart but couldn't apply the information. Froze up. Got eaten. I'm not having another apprentice go the same route. We lose far too many people to these monsters."

People including the last police chief.

Laura backed down, uneasy. "You're the one assigning tests in front of an infestation. Let's go beyond the books and backstory. What are we doing with it?"

"The unpredictable, to confuse the hive mind."

"How do we do that?"

"My guess is the chimney."

"Are we going to use it like a Pit?"

"It's probably sealed off at the bottom since this Quarter has been converted to central heating, but we can still get it. A chimney here is near twenty feet. We can jump down. It won't expect that."

Laura leaned back and glared at his impassive face.

"Twenty feet." She was sure her voice carried her indignation.

"Yes," he replied, like he didn't see a problem.

"You're expecting me to jump twenty feet down a chimney shaft, into the lair of a monster."

"You, certainly not. I'll take care of this one. Stay back with the police. Maybe if you're with them you can impart some semblance of sense." He turned and walked back toward the police, barking something about a ladder.

There were no ladders nearby, and with all of the neighbors evacuated to another location it wasn't viable to ask them for help. After some haggling, Chief Albright called in one of the heavy-duty robots. The bot was nearly as tall as the house, even in its permanent hunched position. Its eight arms moved fluidly, always shifting in movements that made Laura think of spiders. She hated these things. She kind of understood that the drive mechanics had to replicate the human form—something about the human body being the most perfect of all machines, she'd heard her neighbor ramble about that before—but never understood why they pursued it when the outcome looked either unnervingly fake or downright creepy.

The robot rolled in close to the building, mechanical hands looping around to skim the stairs, the doorknob, the gate. Judging by the dust and the amount of smashed brick it carried in the metal basket on its back, it must've been helping with some demolition site. They all looked up at it, and Laura shuddered at the sight.

"Will that do?" Baxter muttered, dubious.

"It better," Albright grumbled.

"It will," Clae assured them.

He deposited the briefcase on the ground, planted his foot on one of the wheel spokes, and pulled himself up. Now off the ground, he pulled his bandana over his mouth and nose and fished a set of goggles out of his coat pocket. Once they were secured, he looked back, eyeing Laura in particular.

"Keep an eye on things out here. I doubt it'll make a break for it, but you can't always apply logic to monsters."

"You're sure you don't need backup in there?"

"You don't have proper protection. We haven't gotten that kin-treated equipment for you yet. You're as good as a sitting duck."

The bandana around Laura's neck was saturated with kin, but it was just a scrap of cloth. She suspected it would do her no good in this situation.

"Next time, though?"

"I'll consider it."

"What should I do if I see anything happening?"

"Your instincts are good. Follow them."

Because that made so much sense.

Clae turned, grabbed hold of the trash container on the robot's back, and heaved himself higher. A series of bumps mimicking a spine provided footholds on his way up. He balanced at the top, wavering on the robot's head and judging the distance before taking a leap. He soared and landed soundlessly on the shingles. He must've activated the magic-producing amulets in his boots. Pausing a moment, he turned and gave a thumbs-up. A policewoman waited on the other side of the robot, elbows deep in a control panel. As she made a twisting motion, one of the robot's limbs moved, scooping up the briefcase and bearing it to the roof. Clae retrieved it and crept away, disappearing from sight.

Laura shifted her footing and looked around at the gathered people.

Even without the excuse of shepherding a civilian crowd, their police squad stayed several houses away, watching the house as if afraid it would explode at any moment. Only one seemed interested in getting closer: a young woman in an ill-fitting uniform, who stepped slowly forward. Laura tried to wave her back again, but only caught her attention.

"He's going in?" the woman whispered. "I thought a mob hit would mean the po—*we* would go in first."

No wonder she was sneaking closer. She wasn't aware of *the situation*. Laura had been under the impression that police had it drilled into them from day one, but on second thought, a new recruit might spill the secret, believing they were doing the right thing.

"Your squad hasn't filled you in yet?" said Laura.

"I—A little." The woman stuck her hands in her pockets, as if tempted to pull something out. "You're . . . Sweepers?"

"That's right."

"And you're the spiritual successors to the MARU? You tackle mob business?"

"Something like that." Laura wanted to say more—always had—but contracts were a damnable thing. She could hint at the bigger problem, though. "You're aware of infestations, right?"

The policewoman looked lost. "Like rats?"

"No, like—" Laura shot a glance at the chief, judged Albright far enough away. "I mean monsters."

It took a moment for the implication to set in, and the woman's eyes widened. "Wait, a monster? There's one in—"

"That's why we're going in first. Don't worry." Laura threw on her most cinema-star smile, hoping she was convincing. "My boss is an expert."

A thunk from the roof caught her attention and she whipped around. More sounds reached her ears; was the creature trying to get out? But it wouldn't. Leaving the house meant facing sunlight, and sunlight burned . . . but it wasn't perfect repellent.

"What was that?" the policewoman squeaked. "You don't think it's—"

"It's fine," Laura assured her, but wasn't too sure herself. "I'm going in to check it out. You head back to the group, right? If we need help we'll shout."

It wasn't the initial plan, but better to move in and understand what was going on than get caught by surprise, right? Laura pulled her own bandana up, goggles down, and the world was tinged slightly orange. She climbed the robot, clinging to the trash container and the bumps on its back. It was hot from the sun and her hands stung, but she gritted her teeth and kept on until she pulled herself onto the robot's shoulders.

She could see Clae kneeling by the chimney, fussing with it while the briefcase lay open nearby. Nothing looked wrong. Did he make the noise on purpose? It could be something she didn't know about yet, something routine on big infestations. She'd only dealt with small ones and training exercises, so didn't know whether to worry or not. She glanced down, noticed the drop, and snapped her head up. Climbing up had been manageable but she hadn't thought of how to climb down. She wavered a moment before deciding, hell with it, she'd tag along with Clae anyway. She'd never be a good Sweeper if all she did was sit on the sidelines.

An amulet of her own was clipped to Laura's belt: a pale gray circle the size of her palm, round and curved outward with simple line carvings to form a smiling downturned face. One tap and a silent command activated its magic, and she felt a faint echo from the smaller amulets in her shoes. While she hadn't been on a lot of infestation jobs, she had enough practice with the amulets that it was almost effortless to jump, gravity halved, using the robot's still-raised hand as a stepping-stone to reach the roof. The click of her heels on the shingles was quiet but still noticeable, and Clae looked around.

"The duckling's here to wing it, I see. Didn't I tell you to stay down there?" he scolded, but with no real force. Maybe that had actually been a test to see if she would follow. He'd sprung stranger ones before.

"I heard noise. Is this some kind of routine you didn't talk about before? Because I was pretty sure we were supposed to be *silent*."

"I was testing," Clae explained. "Seeing how nasty this infestation is. I think we've got an introvert on our hands."

"Introvert?"

"It's shifting down there, but not reacting otherwise. Either it's digesting or it's just shy. They're rare, but introverts exist. Shouldn't be as hard to root it out, either way. Meals slow them down too."

"Great. Still doing the chimney plan?"

"Naturally."

Laura sighed. She tapped the amulet on her belt again, giving a new order, and the magic shifted so she could walk more easily—the roof slanted toward the neighboring house, so without magic she'd have to crouch and shuffle to keep from falling. Despite her using three amulets at once, they worked in unison and could only handle one specific instruction at a time, so as she tiptoed to the other side of the roof her feet made more noise than the initial landing. The chimney wasn't a big structure, jutting a foot up at its deepest side and made of white-painted brick. Some sort of metal covered the top.

"Is this the seal you meant?"

"The chimney's likely blocked down at the bottom too."

"How are we going to get through it?"

"We'll remove this and check out how it's stopped up below."

Clae pulled a screwdriver out of his pocket. He frowned at the screws and fit the tool into the grooves. It wasn't the right size and on a few twists it lost its grip and skipped right over into the next groove, but Clae was determined and he worked fast. It wasn't long before the first screw was out and rolling down the roof. Laura didn't bother to catch it, so it dropped away between the houses.

"So, where did it come from?"

Laura was surprised for a moment, and gestured down at the house below. "It? Well, it got into an amulet. That's where they grow."

"Yes, but where did this broken amulet come from? What type of family lived here?"

"Second Quarter, obviously. Pretty wealthy. As far as I can tell, no one important. Why?"

"We need to rule out the possibility of murder."

This being the source of the "mob business" the policewoman had mentioned. Things like this one were sometimes planted in houses to assassinate the residents. It wasn't nearly as common as the Council liked people to believe, though.

"For all we know, they could've had jealous neighbors."

"Would this family use amulets, be able to afford the upkeep? Would there be one in their house?"

"I don't think so." Laura glanced at the rest of the street and the neighboring ones, all the same with thin houses in row upon row. "There can be much bigger houses in Second Quarter. Someone wealthy enough to own amulets would probably be in one of those. Since it's near the outer wall this is a lower district, so amulets aren't so common."

"It's true. Magic users, even in the higher districts, tend to be closer to the inside wall and the First Quarter." He focused on the next screw.

"So in this lower district, amulets aren't common. One wouldn't be in their house. Why do we need to know this?"

"Because amulets can be obvious, and if the family didn't own an amulet, the killer wouldn't set one in plain sight. Judging by the average design of the houses here, the fireplace will be very big, very open, very obvious, so the amulet won't be sitting there. We won't be dropping right on top of it or risk breaking it further by jumping down."

Clae removed the last screw and gingerly moved the cover, setting it down atop the briefcase so it rested against the chimney and ran no risk of falling. Clae peered down the chimney. Peeking around him, Laura could only see darkness.

"We're seriously jumping down there?"

"Just activate the belt and boots."

"I hear chimney sweeps get stuck in chimneys, and those are just kids."

"Far as I can see, this one's big enough if we go down straight."

He climbed onto the edge of the chimney and gave her a short, mocking salute. Before she could comprehend what he was doing, he hopped into the air and did a pencil dive right down into it.

"Clae!" She grabbed the edge of the chimney and leaned over, trying to see if he was okay.

A thunk came from below. Laura flinched.

"Clae?"

"Shush."

Well, he *sounded* okay. Laura crouched farther down, wrinkling her nose as she eyed what little she could see of his dusty brown coat.

"How is it?"

"Brick," he replied quietly. Laura could barely hear it. "We'll have to force our way through."

"How's that?"

"I'll take care of it. Just grab the drill from the case."

Laura searched through the strange devices inside the briefcase. She made a mental note to ask what some were, but she did recognize a portable drill. She pulled it out, checked that it worked, then leaned over the opening.

"How should I get it down?" She glanced at the toolbox. "Is that wire okay? Can I lower it with that?"

There was silence from Clae's end. Laura began to think he'd heard the monster down there, but he replied, "Sure. Just be careful with it or you'll get stung."

Laura pulled out the wire and unwound it. The material was metallic gray, somewhat malleable. She wrapped it around the drill, using multiple angles in the hope it would hold better. When she tied a knot it sparked. It wasn't painful, but still a surprising sting. She cursed the mutinous equipment as she tied it tighter, then leaned over the chimney and began to lower it. Every time it dipped farther down, the knot glowed red, fading just in time for it to duck deeper again. There was movement on the line as he caught it and undid the knot (though not without some faint cursing as it stung his fingers too).

"Right, you can bring that back up."

Laura reeled the wire in, wrapping it around her hand and setting it aside. From below she heard a faint, grating, whirring sound. He'd started drilling. She settled herself on the roof, ready to wait awhile.

It really did take a while, but not as long as she expected. She'd been checking on the police—the woman she'd spoken to had fallen back but still watched the house with rapt attention—when she heard a faint sound from the chimney. She hurried over.

"Did you say something?"

"I said it's done."

"Do you need more equipment, or—"

"I'm coming up." A shuffling sound.

"Need any help?"

"Nah."

She sat and waited, watching carefully as the dusty coat grew closer, his form becoming more discernible as he shimmied awkwardly up the flue. A few wisps of ashy blond hair snuck into Laura's sight and she shoved them away with one hand. In the process she skimmed her face, and was irritated by the amount of sweat there.

Clae finally emerged, fumbling to keep from getting stuck. His amulets did a good job getting him up, but didn't seem to have the capacity to push him *out*. Despite his earlier scorn, Laura grabbed on and helped heave him onto the roof. He looked as sweaty as the policeman before, a few looser waves of hair sticking to his cheeks and forehead. Laura fought the urge to tell him to take off the damn coat.

"We've got a hole," he announced tiredly. "It's not huge, but it's enough."

"Enough for what?"

"The Bijou."

"Run that by me again?"

"*Bijou.*"

"I still don't know what you're talking about."

Clae rolled his eyes and turned to the briefcase. He replaced the drill, grabbed the coiled wire, and unraveled it. He trailed it down the chimney, looking very focused as he did. Once satisfied with that, he reached into the briefcase and picked up what looked like a marble. There was a swirl of sparkling gold inside and a hole bored through the middle.

"Bijou."

"Isn't that a bead?" questioned Laura, and he tutted at her.

"No. Everyone has beads. Beads are common. Useless. These are special. They're little grenades."

"Oh." She looked at it with newfound respect. "You didn't bring those up before."

"I have mentioned them," he defended, but elaborated anyway. "They're not exactly 'aim and shoot,' and a hell of a lot more difficult to practice with."

"More difficult than Eggs?"

Clae nodded at her understanding and threaded the wire through it. "Hand me five others, one at a time."

The Bijou were warm in her hands, but pleasantly so. She gave them to Clae one by one and he strung them on the wire, using one hand to keep them up. Once they were all on, he adjusted the wire so it stuck straight down.

"Now, there's going to be a big bang," he explained. "I wouldn't be surprised if the house is damaged as a result. But the monster won't die so easily. You've got an Egg?"

Laura patted the bag on her own belt, partly to reassure herself. "I've got two."

"Good. Stay steady and be ready to jump."

". . . Really?"

"Really."

With that, he let go of the Bijou. They slid down the wire without a sound, careening into the dark. Clae flicked the tip of the wire. It sparked like before, but now that spark traveled after the Bijou like flame down a fuse. Laura watched it descend almost halfway down before realizing what was going to happen, and clutched the chimney again.

There was a hiss below, and then the promised "bang." The entire building shook, creaking and groaning as the walls twisted and warped. Shingles leapt off the roof at random points, others sticking straight up instead. Smashing sounds came from the front as windows blasted outward, and through it all golden light shone like a beacon from the chimney and there was a terrible, screeching, wailing noise.

Laura had trouble just keeping upright and steady, but Clae gave a whoop and leapt down the chimney. Laura didn't want to be left behind. She clawed her way up, swatting at her amulet for a new command as she did, clambered over, and dropped into the light.

2

THE TWO-MONTHER

Laura couldn't see a thing in the chimney for the light, so couldn't figure out where the bottom was. Her descent was slowed enough that her feet hit the ground without much force. She lurched out onto the hearth, snapping her head up.

The Bijou were still working. They'd scattered across the ground in random directions and glowed white-hot. Fountains of sparks hissed out of them, raining down on the floor to swirl and leap as if they had minds of their own, bathing the whole room in stark white flashes.

The creature they were after was along the side of the room: a hulking black shape taking up the entirety of the wall, a slimy-looking viscous mass. It slipped, slid, and bulged at varying points in a form otherwise shapeless, no bone or structure but an impossibly agile and elastic *thing* that glinted iridescent red as the Bijou's light glanced off it. The creature drew back from the sparks as it would from natural light. When one flare hit, it shrieked and burned like acid, glinting angry and voracious. The monster roiled away, affected patch drying out and leaving a thin black cloud in its wake.

Clae stood nearby, gun in hand. He aimed and shot, and the bullets exploded on impact with flashes of gold. The creature writhed out of the way, sliding up the walls again. Portions spun out from the main mass, forming ropelike appendages. It swiped wildly and Laura had to leap aside. These limbs collided with the wall; instead of breaking through they spattered on impact, staining the wallpaper. In unison they swung sharply right. Laura dropped to the floor entirely this time. She flinched as one of the Bijou rolled close, spitting enough for her to feel the heat on her face. The closest limb bent back on itself to avoid the sting, but the others continued to lash. Chairs and end tables overturned, a lamp smashed to the floor, and objects toppled from the mantelpiece. A smell like burning tar settled over them.

Clae ducked under a limb, straightened, and shot. This time he hit somewhere in the middle of the target, causing it to shudder violently. He got two more bullets in before the monster squalled and collected itself. It sucked in its limbs and hastened to retreat. Soon all of it seeped and squirmed through the door it had been blocking. Clae gave chase, kicking two of the Bijou after it. They squealed and flared brighter, rolling through the doorway as Laura scrambled to her feet.

"Wait up!" she gasped, running after him.

"You *hurry* up," he shot back, not bothering to look at her as he ran into the hall.

There was another gunshot before Laura reached the door, and she looked around, trying to figure out where everything was. This was the front hall. A few doors were on the opposite wall, and a stairway rose on this side of the hall, the bottom just touching the top of the doorframe. Laura couldn't see the stairs themselves from her position owing to the gloom and the railing, but Clae stood by the bottom, gun raised.

"It's upstairs!" he shouted.

His hand went to the bag on his belt, and he took out an Egg. True to its name it was shaped like a large egg, glinting a darker yellow than the Bijou through its glass casing. He nicked the metal lid against the amulet on his belt and tossed it up the stairs. The Egg flashed as it sailed through the air, and Clae scuttled back. He grabbed Laura by the arm with a bruising grip and dragged her into the last room. She nearly tripped over her own feet, but didn't complain. Clae slammed the door right before the Egg went off.

The Egg let out a roar, the building shuddered, and the monster gave another wail. A tinkling sound followed, seeping across the ceiling, spreading and getting louder.

Clae whipped the door open and raced out. Some remnants of the Egg's glass had fallen through the railing. They spat fitfully, like tiny embers. Laura hopped around them as Clae charged up the stairs.

Laura stopped short before the stairs. What Bijou hadn't been kicked had shrieked their way right after them but bumped uselessly against the bottom step. She made to jump through once, twice, but thought better of it and started kicking at them. They veered away, some rolling to follow the presumed upstairs hallway, the others slinging themselves right back toward her. She jumped before they converged again, hoping that little delay hadn't left her too far behind. Clae wasn't far, only a few feet into the hallway. The creature writhed, shifting its slimy shapelessness to cover the space in front of him from floor to ceiling. One goopy tendril lashed out. Clae jumped out of the way just in time, and it hit where his feet were with a loud crack. It kept swiping, reluctant to pull its whole bulk closer, and Clae kept dancing out of the way. Laura watched in mixed fear and amusement.

"Uh . . . what now?"

Clae fired a shot near the ceiling. The creature flinched away before it could hit, emitting a guttural grumbling noise. Once the flare went off, it went right back.

"It wants to take a stand. Probably means we're close. I'll guess the amulet is in one of the rooms up here."

"How do we get past it?"

He stepped back. "I'm going to shoot. You roll an Egg where I aim."

Laura fumbled with the bag on her belt and pulled out one of the Eggs. She gripped it tight and tapped it against the amulet on her belt. The glass portion of the casing cracked and the liquid inside started to glow, bubbles appearing as it began to simmer. Clae shot near the ground now, and Laura rolled the Egg like a bowling ball. Much to her relief, the Egg's path didn't veer off much. It bounced into the open space that had been vacated, just before the creature descended again. The glow vanished from sight and the monster squirmed oddly, but Laura didn't see any other reaction before running back around the corner. Clae ran to the stair below her, just in time before this Egg went off. The floor shook and Laura clung to the railing as the creature shrieked again, so loud it hurt. More Egg shards flew out, scattering along the ground.

As soon as Clae saw these, he hopped back onto the landing and charged down the hall. Laura was hot on his heels this time. The Egg pieces crunched and popped underfoot as they ran, caught up by their shoes to follow along like a wake in water.

The monster had vanished from the hallway, leaving a slight haze of darkness from its burns. While Laura had no idea which room it retreated to, Clae seemed to have a built-in radar. He kicked open the door to their left. Laura followed him in, a second Egg ready in her hand.

This room looked like it belonged to a little girl. The small bed was draped in pink with dolls arranged neatly on top. Girly knickknacks—fake rings, hair accessories, model animals, and the like—were scattered on the white dresser and floor, little things Laura hadn't been able to afford when she was a kid. Their quarry was nowhere in sight, but the window was still covered by curtains.

"Keep an eye out," Clae muttered, slinking over to the bed.

He knelt down, peering underneath. Getting the idea, Laura peeked under the dresser. She saw dust bunnies and a stray comb, but no sign of what they were pursuing. On the other side of the room Clae switched to inspecting the dolls. With the tip of the gun he gingerly tapped them aside, searching through the pile for an amulet. Laura yanked the curtains open and glanced around, checking whether the sudden influx of light had revealed its hiding spot, but found nothing. She moved to the next spot she could think of: the closet. She opened the door, pushed aside dresses on hangers, and squinted, but the door blocked the light from the window.

She shook the Egg, and the liquid inside started to glow weakly. Holding it up and out illuminated the dark corners. There was a moment when she thought she saw something on the floor, but then darkness swooped down from above.

Laura took a step back with a horrified squeak, because now the creature was hanging in front of her face. Its slimy body slid down the woodwork and hangers in stringy tendrils, spinning about the sides and expanding enough that the closet creaked under the strain. There was movement in the middle of the mass, some sort of flicker of a different texture. A split second later she realized it was a set of eyelashes—made obvious as an eye snapped open. This single eyeball was as big as her head, with a crimson iris, bloodshot, wide and ugly and terrible.

Laura found herself rooted to the spot. She knew she had to escape, but she couldn't so much as move a finger, couldn't look away. She was completely convinced she'd die horribly when something rested on her shoulder. It was Clae's elbow. His arm was outstretched, gun in hand, and he shot the creature in the eye. It screamed again, tendrils flailing. The redness of its eye turned away, and with this distraction Laura could move again. Clae dropped the gun and pulled out a second one, lifting an arm to keep her behind him. Laura stumbled back as he unloaded the gun into the monster. It thrashed and shrieked, but this time he stood his ground, eyes narrowed near to slits against the flashing light. Even when it pounded at his side, he didn't flinch.

With one final screech the monster contracted, then expanded further. A wave of darkness surged out from it, dissipating into the air. Laura shut her eyes, and her hand flew up to press her bandana closer to her face to block the smell. The first time she'd experienced this, she was nearly knocked out and ended up sick for days. This time the goggles and bandana did their job. A wave of heat washed over her, but her eyes didn't sting and she could barely smell a thing.

She opened her eyes to see that the creature was gone. The only signs it had been there were the ugly cracks in the closet, hangers in disarray, and the faint haze of darkness even now fading from view. Clae lowered his gun and snorted to clear his nose.

"You've still got that Egg, right?"

"R-right," she replied.

She clapped the Egg into his outstretched hand. He squatted, gesturing with his fingers for her to do the same. He brushed aside a fallen dress, picked up some shiny heeled shoes, and set them down out of the way.

There where the shoes had been were shards of a broken amulet. It looked like its outside was once painted bright colors, and the form of a still-intact wing made Laura think it was shaped like a bird.

Clae knocked the Egg against the wall before cracking it entirely over the amulet. Gold liquid seeped out onto it, prompting a hiss. Some black smoke escaped but vanished quickly, and the amulet absorbed the liquid with a sound like a sigh.

"There," Clae murmured. "You can relax now."

"That's it?" said Laura. It hadn't taken much more to finish off the last few, but the last few hadn't had *eyes*. The very thought of them made her shudder again. "Are you sure you don't need to shoot it again? Use another Egg or three?"

"This step is the same no matter how old the beast is. Once the cloud is gone, it's dead. You just need to soak it so we can transport it without another one taking root."

"And once it's soaked, it won't sprout eyes?"

"Not until the next one roots itself. You should learn to avoid the eyes. They immobilize you."

"You say that as if all of them have eyes."

"They do."

Laura made a gagging sound. "I don't remember it on any of the others!"

"They don't always open them. All infestations have eyes. Some of the more creative ones think up other details. It's not like they need the extra senses, but they know it gives their victim a fright and that's what they like. Close your eyes and try to avoid them or you're easy pickings. Eyes are good targets, though. Hit them there and they die twice as fast."

"How am I supposed to hit it if I can't look at it? Just guess and throw an Egg? Don't we have some kind of equipment for that?"

"Other cities are doing research into it, but at this point we've got nothing. That's why Sweepers move in groups. That way if one of you gets caught, the other one can retaliate. Case in point." He gestured at the amulet.

"What happens if we both end up looking at it?"

"Then we're probably dead."

"Thanks. I needed that in my nightmares."

Clae took a small wooden box from his pocket and picked up the pieces of the amulet, depositing them inside. After a while he asked, "So what do you think?"

"About evil eyes?"

"Whether it was a murder or not."

"Oh." Laura looked back at the closet. "Well, amulets don't belong in a little girl's closet. I think there's a good chance it was planted there." Clae hummed noncommittally and Laura felt a prickle of irritation. "I know this looks nothing like a mobster plot, but you said it yourself: mobsters are far from the only thing spreading infestations. Someone else could've done it."

"There's also a chance that a child finds an amulet, becomes entranced by its looks and hides it away, only for it to be forgotten in the back of a closet. And if one day she knocks it with some shoes, drops a jewelry box on it, it happens to break . . . well, who would know to call for help?"

Laura looked back at the closet and the shoes, feeling her stomach twist. She saw Clae watching from the corner of her eye.

"And what have we learned from this exercise?"

"Infinite possibilities?" she guessed weakly.

"Exactly," he replied. "The Council and police don't seem to care, so if someone's going to make the connections, it'll have to be us. But there's something worse. What we should really be thinking about is that." He pointed up at the closet walls. The discoloration there had set in to the point where it looked like sickness oozed from the wood, mottled and weeping black sap from the cracks. "Have you ever seen something like that?"

"Not caused by an infestation, no," Laura murmured. "Actually, not at all. This looks poisonous. Should we be breathing this close to it?"

"Normal infestations don't leave damage like this until they grow much bigger. This was inflicted, not just a side effect. They don't usually think of such things until they're grown and aiming to frighten their prey."

"But two months—"

"You'd need at least ten weeks for damage like this."

"So what does this mean?"

"Hopefully nothing but a maverick." The little box snapped shut and he stood up. "Come on, let's get out of here."

They walked back along the floor strewn with debris, and down the stairs. The Bijou still spat fitfully on the ground and rolled after them as Clae messed with the door's multiple locks. He got the first two open, but the third one gave him some trouble and he ended up breaking it and kicking the door open.

The sunlight was bright, and even with goggles her eyes squinted in reaction. She tottered out of the house, nearly tripping down the stairs. She kept Clae's coat directly in front of her as her eyes adjusted.

Broken glass crunched underfoot as they exited through the gate. The cleaning robot was exactly where they'd left it, and beyond it down the street remained that crowd of policemen. Clae made a beeline for Baxter, who hurried to meet them.

"Are you all right?" He looked so terribly concerned Laura felt like a child. "It sounded terrible! That thing didn't hurt you, did it? I—"

"We're fine," Clae butted in. "Where's that chief of yours?"

"I'm right here."

Laura looked around to see Albright approaching, a stack of papers in her hand.

"Clay Sinclair." She glanced down at the top page. "You—"

"Clae," Clae interrupted again. "Clae. Like '*Cly*de.' Ends like 'Amic*ae*.' We've been over this before."

"*Clae,* then," the policewoman corrected herself, brows furrowed in irritation. "I wouldn't do so otherwise, but with the increase in infestations lately, I had someone look up your file. You've got quite a record of *incidents.* More than any of your predecessors."

Clae sneered. "Not my fault you're not getting warnings out."

"You're the only one who gains anything from these things." The accusing edge to Albright's voice made Laura bristle.

"Gain?" Clae quirked an eyebrow and jabbed a finger back at the damaged house. "You think I like that shit? No. Whatever you're trying to accuse me of, it's your own fault. I'm just the cleanup."

Before she could say anything else, he held out the little box and kept talking.

"I've got the amulet right here. The infestation's been exterminated. It took root in the back of a closet on the second floor, the room with all the pink. Can't miss it. You'll have to burn that closet and everything in it. Taint isn't usually a health issue, but this one's not salvageable."

The policewoman frowned. "Mr. Sinclair, I think you're misunderstanding me. I just need to be sure that the appropriate steps are taken to—"

"*Appropriate steps*?" he laughed. "As if you care what's appropriate."

"I'm not the one who set these regulations in place. I'm just the one who has to carry them out."

"Then don't ask me questions you don't want answers to."

Clae turned around, dismissing her entirely. He picked out another police officer and pointed at her. "You. Make yourself useful and get my case off the roof. Don't look at me like that, I killed the thing already. Go on."

He walked off. Laura hurried right after him—Albright looked ready to explode. Clae meanwhile had managed to harass the other officer into retrieving his briefcase. As the poor woman clambered up the bot, Laura asked, "Should you really have talked to the chief of police like that?"

"Why shouldn't I?"

"Because she's the *chief of police*. Couldn't she throw you in jail for spite?" He only gave her a raised brow, and she amended, "She could make your life miserable."

"As if she doesn't do that already."

"Excuse me," came a voice from behind them. The same policewoman Laura had talked to earlier now stood next to them, a notepad and pencil clenched in her hands. Clae eyed these reluctantly.

"That's not much to make a report with."

"It's not for a report. Or at least, not a police one," said the woman. "I'm not actually one of the police. My coworker said this was the only way to get to the truth."

"Coworker?" Laura echoed, but she had an idea of what this was.

"I'm a reporter," said the woman. "I've been following the so-called MARU testimonials over the past year, and it just—None of it made sense. I wanted to tag along on one of your actual jobs and figure it out, and between what just happened and the way you spoke to the chief . . . This wasn't a mob hit at all, was it?"

Laura wanted very much to say, *Yes, of course, finally someone's figured it out,* but instead gritted her teeth.

The situation of Amicae was the laughingstock of any proper Sweeper operation. The country was carved as it was because of infestations,

Amicae's fortress of a city built exactly as it was because of infestations, but almost a hundred years ago Amicae's Council had claimed they were impervious to such creatures. *Nothing gets past these walls,* the councilors even now were happy to declare. The truth of the matter was that infestations had gone dormant or targeted other locations, so Amicae went through a brief period of peace. It was very brief. Infestations came back with a vengeance, but by then the damage had been done. Propaganda was spread, and the Council was loath to admit they'd been wrong, or that Amicae could possibly be vulnerable.

We, the friendly city, are the safest place in all of Orien, they boasted.

There's no need for alarm—there's no such thing as an infestation in the city. There's nothing to be afraid of.

But there were many things to be afraid of, just as many if not more than there had been before the claim was made, and the Sweepers were woefully unprepared. It didn't seem like something Clae would allow to go unchallenged, but he sat in his shop and stewed in his anger. Other Sinclair Sweepers had tried challenging it in the past. They'd been charged as traitors to the city, labeled terrorists by every newspaper, and sent to rot in jail. If Clae was gone, his duties would be passed on to some clueless policeman to be utterly botched, and that was something Clae Sinclair wouldn't allow. *Besides,* he said, *it's been too long. It'd be like trying to convince people the sky isn't blue.* Instead he continued challenging behind closed doors, sending nasty letters detailing specific jobs to the councilors and hounding their offices on the rare occasion he had off; Laura had helped write a few of these, and in return had gotten a brief form-letter reply telling her to "stop talking about things you know nothing about."

The Council knew its claims but it had some ties to reality. They kept the Sweepers—even if the office was enormously downsized—and gave these workers huge benefits, all under the condition that they never share information about infestations with anyone. To the public they said that Sweepers were a practically defunct section of the police force, the last scraps of the once-great Mob Action Resolution Unit, only revived because the mobs had learned how to breed infestations and used these *rare* beasts in mob wars.

If Amicae actually knew about infestations and how they worked, countless people would still be alive. The little girl in this latest house could've been out playing hopscotch with the other neighborhood kids, but no, her house was ripped apart, her family dead, and all the neighbors packed away neatly so as not to witness something that shouldn't exist.

Laura absolutely hated it.

"Mobs are ever elusive," Clae said at this moment, but he had the look of annoyance in his eyes too.

"Just say yes or no, whether this was a mob attack," said the reporter.

"Where do you get the idea it wasn't?" said Laura.

"It makes no sense! I asked the neighbors about this family, even the aunt about this family, but nothing links to the mobs. Besides, mobsters are all about finesse. Doesn't this place stink?"

"All infestations stink," said Laura. "It's part of the job."

"Not literally, but—" The reporter paused. "You can't say." And they didn't; Laura pretended to watch the robot and Clae observed his pocket watch. "Is it the audience? If I can make an appointment—"

"I only make appointments with clients," said Clae.

"You must have a lot of them, if it takes up all your time."

"I wonder."

"Got it!" came a triumphant cry from the roof.

Clae walked over to the gate and called, "Toss it down!"

"You're sure?"

"Just do it already."

After a little hesitation, the briefcase came sailing through the air. Clae leaned forward enough that it looked like he'd topple over the fence, but managed to catch it. He opened it, checking inside as if to make sure nothing was stolen. "Job's done. Let's go."

"If you can't talk, who can?" said the reporter, following. "If people are in danger—"

"We're really not the people you need to—" Laura broke off. The crowd of police was approaching, and something about their expressions made her think that maybe the reporter's disguise wasn't as good as she'd thought. "I think they've figured you out."

The reporter glanced back and bit her lip. "Are you sure there's nothing you can tell me?"

"If you want to know the exact details of all infestations we deal with, you'll want to speak with the Council," said Clae. "They get reports of all monsters we're called out for. I'd recommend talking to Victoria Douglas."

"Victoria Douglas," the reporter breathed, scribbling this down. "Thank you."

"Thank you for paying attention," Laura muttered.

"Mr. Sinclair, what are you talking about over there?" Albright demanded.

"It's your policewoman, isn't it?" Clae called. He turned back to the reporter and said, "Might want to run for it now."

And she did. With a shout, a few policemen ran after her.

"Godspeed, reporter lady," said Laura.

"Godspeed, *us*," Clae hissed, pushing her toward the trolley stop, and she realized that the other police were moving to head them off. They hightailed it.

The trolley itself was only just leaving, slow enough that Clae and Laura hopped up onto the back of the car and squeezed inside. There were more people this time, all startled by their presence. It didn't help that there were shouts behind them. Clae dusted himself off and grabbed the rail overhead as he had before, as if nothing was wrong; Laura decided to act the same.

"Laura."

"What?"

"It's a Tuesday. You can go home early."

Laura wasn't sure whether to rejoice or be suspicious. "Are you sure?"

"They'll be coming by the shop soon to interrogate me on what I said. It's not like they can fault me for saying 'ask the Council,' but I doubt they'll be polite about it."

"I was there too," she pointed out. "They'll want to hear my end of it too, I'm assuming? May as well get it all over with at the same time."

"You haven't been a Sweeper long, so they'll probably skim right over you."

"I've been a Sweeper for months."

"They don't know that."

"What?"

"I delayed telling them."

That explained why it took two full months for her to be summoned to the police station and lectured on *the situation.*

"They probably think you're a real pain," she said.

"Better a pain than a comfort," he shot back.

"But you're sure you don't want someone else there?"

"No. Besides, I'll be starting up the Kin again. If you think it's hot in there now, you're in for a surprise."

"You could teach me how to use it."

He barked out a laugh. "Try again in three more years. I'm not trusting you with something that big yet."

⸙

Acis Road played home to theaters (musical, cinema, or otherwise), business offices, churches, and other important buildings Laura had never bothered to investigate. It traveled in a big circuit throughout the Third Quarter, but the stretch with the Sweeper shop sat away from all of them— in fact, this was the least busy part of the loop. For a stretch of a little over three miles there was nothing special, and the Sweeper shop sat smack dab in the middle. The same block contained an old bookstore, a bakery, a pharmacy, and a boarded-up pawnshop. All the buildings shared the same styled front: one large door sunk to be cast in shadow, with a little window right above it and two big windows protruding to display the goods inside. Smaller windows dotted the second floors, which served either as more shop/storage space, or, in Clae's case, the owner's home. The bakery swelled twice as wide as any of the others, but apart from that only different colors and wooden signs over the doorways set them apart.

The Sweeper shop was a dark forest-green color, discolored and peeling in places. The sign overhead read, in faint yellow lettering, SINCLAIR: AMICAE SWEEPERS.

Clae unlocked the door with a big old key, and the two stepped inside.

"Hang on."

Laura lingered while Clae walked behind the counter and searched beneath it.

"Here." He held out two Eggs. "Now get out."

Polite as ever.

Laura made a face but took them anyway. She stuffed them in her bag, grabbed the bicycle, and wheeled it to the door. "I'll see you tomorrow."

Clae waved his hand, already back to inspecting the Kin. Laura had gotten used to being dismissed like this. The door creaked open and the bicycle tires bumped down the three steps. She brought it down to the sidewalk and was about to get on when she noticed Mr. Brecht.

A skinny man whose hair had gone gray and thin, he wore a small pair of glasses on an enormously hooked nose. He ran the bookstore in the dull black building to the right of the Sweeper shop, and people generally considered him a touch insane. Some claimed that his desk and chair were up against the wall only a foot or so away from that room behind the curtains, and that his occasional madness stemmed from whatever was hidden there. Laura highly doubted it, but it was a popular theory. Today must've been one of his clear days, as his movement seemed more cautious than prowling.

"Hello, Mr. Brecht!" Laura called.

Mr. Brecht paused, teetering on the last stair as he looked at her.

"Ah," he muttered. "Yes . . . Hello, Miss Kramer. Lovely day. Lovely day."

Laura didn't necessarily agree, but nodded anyway. "Good business today, sir?"

"A smattering. What of you?" He eyed her disapprovingly. "Looks like you've been . . . ah . . . ambushed by a chimney sweep."

"We jumped down a chimney, so close enough."

He seemed completely unfazed by the news. "Hm. Well, bathe."

"Right."

Laura swung her leg over the bike. She was about to start pedaling down the road when Mr. Brecht squeaked, "Ah, Miss Kramer?"

"Yes?" She looked back.

After a moment of hesitation, he mumbled, "I advise the Tiber Circuit."

"Oh? Okay then."

Mr. Brecht nodded to himself, stared at the other side of the street for a moment, then turned around and headed back inside.

Generally Laura followed the canal route home, but she'd left early. She could afford to take the long way.

The Tiber Circuit was one of the bigger roads in the Quarter, but as it was farther from the inner wall, the attractions and shops along it were cheaper and more plentiful. There were also a lot more people. Laura had to slow down and maneuver carefully so she didn't run over anyone.

The noontime crowd milled in a conglomeration of earthy and muted colors: coats, vests, and pinstripes most common in various shades of brown. The men wearing these styles sported carefully maintained facial hair, some with handlebar mustaches, some appearing to have small animals glued to their faces, still others who didn't give a damn at all and ended up with frizzy patched beards. The young man selling papers on the corner had patchy stubble of his own that didn't fit his boyish face or childishly styled shirt and suspenders—no one over the age of eleven should be allowed to wear suspenders with stars on them. The women tended to have brighter styles, but even if the lady who blocked Laura's path wore a red dress, it was rusty red and didn't stick out much. Most of the women wore dresses, though some made the same choice that Laura did, donning fitted shirts and vests—still in brighter colors than men— to match pants. "Lady trousers" weren't extremely popular, but the initial backlash had died away, much to Laura's relief. She couldn't imagine riding a bike or doing her Sweeper job in one of those loose dresses. The little girls didn't seem to mind them, but she figured they'd learn eventually; for now they were stuck in ugly patterned dresses that made them look like pudgy baby dolls.

Laura was a little frustrated she couldn't just ride in the street and avoid the crowd altogether, but the problem with the street was exemplified as a little boy steered his bright red bicycle into the road, thick white tires bumping over the curb, and a car screeched to a halt on its own bicycle-shaped wheels. The driver leapt up from his cushioned seat to lean over his windshield and shout, just about ready to fall out onto the green hood of his roadster while the boy looked on in confusion and fright and yet another car swerved, puttering around them. Going out there could easily mean getting run over by one of those boxy automobiles; the best bet was to stay on the sidewalk. Laura looked around, keeping an eye out for whatever reason Mr. Brecht suggested the route.

She paused a moment in the shadow of the great equestrian statue of Queen Terual XXIII. The open space of Battle Queen Square provided some relief from the crowd, but not by much; she still had to wheel past sightseers vying to get a look at the statue's plaque. As she dodged a particularly noisy man in a jacket and tie (history scholar, judging by the enthusiasm as he raved about centuries-old military maneuvers), she spotted it. The library rose on the side of Battle Queen Square, all pillars and mismatched stone, and on the side was an assortment of tattered movie posters. They were pasted to the wall, but vandalism had got them in bad shape. Laura coasted up to them and hopped off the bike. She patted herself down, searching, and pulled a pocketknife from her bag. She walked up to the posters and squinted, picking out the untarnished parts she thought best, and scraped them off the wall as best she could. It was a good haul, she thought with pride.

Amicae sheltered its citizens from far more than infestations: anything that came from another city was a potential threat, since other cities knew and appreciated the dangers of monsters. Many foreign films featured them even as a background detail—*in a city!* Amicae bemoaned, as if the idea were ludicrous. They couldn't very well cut out entire scenes of films to preserve Amicae's delicate sensibilities (other cities were outraged at the very idea), so most pictures here were filmed on-site or made a big deal of the infestations being in the wilds and staying in the wilds. An entire committee had been set up to vet their quality before allowing films, books, souvenirs, or any other materials to enter. As a result most people had no idea what other cities were like. Laura was an avid cinemagoer (number one drain on her budget), and even she had difficulty picking out the most famous landmarks of other cities. She knew pieces of Coronae thanks to a book she'd clung to since childhood, but Carmen came next on the list, since it produced such a glut of films; it made sense that out of fifty candidates a year, Amicae could allow one or two. One of the posters here was from Carmen, and she was thrilled to recognize the skyline behind the illustrated protagonist. Some careful scraping, even more careful peeling, and she had a city in her hands. Beside the film posters were smaller pieces advertising local events, spanning all the way from mid-Fourth to outer Second Quarters; she made mental note of a few—particularly the one about bicycle races and the outdoor theater on the east side—before returning to the brighter, flashier pieces. She hadn't found such a variety since the time she'd ventured into the upper Quarters, but the last time she'd tried that people had chased her off for vandalism. Upper Quarters always seemed fussy when the "bottom dwellers" came to check things out. Once she got these pieces in more or less decent shape, she put them between the pages of a large book in her bag—something she carried around for such occasions—and got back on the bike, quietly thanking Mr. Brecht and his eagle eyes.

At nearly four o'clock on the dot, Laura turned onto her street. It was called Cynder Avenue, named for the Cynder block of apartments where she lived.

The bumpy road was full of potholes, but no cars came by this part of the Quarter to be bothered by it; no one was wealthy enough to own or ride in one. Laura rode her bike on the sidewalk, which was also cracked and uneven, but much easier to navigate on wheels—good news for the old bike. She disliked riding it over cobblestones and uneven pavement, but it was faster than walking, and the trolleys never quite synched up with her schedule, despite them being free if she showed off the Sweeper ring on her right hand. So bike it was.

She arrived alongside the hulking, dark Cynder building and hopped off her bike, wheeling it to the door of the first apartment so she could knock. Old Mrs. Haskell made a habit of keeping other people's bicycles in her apartment, as there was no other place to park them in this area where they wouldn't be stolen and people weren't keen on dragging even lightweight bikes up multiple flights of stairs. Laura lived on the top floor, so she was very grateful for the old woman's kindness. Though that kindness only seemed to go out to those with jobs or seeking employment. Mrs. Haskell didn't like deadbeats. It didn't take long for Mrs. Haskell to come to the door, stutter through her daily greeting, and take the bike. That done, Laura headed up. The stairs were dirty. Dust and litter gathered in the corners, and scuffs showed where people had walked. Cracks and flaked paint crisscrossed the walls and floor, but it was still in much better shape than the road. Laura took the steps two at a time. One step. Two. Three. Four. Landing. Turn. One two three four. Second floor. Turn. She kept going until the fifth floor before resorting to one step at a time, all the way to the eighth floor. She took a left, following the hallway down two doors, and tested the third's doorknob. The door swung open for her and she leaned in.

"I'm home!"

"Laura?" came a startled response from inside. Her aunt Morgan entered the hallway, blond hair a mess and brow furrowed in worry. "You're home early."

Laura stepped inside and shut the door, reaching down to undo the buttons on her boots. "We had a bigger job today, so after that Clae sent me home."

"But he's not laying you off?"

"No. Seriously, who else would he hire? Everyone else would quit."

She set her boots aside and stepped up into the main part of the apartment. Morgan moved aside to let her through, and Laura slinked to the living room to sit down and pull out her book of poster scraps. A piece of Vir's Arc of Valerian slipped out and she had to fish it back from under the couch; she'd completely forgotten it before. In any case, Morgan seemed happy to have company again.

"Did anything exciting happen today?" she asked as she headed back for the kitchen and the smell of her newest culinary experiment.

Laura laughed. "You have no idea. We had to go down a chimney today."

"You what?"

Wait. No, she shouldn't have said that. Laura sat up straight again, mind racing.

"It's okay! We had equipment, we weren't in any danger. We just had to climb down and grab an amulet before anything happened to it. Nothing big."

Morgan didn't look convinced, but backed down. "If you say so."

Laura didn't like lying to her aunt, but the alternative was a nervous breakdown she didn't want to experience. She also doubted Clae would appreciate some strange woman barging into his shop to yell at him. As far as Morgan knew, Sweepers led boring lives of gathering inventory and bringing amulets to be recycled. The contract of "tell no one" extended to family members, but even if it didn't, Laura would've avoided the subject. She'd steered Morgan away from the story that they handled mobsters, let alone all infestations. She dreaded mentioning the hefty compensation for families if Sweepers were killed. The simple fact that existed would be enough to send her aunt swooning. Morgan kept dropping hints for Laura to quit the job even now—learning the magnitude of the work would catapult that into all-out harassment.

Before Morgan could say anything else, another voice interrupted.

"Mommy?" Her cousin, Cheryl, stood in the doorway of one of the bedrooms, blue eyes wide and a sodden colored paper in hand. "Mom, I spilled the paint."

Morgan hurried over, taking the paper and motioning for Cheryl to show her the mess. Laura breathed a sigh of relief. She picked up her book and headed for her room before she could regain attention.

Her room wasn't big, but it wasn't small either. It had space for her thin bed, desk, chair, and closet. A big curtained window took up a chunk of the far wall, doubling as a glass door to a thick balcony. The left wall wasn't a true wall, more of a glorified fabric screen separating her room from her aunt's. Even now she could hear Morgan chiding Cheryl about the dangers of spilling paint. The rest of the wall space in the room was cluttered with a variety of papers, all stuck to the wall with tacks and adhesives.

Laura had the habit of collecting discarded papers and sticking them up on her wall. Morgan had never figured out what it all meant, since this grand, ragged collage seemingly had no theme: a tattered monochrome photo of sunset over Amicae hung near her headboard, a colored drawing of an Avis-based opera singer gaped near the closet, and closer to the ceiling sprawled a faded, color-coded guide to trolley routes. In a stroke of middle school inspiration, Laura had dubbed it "Where Am I." She'd lain on her bed, glared at the pictures while the rest of the family clamored about the apartment, and chosen exactly where she wanted to be.

Now, at age twenty, she hadn't been to any of the other cities and had far fewer escapist fantasies, but the pictures were still intriguing and the other cities existed whether Amicae acknowledged them or not. She felt a little more kinship to them now.

After fishing tacks and pins from her desk, she knelt on her bed, transport book beside her, and plotted where to put the Carmen skyline. She was debating whether to deconstruct the whole thing and attempt to redo it in actual, directional order when footsteps announced her aunt's presence.

"The art vandal strikes again. Where did those come from?"

"There were some posters on the Tiber Circuit. Can you tell? It's Carmen." Laura settled on putting it above a matching Carmen automobile before snapping the carrying book shut. "How bad was Cheryl's mess?"

"She's out of red," Morgan sighed. "Spilled the entire container. Luckily it was only on the floor, not the sheets."

"That's good. Easy cleanup, right?"

"She's still expecting a replacement, though. Could you talk to the lady at the craft shop on your way to work tomorrow? You always seem to get a discount out of her."

That mostly being because she bought things off of Clae's supply list at the same time and claimed Sweeper benefits. She couldn't bluff that watercolors were part of the job. "She hassles me about pins. I hate to see what kind of fit she'd throw over paint."

"Then maybe you could convince Charlie to help out? He's so bright, I'm sure—"

"No. Not happening." Laura shoved the book back into her bag with more force than necessary.

Morgan sighed and shrugged in defeat. "All right. I'm sure he'd be willing, but I'll see what I can dig up myself."

"You'll do fine." Laura glanced back at the screen. Cheryl was probably behind it, working on another "masterpiece" already. Not like she needed the red to begin with.

3)

(THIS JOB IS) THE PITS

When Laura was five, her favorite place in the world was an offshoot of the Tiber Circuit. Paglia Road was packed with vendors and their wheeled carts, there on Saturday mornings but gone whenever a policeman sneezed nearby. She hadn't lived with Morgan at the time but her aunt would take her on little trips, snooping among secondhand fineries and stolen loot. The real reason for the trips was probably the man in the tweed jacket: Morgan's boss and Cheryl's father. This was before the times of tears, the pregnancy and banishment. He apparently came here to visit a cousin, a peddler who hadn't made it so well in the business world. Morgan would arrive, exclaim "What a coincidence!" as if she hadn't been planning it the whole morning, and lean in to speak with the man with stars in her eyes. He'd comment on little things. Things Laura felt queasy about as she grew older. Morgan's state of dress, for instance. Compliments on her subservience. A glance at Laura and a mention that "I can see you'd make a great mother." The whole time his eyes dragged over her, unashamed. Morgan drank it all up.

Later Laura wondered if the entire series of trips was a way to show off that aspect; that Morgan only tolerated her as a prop in her bid for marriage. At the time Laura just thought that Morgan was the best aunt in the world, made better because tweed-jacket-man's cousin ran a cart of books. Supposedly he gathered items that fell off trains. Most items were damaged but the price was good. Laura dug through crates bigger than she was, sifting through torn paperbacks and bent covers. Most of the books were meant for other cities, nothing like Amicae's style and holding far different stories. It was one of these books in its too-big crate that changed her life.

We Are Coronae, read its title in thick black letters, its cover gone and pages wrinkled by water damage. Coronae, the capital city. Laura was a little girl with a mind full of princesses, knights, and Battle Queen Square. Of course she took the book. She spent afternoons alone in the house flipping through illustrated pages. It detailed life in Coronae's five Quarters, featuring black-and-white drawings that ruled the pages in (seemingly) epic poses. She'd picked it for the princesses, but found something better.

To the first heir goes the city's knights, the book informed. *To the second is the merchant guild. To the third the Sweepers. Does that mean they are below the knights and merchants? Far from it! While the knights are the ribs and merchants the organs, the Sweepers create the backbone of our great city: we could not stand without them.* Below the text stood a man in ornamental armor, twisted in motion with a sword in one hand and the other raised above his head. He gripped the sun in his fingers. Shadows fled from him, jumbling with the words, *None put terror into the fiends of Orien like the Sweepers. While small in numbers, they are the bravest men of Coronae.*

The following story showed the Sweepers attacking a monster in the wilds, and as she kept turning pages she realized the Sweeper was everywhere. Background or forefront, in every important spread he was in the crowd. *He* was important. Soon her favorite game was Spot the Sweeper. When her friends played cops and robbers she'd squint at the sun, raise her hand as if to seize it, and cry "I'm the Sweeper!" before jumping into the game. The problem was, no child had ever heard of Sweepers. These were days of ignorance, where infestations were only to be mentioned in museums, and the closest thing to Sweepers one could find was the still-operating MARU. Adults kept their mouths shut; who wanted to inspire a little girl to be a mob breaker? Boys kept sniggering and handing her brooms. Years went on and Laura came to the sad conclusion that Sweepers were as foreign to Amicae as the princess; it wasn't like Sweepers had any enemy to fight in Amicae anyway. That changed in her second year of middle school.

It was an offhand mention in the paper: *Head Sweeper Clae Sinclair led the motion for amulet management reform in the Council chambers last Sunday.*

"Morgan!" she'd screeched, leaping from her chair so fast Morgan jumped and Cheryl started crying. Morgan groaned and fussed over her daughter, back turned as Laura held up the page like a trophy.

"Look! Sweepers! I told you we had them! I told you they exist!"

"That's great, Laura. Grab your bag, we're going to be late."

"It's just like the book!" Laura flipped through pages but found no pictures so rifled back to the front. "They're in the Council, so they must be—"

"Honey, don't you have some better things to worry about?" Morgan rearranged Cheryl's scarf and ushered her toward the door, grabbing Laura's bag as she went.

"But—"

"It's just—It's too early."

Morgan rubbed her head, probably fighting off a migraine from the week of late nights catering. She probably didn't mean it so badly, but the high spirits fled out of Laura so fast she could feel herself deflate.

The newspaper joined the book in her cramped closet. She tried to be the kind of person Morgan didn't get migraines over. Quiet, submissive, all about presentation. It made her feel boxed in tight, but hollow all the same. She hated it. She wanted to run. She wanted to be important. The bravest in all the city. How awful was she to be jealous of a proud drawing, an impossible man with the sun in his hand?

Later she learned that such men were entirely possible. In fact, they were downright annoying.

———— ∞ ————

On the morning of August 20, 1233, Laura held one of the side handles of a luggage trunk while Clae supported the other side. The trunk itself was faded green, heavily enforced with black metal bars and a large silver lock on the front, collectively the weight of a small child.

Laura grumbled under her breath and shuffled, switching hands because the metal handle cut circulation to her fingers.

"I hate these handles," she stated, for good measure.

Clae grunted like he was paying attention, but he was busy looking at his pocket watch. It was a nice watch, good quality and well maintained—one of those rare models with a little window and a changing background, like some grandfather clocks; depending on the time of day it rotated to the sun, moon, dawn, or dusk—but it didn't warrant that kind of attention. Well, she didn't think so until he pocketed it and growled, "He's late."

"He" being the man who was supposed to let them in for the elevator.

They stood in front of the inner wall of the Third Quarter. The buildings stopped ten feet from the wall, leaving a cobblestone road following the curve. The wall itself was faintly yellow with a rough stucco texture, a door set in the middle just in front of them: a rusted slab of reinforced metal. While not the largest of the scattered doors, it was one of the Sweepers' most frequented ones.

Through that door lay the inner workings of Amicae—all the big machines and industry, where non-magic energy was created and amulets were recycled, also the best way to reach their destination.

"Maybe they're behind schedule?" Laura guessed. "We're not their biggest priority, are we?"

Clae huffed. "If they don't get here in five minutes we'll climb the ladder."

"You really think we can climb a ladder with this?"

"With determination? Yes."

With his face a permanent blank slate, there was no way to tell if he was joking. Luckily Laura didn't have to fear for long.

The door squealed. Gears at the top corners turned and the door rattled, moving upward to vanish entirely. For a moment only gloom was visible, but a wiry, middle-aged man with sunken brown eyes and a soot-streaked face came into view.

"Sorry 'bout that," he coughed. "Supervisors, ya know."

"I don't know," Clae said flatly.

This man was far too used to Clae to be bothered. He was the same one who let them in, three times a week and at each of the three doors, the entire time Laura had worked as a Sweeper. Instead of complaining, the man scratched at his beard, staining the graying whiskers blackish with soot. "Either way, I'm here now. Come on in. I'll get ya ta the elevator."

Laura and Clae shambled in with the trunk between them, Laura taking care not to bump it against her legs. The man closed the door behind them as they stepped farther into the gloom.

There was a lot of smoke. Not like the smoke from cigarettes, but steam from boilers and black industrial smoke. Vents piped this to the outside, which was why some days Amicae looked like a dying fire. What smoke hadn't escaped in vents rose through the empty core of the city, sifting through and across walkways and obscuring visibility. What Laura could clearly see was the wall they stood by: a factory making machine parts took up all visible space to her right, and on the left curved a set of stairs, caged and leading off into darkness, while below it lights glowed from a pub for workers, and various walkways branched off into the air until they were obscured by the smoke. Above, the underside of some other establishment jutted out of the wall. The noise was a cacophony: gears and pulleys and machines on the wall turned continuously in squeaks and clacks, exerting force on something far beyond Laura's view; a droning hum emanated from the vents while elevators clattered and whirred out of sight, footsteps clinked on metal, the boilers growling and coughing and spitting like animals, and faintly, far below, the deep smashing sounds of mining tools.

Laura felt her ears move in response. She thought if she were a cat, they'd be flat against her head.

The man walked ahead, onto the closest metal walkway. The thin railings only came up to the bottom of Laura's rib cage and she didn't put much faith in them, so she was pleased that it was only wide enough for two men shoulder to shoulder, not two people and a trunk. They walked single file, Clae leading, and Laura could walk down the middle of the path.

They passed two workers, who had to squeeze past them. One ignored them completely, but the other must've been new, because he ogled them in their cleaner clothes and nearly tripped over his own feet. Sweepers came through here three days of the week, Monday and Wednesday and Friday, so veterans were used to them. They openly stared the first two weeks Laura appeared, but by now Sweepers were old news. They passed either unnoticed or unimportant.

Their group turned left onto a branching walkway through a cloud of smoke. Laura walked through the cloud with eyes closed and breath held, led by the jerking trunk. At the end of the walkway was another caged area, this one built around a shaft. Inside she could see cables moving. The man leading them hit a button on the panel to the side, and they stood out of the way to wait.

The elevator arrived with a loud, rumbling, clanking noise. Laura could see through the grilles that it was packed with men from the mining area. The grilles rattled open and men filtered out, too tired to talk as they shambled toward the nearest tavern. Clae and Laura boarded the elevator, and the man gave them a short wave.

"See ya later, son. You know how ta get down. Just don't take too long, or my supervisor'll pitch a fit."

Clae exhaled slowly. The man took this as a response and hit the button again. The grilles rattled shut and the elevator jerked upward. Laura looked out at the view, the workers and walkways and machines, then turned to Clae. "What's that man's name? I've never asked."

"Does it matter?"

"I'd feel better knowing his name."

"Why? Does he know yours?"

As far as Laura knew, that man just knew her as Sweeper Number Two or something. She frowned at the thought and adjusted her grip on the trunk once more.

"I've been doing this for twenty years and he doesn't call me anything but 'Sweeper' or 'son.'" Clae shrugged. "Why bother?"

"You've been Sweeping since you were five?"

Clae glanced at her again, and she couldn't tell if it was in exasperation or acknowledgment.

There was a whooshing sound as the elevator entered an enclosed shaft, this one solid wall instead of grated metal, so the light cut out. Other sounds were harder to hear, but the elevator's noise rumbled and echoed louder than ever. There was no point in talking now. It was too loud to hear voices, and this part would be over soon enough. Laura kept her mouth shut for another two minutes, and the elevator emerged into sunlight. It jerked awkwardly as it reached its highest point and stopped. The grilles opened once more. Laura had to be careful to step down—the elevator stopped three inches higher than the ground.

They were, essentially, on top of the world. Or Amicae, at least.

Before them spread a sea of soaring roofs and grand architecture, the First Quarter. It was bright, clean, and even from this vantage point the buildings were ornate. Even the walkway they stood on was decorated like an over-the-top version of the old aqueducts: built more like a bridge, thick and tall, made of the same material as the yellowish wall, but with great wide arches that made it delicate and beautiful enough to match the Quarter it belonged to, letting in more light than it blocked.

The breeze blew Laura's hair about, but she didn't mind the respite from the heat.

Clae led her left. The path spread wide enough for them to walk abreast of each other, with a good amount of room between their feet and the railed edge. On the side of the pathway ahead was a large round area, an external supporting pillar that followed the wall and disappeared into the ground of the Second Quarter. On the top surface a circle that looked like copper stuck up, the raised rim stretching to accommodate a five-foot opening currently covered with multiple metal slats, all curved triangles whose points met in the middle.

They set down the trunk. Laura sat on it while Clae moved off to the side of this circle. What looked like a handle for a valve jutted up there, a foot off the ground. He grabbed the wheel and started turning it counterclockwise. It squealed in protest with every twist. As it moved, so did the slats in the circle; slowly they inched apart, retreating out of sight. With not enough room for two people to turn the handle, Laura watched. In the meantime she shook her hands, trying to get some feeling back into her fingers.

"Why don't you want to know that man's name?" she asked, lacking anything better to talk about.

"Because I don't care."

"Not at all?"

"Not at all."

"Why not? He's there every day we come through here."

"He may not be next time, you know." He finished with the wheel and sat back on his haunches, looked back at her. "Besides. Should I know the name of every machine I walk past in the morning?"

Cold.

Laura sniffed angrily, but said nothing. She slid off the trunk and opened the lock. With the lid lifted, their load caught the light. It looked like one of the regular Eggs, but the size of a watermelon, with handles on either end and on the metal framework of the middle. Clae helped her pry the object out of its cushion. They grabbed it by the ends and hauled it closer to the metal ring.

The slats had gone from view, leaving a gaping hole with metal sides. It descended into blackness, the contents and bottom far, far out of sight. This was one of the three Pits in Amicae. The workers below called them chimneys for some reason—Laura knew this because her father was a miner—and they went farther down than any of the machinery. It was where they put broken amulets, so they were easier to take care of. There was no way to stop infestations from forming, so containment and monitoring was the best they could do.

They set the giant Egg down very gingerly by the lip, and Clae dug through his pockets. He pulled out the little box from yesterday, opened it, and upended it over the hole. The broken amulet tumbled out, soon swallowed by darkness. That done, he shoved the box back into his pocket and returned to the Egg. Laura helped him roll it so he had one end propped up. She held the Egg steady as he twisted the end off, careful not to spill any of the contents. He set the cap aside, grabbed the handles on his side, and looked up at Laura. Their eyes met and she nodded.

"Three," he counted, tipping the glass. "Two, one."

On "one," the Egg tipped far enough that its contents spilled over into the Pit. They slowly kept it pouring, tilting gently so the liquid went at a steady speed.

The liquid seemed to defy gravity. It first slid down the wall closest to them, but then a ripple went through it and the mass changed course, veering sideways and up like a crashing wave, then surging back down before seemingly hitting something and splashing around it. It kept going like that, frothing and wheeling down in a golden spiral with a noise that sounded like faint laughter.

Once all the liquid was out, they pulled the case back into an upright position. Laura peeked down the Pit again to see the liquid shining far below, like fire from deep inside the earth.

"Put this back in the trunk," ordered Clae, straightening up and going to the knob again.

The empty Egg being much lighter, Laura carried it back and settled it in with no trouble. She shut and locked the trunk while Clae closed the Pit. A hissing sound escaped the dark, like the deep breath of a beast. That meant an infestation had begun over the last week. Good thing they were on a routine. Clae paid it no mind, and the metal slats closed over the Pit completely.

"Right." Clae wiped his hands on his pants. "Let's get going."

Job done, they picked up the trunk between them again and went back to the elevator. Clae pressed the button, and while they stood to wait, Laura used one hand to dig in her vest pocket, pulling out a beat-up pocket watch with initials that weren't hers. She checked the time: ten forty-three.

"It's getting close to lunchtime," she hinted.

Clae's attention was completely absorbed by the elevator button.

"Maybe we should stop for lunch on the way back," Laura pressed.

"Hm." Clae scratched at his neck.

"Maybe we can find lasagna?"

Clae had no life outside of Sweeping and hunting for a good lasagna; Laura had tagged along with him on a few of these lasagna-inspired trips, and decided that he hadn't eaten any in years because he turned his nose up at all they came across. He didn't seem interested in the idea at the moment either. She sighed and looked away. The breeze had vanished, the heat from yesterday returning. She wished it would rain.

The elevator arrived with a retort, smacking against the top of the shaft. They walked in and the grille closed behind them. Clae reached through the grille and hit the button again, pulling his arm back fast as the elevator began to rattle down.

The bearded man waited at their stop.

"Done, huh?" He grinned. "Doesn't seem like it was too bad."

Clae grunted as they stepped onto the walkway.

"It was fine," said Laura.

The man smiled wider. "Good, good! I'd hope a young lady wouldn't have too much trouble."

He probably thought he was being polite, but Laura's mind went back to Morgan, *You could convince Charlie to help*—Her smile froze.

"It's no trouble at all."

"I suppose not! You've got this fine 'gentleman' here ta help!" The man laughed, clapping Clae on the back.

It was almost worth the sting to see Clae stumble forward, shock and displeasure on his face clear as day.

"Touch me again and you will regret it," he hissed, and the man stepped back in surprise.

Clae's step quickened and Laura hurried to keep up, fighting a smirk. The man followed close behind.

"Sorry, didn't realize ya weren't the touchy type. No offense meant."

Clae gave off a peeved aura even while his face had reverted back to neutrality. He stood stiffly by the door to the outside and refused to speak until the man opened it. Laura blinked rapidly at the sunlight.

"Have a nice day!" the man called after them.

"I hope he has some fine gentlemen to help him, too," Laura grumbled. "If anyone needs help carrying shit, it's not me."

Clae eyed her shrewdly. "Not in the forgiving mood today?"

She'd half hoped he hadn't heard that, and tried to wave it off. "It's not important. Just touched a nerve. Where are we going next?"

Clae huffed but he walked to the right, not straight, the wrong direction for the shop. Laura felt victorious. She swung the lighter trunk, a broad smile on her face as she pondered where they'd eat. Maybe the diner on the west side, or the Averill family restaurant. Probably the Averills. That was closer to the shop.

Clae led her straight to the Averills' restaurant. He pushed the door open with more force than necessary. The Averills were used to his moods, even if some customers looked up in surprise. The restaurant's single room looked much smaller than it really was, the long bar on the left doing little to help the illusion even with the number of cushioned metal barstools bolted down before it. Wooden tables and chairs jumbled on the right, crowding up the rest of the space. The walls were a warm woody brown color, changing a foot from the ceiling into bright designs dotted with painted birds. All the other customers sat around tables while Peggy Averill wove between them, notepad in hand, and Dan Averill lounged behind the bar.

Dan's eyes followed them as they walked over to one of the nearest tables. Laura sighed as she finally set the trunk down. She knew the menu by heart at this point, but picked it up to scan anyway.

"Hey, you two!" Peggy Averill stepped around the trunk to reach their table. "What do you feel like today?"

"Cocoal," said Laura.

"Okay then!" Peggy's freckled face broke into a smile. She didn't bother writing it down; it was the usual order. "And you, Mr. Sinclair?"

"Water."

"As usual. You going to finally try our lasagna?" Clae's strange hunt for lasagna was as much a secret as his drapes: not known to the majority of the populace, but within the two-mile radius of his shop, the subject of much gossip and speculation.

Clae's nose wrinkled imperceptibly. The previous few occasions they were here he spotted other customers eating the lasagna and came to the conclusion that it must be terrible, just from one glance.

"Teccinia." He held out the menu.

Peggy's mouth twisted but still smiled. Like she was trying not to laugh at a stubborn child. "Should've known."

"I'll try the lasagna," Laura offered. "Who knows, maybe if he sees it up close he'll change his mind."

"Doubtful."

"It could happen."

"Counting on it," Peggy laughed, scribbling down their order. "I'll be back in a minute."

She took Laura's menu and walked away. Again, much like the situation with the drapes, the nearby store owners had bets on where Clae would finally eat lasagna. The drape bets had died down, since there was no way to know what was back there, but lasagna bets were safe and much easier to find out about. Peggy had admitted that Dan placed quite a bit of money claiming that the Averills' lasagna would finally win him over. Laura leaned over the table and whispered, "You do know about the wagers they have going, right?"

As if he could possibly be in the dark. He sniffed disdainfully, but his mouth quirked in what she'd pinpointed as a really small smile. "What of it?"

"At this point I'm convinced you don't even like lasagna. You just like seeing them trip over themselves, don't you?"

The smile widened. "Again, what of it?"

"You realize that you can determine the winner at any moment?"

"Something I'm not inclined to do today."

"Of course not. I'm just not above helping things along. I may not have bet anything, but I like the idea of an Averill win."

"I'll probably choose somewhere else out of spite."

"Do what you want. My only requirement is that you tell me beforehand, because I need to be there to see it. I'm pretty sure tears will be shed."

And that smile actually showed teeth. She was getting better at this.

Peggy returned quickly. She put two glasses down before them, one full of water, the other with dark, froth-covered cocoal. Cocoal was typically a children's drink, but Laura liked sweet things.

"The food won't take long," Peggy informed them before retreating once more.

Laura used her straw to prod the cocoal foam. At the movement the foam fizzed angrily and turned from brick brown to off-white, and for some reason she was thrilled.

The door opened behind her, but she didn't pay attention until a shadow fell over the table. Mrs. Keedler had arrived. She was one of the owners of the bakery on Acis Road, a heavyset woman who towered a foot above her baker husband, with a ruddy round face, red hair, and kind gray eyes. Laura didn't see her much these days, but they'd crossed paths enough to know each other's names and be friendly. If anything, Mrs. Keedler was a bit motherly.

"There you are. I should've known you'd be here." She spoke with none of the wariness most people tended to use around Clae. If anything, she sounded angry. Clae looked up at her.

"Did you want something?"

"There's a woman by your shop. Been there at least forty minutes. I wouldn't mind, but she's very adamant about seeing you. Keeps walking up and down the street and badgering the other shops, like we're hiding you in the storeroom or something."

Clae looked at her for a while, contemplating. "Who is she?"

"Some *gentlewoman* from the First Quarter. Didn't see fit to give us her name." Mrs. Keedler's face grew thunderous. Whoever this "gentlewoman" was, she must've been really rude to get her this annoyed.

"Have you tried telling her off?"

Mrs. Keedler gave him a look that could dissolve the foam in Laura's cocoal.

"Apparently," Clae grumbled.

"I'll give her one thing, she's persistent," Mrs. Keedler muttered. "When are you going to be back? So I can get her to leave."

"I'll be back soon enough."

"But *when?*"

"After I eat."

"I don't think you understand—"

"Oh, I understand perfectly. But if this woman's as spoiled as you make her sound, I'm not about to cater to her whims. Let her stew awhile."

"Clae Sinclair, you've known me for more than ten years, and you know I am above petty rudeness, but today I am *tempted.*"

"Don't worry. I'll pick up your slack and be extra rude when I get back," Clae assured her.

Mrs. Keedler rolled her eyes. "You'll be the death of me."

"So you've said, yet here you are, ten years later."

Peggy Averill returned, supporting a tray with two plates. She skirted Mrs. Keedler, who watched with some irritation that melted into intrigue.

"Are you eating lasagna?"

"Lasagna's mine," said Laura.

Peggy set out the plates and quickly retreated. Mrs. Keedler looked down at the food for a moment. She was among the people who threw her money in with Dan, so it was probably in her best interest to leave Clae alone with the lasagna (as for the drapes, she placed a bet that Clae was hiding a cursed spinning wheel); Dan for one was watching them like a hawk.

"Fine, but try to hurry up. It's only a matter of time before Mr. Brecht resorts to murder."

"Keep him on a leash. I won't be long." Clae waved her off.

Mrs. Keedler left, and Laura turned her attention to the food. The lasagna looked and smelled delicious, not that the flat greenish teccinia pasta didn't. Laura paused with a forkful halfway to her mouth and said, "Smells good." Clae eyed her as if daring her, and her own smile grew. "Too bad about that wager, because this is all mine."

It didn't take long for them to finish. After paying Dan at the bar, they picked up the trunk and left.

Clae set a brisk pace. They made it back to Acis Road within fifteen minutes. By the time they turned the corner, it was obvious something had happened. The entire street was dead silent—the one customer leaving the bakery had her nose in the air like she'd been terribly offended. Eyes watched from store windows as they walked past.

"This woman must be awful to have this kind of effect," murmured Laura.

Clae didn't reply, probably because he'd spotted her.

The woman stood across the street from the Sweeper shop, wearing a slightly out-of-date, pale yellow dress that hugged her thin frame nicely though the long sleeves were baggy and the skirt brushed the ground. She had a matching hat with a huge brim and mountain of flowery adornments. Her stance was stick-straight; between the military posture and that god-awful hat, Laura disliked her on sight.

The woman spotted them and turned, looking severely displeased, the kind of expression that belonged on a stern old nanny, not on someone just older than Laura.

"Mr. Sinclair, I presume?" she questioned icily.

"Correct." Clae looked over her with what Laura judged to be disdain. She entertained the idea that he equally disliked the giant hat.

"Your door is locked," the *gentlewoman* sniffed. "Do you not keep hours?"

"I tend to work those hours," Clae retorted, gesturing to the trunk.

He crossed the street without further ado and unlocked the shop, tugging Laura along inside. He didn't look back. Laura helped him set the trunk behind the counter, then moved to lean against it while he fussed over the Kin. It took half a minute before the woman came in, her face forced into some semblance of politeness.

"Mr. Sinclair," she trilled, sweetly now, "is this office open or not?"

"Obviously." He didn't look at her, though.

"Then may I make an appointment?"

"Unnecessary. Take a seat."

The woman looked around for a chair, and Laura gestured widely. "Take a stool, any stool."

There were three stools, not counting the one Clae was using, but the woman didn't sit down.

"I'd prefer to stand."

Clae finished twisting one of the parts tighter and finally gave her his attention. He put his elbows on the counter, laced his fingers, and leaned forward to rest his chin on the interlocked digits, eyes wide and probing.

"My work doesn't typically come to me. So what's so important that you sought me out instead of going to the police?"

"When monsters are involved aren't we supposed to find a Sweeper?"

Laura straightened. It was rare for people to know about their actual title, and still rarer for someone to talk so casually about infestations, like they existed. She was impressed, but Clae wasn't.

"Regardless, I tend to get my news from police. What makes you so special?"

The woman giggled humorlessly, then straightened her face. "My name is Mary Sullivan. It's been about two years since I married into the

Sullivan family. They're very wealthy and influential, if you didn't know. My father-in-law has run into some troubles, though. During this time I've noticed that there have been several attempts made on his life—"

"Assassination?" Clae's right eyebrow rose.

"Yes."

"That's not our job. Go to the police." He turned away.

Laura was both gleeful and annoyed: gleeful because Mary Sullivan acted way too pompous and it was entertaining to see Clae ignore her, annoyed because obviously the woman had a problem and he couldn't be bothered to help.

"But the assassination attempts have been made by the mobs, with amulets!" Mary exclaimed, and Clae paused. "They've been planted all around the house. It's a miracle the maids have found them. Behind the pictures, under chairs, in the fireplaces—"

"If you've found them all, just turn them in and be done with it."

"But that's the thing, they've stopped! We haven't seen any amulets in nearly two weeks! And I know these mobsters aren't about to give up. My husband and father-in-law refuse to listen, but I know there has to be one hidden somewhere in the mansion. I've come here to ask you to remove it."

"Look. We're like terriers," Clae grumbled, turning back around, "minus the tracking. We're here to uproot the problem. I'm not about to take an entire day or more out of my schedule for some unfounded paranoia."

"Terriers?" Obviously Mary had no clue what he was talking about.

"Yes, terriers. Dogs." She still looked baffled, and Clae heaved a long-suffering sigh. "Oh, hell. Terriers, hunting dogs. They were bred to hunt down smaller animals and dig them out of their burrows. But for the terrier to work, there has to be prey. Which there may not be, in your case. I'll say it again. Work this out with the police."

Mary's mouth twisted. It seemed physically painful, but she said, "I'm sure I can make it worth your while."

Laura straightened, interested, but Clae didn't share her enthusiasm.

"I doubt you have anything I'd want."

"Well, how's this: If you see anything in the mansion that catches your fancy, you can have it. If you solve the problem, of course. And if you don't like anything, the Sullivans will personally fund your exploits."

"I'm already funded by the city."

"But I'm sure you wouldn't mind a little extra to cover any other expenses?"

Laura's eyes flicked from one to the other. She for one would be very happy with a larger paycheck. With a raise she could get out of her aunt's apartment and away from all the guilt and, more importantly, the neighbors. She sent Clae a pleading look, but he didn't catch it. He looked at Mary like she was a puzzle.

"You seriously think there's an infected amulet hiding in there."

"Yes."

"You could easily lose a lot of money on this if you're right. And what if I decide I like Daddy-in-Law's favorite chair?"

Mary's grip tightened on her purse. "I'm sure he'll be more than happy to give it up. Life's more important than a chair."

Clae leaned back. He didn't look satisfied with this answer, but relented.

"Fine. Just know that we're not overly concerned with the well-being of your house or possessions."

"Meaning?"

"Meaning if I need a grenade I'll use a grenade, whether or not I'm near a china cabinet."

Mary looked momentarily scandalized, but drew herself back together quickly. "Very well. You'll come tomorrow."

Tomorrow they didn't have Pit duty, so the day was open, but Laura still disliked the assumption.

"Fine. We'll arrive around eight in the morning."

Laura made a strangled sound. "Breakfast!"

"Yes, provide breakfast," Clae added.

That wasn't what Laura meant, but she'd roll with it.

"That can be arranged." Mary nodded.

"Good. Eight o'clock. See you then."

Clae turned and walked back behind the black drapes. Mary took a step as if to follow, then looked back at Laura.

"That's it?" she asked. "No directions? No other arrangements?"

Laura leaned back and called, "Hey, Clae! Do you need directions or anything?" There was no way he couldn't hear her, but he didn't reply. She waited a minute before turning to Mary again. "I guess not. If the Sullivans are really that important, I'm sure we'll find the place easily."

"If you're sure."

Laura shrugged. She moved off down the counter and tried to look busy with the Kin. After some hesitation Mary made for the door. She paused halfway out and glanced back. She looked Laura up and down.

"When you come tomorrow, be sure to dress appropriately."

With that, she was gone. Laura looked down at herself, then back up at the door.

"Does she have something against pants?"

Clae peeked out from behind the drapes, suggested, "Get a bloomer dress," and vanished again. Laura felt tempted to chuck one of those hissing Kin flasks after him.

4

SILVER-COIN EYES

Laura didn't own "appropriate" clothing. Her only dress might have been loose like current fashion dictated, but it was loose and baggy in a way that made her look like a child in a flour sack. She passed it up entirely, choosing to wear her cleanest white shirt, vest, and pinstriped pants. They still showed some wear. Clae's own pinstriped vest frayed along the collar, but he appeared to have made some halfhearted attempt to look decent. His old coat ruined the effect.

They both looked shabby, lingering by the gates of the Sullivan mansion at 7:54 the next morning.

Last night Morgan had been happy to share just who the Sullivans were: for three generations they'd reigned as Amicae's sewage kings, but what the Third Quarter knew them best for was their humanitarian efforts. One of the scholarships Laura had chased in school, the same one that Charlie won, was supplied by this very family. She'd marveled at the amount of money, but she could see now that they could readily afford it. That much was obvious just from their enormous lawn. Half the Cynder building could've fit on that lawn. It had been manicured to perfection:

uniform green grass, pure white driveway loop with an elegant fountain stuck in the middle, bright flowers and hedges placed strategically. There weren't many gardens in Amicae to begin with, so this was overwhelming. And the *house*. It was so big and ornate, Laura thought it could be a modern-day castle.

"Only one family lives here?" she muttered, leaning to see better through the bars on the gate.

"And the servants," said Clae.

"They can't possibly have enough servants to fill that thing. What would they all *do*?"

"Does it really matter?" Clae took out his pocket watch, checked the time, and scoffed. "She's late."

"Maybe she expects us to be fashionably late?"

"Then she's an idiot."

Laura peeled her eyes from the house to study him, unimpressed. "You think everyone's an idiot, don't you?"

"The shoe fits."

"Excuse me."

A middle-aged man with graying hair and a black suit was walking toward them. He looked mildly suspicious.

"We're here on business." Clae held up his briefcase. "Mary Sullivan scheduled an appointment for today, eight o'clock sharp."

"An appointment?" The man stopped before the gate. "What kind of appointment?"

"We're here to check up on any amulets in the house. Make sure they're all working properly."

If anything, that just made the man even more suspicious. "Would you mind if I consult the lady about this matter? Just to be sure."

"We had an agreement, eight o'clock. Put us in the parlor or something," Clae insisted.

The man looked highly reluctant but opened the gate. He led them up the driveway and opened the door to let them inside. The lavish interior matched the outside. Outshone it, even. The entrance hall fit two large paintings on either wall, an intricate rug on the floor, a table with a mirror, and an umbrella stand. The décor had warm colors, and despite the amount of dark wood paneling it seemed cozy. The man directed them through the hall to the right and through another door into a parlor.

"I will alert Mrs. Sullivan to your presence. Please make yourselves comfortable."

The door clicked shut behind him, and Laura wasted no time sitting on the oddly shaped love seat. It was cushy, but not too much so, and she liked the rosy pink upholstery. Clae took the winged red armchair opposite her and rested the briefcase on his knees; he inspected the wallpaper, which was pale yellow with dark patterned designs reminiscent of pineapples.

"So what do you think?" she asked.

Clae reached out and plucked a dog statuette off the table beside him. He turned it over in his hands, shook it next to his ear.

"That one's good," he muttered, setting it back down. "A house this size, this wealthy, probably has a lot of regular amulets around. One of them could be sabotaged or replaced. Maybe a broken one could be hidden again. There's no way to tell without searching every room."

"With the amount they have, do you think it's just a case of neglect?" said Laura. "It's not like they know not to let amulets run dry. It may just be an accident."

"She did say the amulets were planted," he pointed out. "That implies she didn't recognize them, or at least they were infrequently used."

"But mobsters? She seemed adamant that they were behind it. Why would they target the Sullivans?"

"Why do mobsters target anyone with money? The number of attempts worries me, though."

The door opened again. Mary Sullivan swept into the room, wearing another of those just-a-little-out-of-fashion dresses, hair done up in a twisted mass atop her head.

"Mr. Sinclair!" Mary sounded overly sweet and looked much happier than the situation called for, possibly because that man from before lingered just behind her. "You came after all!"

"You did schedule an appointment."

"Yes, but—pardon my saying so—you seemed like the type to show up late," she lilted, with a high-pitched laugh.

"That's unprofessional."

"Many professionals would disagree. But enough of that. I need to introduce you to someone."

She moved aside and the man, probably a butler, did the same. A third person walked in, a man who could easily be Laura's grandfather. He stood a few inches shorter than Mary, wrapped in a tailored brown suit fancy enough that it almost canceled out his paunchy stomach, with a watch chain strung across his front. His hair was graying and in need of a trim, windswept in a way that would make him appear amiable if his eyes didn't have that predator's glint. His thin lips pursed in a smile under a thick mustache, and he stepped farther into the room, stretching out one hand toward Clae.

"This is my father-in-law, Frank Sullivan. And this is—"

"The head Sweeper," Frank interrupted. "It's a pleasure, Mr. Sinclair."

Clae's eyes narrowed but he stood to greet him, swinging the briefcase out of the way and reaching with his own free hand. "Likewise. Though I was under the impression that you weren't going to appreciate our visit." He glanced at Mary, who smiled like she knew this would happen.

"I didn't realize you were coming at first. That was all Mary's doing," Frank replied as they shook hands. His tone told Laura that this was not a smart move on Mary's part. "But it's wonderful timing, all the same. I wanted to talk to you about a problem my men ran into while digging."

"Problem?"

"Yes. I'm sure you know the Sullivan brand? I own the largest of Amicae's sanitary companies, and as the population increases, the more sewage pipes we need. I had my engineers plan a new route for a main line, but the problem is that there's something of yours in the way. I believe you call it a Pit?"

"You think you can convince me to move a Pit?" Clae snorted.

"Not necessarily." Frank still smiled, but the sight of it made Laura's skin crawl. His gestures and appearance would be good-natured in another person, but on him they seemed to serve as the coloring of a poisonous creature: a warning.

"Then what do you want to talk to me about?"

"I'd like your opinions on the line. Here, let me show you the plans."

He held out his arm, directing Clae to the other end of the parlor. Clae followed him to a wooden table with papers on top. These turned out to be blueprints, which Frank unrolled and started to explain. "Now you see, here is the Fifth Quarter line, and here is where the paths intersect."

Mary sat on the love seat next to Laura. It was less a refined "sit" and more of a "flop," as if her legs had failed her. She watched the two men with cautious eyes.

"Are you okay?" Laura asked quietly.

"Oh, I'm fine." Mary waved a hand as if to shoo away her worry.

"Are you sure? You look kind of pale."

"Pale is fashionable."

Not that level of pale, Laura wanted to say, but Mary had begun fixing the folds of her dress, so she felt dismissed. Over at the table Clae leaned back, partially blocking one of the windows as he regarded the still-explaining Frank Sullivan. The room was just large enough that Laura couldn't make out his words, though his tone was certainly sardonic. Clae butted in with a snappish response, and Frank looked up from the blue-prints to chuckle.

"No offense, but your father-in-law is kind of creepy," Laura whispered.

Mary let out a breathy laugh. "I suppose it gives him an edge in the business world. People know better than to mess with him."

Some people would know better, but judging by the irritation subtly growing on Clae's face Laura's boss was not one of them. He said some-thing else, which Frank found still more amusing, and soon they were both standing straight and staring at each other as they talked, voices rising toward displeasure.

"Excuse me, but would you like a refreshment?" the butler asked, looking at Mary.

She glanced over to Laura, then replied, "No, I think not. Our guests were promised breakfast and it would be rude to leave them unattended. I'll have something then."

"That would be now." Clae stormed back over to them, and Laura hopped up in response.

"That was fast," she observed.

"Mr. Sinclair doesn't have his father's patience," Frank chortled, walking past them and pausing in the doorway once more. "I'll be in touch later."

"Call the Council. It's city property," Clae retorted.

"Of course it is. Well, go ahead and eat something. You have no other business here, so after that, leave."

Frank vanished into the hallway. Clae simmered in silence while Mary stood and tried to calm the tension. "My father-in-law may seem unkind, but he really is a great man." Her stutter undermined her statement. "Please don't mind him. Here, I'll take you to the dining room. Your food should be ready."

Laura followed, eager to leave the tainted parlor behind. Mary led them out and down the hallway, where more paintings and unnecessary objects cluttered the walls. They walked into a large dining room. The table itself stretched what looked twenty feet long, heavily ornate with a grand set of matching chairs. Windows let in shafts of light around two walls, and expensive china glinted on the table. Two servants stood along the longer, painting-covered wall next to another door. At the head of the table sat a man who looked about thirty, with mousy-colored hair and the same eyes as Frank Sullivan. Between those eyes, his clothes, and the way he sprawled across the chair as if he owned the place, Laura guessed this was Mary's husband. Mary didn't look overly pleased to see him, oddly enough.

"Good morning," he greeted, lowering his newspaper. "And you are . . . ?"

"This is Mr. Sinclair and his assistant. They're here to check up on the house." Mary walked to his side and took the nearest seat. "Mr. Sinclair, this is my husband, Henry Sullivan."

Henry straightened up in his chair, in the manner of a prideful king on his throne.

"Sinclair? I've heard that name before. You're the Sweepers, aren't you?"

"That's correct."

"Of course!" the man laughed. "Sit down, sit down! You must be a psychic, sir. My father was going to call to speak to you today."

"He already did," Clae sneered.

Laura gave him a wary look, but the butler gestured them to the seats halfway down the table, so they slowly sat down. Mary motioned at the other two servants, and they left through the other door. Henry paid them no attention.

"Still, it's perfect timing. I'm sure my father has already explained the situation. Could you be convinced to redirect the path of that—"

"No."

The word was loud and sharp. Henry paused. Mary looked embarrassed that this was happening again; she turned her head away from Henry and raised one hand so he couldn't see her wince.

"Are you sure? It's a rather large structure in a rather bad place."

"The Pits were constructed long before your pipes, and they will stay long after," Clae growled.

Henry laughed again, but this time it held some malice. "Look, sir, it's true this thing's been around for a long time, but that's just it. It was constructed before the larger boom of industry. The people who made it didn't anticipate the needs of today. The Pit is blocking space that could be used for countless other needs of our city."

"The Pits cannot be moved," Clae insisted, and Laura wondered if this was the exact same argument he'd just had with Frank. "You can't just pick one up and put it somewhere else. You can't redirect its course. You do that and you screw up the entire system. And then this city won't have needs. We'll all be dead."

"Don't you think you're overreacting?"

"No, you're just stupid."

Laura resisted the urge to bury her face and cry, because damn, Clae was stupid. Getting big wealthy businessmen to hate them was a bad, bad idea.

"Sir, I do my research—"

"Obviously not, if you think the system can be *tinkered* with. It's very specialized, and too much has been removed from it already for damnable industry. The only remaining components are the critically necessary. You will not touch them."

"Amulets aren't that much trouble," Henry grumbled. "There hasn't even been a regular infestation in Amicae for a hundred years. So long as you keep the mobsters out, what's the point?"

Clae's lip curled. "You're saying that because you don't know shit."

"Excuse me?"

"People have been killed by amulets. Sweepers have been killed by amulets. People have tried to kill *you* with amulets. If you can talk about them so casually, you're obviously ignorant."

Henry sat back in his chair, face thunderous. "You're right. Attempts have been made on my family's lives with amulets. But we're still here. How do you explain that?"

"Sheer dumb luck."

"Not luck. Skill and knowledge."

"Bullshit."

"You're not the only one with access to records of these incidents. I've gone through them and—"

"If you're so well versed, why was I hired to inspect your house for more infected amulets?"

Mary made a small, sharp gesture that clearly meant *shut up,* and Henry looked at her angrily.

"They've been hired to *what*?"

Mary looked frazzled for a moment, but sat up properly and folded her hands, head held high. "After so many attempts on your life with the same technique, I believed it best to do a thorough check."

"Unnecessary. Completely unnecessary." He gave Clae a dirty look.

The servants returned bearing plates of food. They walked confidently, but their eyes darted around as if looking for a threat. They probably heard the spat and got skittish. The plates were set in front of Laura and Clae and the servants hurried back through the door, returning only with tea for Mary. Laura—accustomed to eating porridge for breakfast and maybe some fruit or bread with it—thought this must've been an early-morning feast. A magnificent omelet sat in the middle of the giant plate, surrounded by a small pile of toast, some bacon, hash browns, and a bowl of diced fruit.

Laura glanced around quickly. Tension hung like a cloud over the table, but her stomach began to growl and she pressed her elbow into it, hoping no one heard it. If they did they made no mention—Clae and Henry seemed to be in a staring contest. After a few more moments, she decided she didn't care anymore and picked up her fork. The omelet was amazing.

Clae picked up his own fork, cut off a piece of his own omelet, and was bringing it to his mouth when Henry spoke again.

"We don't need your assistance here. If you're not going to negotiate the situation with the Pit, then you can leave as soon as you're done."

Clae's fork changed direction, stabbing into the omelet with a sharp retort against the plate beneath.

"You made an appointment, and that appointment will be upheld."

"I did no such thing, and the woman has no authority to schedule anything." Henry gave Mary a scathing glance.

What kind of husband referred to his wife as "the woman"? *Probably men like Charlie*, Laura's mind whispered, and she stabbed at her food with more force than necessary.

"Like it or not, a deal was made. I've already wasted far too much time and energy getting here and being harassed by you people. I'm going to do what I came to do."

"No, you're not. I want you out of this house."

"Too bad."

Henry looked ready to blow a fuse. Clae picked up part of the omelet again, nearly took a bite, but—

"You're one of the most ill-mannered people I have ever had the displeasure to have in this house."

Clae's wrist moved like a hinge, dropping down so the fork pointed straight down and the food fell back onto his plate.

"Thank you," he deadpanned. "*So* glad to know I'm properly catering to your whims."

Laura ate faster in case Henry decided to make good on his word and kick them out.

"You have no sense of class, do you?" the man grumbled.

"I should hope not."

Clae picked up some food for the third time.

"You—"

Clae looked up and fixed Henry with his blankest look. "How shameful. You won't even let your guests eat in peace."

Henry's face twisted and he gritted his teeth, but he stopped talking. Agitation still hung over them, but not quite as bad. Laura slowed her eating—wolfing down toast as she'd been doing wasn't exactly ladylike, and she felt pressured by the surroundings to at least pretend to be proper. They managed to eat the rest of their food in relative peace. Laura finished first and sat there awkwardly until Clae was done. He hadn't even set his fork down before Henry declared, "As I said before, we don't need you here. You will be escorted back to the door."

Clae folded his arms but showed no other emotion. Mary squirmed.

"I'll take them back," she said. When Henry eyed her like an insect she continued, "I'm the one who called them here, so I feel responsible."

"Fine. Just get them out."

Mary stood, and the other two rose to follow her. They were quiet as they walked through the halls, but Mary stopped when they reached the entrance hall.

"Please search the mansion," she pleaded. "I know Henry is, well, *upset*, but if they don't know, it can't hurt."

"You do realize they've got all the servants to keep watch for them," Clae pointed out.

"I'll talk to them. Please, I don't want my family to get killed because they're stubborn."

Clae looked around at Laura as if gauging her interest level. She smoothed her face into blankness and raised her eyebrows. She didn't know what he was looking for, but it was probably best to look like she was paying attention. Her insides squirmed as he continued to stare, but soon enough he looked back around.

"We'll stay. But you'll supply us with food at mealtimes."

"Fair enough. How long do you think you'll be here? I'll have to alert the cook."

"How the hell should I know? I don't know how much crap I'll have to sort through."

Mary's mouth quirked in contempt, but she nodded. "Please begin immediately."

She walked around them, heels still managing to make somewhat threatening sounds even against the floor rug. She vanished back into the dining room, and the two began their search of the mansion without another word.

It was very slow going.

All the rooms were cluttered with objects like statues and ornate clocks and decorative lamps and "things of beauty," walls almost hidden under pictures both large and small to the point where Laura had to wonder why they bothered with wallpaper if no one could see it under all the heavy frames. A few items turned out to be amulets, but mostly not. She and Clae sifted through every room with their own amulets in hand, waiting to feel a faint pull or hear low humming. There was no other reliable way to find an amulet.

The fantastic problem of amulets lay in their limitations and their so-called intelligence. They came in thousands of different shapes and sizes, their magic hollows too precarious to ever be handled by an assembly line. Instead they were churned out by artisans, who were happy to carve the outsides into the extraordinarily strange and the strangely ordinary. No amulets could be lawfully sold until an inspector surveyed the work, recorded its details for the police, and determined that the magic hollow was properly secure. If an artisan messed up on the hollow, they'd be put out of amulet business permanently. *For cheating your customers with shoddy craftsmanship,* inspectors claimed. The real reason was because it was prime real estate for a new infestation.

The size and material of an amulet determined "intelligence." The larger an amulet, the larger its accompanying hollow, and the material involved could increase the amount of wear or allow for more efficient magic conductivity. Gin amulets carried by Sweepers were by far the most efficient, but a close second was made with a pearly white stone called Niveus: hard to find in solid deposits but streamlining magical use to the point that they reacted in an instant and made the same amount of magic last twice as long as any other amulet material. This type they found in abundance here at the Sullivan mansion. Laura found one in the shape of a white horse, one of two flanking a clock above the mantel in the library, and it reacted so easily to her own amulet's presence that it actually began to sing.

"Cut that out," Clae snapped from the game table. "The last thing we need is rumors that we're reprogramming the house."

Laura ran a finger over the little carved mane, giving a low hum of her own. The Niveus went silent again, but she could feel its energy swirling under the surface, seemingly eager. Clae eyed her but didn't comment; he'd come to terms with her weird amulet proficiency a while ago.

"How many amulets does your family have?" he'd questioned, during the first week of her employment.

"Zero," she'd replied, and had no idea why he looked so grumpy about it.

"How many did you *grow up with*?"

"None? They're expensive. We'd never be able to afford upkeep."

He'd rifled through her old résumé, squinted at the list of schools. "These places didn't have any available to students, did they?"

They hadn't, she said, and he'd looked at the ceiling as if questioning all existence.

It turned out that amulet "intelligence" only went so far, and how far you could push your amulet was directly tied to earlier experience and imagination. People who grew up with amulets in the home used them so frequently it became second nature, but the drawback was that an amulet needed orders. Installed amulets were usually given only one order, the same as a light switch, and users had trouble accepting that they could use them to do other things. They simply expected. Which wasn't far from what Laura did. She had trouble differentiating between the viewpoint Clae tried to relate to her and the one she'd slid into by default. She supposed it had something to do with wording. Most people ordered "make me run faster" with most attention placed on the words, as if trying to get wishes out of a genie. Laura merely thought "faster," and the amulets reacted to the million different connotations of "fast" in her brain.

Of course, each amulet required different handling. Where her own amulets had the feel of an old but loyal dog, the Niveus on the mantelpiece had more the feel of a kitten with toys in sight. She could feel its faint, tugging insistence even as she crossed over the room to peek behind a heavy picture frame.

"Do you ever get the feeling that amulets like you better than their actual owner?" she asked conversationally.

"We're much more magically saturated. They may think we're . . . *kin*." He paused at a side table and picked up a drink coaster to hold closer to his ear, but frowned and set it down again. "Magic likes other magic. It's not smart, but it knows that much."

"How many have you found so far?"

"Twelve."

That was twelve more than anyone in the Cynder Block owned. What did these people even need so many for? She asked this aloud, and Clae replied, "Status. Flair. Laziness. God only knows, it's not like they have a lot of other use judging by the placement of the ones we found."

"But they have use for others."

"Wait until you see the kitchen."

Laura bit back a groan. "Kitchen. Why do I feel like I should dread that?"

Clae gave a light snort that could pass as a laugh as he walked along a shelf, trailing a finger along book spines. He stopped halfway down and tapped a certain title.

"Amulets are usually used in houses for things like heating and lighting," he mused. "I wouldn't be surprised if they use amulets in the stove and ovens. Better than coal or gas, won't give off fumes or smoke, and generally easier to control the heat."

"How many would they use?"

"One per appliance, I'd guess. For the bakery ovens the Keedlers use six. They claim it bakes everything more evenly."

Clae grabbed the book and pulled it forward. Despite the force it stayed on the shelf, simply tilting outward. There was a grating sound to the left. Before their eyes a small portion of the wall slid sideways, revealing a narrow hall.

"Is that a secret passageway?" Laura gasped, hurrying over to it.

Clae followed and inspected it. "Not so much secret. Servants probably use it to walk around without being seen, or the owners to escape tedious guests."

Laura thought it must've been the latter. They'd already run into a veritable army's worth of servants in stereotypical maid dresses and suits, who'd all fled upon seeing them.

"Should we go in there?"

Clae made a humming sound, glancing back at the library. "Might as well. There's probably no amulet in there, but it might lead us somewhere we couldn't get otherwise."

He stepped over the raised threshold. Laura hopped after him. The narrow hallway was constructed of dark wooden paneling, a color that made the already-dim area still gloomier; the scant lighting shone from small naked bulbs on the ceiling, buzzing with electricity. The edges of Clae's coat billowed as he walked, brushing against either wall. Laura couldn't see very well around him, so she had no idea how far this hall went.

Every once in a while they stumbled across more thin doors that, when opened, led to rooms they'd searched before. They didn't linger long with these, just kept moving. As they closed one on an elaborate bathroom, Laura grew tired of the silence.

"Sullivan mentioned your father before. Was he a Sweeper too?"

"The head Sweeper, yes."

"Oh, that's—" *Impressive,* she wanted to say, but then she remembered the distinct lack of other Sweepers currently, the obvious fact that Clae had inherited the title somehow, and winced. "I take it he didn't retire."

"In a manner of speaking, he did."

That confirmed her suspicion. Sinclair Senior had probably died on the job like most of Clae's apprentices. Best steer away from that memory if possible.

"Is he the reason you became a Sweeper?"

"Kind of. There wasn't much choice at the time." He pulled out his pocket watch and squinted at the ticking hands. He rolled his eyes, pocketed it. "But I suppose I'd never considered any options before that anyway."

"Why wasn't there much choice? Were you in another Sweeper drought like this one? Wait, how old were you? My age?"

"It was a significant drought. No one else was—What is that?"

He stopped short and frowned. They had reached another door, though this stood only half the height of the others. They knelt down to inspect it.

"Is that an actual door?"

"Certainly looks like one."

"Who uses a door that small? A dog?"

"A child could use it."

"Maybe a tiny child."

"There are such things."

"But it's not fake?" As she said this, Laura reached out and twisted the doorknob. The door swung inward, revealing another small passage beyond.

Clae ducked his head to see better. "This is inaccessible enough that no Sullivan would investigate it. Probably a good place to find a planted amulet."

He tossed the briefcase into the little passage, and it made a loud retort against the hard floor. With the ceiling too low to stoop, he crawled in after it. Laura followed, pulling an Egg from her bag and shaking it for some light. Clae set his hands on the case and pushed it along the floor as he crawled, producing a scraping, shuffling sound that grated on Laura's nerves. While it was tight, she wasn't stuck crawling directly behind him. They crept through the passage for what had to be ten dull minutes, and gradually something reached Laura's ears. Music. A warbling male voice echoed around them, muffled and distorted in a way Laura immediately recognized as the sound of a radio. The sound grew stronger the farther they went until they reached a roadblock. A grate separated them from whatever was beyond—Laura could glimpse the detail of the frame as she leaned to see around Clae. He looked through the grate, at what she couldn't tell, and there was a small shift in how he held himself.

"Something interesting?" Laura wasn't sure what that shift meant, but it had to be significant.

"Perhaps."

"Like amulet-interesting, or—"

"Aha." His head rose sharply.

"Did you find one?"

"Better." He actually sounded kind of excited. He shifted, pressed against the wall. "Come here and look."

Confused, she did as she was told and squeezed into the spot next to him. It was an uncomfortable fit. She resigned herself to feeling like she was being crushed against the wall.

The grate seemed to be a vent cover, set near the top of a room along the ceiling. Apart from its maybe being a vent, Laura couldn't guess its purpose. The room itself looked like another parlor, walls almost hidden, floor strewn with cushy chairs and tables and pianos and other rich furniture. A radio sat wedged between one of the chairs and the wall, its arched form crouched on a rickety table as the next verse sang from speakers shaped like church windows. There were two people there. Mary paced, circling an armchair in the middle of the room with long strides that made her skirt swish loudly. The other was a young man, maybe Laura's age, who stood with his back to the window on the other side of the room. Judging by his suit he was another one of the servants, but he stuck out in a way none of the others had. Not because of his ridiculously long brown hair, though. Laura wriggled a bit further, squinting to try and figure out what was so special, and she came to the conclusion it was his eyes. His eyes were gray, but not the dull gray she saw every day; they were bright and shining, like brand-new silver coins. Those eyes were fixed on Mary and her progress.

"A problem?" he muttered. The conversation had probably been going for a while.

"Yes," answered Mary, wringing her hands. "So we have to keep them out of the way as long as possible."

The servant stayed silent, just stared, and something about his lack of expression reminded Laura of Clae.

"What do you think?" Mary fretted.

"I have no opinion."

"Surely you must have some idea."

"Being under the employ of Mr. Sullivan, it would be detrimental to follow a scheme such as this."

Mary scowled at him. "Oh, you just don't want another whipping."

"I'm sorry, did she just say 'whipping'?" Laura hissed.

"Shut up and watch him."

"What about him?"

"His mouth."

Laura craned her head about to look at Clae, giving him an incredulous, concerned look. "Why should I be looking at this person's mouth?"

"*Just. Look.*"

Laura huffed and went back to staring at the servant's face. It was hard to look at his mouth instead of his eyes, because as much as she didn't want to admit it those were gorgeous. But he was speaking again.

"—best interest," he was saying. "If you'd really like an opinion—"

"There." Clae scooted forward too, eyes like a hawk.

"What?" Laura squeaked. "What did I miss?"

"Weren't you watching?"

"Sure, but I didn't see anything."

"That's just it." When Laura continued to look clueless, he clicked his tongue. "Look closely. You hear it, but his mouth doesn't move for it."

"Hear what?"

"The word 'you.'"

Puzzled, Laura looked back at the servant, ignoring his eyes completely.

"I'm not asking Jeremy, though," Mary groused, "I'm asking you. He'll listen to you."

"I think there's a misunderstanding. He doesn't listen to me, he *keeps* me. There's a difference."

"It'll work! Just tell him the fates say to go to the Second Quarter and turn three circles on a bridge or something! I don't care, whatever keeps him out of the way."

"It doesn't work that way." The servant's deadpan expression drifted toward a frown.

"Then how does it work?" cried Mary, exasperated.

The servant hesitated. "That doesn't matter. It won't work for your plan."

It might not have exactly been a "you," but his mouth didn't form the word "your." Laura heard it clear as day, but it hadn't actually been said.

"What the hell is going on?" she whispered.

"Magic," Clae answered.

"He's got an amulet strapped to him?"

"No. There's a group of people who can use magic without amulets, and this is their distinctive trait."

"That's impossible. People can't just wave their hands and use magic. That doesn't even make sense!"

"There aren't a lot of them, and they're mostly in hiding. People went after them with a vengeance during the witch hunts, so they went underground and never resurfaced. These Magi have stayed out of the limelight for centuries."

"And you know about them how?"

"Urban legend, obviously."

"But why would anyone want to use magic on something so small?" Laura gestured at the room and nearly bashed her hand against the grate. "It's not like most people would even notice."

"It's involuntary. Only known innate magic that can affect other people."

"Say what?"

"Magic user, that's all you need to know." Clae seemed utterly unenthusiastic again, and Laura wondered if she was supposed to pick up on something important. "Now let's get going. I don't know what they're talking about and I'm not much interested."

5

WHAT DO YOU HATE?

They continued along the main passage again. It took them to a grandi-
ose red bedroom with a canopy over the bed. Why a secret passage
spanned from the library to a bedroom Laura had no idea, but she didn't
waste time questioning it. They explored the rooms in that wing, finding
two more harmless amulets—one in a bathroom and the other in a box
in another bedroom—scared two more servants, and ended up in another
hallway as noon rolled around.

"What kind of lunch do you think they serve in a place like this?" said
Laura, rubbing at her amulet; it still buzzed with energy after having
bumped into another Niveus amulet. It wasn't her fault she hadn't seen
the thing coming. Who made an amulet out of a doorknob?

"Possibly potato peels," said Clae.

"They wouldn't."

"You never know. Rich people like strange food, and Ralurians have
managed to make peels into a delicacy."

Laura had seen a poster advertising something similar near the cine-
mas, but it had also prominently featured a dish she'd discovered to be

nothing more than fried goat testicles. "I'm more convinced that's a joke they're pulling on the elite."

"More power to them."

"I am interested, though, and it is about that time. Should we head to the kitchens?"

Clae hummed as he opened a large door at the end of the hall. "The kitchen's on the other side of the house. This is a shortcut."

"How would you know about shortcuts in here?"

Clae held the door open wider. The door led into a spacious ballroom with meticulously cleaned floors and tall stained-glass windows spilling colored light everywhere. The crystal chandelier glinted, enormous in the center of the ceiling.

"This place really is a castle," Laura muttered, awed.

"If it was built with a normal plan we'd be done by now," Clae grumbled. "Come on."

They descended a flight of stairs onto the dance floor and made a beeline for the other side. Halfway across, that door opened. The butler stepped through, and his eyes lit up in recognition.

"There you are. We were wondering where you'd gotten to. Mrs. Sullivan tells me she promised you lunch. We have plates set out for you in the kitchen."

Laura perked up. "It's all ready?"

The butler checked his pocket watch. "Mr. Sullivan walks around the mansion at this time, and the lady wants you out of sight. If you'd follow me, I can take you to the kitchen."

They were led through more hallways, and down another flight of stairs into what looked to be a servants-only area. No paintings, trinkets, or wallpapers here, just blank walls and floor, darker than the rest of the house.

The kitchen was as big as the Sweeper shop, give or take. On one side stood two big ovens with enamel coating. Cupboards lined the walls, pots and pans hung from the ceiling rack, and a huge wooden table stood in the middle, covered in supplies. There was a wide space left that looked like it was once a room of its own, but the wall had been knocked down. Another long table and chairs were there, a poor imitation of the set in the dining room. That room was mostly empty. The kitchen itself was full of people hunched over stovetops, mixing things in bowls, fetching supplies and nearly tripping over themselves as they hurried things from point A to point B. It was a madhouse.

"Wow," Laura marveled. "Is it always this crowded?"

"Tonight is a special occasion." The butler elaborated no further. "Your lunch is on the table." He gestured to the long one on the side, and now that Laura paid more attention she spied two places set. "Please return to your job as soon as possible. The master of the house isn't fond of your presence, so it would be best to finish quickly."

Laura felt chided. She frowned. "Right."

Clae didn't speak at all. He ducked around a scullery maid and headed straight for the table. Laura had nothing else to say, so she followed. A large platter sat there, covered in small sandwiches with no crust and accompanied by two bowls of soup. They sat down and Laura eyed the soup suspiciously.

"What is this?" She spooned some up and watched it dribble, chunky and red-brown, back into the bowl. Clae leaned over his own bowl and breathed in deeply.

"Canir."

Canir were animals found outside the city: big, hairy beasts with legs like a dog's that ended in cloven hooves, a doggy body and head, curved bull horns, and a goat tail. They were typically very mean-tempered, though she'd heard of them being tamed.

"Isn't that expensive?"

As soon as the words escaped she felt foolish. Of course it was expensive, but the Sullivans were rich enough to afford it.

"Of course," Clae agreed. "Might want to stick with the sandwiches, though."

Laura frowned and shoved what was left of the spoonful into her mouth. The soup had a sharp tang, powerful enough that she shuddered and made a face. *Way* too strong.

Clae popped a sandwich into his mouth, probably to hide his snort. "I did recommend the sandwiches for a reason."

Laura pushed her bowl away and grabbed for the sandwiches. She ate two, looking around the room and kitchen beyond, and froze when she noticed someone looking back. That servant with silver eyes stood in the corner. He lurked just out of the way of the others, hunched and watching them like a hawk. Laura's mouth was full, so she just waved her hand weakly in greeting. He didn't react at all. She leaned to the side and mumbled, "I think we've got a stalker."

Clae glanced up, spotted him, and looked at her.

"Indeed."

He said no more. Whatever excitement he had before was gone. Laura was somewhat disappointed. While he kept eating, she looked back at the servant and called, "Hello!"

His eyes narrowed. Or, maybe they did. The movement was so slight she couldn't tell if it was movement at all. There was no other reaction, so she gave up. In a short time the sandwiches were gone.

"Back to the ballroom?" Laura grunted, stretching.

"We're here already. May as well check the kitchen."

That would be quite the undertaking with the crowd, but Laura didn't voice that. She pulled out her amulet and followed Clae. It was hard to navigate in the kitchen. The number of people left only a thin path they could easily access, and even then a maid would jump in front of them, from table to counter, with bowls of chopped ingredients. Laura got bumped into six times before she was even halfway across the room. She was buffeted by these touches, but Clae stood against them like a rock and shoved past them in his search.

One maid didn't look where she was going and ran right into him. She dropped her bowl with a squeak of surprise and the whole load of chopped potatoes spilled onto the floor. The clang of the bowl against the tiling made everyone jump.

"What the hell is going on over there?" someone shouted.

The maid stayed rooted to the spot, trembling, as what seemed to be the head cook walked over. The cook was short, with a weather-beaten face and one of the biggest noses Laura had ever seen on a woman. Her beady eyes took in the spilled ingredients, the terrified maid, and then Clae.

"Who are you?" she demanded, locking in on the stranger. "What are you doing in here?"

"Inspection," he responded.

"Inspecting what? Hoping for scraps? I don't have time to waste on some Fifth Quarter bum and his angelina. Get out of my kitchen."

Laura didn't know a lot of hobo slang, but she knew enough to be insulted. An "angelina" was a hobo's companion. Some of the lower Quarters used it like an insult, so nobody named their children Angelina, for fear the poor girl would automatically be assumed a whore. A few people in the Cynder Block called Morgan an angelina, since she'd never been married. She got into a relationship with her boss, ended up pregnant, and he fired her. That was how Cheryl came along, and that was how Laura got to know the term. Because she lived with *that angelina* on the top floor.

"The family hired us. We're doing our job," Clae growled.

"I said get out of my kitchen."

"I'll get out when I damn well feel like it."

Laura jumped in before Clae could do any more damage.

"I'm sorry!" She rushed over, careful not to tread on any fallen potatoes. "This really is an inspection. We were hired by Mary Sullivan."

"That little pup?" the cook snorted. She was still angry, but the name placated her some. "What's she got against my kitchen, eh?"

"It's not the kitchen, she wants us to check the whole house. She wanted us to look at all the amulets to make sure they're working properly."

A shadow crossed the cook's face. "Ah, still worried about them assassination attempts?"

"We're just looking for the amulets, checking they're okay, and moving on. We'll be out of your way in no time."

The cook eyed her for a minute, then motioned with her hand. The maids hurried back to work.

"We've got five amulets in here," she told them. "Four to work the ovens and stoves, another for the refrigerator. Check 'em and leave. We've got a dinner party at six and too much to do to waste time tripping over you."

"Right." Laura inclined her head. "Sorry to bother you."

The cook snorted and walked away. With her back turned, Laura glared at Clae.

"Do you always have to piss people off?" she whispered.

"They shouldn't provoke me. Hey, you! You with the mane."

On the other side of the room, the servant with silver eyes froze. He ducked as if bracing himself, and slowly turned his head to look at them. He held the dishes from their lunch, presumably taking them to the sink.

"Get over here," ordered Clae.

"What are you doing?" asked Laura.

"My job, obviously."

The servant slinked over to them in a manner that made Laura think of a mistreated dog.

"Yes?" His voice was barely audible.

Clae leaned in, inspecting him for a moment longer, then asked, "Is there something you don't like in here?"

Laura was completely lost. Apparently so was the servant. His brow furrowed.

"Excuse me?"

"Is there a place or an object in here that you don't like? Something you want to avoid."

"My apologies, but I'm not among the kitchen staff. I'm not familiar with this area," mumbled the servant.

"I'm not asking the kitchen staff, I'm asking you." It sounded a lot like what Mary said earlier, but Clae's voice held no irritation. He sounded genuinely interested. "You don't need to have any reason for it. If anything, irrational fear sounds just like the thing we're looking for."

The servant continued to look dubious. "Again, I don't know this area."

"Then walk around it. If there's anything, tell me."

The servant took a step to the side and paused. He stared at Clae as if gauging his honesty, then began to walk. As he wove into the crowd, Laura muttered, "What's going on?"

Clae leaned down and whispered, "Once upon a time there were people who could use magic. Not like witches, none of that nonsense, but honest, innate magic. And once upon a time other people started to attack and abuse them, so they fled into the wilderness. In the wilds they met the monsters we fight today, and they lived generations with this predator. Their magic hones their instinct, and instinct says where not to go."

"So you're saying," Laura murmured, eyes tracking the servant's progress, "that he'll pick up on the presence of a broken amulet?"

"If there's an infestation he'll avoid it and hate it, even if he doesn't know why."

"You know a lot about this urban legend."

"Of course. Got it straight from the horse's mouth."

"What's that supposed to mean?"

"Nothing you'd be interested in."

Laura wanted to say that yes, she *was* interested, but the servant walked up to them again. He made it all the way around the room in record time, without so much as brushing against the maids. Laura was quietly impressed.

"Well?" Clae prompted.

The servant was silent for a while, watching them reproachfully. "I don't like this *house*."

"The whole house?" Clae paused, then asked, "Is that a dislike or a fear?"

The servant kept his mouth shut. Clae glanced at the cook, who was watching out of the corner of her eye, and leaned closer. "It's different, isn't it? The dislike and the fear. What makes you afraid? What, specifically, do you hate?"

The servant didn't answer for a while. Laura was convinced he was done talking, but then he sighed, "The refrigerator."

"Refrigerator," Clae echoed, and he gestured for Laura to follow.

The refrigerator was a converted icebox built into the wall: a big white door with no decoration save for the large silver handle and lock. The servant trailed after them but halted a few feet away. Clae ran his hand over the door, eyes flicking from top to bottom to lock. Laura walked up beside him and held up her amulet. She felt no pull, and frowned.

"I'm not getting anything."

"Maybe they set up a countermeasure," Clae mused. "Or maybe the refrigerator itself is messing with it."

"So what are we going to do?"

"Open it up, of course." Clae turned around and started shooing the maids away. "Women, back. I said back up. *Get out of this area.*"

Laura assisted him by nudging a few more disgruntled maids away, and soon the entire area between them and the table was empty. The cook squeezed to the front of the crowd.

"What is it now?" she demanded.

"You may have an infestation in here. Best to keep a distance if you don't know what you're dealing with," Clae informed her.

"An infest—You can't be serious."

"I am entirely serious."

The cook turned her glare on the servant and growled, "What kind of bullshit story did you feed them, you little—"

"Hey!" Laura interjected. "He might've just saved your life by pointing this out!"

The cook scoffed. The servant didn't seem surprised by the hostility or grateful for the interference. He watched dully as Clae reached for the refrigerator handle.

"Laura, Egg."

Laura pulled one out. Clae set down the briefcase. His freed hand disappeared under his coat, presumably gone to the gun holster on his belt. He glanced back at Laura and she flashed a smile.

Satisfied, he unlocked the refrigerator and yanked it open. It was done lightning quick, and almost immediately he was a few steps back, gun raised. The maids scrambled back farther; apparently his speed spooked them. But it didn't look like there was any reason to panic. The door made a loud, unhappy screech on its hinges as it slowly swung open the rest of the way and bumped against the wall. Otherwise it was dead silent. The servant drew farther away, practically plastering himself against the table.

Clae took a few small steps closer, and when nothing happened, sped up. He edged around it, pointing his gun at the cold foods inside. It was mostly dark and Laura couldn't see much of anything, just part of a bowl with something draped over it.

"Well?" she called.

Clae lowered his gun, stance relaxing as he looked back.

"Do you have a set of tongs?"

"Tongs?" the cook repeated, bewildered.

"Yes. Get some."

There was a slight pause before all the maids rushed away in search of tongs. Laura didn't sense much urgency in Clae's stance, so she approached.

"Does that mean something's in there?"

He set hands on her shoulders and guided her in front of him. "It's in the back corner. On the left. Hard to make out, but there."

She squinted. For the longest time she couldn't see anything in that corner, but then there was a small wink of red. She inhaled sharply.

"How big?"

"Not very. Look, I'm going to reach in there and pull it out. You douse it with kin."

Behind them someone managed to get ahold of some tongs. There was a scuffle as the maids squabbled over who would hand it over. Somehow they forced it onto the servant, and he slinked forward with a sour expression. Clae grabbed the tongs from him without a word, and he hurried back to the crowd.

After testing that they worked right, Clae went up to the refrigerator and stuck the tongs inside. Laura shook the Egg as she waited, fidgeting. There was a clinking noise as Clae fished around, and he backed up. As he got clear and turned, Laura could see the amulet.

It was four inches tall and an inch thick, rounded; she couldn't tell any other details, as the infestation happened to be oozing all over it. At the touch of light the little monster began to quake, tightening its grip on the amulet and thinning down as if that would make it invisible.

Clae set it down on the floor and hissed, "Quickly!"

Laura dropped to her knees and cracked the Egg on the floor. The fractured glass began to drip right away, but she held it over the amulet and used the nail of her thumb to open the crack wider. Kin liquid poured out onto the creature. Immediately it let out a shriek, and the amulet wobbled precariously. It wasn't a very big creature, and the kin was already burning it away. The creature's surface spat and boiled like hot water; thin blackness wafted from its injured form.

Laura watched this with some relief, which quickly turned to horror as it jerked hard enough to tilt the amulet. Blackness surged out from under glittering kin. A tangle of burning tarry arms swelled up to whip at the tile. One caught Laura's belt hard enough to knock her off-kilter. It curled about to get a grip, but she scurried away before it properly identified her. Clae pulled out his gun and aimed a bullet at the arms closest to her. It missed, but the resulting bang and flash was enough to cause the limbs to jerk backward. The maids shrieked and scattered. Laura pulled out her second Egg and lifted it so Clae could see.

"Where's the best place for this?" she called.

Clae let out a grunt as he circled closer. "Keep that ready and stay out of reach. We need to cram it back in first."

He doubled over to avoid one of the tendrils; it crashed into the table behind him, causing everything atop it to rattle. By doing that, the creature seemed to reveal a soft spot. Clae raised his gun again and concentrated his fire on the amulet. The central mass had overshadowed its root amulet completely; it jolted back at the force of the bullet, and its arms squirmed back for protection. More bullets made it tumble, flash after flash chasing it to the corner by the refrigerator door. Darkness swelled and smoked there, convulsing at each blow.

"Get it while it's pinned," said Clae.

Laura cracked the Egg against her amulet and tossed it. The bubbling liquid glowed as it flipped through the air, and landed dead center. As soon as it hit the monster, glass shattered and kin surged out. The monster screeched as it burned away.

Laura used one hand to yank up her bandana to cover the lower half of her face, just in time. The creature squealed and let out the same dark wave as the last one. While on a much smaller scale, it carried the same stench. Laura caught a whiff of it. She was glad she hadn't eaten that soup or it would probably be coming back up. Behind them two maids collapsed in a dead faint.

"What was that?" the cook choked, eyes watering.

"Defense mechanism. It's just a smell," Clae explained, slightly muffled by his own bandana.

Hacking and coughing, the cook stumbled closer to get a better view of their work. She looked even more troubled.

"That's not one of ours."

The amulet was a little carved totem pole. There weren't any protruding pieces, but it was brightly colored. The paint was extra vivid against the smear of black left on the floor and wall. Clae scooped it up.

"The ones we use in the kitchen are white. They look like seashells."

Laura leaned in to get a better look at it. "I guess Mary was right?"

Clae hummed. He glanced over to the crowd of maids. "Anywhere else that felt like this? And don't lie."

The servant looked like he wanted to be anywhere but here. He shook his head quickly.

"You're sure?"

"There's none I know of."

Clae nodded and pocketed the amulet. "Good. Laura, come on."

He hefted up his briefcase again and strode toward the door. Laura followed Clae down the hall. He was quiet, and he looked contemplative.

"Since we found one, does that mean this job is finished?" she asked.

"Where there's one there might be more."

"Your gray-eyed buddy said he didn't feel any others."

"He said he hated this house."

"So?"

"If he hates it and now realizes it's in danger, what's stopping him from 'forgetting' and allowing this place to be destroyed?"

Laura's step faltered. "That's kind of extreme, isn't it? Besides, he'd die too."

"Maybe that doesn't matter. You know, when Magi are out in the world on their own, it's not usually because they want to be."

"So he'd lie about this."

"There's a chance." His eyes were pensive. As he walked, the hand in his pocket opened and closed his pocket watch in a slow series of sharp clicks. "Not everyone has a perfect life, certainly not a perfect family. When it gets bad it can drive you to lengths other people can't understand."

Somehow she got the idea that wasn't just about the servant.

"Besides," Clae continued, "I recognize the amulet. It's definitely a mobster job. The Mad Dogs, specifically."

Laura sucked in a breath. The Mad Dogs were notoriously bloodthirsty, but they tended to operate only in the lower Quarters. "How would you recognize it? Is there a signature?"

"Nothing like that. This amulet was stolen out of the Sweeper stores decades ago. The ex-apprentice who did the deed works as one of the mobster Sweepers now. They probably stored it to fester. Must've recycled it a few times by now, of course. That new infestation was pitiful."

He'd mentioned before that the mobs had something of a Sweeper force of their own, but she'd never thought there was any crossover. The knowledge weighed like a dark cloud.

"Can we report this ex-apprentice to the police?" she asked. "If we could catch him—"

"Say that again and actually think about it. *Let's report a mobster.*"

Dangerous, for one, and also useless. There were plenty of mobsters whose identity had been revealed in the press but remained at large. Many arrests were attempted. Very few succeeded. Most ended bloody. With the MARU defunct it wasn't like there was power enough to do anything with the mobs.

"Then what can we do?"

"Not much beyond dismantle any bombs. As much as the city likes to pretend, we're not the MARU. We can't afford to run after a pack of murderers. Focus on the here and now."

They searched the rest of the mansion. Many more oddly placed passageways and vent covers were discovered, along with more amulets and a room full of taxidermy animals where Laura found a canir; it looked menacing even when dead, and Laura was only the height of its shoulder. There was nothing out of the ordinary beyond that.

They wound up back in the main entryway, looking down at the door from the second floor. It was close to three thirty.

"Where do we find Mary?" Laura sighed. "I think we can safely say we've checked all those nooks and crannies."

"God knows." Clae sounded disgruntled. He ran out of patience somewhere around the taxidermy room. "Someone's bound to come through here eventu—Hey!"

He sprang forward to lean over the rail. On the first floor a maid with a duster shrieked in surprise.

"Who's there?" she cried.

"Where's Mary Sullivan?" Clae called.

The maid looked around wildly. For some reason she didn't think to look up. "I-I'm warning you, don't threaten me—"

"Oh for god's sake, just tell me where the woman is and get going!"

The maid squealed at the tone and covered her head in fear. "The parlor!" she wailed.

"Then go get her!"

"Yes, sir!"

The maid dashed out of sight.

"Look at her go," Laura remarked, impressed by her speed. "I wonder who she thought you were?"

"As if I care. Come on, she'll probably come by sooner than later."

They took their time descending the stairs, and were nearing the bottom step when Mary walked in. Her expression went from haughty to exasperated at the sight of them.

"So it was you," she grouched. "Do you enjoy scaring young girls so they think an evil spirit is talking to them?"

"Is that what she thought I was?" Clae sounded completely uninterested.

Mary sighed and massaged her temples. "Forget it. Did you find anything?"

"We did."

Her head jerked up in surprise, and Clae pulled the amulet out of his pocket.

"This was sitting in the refrigerator in the kitchen. Your chef confirmed it's not one of yours. We got rid of the creature that was inside."

"But where did it come from?" gasped Mary. "I mean, who—"

"That's not my job. I told you, terriers. Call the police already."

"Is there any way to prevent more from getting in? To stop this from happening again?" asked Mary, sounding desperate.

A muscle jumped in Clae's cheek. The truest response was that it was impossible to stop the spread—wouldn't other cities have figured that out and created the grand utopia Amicae painted itself to be?—but Clae chose the next option.

"Stop the source. You want the Mad Dogs to stop lobbing monsters into your house? Have Daddy-in-Law stop pissing them off."

"The Mad Dogs?" The mention otherwise shocked her into silence. It took a moment for her to recover and say, "There's nothing else we can do?"

"Absolutely nothing." Clae pocketed the amulet again. "And now there's the matter of payment."

"Yes." Mary folded her hands together and schooled her face into neutrality. "Did you find something, or will I be supporting you?"

"Oh, I found something."

Laura eyed him with surprise. She hadn't noticed him mention or linger over anything. What he might've wanted, she had no idea. She was sad there wouldn't be a pay raise, though. Sweeper pay was decent as it was, but not quite enough for her to be confident buying that new apartment.

"What is it, then?"

"That servant of yours. You know, the one with the gray eyes. He's got hair about this long."

Clae gestured somewhere around his waist, but neither of the others said anything. They were too busy staring at him in incredulity. A person? He was asking for a *person*? Amicae hadn't dealt with slaves in near one hundred fifty years; people couldn't just be traded around like that.

"Are you serious?" Laura laughed uncertainly.

"Completely." Clae kept his eyes on the other woman. "You said anything, and I want him."

Mary was nervous. It didn't take a genius to know, since she made no good effort to hide it. She wrung her hands in distress, avoiding eye contact. "Are you sure there isn't anything else? A vase, a chair . . ."

"No."

She fretted even more. "He's not really mine to give."

"That didn't stop you before. You were willing to give me anything of your father-in-law's, even his favorite chair."

"But that's a chair, not a person."

"Anything. A body is a thing. A person's a body, so it counts."

Flawed logic. Definitely flawed logic. The ridiculousness of it made Laura want to smack him. She wanted to smack them both, because this conversation shouldn't even have happened.

"Are you trying to argue with slave logic?" Mary squawked.

"He wouldn't even be here if you weren't keeping him like a slave."

"For your information, the Sullivans have been nothing but kind to that boy!" cried Mary, puffing herself up. "They took him in as a child, fed him, clothed him—"

"*Abused him.*" When Mary faltered, he hissed, "Did you think it wasn't *obvious*?"

Laura remembered the way that servant reacted in the kitchen, like a wary, mistreated dog, and how Mary had been talking about whipping. Her stomach did an odd, sympathetic flip-flop, but she still wasn't keen on where this was going.

"He's treated just as civilly as the rest of—"

"Don't try to bullshit me, woman. We made a deal."

"But you don't even care about money! Why would you want him?" Mary practically shrieked.

Laura couldn't make any connection between the servant and money, but before she could think too hard on it someone else came into the hallway. It was Henry.

"What's going on here? Mary, why were you shouting?"

Mary buried her face in her hands and shook her head. Her husband looked up at Laura and Clae, and his expression clearly blamed them, even if he didn't know what for yet.

"What are you still doing here?" he growled. "I thought you were thrown out!"

After a moment Mary's hands slid down and she forced calm as she said, "I told them to do their job anyway. I said if they found something they could have anything from the house as payment, and they found an amulet planted in the kitchen."

Henry's face contorted. He seemed to war with worry over the danger, and anger. He settled on the latter.

"Why would you make such a stupid deal? And with my father's property! You own none of this, nothing!"

"You were in danger! We were all in danger! What was I supposed to do when he refused to accept money?" she yelled back.

"What is it he wants, then?"

"He wants Okane."

Clae gave a loud snort, but Laura didn't catch the joke. Henry's face was dark as a thundercloud.

"That's not happening."

"Oh yes it is," said Clae, "because that's the deal. God forbid the Sullivans go back on their word. Who knows, this little old Sweeper might spread some rather unsavory accounts of your activities, and what exactly you're hiding around this house." That was a bluff and Laura knew it. As far as she could tell they'd found nothing incriminating. "Of course, I could just go to the police about that *slave*. They wouldn't even question me about it. We're quite well acquainted, you know. Either way you lose him. Best take the option that doesn't drag your name through the mud. Your choice, of course."

Mary's expression was one of horror, and Henry looked just about to blow his top.

"You have nothing," he spluttered angrily.

"Is that a chance you're willing to take?"

His voice was full of confidence, even with a face the very picture of a clean slate. Laura was impressed by this if not by the blackmail. If the police caught someone with a slave they could be thrown in jail for a long time, and if someone like the Sullivans had their names stained with that, no one was likely to want anything to do with them. Business sunk. Pit disaster averted. Either way, Clae got the better end of the stick.

They seemed to hold a staring contest. The intensity of Henry's glare made Laura happy she wasn't the target, but Clae stared back with no concern. The silence pressed on for what felt like forever, but Laura could see Henry breaking. The muscles of his face twitched and jumped, his jaw clenched, and his eyes narrowed. Laura had to shift her weight by the time he spoke.

"Fine. Fine."

He turned and brushed a hand against one of the amulets they'd found earlier, a slight detail of the umbrella stand, and a short time later the butler arrived.

"You called, sir?"

"Get Okane," Henry ordered.

The butler's eyes flickered to Clae and Laura but he inclined his head, murmuring, "Yes, sir," before vanishing the way he'd come.

Did this mean Clae had won?

Laura looked around at the others. Mary's face was downturned, Henry's flushed red. After a while footsteps broke the silence again. The butler returned, silver-eyed servant in his wake.

"—called for me?" the servant said, again barely discernible. Now that Laura paid more attention she saw the delay in his speech, and didn't hear the word at all.

Henry eyed him venomously for a moment before saying, "Okane, you're not staying here anymore. You're going with them."

Confusion flickered over Okane's face. "Sir?"

"Go," growled Henry, turning away. "Now!"

"Hang on," Laura cut in, confused. "Doesn't he need to gather his belongings? He must have clothes, or—"

"Get out!" Henry roared.

It was so loud Laura jumped in fright, and she wasn't the only one. Clae was singularly unaffected.

"Come on, then." He beckoned to the servant.

Okane hurried over and Clae waved them on to the door. He glanced over his shoulder as they left.

"Pleasure doing business with you," he purred.

Henry snarled, and Mary choked back angry tears.

Out on the front step, Laura eyed this Okane person shrewdly. He looked right back from the corner of his eyes, distrust clearly stamped on his features. Clae shut the door with a loud click and glanced between them.

"What are you waiting for? Get walking."

Okane moved at the pace of a snail, but they began the trek toward the main gates. Laura itched to ask what was going on, but she didn't like the idea of asking when the subject of her uncertainty was *right there*. Luckily said subject was just as uncertain as she was.

"If I may ask," Okane ventured, "what exactly is going on?"

"You're switching jobs."

"I'm what?"

"Switching jobs. You're going to be my apprentice now."

Laura almost tripped and fell flat on her face. She was glad she didn't, but that relief was eclipsed by shock. Apprentice? He was supposed to be an apprentice? But that was Laura's job! She'd been doing well, too, and she didn't think she was too annoying. Was it that Clae wanted a complete pushover to follow him around instead, with no questions or concerns, just blind faith? Did he not like a chatty girl? Was it simply because she was a girl? Another glance at Okane and he was altered in her mind: no longer a sad-eyed pretty boy but a threat.

"Don't make that face." Clae bumped her knee with a corner of the briefcase. "Sweepers can have more than one apprentice."

Laura was relieved, though not by much. She hadn't had to compete with anyone in this job yet, and wasn't a fan of the idea.

"But I work for the Sullivans," Okane insisted.

"And they've given you up, so you can work for me. If you want the job."

"They won't let go of me that easily."

"Look, kid." Clae's eyes carried a hint of irritation now. "They may not like me, but I've got at least half the police department to back me up. The Sullivans have no hold on you now."

As if to directly counter that statement, the door swung open behind them and Frank Sullivan stepped out. His earlier calm was gone; instead the animosity bubbled to the surface, twisting his features.

"Bastard!" he shouted. "You goddamned, underhanded, flea-bitten bastard! Get back here!"

Laura gawked for a moment before Clae jabbed her with the briefcase again and hissed, "Get moving!"

The three of them sprinted down the rest of the driveway with Frank hobbling along behind, raging all the way. He was nowhere close to catching them, but there was still the gate. They reached it at full speed and practically smacked into it. Clae shoved the briefcase through the bars, clicked his heels together, and began to scale the gate. Laura clicked her own heels together. As the amulets there activated, she felt gravity's hold slacken enough that she could climb more easily, gripping the iron bars and heaving herself up. Okane scrambled up after her, doing well for someone without an amulet's help. They vaulted over the spikes on top and landed heavily. Laura was sure without the magic she would've broken one of her ankles. She glanced back to see Clae still on the other side. He was near the top, but he reconsidered and jumped back down. He charged back toward Frank. The businessman faltered in his tracks, then turned tail at the sight. Clae chased him a good ten feet up the driveway before dashing back to the gate and vaulting over it. He landed next to Laura and scooped up the briefcase, glancing over at her.

"Come on. I can scare him, but he probably has security. Best get out of here before they show up."

Laura nodded, and they fled the scene.

They only stopped running at the cable car platform, and by that time Laura was completely winded. She leaned against the platform rail and panted there for a while. Okane breathed hard too, but Clae regained composure quickly. He knelt down and opened the briefcase to check if anything was broken. The cushioned lining must've done its job, as he nodded and closed it again.

"What were --- saying, before?" Okane wheezed. It was so quiet Laura guessed they weren't supposed to hear it, but Clae replied immediately.

"They're sore losers, but they're not going to get you again."

Okane recoiled. Clae caught the movement and sighed. He held out one hand, palm up, and forced himself to relax. He spoke something in a different language, the words choppy—obviously he wasn't fluent. Slowly Okane relaxed too, staring at Clae like he was some alien creature. Clae said nothing more, simply knelt there with hand outstretched.

After a while Okane asked, "Who are --- people, anyway?"

"Sweepers. I'm Clae Sinclair. This is Laura."

Okane's brow furrowed. "--- clean floors?"

Laura's gasping for breath dissolved into a fit of giggles, even if it wasn't that funny, and her lungs were further deprived of oxygen.

6

SILVER IS NOT GOLD

The next day, Laura fretted over the new addition.

She was a little upset that Clae had hired Okane. She didn't want to be replaced as favorite—even if she was the only one that could be considered such before—and was unsure how to act around Okane himself. After a short conversation about what Sweepers did (and how there were absolutely no brooms involved, they weren't chimney sweeps), he clammed up and skulked around after them like a sulky shadow. He absorbed information well, but trying to pry anything from him proved a hassle. Though Laura had left rather early. Maybe Clae cracked him at some point later on?

She didn't much like him. He'd given her no reason to. He was competition, the cuckoo in her nest, and damn if she was going to let him worm his way into Clae's good books when she'd spent a good three months cracking the cover. But she supposed she'd at least act civilly. He was in a bad situation and maybe he'd get better.

She decided this as she wheeled onto Acis Road. She braked her bike outside the door to the Sweeper shop and lugged it up the stairs. Opening the door and maneuvering the bicycle around it, she spotted the others quickly. The giant Egg sat on the countertop, Clae explaining what they were going to do with it while Okane nodded absently.

"There you are." Clae noticed her and broke off mid-explanation. "Come on. Get this in the trunk and let's get going. We don't have all day."

He was rude as ever, but for some reason Laura took it personally this time. She leaned her bike against the wall and sulked over. The trunk lay open on the floor. She grabbed one end of the Egg and waited for Clae to take the other, but he didn't. Instead he looked expectantly at Okane. Okane hesitated, but grabbed the other handle. A hot flush of resentment crawled up the back of her neck.

"Careful, now," warned Clae. "You break that, and I break you."

Laura pursed her lips but lifted her end. Okane copied soon enough, and they heaved the glass case off the counter. Okane floundered. For a moment Laura was terrified he'd drop it, but he steadied himself, and with a little difficulty they lowered the Egg into its place in the trunk. Clae snapped it closed and locked it, then stepped back.

"You two are carrying that, too. Take care not to drop it."

"You're not helping?" asked Laura, surprised.

"Why should I when I have two apprentices?"

"I thought this was part of the job."

"Why do you care? You're carrying it either way."

True, but that didn't mean she had to be happy about it. She felt like he'd managed to cheat his way out of it.

As they began their walk down the street toward today's Pit, her mood didn't lighten. She thanked her luck that it was Friday and there wasn't much distance to this one; Okane struggled with his half of the trunk, unable to find a position where it didn't bump into his knees or otherwise impede his walking. To this at least, Laura was sympathetic. She wasn't fond of how it ended up messing with her side, though. She kept having to adjust for his changes and frankly, it was getting annoying. Thankfully Clae decided now was a good time for picking up his earlier explaining to Okane.

"There are three usable Pits in Amicae. They're used to store broken amulets, so they can be monitored and 'flushed' regularly. Each Pit is visited once a week. North on Monday, Southeast on Wednesday, Southwest on Friday. The cycle is required to make sure nothing takes root in the amulets there in the Pit. There's no way to prevent infestations from taking root in a broken amulet, and if there are multiple spaces for infestations to fester in one place, they spread faster. Flushing kin down the Pit every week destroys any and all infestations that may have begun over the week. Skipping a week of the Pit rounds isn't life-threatening, but if you leave it much longer, infestations will grow and they will start working. So *don't* fall out of the habit. Every week. Monday Wednesday Friday. Keep up."

"And the Pits can't be moved," Laura added, to show she was listening the other day.

"You try to redirect the Pit, and you'll end up ruining its efficiency and compromising the structure of the city itself. The Pits were in the original blueprints of the city. Amicae is essentially built around them," Clae elaborated.

"Wait, really?"

Throughout her school career Laura learned about the founding and history of Amicae, but Sweepers had only been touched on as being obsolete. There'd been no mention of Pits whatsoever.

"Sweepers were heavily involved in the founding of Amicae, though we fell out of favor with the rise of industry. We had a lot of influence and space in the beginning, people got jealous, and they started appealing to the Council during a long dry spell so there weren't any infestations around to really prove we were needed. The Council decided that Sweepers had no real purpose so didn't need all that room, and as time went on they kept reallocating the space and we had to make do with what we had, even when the infestations started picking up again. Sweepers nearly died out, and we've never recovered." He glanced back at them. "Look at you. Case in point."

"I'm not that bad."

"There are only three of us. Other cities have around twenty active Sweepers."

"That many?"

"They never had the pedestal to fall from, though."

"I was more under the impression it was a cliff," said Laura. "Sweepers were important everywhere. I thought Amicae just purposely let it slip."

"It's a bit different with Amicae. More offensive. Other cities were built up and fortified even in the first years of the infestation's spread, back before anyone knew what worked, and later incorporated all the pieces around the existing structures. Amicae was built well after Sweepers were established, so one was hired before the city was even constructed, and they asked her if there was anything important that may need to be in the blueprints. She took the chance to hijack everything and specialize the city to suit Sweepers: Pits galore, factories for Kin, weapon construction, treatment of clothes . . . anything that could possibly help a Sweeper, she bullied the founders into including it. Once it was all done, the job was so efficient it wasn't until the decline that even one Sweeper was killed. People came from all over to learn techniques here in 'the Sweeper city.' Glory days. And of course, all that space was city-owned property, and able to be reallocated. In the end Sweepers had to scramble and raise money to buy as much of the critical equipment as they could."

So there was more to it, beyond the Pits and the shop? "I'll have to look this up."

"You'd best look for old material. Sweepers have practically disappeared from the history books," Clae hummed.

"No wonder I had to find out about us through a Coronae publication. So, check old bookstores like Brecht's?"

"Coronae?" He frowned but shook his head. "I have some books on the subject too. Remind me later and I'll lend them to you. It's probably more relevant than any glorified story they pump out. Amicae's a pit, after all."

By this time they'd reached another door to the interior of Amicae. It looked identical to the others, and when it opened, right on time today, there was the same man who was always there to greet them.

"Mornin' son." He grinned. "How are ya today?"

Clae blatantly ignored him, but Laura smiled. "We're doing well. How are you?"

"Not bad! Better now I'm gettin' a break!"

He chuckled as he led them inside. Laura took five steps into the dark, smoky atmosphere, and found she couldn't go farther. Okane froze, clutching his side of the trunk like a lifeline as he stared at their surroundings.

"Come on." Laura tugged at her end, but he didn't budge. "What's wrong with you?"

"What are you two doing?" Clae was already a good distance away from them and he looked annoyed.

"He stopped and he won't start walking again!" she complained.

Clae doubled back and tapped Okane's shoulder.

"Hey. What's wrong?"

Okane seemed to shrivel up further.

"Answer me."

"What is this place?" Okane muttered.

"Interior of Amicae. That noise is industry, not a beast. Get walking."

Clae nudged him forward. Reluctantly, Okane began to walk again. Once Clae was sure he'd keep moving, he rejoined the bearded man ahead of them. The man watched in interest.

"Who's that new helper of yours?"

"None of your business."

"Is he just a buddy or is he another apprentice?" the man persisted, stubbornly looking for a conversation.

"I said it's none of your business."

"Well, if he's an apprentice, why's the girl still carryin' that thing?"

"She's tough. She can handle it."

Laura wasn't sure whether to take that as a compliment or not.

It was slower than usual, but they made it to the nearest elevator. The bearded man brought it up, where more miners flooded out, paying them no attention though Okane gave them a wide berth. The three Sweepers boarded the elevator.

"Good luck," the man wished them. Laura decided he had no idea what they were doing.

The grilles rattled shut. Laura swung her side of the trunk as the elevator began to rise, and as a result Okane stumbled.

"Are we just doing the Pit rounds today?" she asked, pretending not to notice. "Just sitting around in the shop the rest of the day?"

"We're visiting the Amuletory afterwards."

"Are we really?"

"What's with that tone?" Clae glanced back. "Yes, we are."

Laura made a face. Clae snorted. They entered the closed shaft. A short time later they reached sunlight again and the grille opened. This location looked nearly identical to other Pit locations, save for different buildings nearby. A steeple jutted up beside the wall, casting part of the walkway in shadow and a spray of rainbow through its colored windows.

Clae made a beeline for the Pit cover. Okane watched him go with apprehension, and Laura had to drag him out. Meanwhile Clae started turning the wheel. Laura could hear screeching as the slats moved. The opening yawned almost completely uncovered before she and Okane reached it, setting down the trunk as Clae finished.

"Right." He rubbed his hands together as he walked over to them. "Like I said before, we'll pour the kin down here. We're not dropping this Egg down, we're taking off the lid and pouring it nice and slow. Take it out, and remember, this is the only one we have."

"Out of curiosity, how long would it take to get a new one?" Laura asked, opening the trunk.

"God only knows. If you don't want to carry this vessel's worth of regular Eggs, you'll treat it carefully."

That seemed aimed at Okane, for good reason. Laura was used to this already. She and Okane took hold of the Egg handles and lifted it from the trunk. Clae hovered over them, twitching badly when Okane stumbled. Laura managed to save it from cracking into the ground twice before Clae intervened.

"Oh for the love of—Just step aside and watch."

He wormed his way in and took hold of some handles, shooing Okane away. He watched them from a slight distance, and Laura felt relieved.

"Thanks," she whispered.

"Don't thank me, concentrate," Clae shot back.

They lowered the Egg gently and he unscrewed the cap. He balanced most of the weight on his leg as he set the lid aside, then began to tip the Egg. Laura helped him steady it and soon enough the kin spilled out, beginning its strange, dancing descent down the Pit. Laura peered over the edge to watch better.

"Don't fall in."

"I know better than that," she scoffed, but drew away all the same. There was nothing to catch herself on if she did end up falling.

"That's all there is to it." Clae glanced at Okane, who seemed just as intrigued with the kin's movement as Laura was a moment ago.

"Really?" Okane muttered.

"Now this goes back in the trunk and we leave."

He and Laura straightened the Egg, and he put the cap back on. That done, they brought it to the trunk to close it all up. Once that was taken care of, he ordered Okane to help carry again. With less weight the trunk was easier to manage.

The elevator ride down stayed quiet and uneventful. The bearded man grinned as they stepped out onto the walkway.

"That was fast."

"We didn't have to wait for the elevator," Clae quipped.

"True enough. I think somebody's behind on the work schedule." The man scratched his head. "Usually the shift changes and people go ta the lower levels round this time."

Laura's heart skipped a beat and she looked around. The noise was the same, the amount of smoke the same, the buildings no different from usual, but . . . "Did something happen?" She may not have been very close to her father, but he was in the mines below. She'd hated dark places as a child, and now, with firsthand knowledge of infestations, the thought was so much worse.

"Nah, if something happened we'd all hear it."

"Are you sure?" she said.

Clae raised a brow at her concern and jerked his head at the elevator shaft. "The interior has an alarm system. If something happened, it'd be loud."

"An absolute racket," the bearded man laughed. "No worries here. I suppose you'll be in a hurry on some other business, then? I'll take ya back to the door."

He led them back the way they came, passing by some workers on the way, who did double takes upon noticing the addition to the Sweeper group. Laura was too busy peering over the railing to notice them. The lower levels were too dark and wreathed in smoke, but at least there was nothing *strange*. No alarms.

⌗

The main Amuletory was located in the Fifth Quarter. The argument for this was so that even the poorer, uneducated people would be able to have access to it. A good idea, but Laura wasn't a fan of walking through the surrounding district.

The ramshackle buildings squatted discolored and old, but were kept up so they were still usable despite obvious disrepair. The dirty streets and dilapidated structures carried a dark overtone, as opposed to the yellowish, brighter air of upper Quarters. The business district managed to be slightly cleaner than the rest, with smaller buildings contrasted with the many-leveled apartments behind them. People stood on flat roofs as if they were porches, even going so far as to bring up rocking chairs or tables.

Through this business district the Sweepers walked, carrying the big faded trunk. Laura had never felt completely safe here, even less so now that they carried something big and potentially valuable. The eyes of those rooftop watchers burned into her.

"How much longer until we get there?" she asked, too busy eyeing their spectators to pay much attention to their other surroundings.

"At the corner, see for yourself." Clae waved a hand ahead.

Sure enough, on the corner twenty yards beyond, the sign for the Amuletory stood out on the sidewalk. The large lettering implied a circus more than a shop. They quickened their pace, passed a store with floor rugs hanging out on display, and pushed open the door to their destination.

The Amuletory was small, only about half the space of the Sweeper shop. Amulets of all kinds were strung up, on the walls, on the ceiling, laid out on tables, and dangling in the window. There was no rhyme or reason to their shapes or colors, simply a giant smattering of everything. In between the piles lay incense burners, which fogged up the room. It was meant to smell good, but Laura felt it like a physical blow. Her eyes watered. The whole store seemed wrapped up in a stuffy, strange *something*, as if it was meant to look like the hideout of some witch. They were selling magical items, Laura supposed, so they might as well go all the way. Play up the gimmick and all.

A woman with heavy eye makeup sat in a musty chair near the back. Her dirty orange hair lay uncombed, and her cigarette only added to the haze. When she saw them, her scarlet lips turned up in a smile.

"Hello," she purred. "Back again, Mr. Sinclair?"

"Obviously. Where's Marshall?"

"On business." She stood and slinked closer, breathing out a cloud of smoke. "What about you, then? Are you here for business? Or something else?"

It should've been obvious that he was here on business—he came in with two apprentices on his heels. Besides, he was Clae.

"Business. Now where's Marshall?"

The woman slid even closer, and Laura rolled her eyes. This woman, Freda Ashford, and the smell were the two reasons she couldn't stand this place. The smell almost hurt, and Freda kept trying to drape herself all over Clae, which made Laura uncomfortable. She really didn't need to see that. In the past she'd begged Clae to just visit a different Amuletory location— there were satellites all around Amicae—but he frequented this one because he appreciated Marshall's attitude. Instead of complaining, she wordlessly pulled Okane to the side so they could deposit the trunk, and inspected one of the amulets in the window. It looked like an ugly theater mask.

"Are you sure *I* can't help you?"

"I believe I've made it clear on multiple occasions that no, you can't. Now go get your boss."

Freda let out a sigh that somehow managed to be annoyed and flirty at the same time, did a strange toss of the head, eyed him a bit longer, then sashayed to the door. She opened it and leaned out; her voice went from silky smooth to a harsh bark.

"*Hey you stinking little shits! Tell Marshall to get back here, now!*" She closed the door and smiled at them again. "He'll just be a moment."

"I'm sure."

Laura sat down on the trunk. There was no telling how long this would take. Okane kept standing, but she ignored him. Maybe if she pretended he didn't exist he'd vanish.

"So how are you today?" Freda gravitated back toward Clae and ignored the other two completely.

Clae didn't comment. He glanced over at the vacated chair, then decided to entertain himself by looking at the amulets.

"Well?" Freda pressed, actually leaning on him, and Clae made a hissing sound and stepped away.

"Back off, woman."

"Just trying to make friendly conversation."

"Freda, stop harassing the man." The deep voice made Laura jump.

Jacob Marshall was intimidating. He was the most muscular person Laura knew, with veins bulging out on his arms and neck. His dark head had been shaved bald and scars wound about on his face and right shoulder. Tattoos rose up his arms, even more sinister when paired with a blind right eye in a pale blue-gray color. His face was arranged in a way that made him look permanently angry.

"Sinclair." He nodded.

"Marshall." Clae turned away from Freda, who looked rather disappointed. "I've got some amulets for you."

"Of course." Marshall walked back toward the chair and pulled a large notebook out from under a table. As he flipped it open, he asked, "How many this time?"

"Didn't count."

"Well then, let's see them."

Clae emptied out his pockets. It was all the unbroken amulets he and Laura had found, or what had been turned in to them, over the past month.

While one function of the Amuletory might be the sale of amulets, its other job was recycling. Amulets couldn't be allowed to run out of magic or they'd become ideal homes for monsters, so a system was set up to get them powered again. People were supposed to turn in amulets to one of the Amuletories, which sent them below Amicae. There they would be placed next to the magic strain: a type of rock called Gin. They absorbed magic from there, and were later returned to the owners. If there were no owners, the newly functioning amulet was put up for sale here. Many

upper-class people either couldn't get down to an Amuletory or were reluctant to do so, and turned their amulets in to the Sweeper shop instead.
Such amulets Clae usually scribbled the owner's name on in pen. Quite a
few of those were dumped onto the table now. Laura recognized the one
from the Sullivan house among them. Marshall took notes on all of them,
documenting appearance and owners and other information, which he
would later share with the police—that way they'd get a better idea of
who had amulets and who to check in with should something arise.

"Twenty-six," Marshall confirmed. "Difficult to get ahold of?"

"The difficult ones tend to be broken," said Clae. "Most of these just
need a refresher."

"Of course." Marshall tipped one amulet to better read the name.

"Any of yours?" murmured Freda, leaning her hip on the table.

"No."

Sweepers had special amulets: theirs were pieces of the magic strain
itself. As such, they never ran out of power. These types of amulets were
rare and generally unknown to the population, but people who did know
would pay amazing amounts of money for one.

"You never do," Freda sighed. Obviously she wasn't in on the secret.
"We'd take good care of yours, you know."

"I'm sure." Clae rolled his eyes, and Marshall glanced up at him with
something that might've been amusement.

"I'll have copies of this sent over to the police."

"Good. Maybe then they'll get off my back. The new chief thinks I'm
up to something."

"You're harmless," Marshall chuckled.

"*Thanks.*"

"Don't mention it."

Clae drifted back and gestured to Laura and Okane. "Let's go."

"You could stay awhile," said Freda.

"Business," Clae repeated, and they left the store.

Once they were outside, Laura took a deep breath of fresh air.

"I thought I was going to die in there," she muttered.

"They do go a little heavy on the incense."

"How can they survive with that much smell in the air?" Laura followed, pulling the trunk and Okane along as Clae walked down the street.

"Sheer determination. That or they live on it. The whole block is obsessed." Clae jerked his head at another shop, which smelled strongly of lavender.

"I hope it doesn't start a trend."

"If the trend reaches us, you and Brecht have my permission to sabotage all of it."

Clae pulled out his pocket watch again. As he did, Laura realized they were headed in a different direction than the cable cars.

"Where are we going?"

"You don't know?"

"Not really."

"The tree."

Ah, the tree. Of course.

7

ROOTS

The tree in question was an eastern maple, at least twenty feet tall. Its trunk and branches twisted and contorted into something entirely strange, with the resulting shape of a leafy mushroom. Today the leaves were dark green, but if it was anything like the decorative trees along the Tiber Circuit, it would turn a beautiful red in the fall. Clae liked to frequent this tree when he had time. Laura wasn't entirely sure why, but he did. It was probably just another of his habits.

"You really like this tree," Laura mused, when they reached it.

The tree was located on the outer edge of the Fifth Quarter, almost teetering over the side of the low wall. Beyond and below, the shacks and military barracks of the Sixth Quarter could be seen. On some occasions Laura had sat with her legs over the side (tempting fate—one slip and she could fall all the way down and kill herself), and watched as soldiers drilled or shooed noncitizens away from official buildings. Clae only had eyes for the tree. He walked up to it, stepped onto a particularly large root, and placed his hand on the trunk.

"It's a good tree," he replied, running fingers across the bark.

"Aren't all trees good trees?"

"This one's particularly good. Here, come closer."

With a sigh Laura trudged over. She entered the tree's shadow, and had to admit it provided nice shade from the heat. She loosened the bandana around her neck in case of a breeze, and craned her head to look up. The sun filtered through the leaves, blinding in spots and simply highlighting the green in others. As a slight wind sighed through, they swayed, and the light winked merrily.

"It's pretty, but I don't see why you like it so much."

"I don't see why you like poster scraps either," he retorted, and she flushed red.

"How did you know about—"

"When you're stuffing old flyers into your pockets all the time, how wouldn't I know?"

Here Laura thought she'd been sneaky about it. "I like the colors," she grumbled. "The pictures are nice."

"And the tree isn't?" he challenged.

"It is," Laura groaned, slumping against the tree and sliding down to the roots. She dragged Okane and the trunk down in the process. "It's just . . . I don't know. Doesn't seem like the sort of thing you'd like so much."

He simply hummed, trailing back around to admire the other side of the tree.

⸺⸺

Laura arrived home at five that evening. She turned in her bike, trudged up the stairs, entered the apartment, and flopped down on her bed without Morgan being any the wiser. She would've gone unnoticed for much longer if Cheryl hadn't spotted her.

"Mom! Mom! Laura's back!"

Laura could hear her voice in the kitchen, and it was one of those times she really hated it. That girl's voice was so high-pitched sometimes it could hurt. Luckily she'd quieted down, more so the neighbors wouldn't complain about it than for this apartment's comfort. Footsteps alerted her to Morgan's approach. Laura tipped her head to the side to look up at her. Morgan stood in the doorway, looking both worried and amused.

"Hello." She smiled when she saw she had Laura's attention. "How long have you been in here?"

"Five minutes maybe?"

Morgan gave a breathy laugh. "I didn't hear you come in. Must've been the stove making too much noise."

"Or maybe Cheryl," Laura suggested, heaving herself into a sitting position.

"She's just excited. One of her friends got a penny doll and now she wants one too." Morgan was quiet for a moment. "Did everything go well today? You seem down."

"I'm just tired. It was a long, boring day. We went to the Amuletory which, you know, I *love*. And then Clae dragged us out to look at his tree and we spent the rest of the time trying to talk to the new employee." She wrinkled her nose and said, "I hope he quits," under her breath.

"Surely he's not that bad? Didn't you say Mr. Sinclair's been having you haul things around for him? That must be men's work. This takes some of the pressure off of you!"

Laura rolled her eyes. "Men's work" this and "men's work" that was a frustrating constant by now. "You'd like to think that, but he's a total goldbrick."

"Is he clever, at least?"

"Not as far as I can tell."

"You don't think he's there to replace you?"

"Clae said no."

They were quiet a moment, and then Morgan asked, "What's his name?"

Laura hummed out the syllables: "Oh-kah-nay. I've never heard of anyone named that before. I think it's another language."

"Is he from another city?"

Laura glanced at the collage, couldn't picture a single place in all the city pieces where Okane would look natural. "Maybe?"

"Interesting. Is he handsome?"

"Mommy!" Cheryl ran up to tug on Morgan's skirt. "I want to eat! When's dinner?"

"We'll be ready in just a few minutes." Morgan hustled back. "Could you get the bowls out? Laura, get the cups."

Laura sulked into the kitchen and pulled open the cupboard. *Is he handsome,* she mouthed bitterly. The conversation had bounced from "how's your day" to "my job may be in danger" to "do you fancy the dingbat you just said you disliked." She really should've seen it coming.

Soon she had the drinks set, Cheryl tottered over with the bowls, and Morgan came over with the stewpot. She put it down on the table, and set aside the two washcloths she'd been using like mittens.

"Right, sit down and let's eat." Morgan started sorting out the silverware, but stopped short. She counted through the spoons and sighed. "I let the neighbors borrow our ladle."

"I thought you got that back last week," said Laura.

"I did, but they were hosting a party and needed it again. Don't look at me like that."

Laura shook her head. Morgan wasn't a popular neighbor, but she was always trying to win people over by being as helpful as possible. This typically resulted in neighbors "borrowing" things from them and Morgan fretting about whether they'd be upset if she asked for the items back. Several times Laura had to march up to doors and demand plates they'd lent out six months ago. The Cynder Block quickly learned that while Morgan deferred easily, Laura was a leech determined to make lives miserable.

"Who'd you lend it to this time?"

"Charlie," Morgan admitted. "Could you run down and see him? I'm sure he'll give it back if you ask for it."

Determination flew out of Laura with such speed she felt suddenly weak.

"Well," she coughed, "we can probably make do with just the spoons."

"It'll only take a few minutes," said Morgan. "Just enough time for the food to cool!" Laura gave her a dismal look, but Morgan made a shooing motion, smiled, and said, "Go on!"

Laura closed her eyes, resigned herself to her fate. Just a minute or two. She could do this. She sucked in a breath, told them she'd be right back, and made for the door.

Laura didn't like Charlie.

Once upon a time they'd been friends, and there was a point in high school when she'd been appreciative of his looks, almost dated him even, but in the past few years he'd gone from friendly to irritating. Morgan hadn't picked up on that change, and Laura didn't want to point it out. She didn't like to acknowledge the reasons.

Apartment number 808 had a large scar in the door, nearly half an inch deep at its worst. She eyed it reproachfully but reached up to knock. Almost immediately a clatter and quiet cursing came from inside. Laura twiddled her thumbs as footsteps grew closer. The door opened.

Charlie was a head taller than Laura, with short brown hair in varying lengths on his head as if he'd burned patches of it off. He hadn't shaved and there were dark bags under his eyes, but those eyes lit up when he saw who it was.

"Laura!" Even his voice seemed brighter. "Haven't seen you in a while. How have you been?"

"I'm fine. You?"

"Never better. What's up?"

"My aunt says she lent your mom one of the ladles. I was wondering if you were done with it."

Charlie's face blanked for a moment. "Oh, yeah! The ladle! I'll get it now. You can come inside if you like."

Charlie retreated into his apartment, leaving the door open behind him. Laura slinked into the entryway but ventured no farther, choosing to watch instead as he rifled through drawers. His apartment was set up the same as the one Laura lived in, so she could see straight into the living room. A wide array of metal parts and tools were scattered on the floor there, and the torso of a robot rested on the worn couch beside a half-eaten bowl of rice. The stare of its mechanical face made Laura shift uneasily, rubbing at her arm for comfort.

Charlie was actually very smart. While other people Laura knew never went farther than high school, Charlie was gifted with scholarships like Sullivan's to attend college. His knowledge grew by leaps and bounds, and it was obvious from his pet projects how much he learned. He liked to build robots and steam machines for various strange purposes, and was even more excited to talk about the processes with people: this being the very reason Laura began to dislike him. Yes, it was wonderful that he was so enthusiastic about what he did, but he talked of nothing else, rarely allowed any opening to respond, and honestly, Laura wasn't interested in the topic. She couldn't care less what wire went where and how these gears worked together most efficiently. It was boring, and the fact that she didn't understand it made her feel stupid. She hated feeling stupid. Clae made her feel stupid all the time, but he at least tended to explain things in simple ways, and he was also her mentor, so he was supposed to be a step above her, knowledgewise. Charlie held knowledge over her head like a trophy. She was certain half of the technical rubbish he spouted was just so he could see the confusion on her face, puff up his chest in pride that this made him superior. She still remembered the year before they graduated high school, her mourning over not making it into Class One—the only group universities or talent scouts would ever consider—and outlining feverish plans to eavesdrop, to sneak her way into the coursework. He laughed at her. *Why would you want to do that?* he'd asked, still half choking on his own mirth. *Class One is for us, not you. What would you do with a degree? Become some doddery librarian? A spinster? Who'd ever want to marry that?* As if that was all she was good for. For weeks after she wished she'd had the courage to punch him in his stupid face, but now she knew it was best she hadn't; Clae had only shown her the proper way to punch something a month ago.

"Here it is!" cried Charlie, fishing out the ladle. "I should keep better track of things, it would make work so much easier!" He laughed to himself as he walked back and offered the utensil. "Have you got some free time? I want to get some opinions on my summer projects, and my parents have had to work late recently. Besides, I want a fresh take on what I'm doing! Class starts up again next week, and if I need to do some fine-tuning, I have to do it fast. You helped a lot just listening to that essay last semester. You know, the one about the faulty sprinkler system in the interior? I almost got full marks on that!"

As if he was actually looking for feedback. Laura had been no help on that essay and she knew it. This was probably just another excuse to see if his explanation went suitably over her head. He likely thought that if he could impress one girl he could wow any female on the examination council. "Sorry." Laura snatched the ladle away and gave one of her fakest smiles. "Sounds great, *really,* but I'm actually busy. Gotta eat dinner and then head back to work. Clae's a slave driver, you know."

Thankfully he bought it. His face fell, but not by a lot. "I hear he's pretty mean. You sure you're okay working for him?"

"Sure, he's all bark and no bite."

"Still, having a tough boss on top of that kind of job?" He shook his head. "Maybe you should look into something more fitting. Didn't the other girls in our class become phone operators? You should've tagged along with—"

"Oh, no, that reminds me!" Laura smacked a hand against her head, hoping she was a good enough actress to pull this off. "Clae's supposed to be calling at six! If I'm not ready by the phone, I don't want to think how he'd react!" Probably with nagging, but he'd never attempted calling the Cynder Block before. "I've got to get going. Thanks for the ladle! I'll see you later."

He looked mildly surprised but laughed again. "Come back anytime!"

Laura had absolutely no plans to return. She hurried back to her own apartment.

Over at the table, Morgan jumped as the door slammed. "That was fast."

"All for the better, right?" Laura kicked off her boots without bothering with the buttons. She was in too much of a rush.

"Funny, I was sure you were going to waste more time over there." Morgan smiled.

"I made an excuse and got out of there as fast as I could," said Laura, setting the ladle into the bowl. On second thought maybe she should've double-checked it was clean.

Morgan looked startled. "Did he have company?"

"No? I'm hungry and he's got work to do."

"Oh. Good. But you don't have to worry about that in the future. We can always warm up food on the stove, and I'm sure Charlie would be so happy to talk—"

"And I do not feel the same," said Laura, spooning food into Cheryl's bowl.

"But it's been so long since you had the chance to talk."

Cheryl looked up from the soup and met Laura's eyes in perfect deadpan. There were times like these where the nine-year-old transcended childish annoyance and they linked perfectly; Cheryl very much knew that Laura disliked Charlie, and didn't like Charlie any better herself.

"Maybe we should invite him over soon," said Morgan, taking her own full bowl. "He always used to come over while you were in school."

"If this is a matchmaking scheme, it won't work," said Laura. "It didn't with your coworkers' sons, and it's never, ever happening here."

"Charlie's such a good boy. You'd do so well together!"

Cheryl mimed gagging. Laura rolled her eyes. This was well-trodden territory and she'd never won the argument.

"Do whatever you want. But forewarning, the Keedlers might be hosting some kind of 'bonding night' for the Acis neighborhood. I might end up unavailable for dinner."

"Keedlers?" Cheryl perked up. "The lady with the cookies?"

Even Morgan joined in on that praise, and the matchmaking topic was dropped for the moment. Laura intended to keep it that way as long as she could.

<hr />

Her simmering feelings finally hit the surface two days later, when she doubled back to return one of Clae's Sweeper books. She'd like to have blamed it on the three infestations they'd had to tackle (all small but nasty, the victims being a chicken coop—complete with six chickens—on the south side, a pet dog not far from there, and two mechanics in their garage), but while they were contributing factors they weren't her limit. She walked into the Sweeper shop, only to find Clae leading Okane out from behind the black curtain. She froze in the doorway to stare, and their hushed conversation came to a stuttering halt as they noticed her presence. Laura wasn't sure what kind of expression she was wearing, but Okane's already pale face went white as a sheet and his jittering worsened. He stepped back in unease, and looked at Clae for help. Clae motioned for him to keep going. Okane glanced back once, then hightailed it to the other door and disappeared.

"What was that?" Laura asked quietly.

"What was what?" Clae sat down on one of the stools and pulled the newspaper closer on the counter.

"*That*," Laura hissed, striding closer and pointing at the place Okane had vanished. "What were you doing? What were you talking to him about? What were you—"

"Calm down. I'm introducing him to the job is all."

None of Laura's introductions included going behind those drapes, and the fact that Okane's did made her blood boil. Why was he getting special treatment? She'd been around longer, she deserved to know more! She deserved to know what was back there!

"You're teaching him differently."

"Everyone has a different learning style," he replied, like it was no big deal.

The fact that he was taking this so easily stung. Laura looked at him, then the drapes, then back again. He couldn't seriously not know about her opinion on the drapes. If he could see she was so obsessed with scraps of paper, he had to pick up on the drapes too. If he hadn't, he was an idiot. That or she was screwed. She was probably screwed either way. Maybe this was like a warning. Acting like it was unimportant meant it was unimportant. Or maybe it was a dare; one she wouldn't take up, because she was angry but she wasn't stupid, and drapes were not worth her life.

This decided, she slammed the book onto the counter beside him and sat on another stool. At first she tried to look defiant, but it kept eating away at her, and eventually she slumped.

"Is it because he's a boy?"

"Hm?"

"You're showing him more things than me. I can't help being a girl, I'm completely capable."

"I never said you weren't."

"But you're—"

"His background requires a different approach." Clae folded the newspaper and looked up at her. His eyes were doing that weird analyzing thing again. "Besides, if I put all the knowledge in one set of hands, what happens if that apprentice dies or quits?"

"Then give us both the info."

"Easier said than done."

Even more easily shown, Laura thought, looking back at the drapes. Her eyes didn't linger there long, though. Couldn't let Clae think she was too interested, right? Unless he was just playing stupid and he really knew and he totally noticed that glance just now. That would explain why his eyes narrowed slightly.

"There's no reason for you to panic. I'm not about to fire you."

"But he'll get any promotions over me."

"With his track record so far? Not likely."

Even with the track record, he got to see behind the drapes. Maybe Laura should start stumbling and slipping up, then maybe Clae would take pity on her and tell her more things as motivation? Unlikely. He didn't do that when she first started, and if she purposely screwed up not only would she hate herself for it, Clae would only get irritated.

"I am your apprentice, though, and you're supposed to be teaching me."

"You've mentioned," he replied dully.

"And you're not teaching me."

"Of course I am. Learn by example."

"Example of what?"

"That's your decision." He picked up the paper again and flipped it up, covering his face. Laura frowned at headlines about a new mob scandal and the approval for some sort of piping project.

"When you say 'it's your decision,' do you mean I should just pick up anything I want?"

"Yes."

"So, in theory, I could pick up the traits of being a blunt, annoying workaholic?"

Clae flipped the top half of the paper down and eyed her reproachfully. "You know what I mean."

"Do I?"

"I'd like to say you're not that stupid."

"You'd *like* to say. What's that supposed to mean?"

"It means stop focusing on Okane and get over it. You're smart. Use your brain."

"Still," she griped, and Clae interrupted her.

"As a side note, don't get too close to Okane with pens or sharp objects."

"What, you think I'm going to stab him or something?" Laura asked incredulously. She might have been upset, but not enough to attack somebody about it. "I'm not homicidal."

"Not just pens," said Clae. He picked up a few of the Kin fasteners; they were the only ones left on the counter, the rest stowed somewhere out of sight. Come to think of it, a lot of the pointier objects around the shop had vanished. "These, too. Your pocketknife. If you can avoid it, don't let him know you're carrying that at all."

Laura's brow furrowed. "Why are you telling me this?"

"I did say there were different circumstances."

"But what kind of circumstances could—"

"Nothing we need to get into at this point. You read that book, right? Tell me what you learned about the sunk Pits."

"But—"

"Book smarts don't go far. We'll clear up misunderstandings while it's still fresh in your mind."

Baffled, she sat and recounted the reading. It took an hour, and Clae never returned to the earlier topic. The black drapes remained static and daunting. Okane didn't reappear.

8

STORMY SWEEPER

When it rained in Amicae, it rained all day. Laura knew this well, so she knew there was no chance the pounding against the windows would stop anytime soon. The skies darkened to the point where streetlamps were lit, but anything beyond that was completely obscured by the downpour.

Laura had met Clae on a day much like this one: the rain had pounded hard enough she felt half dragged to the ground, but she still stood opposite the Sweeper shop, damp newspaper clenched in her hands. The overhang of the boarded shop behind her dripped fat droplets that soaked her stockings. She glanced up at the glow of the lights ahead of her, then back down at the paper.

TRAGEDY AT THE OPERA, announced the headline. *Sunday morning, the sun rose on a terrible scene: the grand opera house of the First Quarter awash in darkness, all her lights and glass smashed. Overnight members of the Mad Dogs mob planted an infestation in the stage, and when city workers rushed to exterminate it, the creature pounced on them. No less than thirty-five members of the police department were lost to us this evening, including well-loved Chief Otto Mumbar. Head Sweeper Clae Sinclair carried out the extermination, though his own apprentice was lost as well.*

The article went on about damages, costs, delayed showings, but she was no First Quarter girl. She was far more interested in the little ad wedged next to this article, almost lost in the patchwork format: *Sinclair Sweepers, hiring all positions.* Following that was a list of benefits. Tax free. Free transport. An astoundingly high wage. She'd thought it was a joke at first, flipped through the entirety of the paper and found no proof of deceit before daring to consider it. *Recompense to family after death* made her stomach twist, but this could be her coveted windfall. Finally, a chance to grab that world she'd glimpsed in the old Coronae picture book. Morgan had scoffed at it before, but now she had leverage: the family had fallen on hard times, after all. Morgan's catering job had hit an all-time low and Cheryl had racked up an ugly doctor's bill. What else were they supposed to do, eat their savings? If Laura could snag this job and its great pay, they could get back on their feet. Morgan could look into her coin purse without wincing while paying for groceries. They needed the money, and they needed it fast. Morgan couldn't complain about the occupation, and if she did Laura could counter easily: factory jobs didn't pay near as much, and if she was about to risk life and limb, she might as well do it for the best deal. The old book and even the vague job description of the ad had her imagining something *big,* but the shabby shop opposite her almost looked abandoned. It made her hesitate, second-guess. Was this some police outpost for surveillance of lower Quarters? It couldn't possibly be a hub of activity for the MARU. If it was, and if they couldn't pay to keep up their building, how could they possibly pay that sum to any employees? Could *the backbone of our great city* be reduced to this state?

No matter.

Laura gathered up her skirt, unfurled the umbrella above her head, and marched for the door. The shop was warm, of course. In the future she found uncomfortably hot a fixed detail, but on that day she stood dripping on the threshold, feeling rather sullen about it. And of course, Clae was there. He didn't make a wonderful first impression, being half wrapped in bandages and probably in a lot of pain judging by said bandages and the bottle of painkillers in one splinted hand. He paused in the process of shaking out a pill and glared at her.

"What do you want?" he demanded.

She took it as a challenge. She squared her shoulders and drew up to full height, ignoring the fact that she looked half drowned. She'd decided on this the moment she committed to tracking the shop down—cast aside that good-girl persona Morgan had loved so much in her school days. If she was going to be the bravest in all the city, she'd do it without hiding.

"I'm looking for the head Sweeper. Is he in?"

He simply stared at her. Another one of those idiots who thought all women belonged at home with a baby on their knee, she decided. Should've known she'd run into another Charlie. Her nose wrinkled and she brought her umbrella down like a cane against the floor.

"I've got things to do today. If Mr. Sinclair is having interviews, let's get on with it."

He let out a sharp bark of laughter. He finally succeeded in rattling two pills into his hand and swallowed them dry. That done, he stumped around the counter. She thought at first that he had a peg leg, but it was really a crutch tucked under one arm; the leg on that side was done up in a splint to match his arm. He hobbled closer and paused a few feet away, something like a sneer on his face. Laura felt on edge, but it wasn't the type of look she'd had from other almost-employers and it definitely wasn't what she expected from a Sweeper. His eyes were dull, tired, like he hadn't slept in a month. They did little to liven the halfhearted look, the flat tone.

"You're in the wrong place. Go back to the union, or wherever they sent you from."

"I came here on my own," she retorted, scanning for any sign of another person.

Clae raised one eyebrow. "Did you now."

"You're hiring, aren't you?" She fixed her gaze on him again, but that look in his eyes made her uneasy; it was like whatever light was in him seemed about to snuff out. She averted her gaze again. "Look, just point me at Mr. Sinclair and we can leave this all behind us."

"You're looking at him." He sat heavily on a stool, placed his hands atop the crutch and eyed her as if gauging a reaction. Sure, she was a little embarrassed to mistake who the man was, but she couldn't afford to let that stop her.

"I'm Laura Kramer." She stuck out her hand. Clae huffed again and raised his splinted hand; she switched hands without a word, and he rolled his eyes. "According to the paper, you're hiring for all positions. I'd like to interview for—"

"I suppose you read the bullshit next to the opera piece."

The paper still crinkled under her arm. She frowned. "You're the one who put it there, aren't you?"

"No. Some idiots did. Idiots who don't know how the job works. All that's in there is garbage."

"So there's no compensation for Sweeper families."

"There's that."

"So it's not all garbage."

"Enough of it is. You don't know what you're trying to get into. Leave."

"Not a chance."

She cast around, grabbed another stool, and set it in front of him. He watched this with narrowed eyes, but didn't protest as she sat right there and rattled off her résumé. He seemed the type to wear down easily at this point. Maybe his head hurt so bad from a concussion he'd hire her just to shut her up, and wearing him down was exactly what she intended to do. If her classmates could talk someone into submission, so could she. Originally she'd come to apply for some kind of desk job—"inventory," the ad had said, oh so helpful—but as much as she went into detail on previous writing experience, volunteering at the school library, he seemed dreadfully unimpressed. Eventually he leaned back, shaking his head.

"Paperwork is covered," he said. "I don't need any help with that."

"But the ad said—"

"I know what it said, and it's wildly inaccurate. You probably even think we're part of the damn MARU."

"I'm willing to learn. Please, I'll do anything!" She leaned forward, pleading. Oh, she hadn't sunk this low before, but the damnable man with the sun in his hand blinked in the back of her mind. It didn't matter how little she could get so long as she could be on board. "I really need the money. If I don't get a job soon, I don't know if my family will even be able to eat!"

"Find a job elsewhere." He heaved himself back up, shaky but determined. "Trust me, you don't want to end up like the last apprentice."

"There's an opening in apprenticeship, isn't there?" She jumped after him, yanking the paper into view and showing off the runny ink of the article. "One just—look, I don't know how many people you've got working here, but surely I could help!"

Clae sped up, but he wasn't as coordinated as he thought. The crutch bashed into the cupboard's side in his rush, hard enough to rattle the equipment atop it. One of the Kin flasks had been perched close to the edge and tipped completely. Without thinking, Laura leapt to catch it. The flask slipped perfectly into her hand, even if she almost ran into the cabinet to get it. The brew inside popped and fizzled brighter gold, which she hoped wasn't a bad sign. She pulled herself up and set it on the table again, grumbling, "Watch where you're going, or you really will break something."

She looked up, expecting the pinched expression again, but his face was completely and utterly blank. It was almost as bad as the eyes before, though they seemed sharper somehow.

"Nice reflexes," he noted, sounding indifferent. "Were you in a sport?"

"Racing," she admitted quietly. Usually employers liked to steer well clear of athletics when it came to proper young ladies. "Why?"

"I have no need for inventory." He limped behind the counter, peered at her through the Kin's tubing, and reached out to tap a finger on a small stone circle she later learned was a Gin amulet. "I take care of all that. What I need assistance in is the practical solutions. The real Sweeping. You said you'd do anything, didn't you?"

Her heart leapt into her throat. Was this real? "Yes?"

"Then would you consider being an apprentice?"

"Of course!" That came out embarrassingly loud.

Clae's eyes narrowed. "Even though you know nothing about it."

"I've read a book or two," she replied, trying to fight down her smile. "Besides, I told you I could learn."

"Then let us hope, for both our sakes, that you are a fast learner."

He held out his uninjured hand, and Laura grasped it. The contract came later, but this was the moment things switched for Laura. In the next few weeks she thought she might have sold her soul to the devil, he pushed so hard, but then amulet training began and she got her hands on that little stone circle. She'd never felt so light before that moment, and when she turned back to Clae to see his reaction, well, she'd never forget that expression.

You're a natural.

No one had ever looked at her that way before; as if she'd done something amazing. She'd never been a natural either. The idea was thrilling.

Now, on a day much like that one, Laura looked out at the rain and wondered what her old self would say to this situation.

On September 2, 1233, Laura had taken the trolley to work; thus she was mostly dry, with the exception of her boots, which sat by the door to dry. She perched on a stool by the counter, socked feet resting on one of the rungs, while Clae talked angrily into the telephone. Up until two minutes ago he'd been on the stool next to hers, reading a book while waiting for the tea to cool.

Laura wasn't much of a tea drinker, but the rain brought cold air, and as much as she complained about the heat, the sudden change made her welcome the warm drink. Her own cup sat by the kettle, untouched. Now that she thought about it, she reached back and held a hand over it. Still too hot, she decided, and let it alone again.

Meanwhile Clae looked tempted to pull out his hair.

"No, I do not—Yes, I get it, you want a bigger 'boom,' but this is completely—No, you—Thing is—This—I—*God damn it, stop interrupting me!*"

The shout inspired movement on the left as Okane jumped. He was hiding again, having found a spot behind the Kin where he could go unseen by anyone not directly looking for him. Despite improving over the last two weeks, he was still standoffish. Laura frowned at him and he just stared back.

"Call the bastard in, I'll tell him face-to-face."

Clae tried to hang up angrily, but the mouthpiece fell off its hook and dangled by its cord. He had to try twice more to make it stay, and by then he was fuming.

"What's going on?" asked Laura.

"Some *idiot*," Clae seethed, "decided it would be a good idea to use amulets as *bullets* for the army. And this idiot's higher-ups seem to agree!"

"But then they'd have to pick up all those bullets, wouldn't they? Or infestations would start out where we can't get them."

"Hasn't occurred to them," Clae hissed. "I'm going down to the police station to set this straight. Watch for any clients."

Laura perked up. It wasn't the first time he'd left her in charge while he ran errands, but it was the first where he had to make a choice about it. She felt herself puff up with pride and glanced to the side to see how Okane took it. He could stand to look a little more disappointed.

Clae didn't look at either of them as he pulled on his coat, and did up all the buttons. He popped up the collar, drew the fabric closer to his neck, picked up his umbrella and walked out into the rain. The door closed behind him, and his ghostly form flitted by the windows and out of sight.

Neither of the two left spoke, so the pattering of rain overcame the room.

The door opened five minutes later. For a moment Laura wondered if Clae got halfway to the cable cars and noticed he'd forgotten something, but the visitor was a girl a few years younger than Laura. She looked like a half-drowned rat, her hair hanging tangled and stringy in a big wet mass.

"I'm sorry," she panted, as if she'd been running, "but I'm a little lost. Do you know where the Keedler Bakery is?"

"Just down the street. Go that way"—Laura gestured to her left—"and look for the big white building. Someone broke their sign, but the name should be on the windows."

"All right, thank you." The girl ducked out again.

Laura turned her attention back to the newspaper. She was halfway through an article on a visiting opera company (she considered stealing away the featured picture of the star singer, but it overlapped with an article on new candidates for the Council which had been circled, its headline underlined in pen; probably not a good idea to take) when the door opened again. She glanced up, but this time, while it wasn't Clae, it wasn't someone lost in the rain. A man entered, shaking his umbrella on the doorstep before closing out the sound of the storm.

"Hello," Laura greeted, folding up the paper and setting it on the counter. "This is the Sweeper shop. Did you need something?"

"Yes," the man replied, "I'm looking for the head Sweeper. Is he in today?"

"He stepped out for a while, but he should be back soon. You can wait in here if you'd like."

"Is that all right?"

"Sure. Coatrack is by the door and you can sit on any stool."

"I appreciate it."

He hung his long, dark coat and his hat on the coatrack, and leaned his umbrella against the wall by Laura's shoes. He then took Clae's earlier seat. Had it been Clae, Laura would've been fine with this, but the man was a stranger and the stool was positioned just a little too close for comfort. She shifted slightly in unease as the man settled himself. He was around Morgan's age, with dark hair and a well-trimmed beard and mustache, eyes a murky brown behind his glasses.

"What's your problem, sir?" Laura asked politely. With those clothes he seemed to be from at least the Second Quarter, so manners were a must. "I may not be Mr. Sinclair, but I might be able to help."

"It's not much. Nothing a young lady like yourself should be worrying about," he responded, in a deep and cheerful voice.

Why was she always "young lady"?

"Are you sure? I've worked here awhile."

"Just a small problem, but I've been told to go straight to the top," the man assured her. "Private business."

Whether "private business" meant secret workplace or family issues, Laura wasn't about to guess. She shrugged, unsure what else to do. They sat there for a while. Laura wanted to go back to reading the paper, but she didn't want to be rude and ignore him. She stared off at one of the big windows. She didn't pay much more attention to the man before he spoke again, and when he did, she jumped.

"Are you the only employee he has?"

"No, there's one more," Laura muttered ruefully, glancing over at Okane.

Okane ducked still further, vanishing almost entirely behind the Kin as the man followed her gaze.

"Oh?"

"He's sort of new to the job."

The man looked around a bit more, completely missing Okane. His hair camouflaged well with the woodwork, apparently. After a while the man straightened himself again.

"So you're the only woman here?" He sounded sympathetic. "Why did you take this job, of all things? If I hear right, it's very dangerous."

"My own reasons. Besides, this pays well." Laura shrugged.

"The MARU hardly seems like the kind of job befitting a young lady like yourself. If you want—" He rested a hand on her leg. Laura froze. The man kept looking at her face with a plastic, concerned expression, but his thumb rubbed at her inner thigh. She was almost too shocked to hear the rest of his sentence. "—I could look into finding you a different job. I have friends I could contact, they own businesses. Maybe you could work as a seamstress instead? It would be much safer and easier."

He was still rubbing. Rage and mortification rose in Laura's chest. Her eyes caught movement—Okane had straightened up to get a better look, probably to see why she looked so scandalized, and realization dawned on his face. He strode toward them, but Laura's mind balked. She was not the damsel in distress. Her earlier conviction steadied, and she smoothed her face into pleasant neutrality. The man took that as a good sign and smiled. In response, Laura reached back, picked up her teacup, and up-ended it over his hand.

While it had left the state of magma heat, it was still really hot. Laura gritted her teeth and held that neutral expression, even as her leg felt like it was burning. The man pulled his hand back with a sharp yelp and cradled it close.

"Why, you little—"

"If that type of service is what you're looking for, you're in the wrong place," Laura said, sweetly as she could manage.

Enraged, the man stood and raised his uninjured hand, but a scraping sound grabbed both their attention. Okane held another stool above his head, loathing written all over his features.

"Touch her again and I'll break this over ---r head," he hissed.

The man stepped back, eyes flickering from one to the other, and

Laura had half a mind to grab the rest of the teapot and chuck it at him. He ended up walking back to the door and grabbing his possessions from the coatrack.

"Heathens!" he barked. "You little swine! I'll make sure your employer hears about this! You'll be fired, and then we'll see who else takes pity on you!"

He crammed his hat back on his head and left, slamming the door behind him.

As soon as he was gone, Laura lost her attempted serenity and swore, patting uselessly at her leg as if that would help the burn. Something white was shoved into her vision. It was a moment before she realized it was a handkerchief.

"Thanks," she muttered, taking it and dabbing at her pants.

Okane didn't reply. He set the stool down and sat on it, still looking peeved. He watched her for a minute, then asked, "What was that?"

"That? That was a pervert," Laura growled.

"No, I mean that." He pointed at the teacup.

"Oh. I saw that in a movie recently." She flushed a little. "It's not terribly original, but it worked."

"That it did."

Laura sighed, sitting down again and setting the handkerchief on the counter.

"What do you think, did I pull off the Clae look?" she asked after a while, wistful. Okane gave her a puzzled look and she explained, "You know, how you can't actually see the emotion on his face, but it's like, there in his *aura*, so it's that much more terrifying. Did I manage it?"

"Not really. ---'re kind of an open book."

"Really?" Laura groaned, propping her head up on one arm.

"It's not a bad thing, though."

Laura grumbled incoherently, but as she did, she realized he actually started this conversation. Nowhere in these two weeks had he done that before. She'd been so busy glaring him into submission he hadn't gotten a word in to begin with, but he hadn't started a conversation with Clae at all either. She shifted to stare, searching for an answer in his expression.

"Thanks, by the way," she mumbled. "For . . . y'know, the stool. And the hanky."

"It's nothing." He looked away.

That seemed like the end of their little chat, but for once he didn't flee to the other side of the room. Slowly, Laura found herself smiling. Maybe she'd earned his respect by pouring boiling tea on someone. He better not be sitting there out of protective instinct. Her smile began to dip back into a frown at that thought.

Two sharp knocks on the door broke her out of her thoughts, and she knew who was there even before it opened. Mrs. Keedler entered the room, snapping her umbrella shut as she did. The bottom of her dress dripped water onto the threshold, but that didn't dampen her spirits.

"Hello, Laura," she called. "Everything all right? I passed some man cussing about witches."

"It's fine. He was a rat, but we took care of it," Laura replied.

Mrs. Keedler looked back at the window with a black expression. Knowing her, she wanted to beat that man with her umbrella.

"Cads. There's more and more of them coming down to lower Quarters because they think they can take advantage of people."

"I hope he comes back when Clae's around, he'd give the rat a good lesson. But forget it. What're you doing over here? The bakery's still open today, right?"

"It is." Mrs. Keedler brightened up. "But I saw Clae go past the window. I've seen too many days when he's put off eating until late at night, and while he's gotten better since you came along, I don't want you to miss lunch just because he's in a hurry."

She walked over to the counter and set a basket there. Flicking away the cloth covering revealed three sandwiches.

"It's not much, but I cut up one of our baguettes. Can't have you starving over here if I can help it."

"Mrs. Keedler, you're an angel. Thank you!"

Mrs. Keedler just laughed. "Don't lie like that. So, is this the new Sweeper I've been hearing about?"

She looked at Okane like she hadn't noticed him before. He shrank, but stayed on the stool.

"This is Okane. We hired him about two weeks ago. Okane, this is Mrs. Keedler. She and her husband run the bakery down the street."

Okane nodded slowly in acknowledgment.

"Not much of a talker, are you?" Mrs. Keedler observed, to which he shook his head. She chuckled. "Well, I hope you've settled in nicely. Clae might be a bit strange, but he's got a good heart. Save him one of those sandwiches."

"I will if he hurries," said Laura.

Mrs. Keedler patted her arm as she drew back. It was a completely different kind of touch from the one that man used, and Laura smiled at it.

"Rain or no, I'm sure he'll be back soon, and I've got to get back. God knows that husband of mine can't last long on his own."

"You sure you can't stay a little while? You could have some tea," Laura suggested.

"No, but thanks for the offer. You two have a nice day. Stay dry!"

Once the woman was gone, Laura picked up one of the sandwiches and took a bite. Okane waited, watching as if he needed some sort of approval.

"Go on, they're not poisonous."

At that, he reached out and took one.

"Mrs. Keedler may be intimidating, but she's actually a big sweetheart. She makes great bread, too." Laura picked at her sandwich, frowning, before thinking *to hell with it*. "If you stick around I think you'll like her."

Okane mumbled something into his sandwich. Silence settled between them, but not the uneasy silence from before. It was a bit more like the silence between her and Clae. She ate her sandwich slowly, to waste more time.

An hour passed. By this time Laura had gone back to the newspaper. She read out the more interesting bits while Okane studied the tubing of the Kin, but she knew by his soft noises that he was listening. It was a little strange to think about; just this morning she'd been dead set on loathing him, but if he was on board with breaking stools over her enemies' heads, he couldn't be all bad. Her eyes trailed after him as she recited the report of recently imported films and how Amicae's golden boy was off to act in some big production in another city. She couldn't see much beyond the glint of his eyes through the Kin, but she could hear another faint laugh. He was almost endearing from this angle.

She was reading about a minor scandal in the Third Quarter (some man messing with the streetlamps, painting silly faces on them so they looked like jack-o'-lanterns) when the door swung open again. This time it was Clae, completely soaked through and only slightly less irritable. He stopped short just inside the entrance, water dripping off his coat, and cast a suspicious look around. He zeroed in on Laura.

"What happened?"

Immediately, Laura panicked. What was he looking at? Had he heard what she'd done to that would-be customer? Had he seen the spilled tea, if it hadn't dried up? She never cleaned it up!

"It was self-defense, I swear!" she blurted.

Clae cocked his head to the side.

"Self-defense," he repeated, disbelieving.

"Yes."

Clae shook his head. He hung up his coat on the rack and yanked off his boots, setting them next to Laura's. He padded across the floor in socks that were miraculously still dry, passing them by to go through the back door. He didn't close it all the way, so the steep stairs remained visible, and after a moment there was creaking overhead.

Laura cast around the room for something to talk about when he came down again. She wasn't keen on explaining why she'd dumped tea on a visitor, pervert or no.

"You live up there too, right?" she asked.

"Yes," muttered Okane, raising an eyebrow. "Why?"

"I just realized, isn't this place kind of small? Are there multiple rooms up there?" Laura gestured at the rest of the shop.

Okane glanced up at the ceiling, as if making sure Clae couldn't see or hear him. "There are rooms. More than I expected for a bachelor."

"Oh?" Laura looked up too, though the ceiling was nondescript and gave her absolutely no insight.

"They're small, but they're furnished. ---'d think a family lived up there."

"This was a family business."

Clae's voice made them both jump. He stepped out from the stairwell in new dry clothes, though his hair remained sopping wet. He sat back down on his stool. Okane drew back as if expecting some sort of punishment for gossiping. While Laura felt a little ashamed too, she wasn't about to flinch away; Clae wasn't the kind to lash out about something like that. He didn't seem to notice Okane's discomfort at all. He inspected the teacup he'd left however long ago, frowned, and quickly downed it. He set the cup back on the counter with a loud clack and clarified, "Family business, family house. We all worked here."

Laura folded the newspaper with slow movements, creasing the folds again as her earlier apprehension drained a little. Clae didn't usually go out of his way to volunteer personal information. The most she'd gotten out of him was the brief mention of his father during their run through the Sullivan mansion.

"And it's not a family business anymore?" she prodded quietly.

"Job has its hazards." Clae shrugged. "Why didn't you heat up the tea?"

Laura blinked in surprise at the change in topic. "Uh, well, I didn't think about it."

At that, Okane picked up the teapot. He made a muffled noise and walked off, which Laura took to mean that he was going to make more. He'd barely reached the stairs when Clae leaned over toward Laura. She leaned back in response, but paused as he whispered, "Self-defense? What, you punch him and all of a sudden he'll sit next to you?"

For a moment Laura was baffled, but then she looked back where Okane had disappeared up the stairs, and it clicked.

"Oh, no, I just—No. He was ready to break somebody's head open but I beat him to the punch."

Clae's head moved minutely, and she knew he wanted more information. She felt flustered and reluctant to say it, but forced the story out. "Well . . . somebody came in, and he . . . um . . . he was here to see you, but he was talking about how a girl shouldn't be here and—" God, this was the very last thing she ever wanted to happen or talk about. She couldn't even form the words but gestured vaguely. "He thought he could . . . take liberties. So when he—Well, I dumped tea on him."

Clae's eyes narrowed, and he growled, "While the tea was still hot, right?"

Laura rubbed at her burned leg. "Definitely."

"Good." He sat back on his stool, pondered a moment. "If he comes in again, tell me."

"Right." Laura tapped her feet together twice, then mumbled, "So you haven't gotten Okane to open up to you?"

Clae made a huffing sound. "He won't."

"You think?"

"No. It's vulnerability. He saw you vulnerable, like he is. You're less likely to threaten him, in his mind."

Was that some kind of insult? Laura's brow furrowed. "He thinks I'm too weak to pose a threat?"

Clae snorted like she'd missed the point entirely. "Forget it."

Nearly half an hour later, as Clae pondered closing early, the man from before returned. He had a shorter, portly man in tow, equally well dressed, and they opened the door seemingly as loud as possible. Okane started at the noise, and as soon as Laura saw who it was, she kicked at Clae's leg and hissed, "It's him!"

She didn't elaborate, but that was enough information for Clae. Right there, at the drop of a hat, he was *angry*. It didn't show on his face but it was there in his eyes, and the menacing click of his pocket watch didn't help. Laura scooted her stool a good foot or two away before she realized what she was doing. The men didn't pick up on his mood.

"Are you the head Sweeper?" The man from before looked much more pompous and annoyed than last time.

"I am," Clae replied, stowing the watch in his pocket and folding his arms.

The man's eyes flicked over to Laura and Okane for a moment, and Laura was sure she saw gloating in his expression. He probably thought he was about to get them fired.

"Wonderful," he said, striding forward. "I'm James Sutliff. It's a pleasure to meet you, sir."

He held out a hand to shake, and it just so happened to be the one Laura poured tea on. It was wrapped in a bandage. Laura felt some pride at the sight. Clae looked at the hand. Just looked at it, saying nothing, something like disgust curling his lip. That was when the man got an inkling that something was off. He cleared his throat awkwardly and took a step back.

"I stopped by earlier but you weren't in. I wanted to see you about some mobster trouble I've been having recently. Mr. Ohler here tells me that it's a rather sorry state"—here his companion dipped his head, flashing a quick, false smile—"and advised I go directly to the top. Your employees were here, but they weren't very helpful. In fact, they were openly hostile. Not to insult the way you run things here, but these two—"

In one smooth movement, Clae stood. He was shorter than James Sutliff, but he invaded the man's space and glared up at him in a manner that made Laura think of a mean little stray dog. He grabbed Sutliff's injured hand in one of his own, gripping tight enough that Sutliff gasped in pain.

"You." Clae's voice was so low that Laura could barely hear it. "I'm sick of you so-called high-class *gentlemen* coming down here and acting as if you own everything. You *dared* touch my apprentice and you have *crossed a line.*"

As he spoke, his grip tightened. Sutliff made an odd noise and tried desperately to wrench his bandaged appendage away. Ohler hurried forward to intervene.

"Mr. Sinclair! Mr. Sinclair, what are you doing?"

Clae paid him no attention. "Get out. If I see you on this street again, I'll rip both your hands off."

He let go. Sutliff stumbled back, injured hand kept tight to his chest for protection. Ohler stood between them with arms outstretched as if expecting Clae to rush for the other's throat, but Clae simply reclined against the counter.

"That was entirely uncalled for!" Ohler cried. "You can't go assaulting your clients!"

Clae turned his gaze on him, and Ohler shrank back immediately. He stuttered for a moment, but Sutliff brought him back to earth.

"You won't get away with this. I don't care how long it takes or how many people I have to go through, I'll make sure you're out on the street!" Sutliff growled.

"I said *get out,*" Clae spat.

The men hesitated, but when he pushed himself up again, they scampered for the door.

"Mark my words, you'll regret this!" Sutliff yelled, even as he stumbled down the steps. "I'll have you all fired!"

The door banged shut.

"You don't think he can actually get us fired, do you?" Laura muttered.

"He can't. We're the only Sweepers as it is, so we're irreplaceable. The City Council will be up in arms if he tries getting rid of any of us," said Clae.

He stacked their empty teacups with no attempt at grace. They stacked well enough without handles, and he picked them up in one hand, teapot in the other.

"You can go too."

"We're closing early?"

"No one in their right mind is going out in this weather. Might as well close up. I'll call if any urgent news comes in." As Clae passed Okane, he gestured with the teapot. "You can go with her to the trolley stop. If that 'client' of ours tries to follow, feel free to crack his skull open."

Okane nodded and Clae vanished through the door to the stairs. Laura leaned over the counter and called after him, "I'll see you tomorrow, then! And, uh, thanks!"

There was a loud grunt, but no other response.

"Will --- be leaving now?" asked Okane.

"I suppose. He said I could go, after all. Typically means leave as soon as possible."

She eased herself up from the stool and made her way slowly to the door. Her boots there had dried. She prodded them to check, then slipped them on.

"Do --- want me to go with ---?" Okane drifted after her.

"Sure. You don't have to if you don't want to, though. It's not the nicest weather, after all."

Okane looked out the window, probably deciding whether it was worth the effort. Laura didn't expect him to come along, so turned her attention to donning her light jacket and fetching her umbrella. She stepped out onto the top stair. There she was protected from the rain for a moment, giving her the opportunity to open her umbrella and step out into the downpour. A following snap sounded behind her, barely noticeable amid the pattering of the storm. A glance back showed Okane following a step behind her, wielding Clae's battered umbrella.

"You're actually coming?"

He muttered something she couldn't hear.

"What?"

"If it's okay, I said."

"It's fine. I just didn't expect you to." Laura shrugged.

He copied the movement and stood there awkwardly. Clearly he wasn't planning on saying any more, so Laura tipped her umbrella. "Shall we?"

He nodded.

They hurried down the street, tramping through puddles on their way to the trolley stop. The stop was out of sight of the Sweeper shop even on a good day, two streets away. There was no shelter at this one, which Laura lamented, but she could deal with it. They waited for a long while. Laura's boots were good protection, but the raindrops were big enough and hit with enough force, the liquid bounced up; Okane's pants were soaked up to midcalf. He would need boots of his own. Laura dug out her pocket watch. They still had some time.

"Why did you tag along?" she asked.

Okane just shrugged again.

"Really?" she pressed. "Because before today I didn't think you wanted anything to do with anyone. It's been weeks and you've only just started talking."

Okane's mouth twisted. He frowned out at the rain, resting the umbrella pole against his shoulder.

"Well, --- didn't like me."

"True, but if I'm mean to you, why do this? Why the turnaround today? And don't tell me you were trying to be my knight in shining armor."

He glared at her. His eyes seemed even more luminescent in the near dark, like they reflected the lamplight. "---'d rather I just watched?"

"No, but I'm not weak like everyone seems to think," she grouched.

"Obviously not." Okane looked away again. "--- at least stood up for ---rself."

Laura tilted her head and peered at his face, trying to figure out what that was supposed to mean. The way he said it almost sounded like an insult.

"And that's a good thing?" He didn't answer, so she went for another approach. "Did you not do that, back with the Sullivans?"

He made a frustrated sound and switched the umbrella to the other shoulder.

"They taught me early. I thought it was useless."

Oh. Well then. Laura drew back. She inspected the handle of her umbrella and began to turn it for a distraction, sending scattered droplets into the air.

So she'd done something he hadn't dared to before. Maybe Clae had been on to something when he'd said Okane felt connected to her by vulnerability. It was just that Laura reacted, and maybe he respected that. She thought back to the Sullivan mansion, the way the cook had snapped at him and the maids avoided him, the mention of whipping and Henry's thunderous face. No wonder he sounded afraid to laugh before. She dragged in a deep breath and spun to face him. He jerked back, eyes wide.

"Well! We're both apprentices now, and I doubt Clae's going to let either of us go if he can help it. I'm not going to let you beat me, but let's try to get along better, okay?"

She held out her free hand, hoping it was enough of a peace offering. Okane eyed it, then, very, very slowly, took it.

"All right."

His grip was loose and rather weak, but they shook, and Laura felt a little better about the whole situation.

9

YESTERYEAR

"Laura."

Okane's voice came as a soft squeak, timid but stronger than it was a few days ago. She looked up from her book to see him drifting across the shop toward her.

"Hm?"

He rubbed at his arm nervously. "Sorry, but I was wondering if --- could tell me some things."

"About the job?"

"Not quite, no."

"Then what about?"

He seemed embarrassed but elaborated, "It's been gnawing at me for a while. What exactly are amulets?"

Laura blinked in surprise. "Are you serious? You don't know what they are?"

"No, not really."

"You didn't ask Clae?" Come to think of it, why would he wait until Clae had stepped outside to ask about the subject? Clae was the one who knew this best, and despite her new efforts Laura knew she was still prickly dealing with her new coworker.

"No. I already look stupid enough to him. I don't want to add to it."

If he was looking for pity, he certainly got it. Laura straightened up in her seat, unclipped the amulet from her belt, and set it on the counter with a loud clack as she asked, "How much do you know about amulets?"

He dragged over a stool, mulling over what knowledge he did have. "I know they give power for appliances."

That was it? Laura pursed her lips as she tried to figure out where to begin.

"Well, let's see . . . Yes, amulets do hold energy, but that energy is magic. Some of them are like this one"—she tapped the smiling amulet before her—"so they're made out of the magic source. That's called Gin. It's a rock found way below ground that has so much magic, it leaks out. But you want to keep that rock down there, because its magic helps ward off bad things and helps all kinds of plants grow. If we didn't have it, we'd have trouble growing all the crops we need here. But Gin around Amicae has gotten kind of rare: in the beginning they had to mine so much of it to pay for construction of the city, and the Council kept leaning on that as a way to pay off debts. Most of the Gin around here is strategically placed and monitored closely, so amulets like this are very expensive. They're more powerful and convenient than regular amulets. Regular amulets are made out of a more common material like other stones or clay, but they have a hollow inside so they can absorb and store magic there after they've been stored by Gin for a while. Common amulets need recharging, while Gin doesn't."

"But they don't all look like that one," Okane muttered.

"People like amulets to be decorative. A lot of them get painted or carved, so they all look different. They tend to be around this size, though."

"What are they used for?"

"Power, of course. For normal people, anyway. It's a nicer replacement for electricity and gas, but if things can go wrong with those, it can get catastrophic with amulets. Plus there's the danger of infestations getting into them, so cities make sure amulets are priced high so the only people who can get hold of them are the ones who can afford to take care of them. Less damage, and easier for the police to track."

Okane frowned, reaching out to prod the amulet. "It's expensive electricity, then. But if amulets hold magic and infestations are killed by magic, why do infestations live in them?"

"That's what they're meant to do. That's why they were made." Laura shrugged. He sent her a puzzled look, and she got the idea he had no clue what she was talking about. "You know, because they were designed that way?"

"Designed?"

"Did they teach you *anything* at that mansion?"

He recoiled, and she decided that must be a resounding no. Leaning back herself, she sighed.

"Sorry, it's just that they had a big impact on how everything works. A lot of everyday things don't make sense unless you know about the monsters first."

"I didn't learn much about the outside," he admitted, rearranging his hands in his lap. "Mobs I know, gas lighting I know, but history? Nothing I can use."

Laura eyed him shrewdly. "Do you even know what country you're in?"

He shifted guiltily but avoided the subject.

"If the infestations were made, who made them?" he questioned instead, eyes fixed on the amulet. "Why would anyone ever make something like that?"

"I don't know, why would anyone make a felin, either?"

He glanced up, apprehensive. "Those actually exist?"

Laura exhaled slowly. He had zero knowledge of the world. She was no teacher, but she could give some kind of overview. She searched under the counter. Clae had bundled a huge number of things down here, along with all the sharp objects. Once she found her prize—a crinkled roll of paper—she had to tug it out from under a stack of angry letters from the Sullivan offices.

Okane tracked her movement and drew back as she spread the document flat on top of her book. The piece in question was a map outlining the three main islands and scattered landmasses, the thirty cities marked by dark triangles with their names printed nearby. Some of its usefulness was diminished by random spots of ink in the mountain areas and colored lines drawn to show where various train routes went.

"Okay," she announced, "I'm going to give you a quick rundown on the history of the Orien Territories."

He looked up with a raised brow. "Orien?"

"It literally means 'east.' When the first explorers from the mainland sailed east and stumbled on the islands, they thought they were at the end of the world. That's why the ocean to the east is called Malamare—it means 'bad sea,' since you'd fall off the edge of the world if you went too far on it. So you are currently in the archipelago called Orien, in the biggest country: Terual." Her finger circled the middle of the largest island, tapped a marker on the southeast side, between a particularly large mountain and a bay. "This is Amicae."

Intrigued, he leaned over to inspect this. His eyes tracked farther down, though, to the darkest-shaded portion of the map, the southernmost of the main islands, which was labeled in pictographic script Laura couldn't read.

"What's this?"

"I'll get to it," Laura grumbled. Of course he'd pick out the source of trouble right away. "Back in 323, Zyra—that's a big kingdom on the mainland—decided they wanted to expand and went searching for more territory to conquer. They were trying to figure out how far they could go when they sailed into the islands. There were already people living here, but what Zyra was really interested in was the Gin. Back on the mainland Gin was scarce, so it was really valuable. People used to use magic in things like weapons, so they thought Orien's supply could fuel their war goals and 'bring them into the arms of untold fortune and prosperity.'" The quote was from an old textbook. "So then everybody wanted the Gin, and everyone wanted Orien. Needless to say the people living here didn't like that, so they put up a fight. Zyra organized crusades to sail in and conquer. They turned it into a holy war—the Orien Conquest—and tried to wipe out the original people completely. But that took a long time and backfired, because the conquerors set up their own kingdoms and hoarded the Gin they could find instead of sending it back. That's how we ended up with four countries."

She gestured at the country names, assuming he'd take it in quickly enough, but paused. He squinted at the print, but there was something about the determination in that squint, how slow his eyes moved . . .

"Can you read?"

"No!" he squawked, loud like the very idea was foolish or incriminating. He averted his eyes from her and the map completely, and Laura was baffled.

What was he, twenty? And not able to read a single word? She opened her mouth to demand what Sullivan had been playing at, what kind of crackpot waste-of-space teacher Okane had as a child, but the knowledge of another textbook flickered in the back of her mind. Slaves were not often taught to read, crippling their independence; it kept them from running away, communicating, or learning. Knowledge is power, and a slave must not have power. There was more to Clae's statements than she'd realized. Kept like a slave, indeed.

Suddenly shameful of her own lack of understanding, Laura shuffled the paper around. She cleared her throat unsurely, making a mental note to try teaching him later (hopefully without such a violent reaction to the idea), and tried to grab his attention again by circling the countries with her index finger.

"The northernmost island is Ruhaile. The biggest island is divided between Terual at the top and New Zyra at the bottom. We just call it Zyra, though."

Reluctantly Okane turned his head again, not all the way, but enough to peer distrustfully at the map again.

"And the last one?"

"Kuro no Oukoku."

A flicker of comprehension crossed his face and he translated, "The Black Kingdom?" before realizing what he'd said and curling in on himself.

"That's right." She nodded, skin crawling. She didn't want to think of what had happened in the past to cause such self-deprecating actions. *Knowledge is power.* She got the feeling, between Okane and Mary, that she wouldn't have fared well at the Sullivan mansion at all. Slowly Okane relaxed, still somewhat tense but blinking owlishly with those abnormally silver eyes.

"The Black Kingdom?" he repeated.

Laura chewed at her lip before continuing.

"It took a long time, but the crusaders either enslaved or uprooted all the natives in their path. The remainder escaped to the last island, and they rallied there." This part had never been in any of her schoolbooks, instead related to her by Clae on a dark afternoon as the overhead light flickered and a storm raged against the shop windows. "The native people knew that the invader's power came from magic weapons; if that magic could be crippled, they'd be as good as sitting ducks. So the natives created an anti-magic monster. Even if it couldn't take magic head-on, it could infiltrate magic containers, interrupt the power, and wreak havoc on their enemies from a place they'd never expect. The problem was, the creature they created couldn't comprehend 'master' or 'ally.' Everything was food to it, and they didn't understand how it grew or spread yet. It escaped their hold, and it ate them."

"All of them?" Okane breathed.

"No, but a lot of people wish it did. Some survivors got on boats to escape to the other islands, but they brought the creature's offspring with them by accident. Infestations don't like water, can't or won't cross it, so if they hadn't sailed out, it would've been confined to Kuro no Oukoku forever . . . or longer, at least. As it happened, the monster did its job. Once it got to the other islands, it spread like crazy. People died all over, and once the mainland got wind of it they set a quarantine on Orien. Nobody can come or go. If people tried to sail to the mainland, they'd be sunk on sight. Go the opposite of the mainland, and you fall off the edge of the world. The quarantine was set up back in 723, and we haven't had people sail here from the mainland since. No contact whatsoever. And the ones left behind? They couldn't be spread out the way they used to be, so they grouped together in cities to defend themselves. That's why we have the big fortress cities today, with the wilds in between—that way Sweepers can keep track of people and stop infestations easily, instead of running all over the countryside and being too late to save anyone."

Okane frowned down at the dark blot of Kuro no Oukoku and summed up, "So it was a weapon in a war that got out of hand, and we're stuck with it all these years later."

"Five hundred and ten years," Laura agreed. "Countless casualties. Amicae is mostly under the impression that infestations aren't a threat anymore, and that's beyond stupid. Their entire purpose is to *infest* so you can't see or stop them, and strike out while your guard is down. It's meant to kill huge numbers of people at a time. It's genocide on legs. Sweepers are critical, because if one of them is allowed to spread, the city will die. It's not like we'll have much help, with the Council's attitude and the mobster Sweepers having nothing to do with us. It's terrifying when you really think about it, how close we are to being erased off the map. I wonder if the natives would've gone through with it if they realized how much damage they'd cause. How they'd almost get wiped out, too."

"Maybe it didn't matter," Okane muttered, barely audible.

Something else Clae had said came to mind. *Maybe that doesn't matter. When Magi are out in the world on their own, it's not usually because they want to be.*

Laura scratched at her arm, unnerved.

"How many of the natives are around these days?" Okane pressed, not catching her discomfort.

"There are a good number in Amicae. Apart from Zyran cities, we've got one of the largest populations. The woman who owns the pawnshop is one."

"She is? How can --- tell?"

"Well, it's kind of obvious. She's got the black hair, the—" She paused, then said, "Sometime I'll bring you past the pawnshop and maybe we'll see her. You'll understand better that way."

"Okay," he mumbled, mystified. "Is Amicae special or something?"

"Hm?"

"The largest population outside Zyra, but there are plenty of other cities closer to that border." He pointed out cities like Vir and Avis. "Why are there so many here?"

"Because it's like the infestations: designed that way."

"How so?"

"Amicae is a newer city, compared to the others."

He nodded. "Made after Sweepers were established."

"Exactly. There are a few reasons why it was made: to bridge the gap between Terrae and some other southern cities, to take advantage of the bay for fishing, and to make a haven. All the cities have nicknames, and Amicae is 'the friendly city.' The main drive behind it was a charity that wanted to make a place where people lost in the wilds could find refuge. That's why an extra level was added to the construction. Other cities only have five Quarters, but Amicae has a sixth. That's why Amicae is partially overrun with noncitizens and refugees from destroyed satellite towns. Those refugees included the native people, since Amicae didn't turn any-one away for a long time. Most of them went to Thrax, since that city had more lenient laws for them, but a lot came here, too. Of course, we aren't exactly 'friendly' anymore. The friendly city took a twist in politics, so here we are, little rights for the poor, slowly crumbling into a caste system . . . and people don't treat them very well. That's one of the reasons so many of them are in the mobs. When the MARU was around, they came down on natives pretty hard even when they weren't with mobs; some sort of idiot tactic meant to scare relatives who were. Oh. You know about the MARU, right? The group everyone thinks we are?"

He nodded solemnly. "The Mob Action Resolution Unit. Back in 1198, the mobs grew full of themselves and started acting openly enough that the Council was afraid we'd descend into a mob-run city like . . . Carmen?" He seemed pleased by her nod and continued, "The Council approved the formation of a police-recruited vigilante squad. Those seven recruits became the massive MARU, and almost ran the city for twenty-eight years. Sullivan took pleasure in their loss."

"'Loss' is putting it lightly," Laura muttered. "The MARU might still be around if it hadn't branched out in targets. I mean, they started going after innocent civilians just because of their race—it was messed up. I don't know why it was allowed."

Okane wore a wry smile. "This is the same MARU that regularly manhandled their informants and murdered any mobster who didn't re-ply correctly."

"True enough," said Laura. "The Silver Kings mob decided they'd had enough. They started alliances. The MARU were good at picking on individual mobs, but a united front? They became the hunted."

She remembered those days well, even if she'd only been in elementary school. Gruesome headlines in the papers told of MARU officers captured, mutilated, or killed outright, pictures drawn of a MARU survivor who'd been doused with acid, and all throughout it were print and pictures of a thick and perfect circle, dribbling paint or smeared in ash. That was the psychological part of the mob threat, serving as a giant target and drawn everywhere a MARU agent went—on the house, on their coat, hung over baby cradles—so agents quit, bent to the will of the mobs, or were driven crazy with fear before being found shot full of bullets in a cramped alley. The MARU buckled and broke. The few survivors were either so horrifically injured that they couldn't return to duty, or so cowed that even upon returning to the police force they fled at the slightest hint of mob involvement. Clae had mentioned that a real revival of the MARU was attempted in fall of 1229, but the mob backlash had been so sudden and violent that it was given up entirely.

"The anti-native sentiment got fanned during that time and never went back down. That's one of the reasons the pawnshop is boarded up. Some brats went and threw rocks through the windows. The neighborhood had to crack down on security for a while to scare them off."

"That's awful. Is the owner all right?"

"She wasn't there at the time. Clae and I came running out when we heard it, so we chased them off." She scowled. The memory still left a bad taste in her mouth. "Come to think of it, I think that's where Clae learned that language."

"The brats?"

"The pawnshop owner. I've never actually gotten her name. Where did you learn it, though? Was somebody in the Sullivan mansion fluent? Was there actually a mobster?"

"My mother spoke it sometimes."

"Your mother?" Laura's interest was piqued. "Where is she—"

The door clattered open, interrupting her as Clae struggled in, attempting to balance two more briefcases in one hand and a strange assembly of large metal parts in the other. He cursed as the door threatened to close on him, and Okane leapt up to hold it. Clae gave him a funny look, but his cussing died down and he stormed farther into the room.

"Where have --- been, sir?" Okane asked, tagging after him and ignoring Laura completely.

"Factories. I've gotten more supplies," Clae answered grudgingly. "What were you up to?"

"Nothing."

Nothing indeed. Laura had lost that conversation. She slumped over the map with some bitterness, watching as Clae deposited the equipment and opened a case. This was the first time Okane had mentioned actual family, and his mother must've been one of those magic people. She would've liked to know a little more about that. Then again, if he had to talk about parents, he'd probably expect Laura to reciprocate, wouldn't he? The thought made her sulk lower. She had her aunt Morgan looking out for her, but her parents had essentially left the picture long ago. Both of them chose to work on long contracts, outside the walls or in the deepest bowels of Amicae, rarely visiting. Her parental plight didn't seem near as bad as his could be, but she hated thinking about it. Ergo, she would not pester him on this subject. Best move on so it could be left forever in the dust.

"Sir, I wanted to ask . . . are those regular bullets?" Okane was looking over Clae's shoulder at the contents of a case; it must have contained supplies for his gun.

"They've got kin in them," Laura supplied loudly.

"Of course they're not regular bullets," Clae scoffed. "If regular bullets had any effect, do you think the military and police would be sitting on their asses?"

Okane ducked his head and muttered something that sounded like "Yes, of course."

Heaving a loud, irritated sigh (someone must've gotten on his bad side at the factory), Clae gestured for them both to move closer. "Here, this is how it works. There are a number of Sweeper weapons that work on a similar principle."

Laura circled around the counter to join them as Clae held up a single bullet, right in front of Okane's face so he could get a good look at it. The object looked like a regular bullet, if rather pale.

"These are specially constructed by a guild of gunsmiths. Their location in Amicae is Cherry Co. You've probably heard of it. They have a specific line in their factory creating these every other month. These bullets are essentially capsules, containing a small amount of kin liquid inside."

"And they get the kin from Sweepers?" said Laura.

"Yes." He gestured at the mess of tubes and bottles on the countertop. "We're the only ones in the city capable of producing this. We pull magic from Gin into liquid form and send it through here to refine it to the point it's useful for weapons. The longer kin stays in this, the stronger it is. Likewise, the longer this equipment sits around, the stronger it becomes. Take this bullet for example. With such a tiny amount of magic inside, normally it wouldn't do much good. We have to store them and let them fester for a year before they're capable of serious damage to an infestation."

"A whole year?" Okane frowned.

"At minimum."

"Is there a big store of them somewhere?" Laura asked.

"Of course. These cases are from a cache we stored away two . . . three years ago?" He mused on that for a while before shrugging. "We have more powerful backups hidden away in case of major problems."

"How old are those?"

"Some of them were stored before I was born."

"Thirty years?" she guessed. He didn't dignify her with an answer.

"There are Eggs and other kin containers stored longer, but bullets we tend to run through fast when guns are in use, so those aren't allowed to age very long. To use them, we have a special gun."

He pulled one of his guns from its holster and held it up for them to examine. It looked like a strange combo of a flare gun and a military-issued pistol, leaning more toward the pistol side. All along the barrel were more pictorial letters, complex but similar to the ones marking Kuro no Oukoku on the map. Clae spun the cylinder, creating a grating, clacking sound, then pulled back the hammer. This time it produced a low hum that Laura had never noticed before, and the symbols on the barrel began to glow faintly.

"When I pull the trigger, the hammer hits the bullet and it flies," he explained, "but on its way out, it passes this." He ran a finger over a small bump halfway down the barrel, what looked like a thin, silvery ring running around the outside. "This here is Gin. Do you know what Gin is?"

Laura knew, of course, but after the explanation earlier Okane was able to nod along too. Clae seemed vaguely impressed and carried on, "When the hammer is pulled back and these light up, it means the Gin here has activated like an amulet. And just like our regular amulets, it serves the purpose of lighting a fuse. When the bullet passes this, its kin becomes active, and will explode on impact."

"So it's something like Eggs. I thought it would be more complicated," said Laura.

"If it were too complicated it would be too difficult to use. Better to keep it simple so we can utilize it under pressure."

"But isn't that like the military was trying to do earlier?" said Okane. "When you were on the phone and they wanted a 'bigger boom'?"

"They weren't planning to use kin capsules, they wanted to use actual amulets. Kin and magic aren't the same. Kin is liquid; magic is more like altered air in a pocket. The liquid is potent and weaponized for our purposes, but aside from burning, the amount in a bullet won't do much damage to anything beyond an infestation. Even the bullet shell itself only does the minimum. Amulets can be commanded to do a lot more on impact that could cause that burning, but it could also have a secondary reaction, a larger explosion, shrapnel, change the properties of its casing, things that would work on human forces or the beasts in the wilds. The problem is, while Sweeper bullets are entirely saturated in kin and made of the wrong material to host regular magic, an amulet shot in the wilds is broken, abandoned, or both—almost guaranteed to be a new host for a new infestation. Even if the Council can pull off their 'Amicae is immune' bull inside the walls, the story doesn't account for the outside. That was easy to shoot down once they actually understood the consequences."

"They realized they needed to protect the satellite towns?" Okane guessed.

"Exactly," said Clae.

"What other weapons were you talking about, that work on the same system?" said Laura.

"The most common form like this is bow and arrows, long-range weapons."

"There are short-range ones?"

"Of course. The Sweepers here used to specialize in short range, but that died out not too long ago."

"Why's that?"

"Because I got to be the only one left, and I like keeping a distance." He spoke without bitterness, more the resigned drawl of one who'd been over this so many times it seemed nothing more than dry fact.

Laura pondered a moment before speaking again. "Do we get to pick out weapons at some point?"

"Apprentices have to stick with Eggs, it's a requirement. It gives you the needed basics. Once you move up you'll be able to pick something else if you want to. Just keep in mind it has to be something I'm able to coach you in. We don't have other teachers for you, and as much of a prodigy as I'm supposed to be I'm terrible when it comes to close combat with these things. May as well ask me to tap-dance."

Considering the woeful number of Sweepers and the limited space, Laura doubted there would be much variety of weapons to choose from anyway. Her eyes trailed over to the open briefcase, the absurd number of bullets lined up inside. If she didn't know better, she'd think he was stocking up for a garrison's worth of guns.

"You're storing most of these, right?"

Clae made a noncommittal noise, and she frowned. He caught her look, then returned his attention to the gun, clicking the hammer back so the glow of the letters faded.

"There are more signs popping up," he said, shoving the gun back into its holster. "Bad ones. We may have to use some of the older stock. Deplete our supplies."

"What do you mean?"

"There's a spike coming. I've seen warning signs in the past, but these? These are different, and they're occurring all over the island. I have contacts with other Sweepers and they've confirmed it. I don't know what to expect, beyond downright *nasty*."

"How bad is nasty?" Okane squeaked.

Clae eyed him for a while, blank-faced and brooding. "I'll put it this way. If you don't take training seriously, you're not going to last long."

10

NUMBERFACE

"Hurry it up!"

Clae's bark lent more speed to Laura's flight. She sprinted across the cobblestone road and down an alley, trying to stay ahead of the pounding footsteps. Okane panted harshly just behind her, and a glance back showed his eyes wide and panicked. That same glance showed Clae gaining fast. With a squeak of fear, Laura smacked the amulet on her belt. With gravity's hold slackened, she charged the wall to her right. The amulets in her shoes let her take three steps nearly vertical on the brick, and she launched herself up, grabbed hold of a large windowsill, and tumbled through the opening. She landed heavily on a hardwood floor and whirled about, pulling a rubber ball from her bag and tapping it against her amulet. She stood ready, waiting for Clae to appear (him being the mock monster, she needed to try to hit him with the mock Egg), but he didn't. Instead, his voice issued from outside.

"Damn it, Okane, you're supposed to be using your amulets!"

"I don't know how!"

"I showed you five minutes ago!"

Laura let her arm go slack, heaving a sigh. This was the third time during the exercise that they'd had to stop. She drifted back to the window and leaned out, looking down at her coworkers. Okane cowered by the wall while Clae, sounding very much annoyed, walked him through how to work the amulets. He'd been trying to explain them for over a week, to no avail; they'd had to leave Okane locked up in the shop while they took care of other minor infestations. Why Okane hadn't gotten the hang of it, Laura had no idea. It was easy for her to use them. Then again, she was a *natural.* She basked in that old praise for a while, passing the rubber ball from one hand to the other, then shouted "Think fast!" and slung the ball downward.

There was a series of snapping sounds, and the next thing she knew Okane was clambering up the fence of the dead-end alley. Here she'd thought it was impossible to climb. Clae remained unimpressed.

"Amulets, I said! You can't rely on fear forever!"

Okane stopped, teetering on top of the wood, and peered down at him. The thin fence wavered beneath his weight.

"I don't like amulets."

"*Obviously.*"

Laura climbed back onto the windowsill and hopped down. The amulets of her shoes slowed her descent so she alighted easily beside Clae.

"Any particular reason why?" she asked.

"They feel wrong," Okane defended. "It's like they're crawling into my head."

"Get down from there before you break your neck," Clae scoffed.

Okane wobbled precariously on his perch, trying to pick his way back down.

"So he's not even using magic to get up there?" Laura marveled.

"Wrong kind of magic. Remember the 'you' phenomenon? That's not the extent of it. His innate magic kicks in with fight-or-flight instinct, but it's uncontrollable. He doesn't think when he uses it, so he can't properly utilize it. One slip in control, and he's dead meat." He paused, then nodded his certainty. "No. Dead. Literally dead."

"He can't use the innate kind at will?"

"What do you think he is, a witch?"

"You're the one going on about magic."

Clae folded his arms, glowered at the fence. "His understanding of magic and amulets is probably like yours. Abstracted. Doesn't have direction. There's nothing else to react to your thoughts, but he's got two avenues to try and he's so used to the natural one he can't switch over. He's not even trying. This is an adrenaline-fueled environment, and if he doesn't get the hang of it soon I can't take him anywhere."

Okane dropped to the ground, stumbling to catch his balance. He gave them a sullen look. "Are we done now?"

"No," Clae snapped. "We're doing this either until you get it right or the sun goes down."

"Really?" Laura groaned.

It was late afternoon and she was sick of being chased down the streets of the Fourth Quarter. They must've looked utterly ridiculous.

"An infestation's going to run faster than me if it's big. You planning on surviving or not?"

"Of course I am, but can't you do individual lessons?"

"He's already getting individual lessons."

"Then what are we doing here?" Laura cried.

"Individual lessons are different. Those are desensitizing."

"I don't like it," Okane butted in, and Clae glared at him.

"If you want to survive this job, you can't panic every time you come across a monster. Did you even make a conscious choice how to use that magic just now?"

"No."

"And that will get you killed." Clae glanced over at Laura and added, "Anselm."

"Anselm?"

"Anselm."

Must've been another dead apprentice. Maybe the "horse" Clae learned all this information from.

Clae turned on his heel, gesturing for them to follow. They trailed behind him onto the main street, and Laura squinted up at the building she'd sought refuge in. It was a hotel with some front windows smashed in, patched over by patterned cloth that might've been old dresses. A woman scowled from the second floor—she might've been startled by

Laura. Laura hadn't been paying attention to where she was going, so she was lucky Clae had been so focused on Okane; otherwise she'd be chewed out.

"What exactly are you doing for this desensitizing?" she asked.

"I sit and stare at an infestation," Okane grumbled.

"A little one. It won't be able to do any damage for a while, and I've been monitoring its growth closely." Clae didn't look back at them, so Laura just stared incredulously at the back of his head.

"Isn't that kind of cruel?"

"What do you think Sweepers are, picnics and butterflies? If sitting you down with the thing you hate will help you keep your wits later, I'm going to do it."

Okane slipped further into his sulk but didn't argue. Laura sighed and folded her arms, unable to come up with a counter. It must've really sucked being around Clae twenty-four/seven, especially with the amulet situation. Maybe she could offer to let Okane stay at her apartment? But then there was Morgan to deal with—would she crow over Laura finally having a "beau," or despair that she didn't invite Charlie? Hell, that might set an awful precedent . . . but she was already dealing with angelina rumors. Laura's mind was obviously running too far; no way would Morgan ever allow a male of any kind to associate so closely with poor, unmarried Laura. Might sully her for future marriage prospects.

The three of them passed by another alley, where a group of children tracked their progress eagerly. One scampered off in the direction the Sweepers came from. The kids here recognized Clae's coat on sight and had a habit of following the Sweepers throughout the Quarter. The rubber balls used in training ended up getting lost more times than not and became little treasures for the kids here. There weren't a lot of good toys in this Quarter, so Laura wouldn't be surprised if these kids worshiped Sweepers like Underyear spirits.

"How do you have another infested amulet?" she sighed after a while.

"Someone turned it in for recycling, just a little late."

One of the children ran by, holding a rubber ball above his head and cackling, a pack of others hot on his heels. Laura smiled at the sight, though Clae snorted in disgust. The laughter faded as they arrived at a low wall of rosy brick. Clae reached up, jumped slightly to catch the top, and heaved himself up. Laura copied, scowling at her arms as she did. Her arms looked pale and brittle compared to Clae's, even if she did have some muscle. She pulled herself on top of the wall and rolled over it to drop in the space between brick and a flower bush. She batted at the bush gingerly, dislodging some thorns from her clothes.

Gardens and green spaces were sparse inside the walls of Amicae, but little oases had been scattered around, this being one of them. The garden lay between two larger brick buildings, fenced in to deter people from cutting through and crushing the vegetation. A path of scattered stone circles wound through dark soil, glittering with colored beads and glass. Laura balanced on a circle with the imprint of childish hands. The plants tended toward dark green with a smattering of lighter green and bright flowers of orange and pink and pale blue. A particularly large, bell-shaped purple blossom tilted in their direction as Clae drifted nearer, its petals curling tighter. It was a Watcher Lily; as a child, Laura had been terrified of them, and even now she gave it a wide berth.

A yelp and crash caught their attention. Okane had slipped on the wall and tumbled to the ground. The thorny bush shook as he scrambled to his feet, its pink flowers closing up. Loose soil coated Okane's front, and he batted it away as best he could, flushing in embarrassment.

"You okay?" Laura called.

"Fine," he mumbled, walking over and studying his hands.

The thorns had pricked a small hole in his sleeve but he escaped getting hurt too badly, with the exception of a long, thin cut on the side of his left hand. The blood appeared extra dark against the pallor of his skin and white sleeve. Clae grabbed him by the wrist and Okane recoiled, trying to jerk his hand back. Clae hung on and scolded, "Calm down, it's just Laura. It's not like she's going to bite you."

Okane deflated. It looked like he was retreating into an invisible shell.

"You really are a bully," said Laura. Clae shrugged that off.

"Look," he instructed, nodding at Okane's hand. "You should know about this too, take it into account later."

Frowning, Laura stepped closer. Yep. Blood. Clae rubbed the spot with his thumb, smearing the redness away from the cut. Only there was no cut. It looked a few days healed, and in a matter of seconds it was like he'd never bled at all.

"What the—"

"Another Magi perk," Clae explained, letting go. Okane held his freed hand close to his chest. "Works fast on small injuries, speeds up recovery a little for bigger ones."

"That's . . ."

"And he's essentially a kin lighthouse when monsters get close. Ideal Sweeper if he gets it all under control." From Clae that might've been a compliment, but it didn't sound like one.

"How have I never heard of this?" said Laura. "The magic thing, that's easy to miss, but instant healing? Doctors would be desperate to figure out how that works. They'd whine about it all over the radios. How on earth—"

"I told you the Magi went underground," said Clae, as Okane shrank still further. "They know very well what the cities would like to do with them, and they're not interested. I wouldn't be surprised if Okane's the only Magi in all of Amicae."

"But even if they were in another city—"

"The natives may have agreed to return, but the Magi knew better," said Okane.

"But if they're not in a city, where are they?"

"Somewhere no city can find them."

A low howl rose in the September air, brassy like it came from a horn, but it continued in a drone that grew subtly quieter, then louder, then quieter again. It sounded distant, but after a minute an echoing drone started up nearby.

"Is that a siren?" Laura looked around but couldn't spot the source.

Sirens were rare in Amicae, only used when particularly bad weather rolled in, but nothing in the cloudless sky hinted at incoming storms.

"We're not about to get a typhoon, are we?"

"No," said Clae.

"Then why—"

"It means there's danger, not just bad weather. Rex has been on the move, hasn't it? Either they've been sighted nearby or some spies managed to get in."

"They're not targeting us, are they?"

"They target everyone."

"Rex?" Okane questioned. "Isn't that another city?"

"The city everyone else hates. They're military-based and belligerent to the point they can be downright stupid. They're obsessed with the idea of reaching the apex of human potential, and seem to think they can reach it through battle. So they go out and attack anyone and everyone. It's a wonder they haven't been wiped out yet. Problem is, trying to interfere with them is like poking a kinral nest. You get swarmed and bitten before you know what's happening."

Okane's brow furrowed. "Then what do we do now?"

"Everyone should be getting indoors so the police can comb the area. By the sound of it the warning is restricted to the bottom Quarters," Clae mused.

"So should we go back to the shop?" said Laura, getting antsy now. She never wanted to meet anyone from Rex, spies least of all.

"They've probably shut down the cable cars and roads." Clae dug his hands in his pockets to fiddle with his watch again.

"What?"

"Keep the spies from getting any further. Trap them, catch them. We'll have to wait in this Quarter until the ban gets lifted."

"If they have to comb for spies, how long will that take?"

"If all else fails we can probably convince the police to let us back through. Sweeper privileges."

"Where do we go in the meantime?" Laura spread her arms out at the surrounding greenery. "We can't just lurk in the garden for god knows how long!"

"We'll wait in there." Clae gestured at a nearby shop, a hunkered-down building with a rough pinkish exterior and no visible signage. The large windows and location marked it as a kind of shop, as did the big cages being hauled inside by a man dressed in black. Laura couldn't identify what kind of shop it was, though.

"You've been in there before?"

"Sure I have. Come on."

He led them out of the garden and across the street, catching the door before it closed behind man and cage. The man looked back at the sound, bleary eyes unfocused and almost looking in opposite directions. His black hair wound in tight curls that sprang out from his scalp in a frizzy mane to hide his ears, gray and white streaking through in corkscrew curls. His gaunt face was waxy and pale; Laura thought this must be what the living dead would look like.

"Sinclair," the man warbled. Between the eyes, the voice, and the fact that she realized he wore a tattered robe and slippers, she concluded he wasn't all there. "Come to visit, eh? Came to visit . . . last week, didn't yer? Got no . . . candy for ya."

"That's unnecessary. We're just waiting in here until they give the all-clear," Clae replied.

"All-clear fer wha . . . t?" The man squinted outside. What did he mean, "for what"? The siren made him go inside too, didn't it?

"Doesn't matter."

Clae grabbed the cage and heaved it up to carry it out of the way. As he did, the pack of rabbits inside squirmed about in anxiety. With the way cleared, Laura and Okane edged inside. The man tottered after Clae and plucked a rabbit from the cage before flopping onto an armchair. A few ratty couches were pushed against the other walls, though the armchair guarded the staircase and a radio squatted in the opposite corner. Gloom and dust settled over everything, lending the aura of a crypt. Laura felt unwelcome, so hovered in the open space rather than sit down. Clae lingered by the window, squinting out the filthy panes at the street while muffled sirens wailed on. The man petted his rabbit, and the animal quivered, eyes bulging.

"No . . . candy," he repeated.

"I don't want candy," Clae retorted.

"Eh?" the man screeched, rolling his head to look at him. "No?"

"No."

The man rolled his head back and clacked his teeth, gaze roving around the room before alighting on the apprentices.

"Anklebiters."

Clae didn't correct him, simply transferring himself over to the couch. Springs groaned and dust shifted under his weight.

"Here," the man wheezed, holding out the rabbit. "Take the rabbit. Take . . . rabbit." Laura stayed rooted to the spot. The man moved the rabbit up and down in his outstretched arms, calling again, "Have the rabbit. Don' . . . hafta buy. Hold rabbit."

He kept insisting until Okane finally crept forward. Taking pains not to touch the man's clawlike hands, he took the rabbit and cradled it to his chest. The animal might as well have been a doll; throughout the transaction it made no movement save for the furious twitching of its nose.

"Nice rabbit." The man grinned.

"How do you know this man?" Laura asked, sinking down next to Clae.

"He's Old Gabe," Clae responded. "Used to be a scientist. He did experiments with the mixture of magic and science, like the robots only bigger, all meant to further Sweeper abilities. My father had him over at the shop a lot, but he was always offering candy and edging around us. He talked strangely in the first place, then got caught in the middle of some experiment malfunction. He doesn't remember much of it but on the odd occasion he does he's happy to say it was an *electrifying* experience. So now he sells stew rabbits."

"Why exactly is he trying to bribe you with candy?"

"Because he's stuck with the memory of me at six years old. No one's really smart at six but even then we knew he was strange. Back when he was smarter his wife was around to send him on wild-goose chases, but she died . . . ten years ago now? During the epidemic. He's harmless these days."

"I'm sure."

Old Gabe didn't look harmless. His eyes were big and mad and fixed on Okane, marking him a victim.

"Rabbits're . . . *fascinatin'*," he slurred. "Y'know. Haven' changed since . . . ever. Born with the world as is. All them . . . Firins? Felons. *Felins*, and muck in th' wilds grew like tha'. Weren' all ugly in the beginning, no sir. Only domestic animals're unchanged by them wilds. Rabbit . . . from th' dawn 'f time."

He grinned toothily but Okane didn't return the gesture. He glanced over at the others for help. Laura would help, but she'd probably just take over as the next target. She gave an exaggerated shrug and pulled a face.

Okane made a pitiful noise. Clae leaned over to the radio and turned dials until it crackled to life.

"—Mershon's got the ball, he's running for the goal, what a game, folks—" Click. "Mr. Frank Sullivan announced today that he'll be backing—" Click. "Shipment of canir furs—" Click. "—regards to the alert—"

Clae's fingers hovered over the dial but this time he allowed the sentence to finish.

"We appreciate the trouble this has caused the citizens at this time, and will do our best to minimize the duration and resolve the problem. Again, if you are outside in the Sixth, Fifth, or Fourth Quarters, please return to your homes or locate a public shelter. Police and militia are standing by to see to your safety. A small hostile group has infiltrated the city, and as such, the cable systems, roadways, and interior doors have been barred. City officials who need to return to the upper Quarters may do so by approaching one of the road blockades and presenting proper identification."

"Hear that? We can go back!" Laura would much rather be bored to tears in the Sweeper shop than hanging out with Old Gabe. Clae hummed a discordant note, and she frowned. "Wait, do you . . . Do you really want to stay here?"

"Identification is the problem. Okane over there"—he nodded toward the hapless victim in question—"doesn't have a proper ID. As far as Amicae public records go, he doesn't exist. The Sullivans either never registered him or got rid of his records. Unless they take Sweeper rings as sufficient ID, we won't be able to get through."

"But he should've got an ID the minute he walked in the city! People can't just mess with public records like that."

"Enough money can buy anything."

Laura leaned further against the couch. "I feel like the more I learn about people, the more I lose faith in the world."

"And that's why you need to be a pain, don't let people walk all over you."

Laura wrinkled her nose. "Better a pain than a comfort?"

"Of course."

"Then you need to start teaching Okane fast. Look at him. He's a pain unto himself."

"Backbones take time," Clae scoffed, making no move to help. "I've been working with Albright to get him a proper identity. Until then we just need to keep him out of too much trouble. Not that I expect him to get arrested or anything."

"That's one of the reasons he's living with you?"

Clae shot her a confused look, as if he hadn't even considered another option. "Where else would he go?"

"I've just gotten a message," the radio announcer piped up. "The Sinclair Sweepers have been asked to return to their headquarters. Why I'm not sure, but the police have requested they avoid the lower Quarters."

"There we go." Laura clapped her hands on her knees. "If they're expecting Sweepers, they'll know what we look like."

Clae hummed again but didn't move. He sounded unconvinced.

Laura stood and walked to Okane. She plucked the rabbit from his arms and offered it back to Old Gabe. "Sorry, but we've got to go."

She tried to sound as sweet as possible, but it backfired. Old Gabe snatched the rabbit back and glowered at her. Laura held up her hands in surrender. Okane shuffled to hide behind her, but with him being taller than both her and Clae, this didn't work too well.

"Sinclairs," Old Gabe sneered. "Al'ys . . . *ruuude.*"

"Comes with the job," Clae agreed, standing slow and leisurely.

"Sssweepers."

"Clean this place, there's rabbit droppings in the couch."

The nearest blockade was located on Nera Street, on one of the sections that broke apart from the main drag and sloped gradually along the inner wall to reach the next Quarter. A line of police cars had been parked lengthwise across the road, blocking the way with another matching line behind it. Policemen and soldiers alike manned the area, and more could be seen over the edge of the wall above. When the Sweepers grew close, the soldiers raised rifles. Almost immediately the police started moving more erratically and there was an audible command to *stand down, for god's sake don't shoot them of all people,* but the soldiers were hesitant to lower their weapons. Clae raised his hands and advanced slower, and the other two followed his example. One of the policemen tried to tame the line of soldiers while another ran toward the Sweepers with a galloping gait.

Baxter again. At least it was someone they knew. Laura relaxed at the sight of him but didn't lower her hands.

"You order Sweepers to come, then try to shoot them?" Clae snarked.

"My apologies." Baxter cast an anxious glance back. "Considering the intruders, everyone's on edge."

"You've identified them?"

"Ah, yes. The chief said specifically to tell you that they had numbers on their faces."

"Oh, that's just *lovely*," Clae hissed through his teeth. He obviously knew the culprits, but the description meant nothing to Laura. Baxter nodded.

"We want you out of the line of fire as soon as possible. Fighting monsters may be your job, but fighting humans is ours."

"Knock yourselves out, I want nothing to do with this," said Clae.

Baxter's mouth quirked uneasily. "Of course. Please follow me. We'll get you through quickly."

He led them to the line of defenders. The soldiers had finally lowered their guns, but their faces were wary. The policemen recognized Sweepers right away—Laura and Clae, at least—but a dark-skinned man in the military uniform stepped to block them. His dreadlocks framed his scowl, and his voice boomed deep.

"Let's see some identification," he ordered.

Clae sighed. "What did I tell you."

"Sir, these are the Sinclair Sweepers. We've worked with them before, we know them."

Nearby police nodded and murmured in assent, but the soldier and his brethren remained unconvinced.

"Amulets have changed someone's appearance before. ID, now."

Clae let out a short, annoyed huff, and stuck out his right arm. The man twitched backward in response.

"The rings," Baxter prompted. "They're like the army crest or police badge. The Sweeper's name is on the inside."

The soldier looked at the hand, at Clae's face, then back down at the hand and back again before assuring himself that there was no chance of an attack. He grabbed Clae's fingers and leaned in to squint at the gold ring.

"'S.S.Am.,'" he read aloud.

"Sinclair Sweepers of Amicae," Clae recited.

The man sneered and let go before waving Laura over. "Come on, you next." Laura could feel thick calluses when he took her hand, and his grip felt too tight. Luckily his inspection ended in a matter of seconds, and he moved on to Okane. Okane had a ring, but he fidgeted and squirmed, much to the soldier's annoyance. He had to be told twice to stop fussing before he got released too. The soldier wasn't happy, but he was placated.

"Get out of here, then. You're in the way." He sent them off.

Baxter accompanied them to the top of the hill.

"The chief herself is on the prowl," he chuckled. "With her on the job, there shouldn't be much to worry about. Of course if you do run into any trouble, then call right away. We've still got people minding the telephones just in case."

Baxter doubled back to his post while they turned onto a thin road, directed toward the middle of the Third Quarter. A few soldiers tracked them from their places along the wall, and some police rushed past, but those soon fell behind.

"So," Laura sighed, "what did that mean, when he said those people had numbers on their faces?"

"It shows they're part of the Rex breeding program. Sure, Rex encourages specific matches, but there's only one declared breeding program, and that's with their Sweepers. The result is a crack force of the best Sweepers in the world. God knows they need them, with all their forays into the wilds outside the cities. But those people don't have name tags. They have serial numbers on their faces, right here." Clae tapped his left cheekbone. "That's all they're ever known by."

"Why would Rex send Sweepers here?"

"If we're judging by the police's reactions, they're here for us."

"Us?" Okane repeated, looking up.

"Yes."

"But why?"

"Because if we're not around, Amicae falls. Without us taking care of monsters and monitoring Pits, infestations would take root and eat this city with no resistance. Then people would leave the walls and become easy prey for Rex troops. There are other ways to destroy Amicae, of course, but the military has plans to counter those. No one has plans with Sweepers but the police, and theirs aren't long-term."

For most of the remaining daylight Laura hunkered down in the Sweeper shop, straining her ears to hear the radio in the pawnshop. At exactly 5:43, a newscaster announced that the hostile group had been caught. Okane was listening too, because he asked, "What's going to happen to them?"

Clae paused in the middle of cleaning a gun and regarded them for a moment, before using one hand to mime someone falling from a great height.

11

HITTING THE GRIT

"Infestations don't spread in a physical manner. They don't reproduce in the way you're familiar with. There are no males or females, they do not divide to asexually reproduce. They do not give birth. There is absolutely no way to prevent the spread. An amulet could be stored in a safe, completely and utterly shut off from the world, and an infestation could take root anyway. It is believed that this happens in part due to proximity and aggression level of another infestation, but experiments show that it happens whether or not there are multiple in the vicinity. The addition of another just seems to speed the growth. Nevertheless, the theory is that this monster resonates with the hollow of an amulet, prompting the absence of anything inside to develop into an 'absence' creature. That begs the question, if a monster can 'resonate' as such, is it possible that other things could 'resonate' and trigger the birth without our knowing? The creature was created by man; perhaps it's still being assisted without us even noticing."

"In a nutshell"—Laura turned to walk backward, addressing Okane—"nobody knows how they get places. Many theories, nothing concrete."

"Ah."

"As such," Clae continued, as if he hadn't been interrupted, "infestations could take root anywhere, at any time. They're more common the further south you are, but Amicae is considered southerly so we're in the red zone. The only way to stop it is by monitoring habitable areas through recording amulet ownership and use, recycling, and monitoring Pits."

Laura knew all of this too, but it must've been new to Okane, because he nodded.

"That's why you two always need to be armed. With no way to predict when, where, or how developed they'll be, you don't want to be defenseless at any time."

"Have you lost an apprentice that way too?" asked Laura.

"I made that mistake myself," Clae confessed, eyes still directed straight ahead. "It was a very unpleasant experience."

He stopped short, suddenly enough that the others almost ran into him. He had led them from the shop forty minutes ago, and Laura wondered if they'd reached their destination.

On their right rose a temple, one of the larger of its kind in this Quarter. Churches dedicated to righteous spirits tended to be on a grander scale and had the run of the city, but the temples and shrines of immortals had clung to existence.

One of the big differences between spirits and immortals was that spirits were all facets of an individual god known as the Spinner, and each facet was invoked to make the worshiper a better person and more deserving of salvation in the life after death; immortals were a pantheon essentially created to explain certain happenings like falling stars and the advent of music, and their worshipers aligned themselves with members of the pantheon and supposedly, if they pleased their patrons, became permanent guests of their kingdoms after death. In both beliefs, those found unworthy wandered a wasteland for all eternity. The spirit ideals were brought over from the Old World before the quarantine or the monsters had even occurred to anyone, while the immortals were more of a native thing. The original inhabitants of Orien hadn't left much more visible influence than their old temples and gods, and their remaining religion was still the object of scorn by association.

The outside walls of this temple were covered in tile mosaics of stars,

animals, and abstract people, the sloping domed roof dark and undeco-
rated. Great stone canir flanked the open doorway with gaping jaws.

"So what's this?" Laura asked.

"The unexpected. Are you ready?"

"Are you telling me there's an infestation in there?" Laura gave him an
appalled look.

"I didn't sense it," Okane muttered.

"That's because it's small," said Clae. "I planted it there. We're having
another training exercise. And you"—he looked at Okane—"are going to
exterminate this."

Okane shrank down. "I don't think I can."

"Laura will walk you through it."

"I'll what?" Laura deadpanned.

"You'll learn through teaching."

"But—" Okane began, but Clae cut him off.

"If we want you in the field anytime this decade, we need to work
harder. Who knows? Maybe you'll do better in the moment than with
tests."

"But you won't be helping," said Laura.

"I'll be observing, but I'm not lifting a finger unless you're about to
die. You're doing this on your own strength with the equipment you have
on hand. If you fail this test, I will have no choice but to spring these
traps on you more frequently, with absolutely no warning, and leave you
to flounder. Unless you want an infestation after you at three in the morning, you'll do this right."

Laura's shoulders slumped. She'd been through this before, the more
practical training, but she'd never enjoyed it and she always had forewarning; several days' forewarning, usually. She didn't appreciate the surprise,
and judging by the pallor of Okane's face he didn't either.

"--- would do that?" he breathed, horrified.

"I would."

Laura had the feeling she'd be doing this mostly solo. That was okay
though, she reminded herself as she pulled herself to full height. She'd
helped take out the Two-Monther. A test like this should be child's
play.

Clae threw a hand up, barked, "Begin!" and walked over to lounge against one of the statues. A man in priestly robes rose up from the statues' shadow to meet him. They must've been in cahoots.

"Right then," Laura sighed, resigned. "What kind of equipment did you bring?"

"An Egg."

"Just one?"

"Yes." He looked at the ground in shame or embarrassment.

"I've got two more." Laura patted her belt. "If it really is small, we should be fine."

"If --- say so."

"Of course we will be! Come on." She led the way through the open doorway.

Ribbons dipped down from the gloomy ceiling, festive colors festooning a wide passage otherwise bleak. Beaded ornaments hung on the walls, methodically spaced, and the dark purplish rock of the floor made their every footstep echo deeper inside.

"I don't like this place." Okane's voice echoed too, and he shied away at the sound. "It's too loud. Don't they listen for Sweepers?"

"There's not a lot we can do, but we can minimize it. Whisper instead and use the amulets."

Laura tapped the amulet on her belt, and magic rushed down to her feet to lessen the noise. It was muffled but certainly audible. Okane copied, and they did their best to sneak into the main room.

The circular main room was lit by an oculus in the domed ceiling. Afternoon sunlight filtered in to illuminate the place, shining down through the huge hole in the floor. Well, it wasn't so much a hole as a drop. The walkway stretched seven feet wide, no railing; the flat part on their level served as a landing as the rest created a spiraling staircase, wrapping twice before reaching the bottom floor. Alcoves lined the stairs, dips in the wall with tiny altars and statues of immortals inside. Jumbles of offerings littered the spaces, candles, coins, art pieces, and even food items crammed in around the statues' legs; more bright ribbons were tied about the limbs, so the statues appeared to have rainbow sleeves and pants. The first statue in its alcove grimaced at its unfortunate wardrobe.

"Well?" Laura prompted as she began to descend the stairs. "Feeling anything?"

"Nothing," came the miserable response. Okane eyed the statues balefully.

"Let me know if you do, okay?"

"Right."

They kept walking, step after step after step until they were nearly two-thirds of the way down and Okane inhaled sharply. Laura stopped short, hand flying to her belt.

"You sensed it?"

"It's . . . it's two more down."

The alcove in question hosted a statue the size of Cheryl, sitting with legs crossed and head downturned, the smile on its face oddly reminiscent of the ones carved into the Sweeper amulets. A royal purple robe was tied about its form, almost eclipsed by more ribbons and an old Underyear wreath hung about it like a sash. A porcelain horse and smaller equine figures cluttered any space not covered by the altar and rotting fruit atop it.

"Anything more specific?" Laura surveyed the mess from a distance before glancing up.

Clae hovered at the very top of the stairs, watching them just as he'd stated before. The robed man stood behind him, yammering something that was lost in the echo of the room, but Clae paid him no attention. Instead the Sweeper met her gaze, held up three fingers, and mouthed, *A.M.* Laura scowled. She doubted he'd plant an infestation in her apartment in the wee hours of the morning, but he'd probably plant one *somewhere*. Every time he assigned one of these tests he got nastier about it.

"It's behind the statue, I think." Okane's voice brought her back to earth, and she looked back at him.

"You're sure?"

"Not entirely. I feel it but it's not enough to pinpoint beyond there."

If Clae planted this, it must've been a small enough infestation to be handled without danger. Maybe they wouldn't have to blow up the statue; that would certainly be preferable.

Laura cast about, skipped down to the next alcove, and pulled a long stick of incense from the offerings. She brought it back up and prodded at the area behind the statue. This way she could search for an amulet and rouse the monster into showing itself, hopefully. It worked. She got resistance on the other end of the stick. A sharp tug, and she let go immediately. Blackness rose up, roiling like a chunky shadow on the wall behind the statue.

"Whoa. Well, we found it."

"Now what?" Okane squeaked.

"Well, uh, we destroy it! Obviously!"

"How?"

"Beat it into submission and douse it. I think we have to draw it out first."

"How?"

"Oh, use some imagination!"

As they spoke, the darkness spread, and Laura got an idea. She stomped. The sound echoed. A ripple went through the monster and it reached out faster. Laura dismissed the magic on her shoes and clattered slowly up the stairs, making as much noise as possible.

"Shh!" Okane hissed. "Keep doing that and it'll attack ---!"

"Exactly!"

The monster oozed out, glinting slimy and formless. It wriggled through the mortar joints, toward the source of the noise. It wasn't fast, and the meager amount told Laura that this was a baby infestation, just grown old enough to feed. She kept stomping, luring it closer. More confident now, it spread. Black eclipsed white stone like a vertical pond.

"Okay Okane, your turn," she said. He went even paler than before, skittering away a few steps behind her. "You're going to attack it with that Egg. Ready?"

Okane patted himself down in a panic before remembering the utility belt. He pulled out an Egg with shaky hands and reeled back to throw it.

"Hang on!" Laura cried, diving forward and grabbing his hand. He balked, twisting his entire body away in response. Laura let go and glanced back to see what made him so panicked. The creature kept its pace, not at their level yet; *she* must've been the thing that spooked him. Maybe she moved too suddenly. At this point it didn't much matter.

"You have to arm them first!" she told him, following his hasty retreat. "If you throw it without activating it with the amulet, it won't do anything. It'll just break. Amulet first, then throw."

Okane calmed down minutely and followed her advice. He clicked the Egg against his own amulet and threw it. They were lucky the infestation was so small and slow, or that little lesson could've gotten them killed. In this case, though, the Egg sailed in a low arc and hit the steps beneath the creature. The glass cracked audibly, and the pair dashed up the stairs to get out of range. The Egg went off with a roar, and golden light danced off the bleak walls. The stairs and alcove offerings shuddered in place. Laura changed direction to charge back down. The place it had been was smeared dark, the stone cracked and mortar weeping smoke. The creature's form had vanished, but she heard its squeaks and squeals of pain behind the statue. It was crippled. One good blow and she could kill it. One, two steps, and she was in front of the alcove. Laura whipped out her own Egg, but stopped short. She wasn't the one meant to do this. She could finish this easily, but it wasn't her task. Something ugly tugged in her chest: *Do it anyway, show your worth, leave him in the dust.* Okane trembled on the step behind her—he looked ready to let her go on, ready to stand aside. That was probably why she forced herself to stop.

"You're the one supposed to be doing this. Here." She tried to hand off the Egg, but Okane backed off.

"--- can do it."

"What? No! This is supposed to be your test, I've already done enough!"

"But I don't—"

"Just take the Egg, lean in there, pour kin on the monster and the amulet, okay?"

"But—"

"Hurry! Before it recovers!"

Okane jumped. He took the Egg, fumbled to pull off the top.

"Just break it!"

"R-right!"

He leaned into the alcove, arm outstretched. Blackness bubbled and smoke rose on the far wall as the creature stirred again. He shuddered and made as if to fall back.

"You've got this, come on!" Laura called.

He forced himself to stay put and crack the Egg against the wall. It hit hard; glass smashed at the force, and he reeled away. Kin liquid spilled out onto the dark spot, hitting the creature with a hiss both audible and visible. Smoke puffed out, twisting thin clouds while snaps and pops issued from the spot. Tendrils shot up and smacked against the alcove walls, dislodging offerings as the creature writhed in pain. With every blow the statue shook; the tendrils twisted and thrashed enough to rip off ribbons. More cracks appeared on the stone walls, tainted dark like smeared tar in the creature's wake. Laura and Okane took hurried steps back. Laura's mind raced. Something so small shouldn't struggle this much. Did they need more Eggs? She held out one arm, ushering Okane behind her as she checked her belt. She could probably hold it off long enough for Clae to get here. But the creature had no interest in them anymore. Soon the noise died. The tendrils lost momentum and slid back down in defeat. One clawed at the statue in a few last, desperate swipes, yanking the statue by its robe and rending the wreath in two. At last it stopped. The tendrils liquefied. They spilled out of the alcove like a waterfall of pitch, carrying offerings with them to clatter and vanish into rancid smoke as soon as they hit the floor. The smoke wound down to nothing. One last hiss and it was certain. The monster had died.

Laura gave a shaky sigh. "You okay?"

"I'm fine," Okane replied, slowly straightening and rubbing his hands together as if checking for glass shards. "I'm lucky. I . . . I think it's dead. Right?"

"Took you long enough." Clae's scoff made them both jump. At some point he'd descended the stairs, so now he stood right behind them. He observed the alcove, the discolored walls and crushed or toppled offerings, with something like disdain.

"At least it's done," Laura defended.

"You keep hesitating." Clae scowled at Okane. Okane mumbled something but otherwise didn't argue.

"You did spring it on us. Maybe if you did a gradual approach he'd have built up a better spine?" Laura suggested, displeasure coloring her tone as she moved to stand by Okane.

"The private lessons are the gradual work-up."

"So those are going well, then."

Neither of them said anything, and that was answer enough. Clae reached into the alcove and fished out the amulet. It was a small, orange-painted horse with the head missing. Its broken form exposed one end of the magic hollow. He shook it, and some kin slipped out of the hole like golden blood.

"Good aim." He sounded reluctant to compliment. "Just know that could easily have gone wrong. Very wrong. So you can't start panicking. You can't hesitate like that. If not for yourself, then for the people next to you. You don't want her to get eaten, do you?" Clae jerked his head at Laura, and Okane looked mildly horrified.

"No!"

"Why am I being dragged into this?" Laura grumbled.

"Because more than one Sweeper's been done in by the incompetence of coworkers, even in just the past few years. She carried you through this the whole time. If she's busy watching your *inept* back, she's distracted from watching her own. Fall behind, and you'll lose her like you lost the haven."

"I can take care of myself." Laura didn't completely believe that, and by the look on Clae's face he didn't believe it one bit either.

"If that's what you're thinking, best start praying now." He gestured back at the beribboned statue.

"That's a good choice for Sweepers."

Laura inhaled sharply and Okane twitched badly next to her. The priest stood on the stair just behind them, wrinkled face pulled up in a good-natured smile. He raised his arm to direct their attention to the statue again.

"This immortal is keeper of the stars. A light in the dark, if you will. I think he would be most sympathetic to your plight."

"Sure," Laura mumbled, forcing a smile for politeness.

Clae, on the other hand, didn't have a polite bone in his body. "Didn't I say we weren't coming for a baptism?"

"Of course!" the priest laughed. "But still, you may want to keep the stars in mind."

On the way back to the Sweeper shop, Okane remained quiet. That wasn't unusual in and of itself, but his pinched face showed he was mulling over something not quite happy, turning it over and contemplating it in a way that reminded Laura of Morgan taste-testing her cooking. *No, that's not quite it . . . maybe if I add more salt? No. Definitely not that either.* She didn't interrupt him, and neither did Clae. Laura instead pondered the possibilities of Immortalist books in the city library. She was sure there was a connection between that statue and the Gin amulets somehow, and she wanted to track that down.

The thought followed her all the way back to the shop (they took the long way, as there were a bunch of men transporting pipes for a new main line to the interior), and it only left her mind when they found the police chief waiting for them. Albright leaned against the doorway, perusing a newspaper as she took up the space. When they approached, her eyes looked up from the print, and she watched with a blank expression as they grew closer.

"What are you doing here?" asked Clae, disgruntled by the roadblock.

Albright tucked the paper under her arm before pulling a comb from her pocket. "We found an unregistered amulet with a small infestation during a search today."

Clae took it and looked the object over before nodding. "You could've brought this to the Amuletory."

"I had some questions for you, too."

Clae exhaled slowly, but invited Albright inside. They filtered through the door and scattered to their respective haunts, taking up their seats on the stools. Just as he had with Mary, Clae sat opposite Albright, behind the counter but in a spot with less Kin than the rest so they could clearly see each other. Laura sat to the side and leaned on the counter with every intention of eavesdropping. Albright didn't seem bothered by it. She focused her glare on Clae, even while Okane shuffled in restless half circles at the other end of the counter.

"What kind of questions did you have?" Clae asked.

"One in particular," said Albright. "I've read up on Sweepers and monsters, but none of the information we have on file explains the increase in infestations. It's happened in the past that we have a lull of several years, even decades with few infestations, and then the discovery rate and damage caused skyrockets. The time length and intensity of the outbreak varies, but it seems an inevitability since the founding of Amicae. What is it that controls this phenomenon?"

Laura blinked and mentally backtracked. It was true: even during the short time she'd been an apprentice, infestations had been cropping up more and more frequently. It hadn't registered as a citywide problem for her, though. She'd been more under the impression that Clae was simply taking her along to the big jobs as she improved, and the city had covered up any others. Maybe that was why this latest test threw her for a loop?

"So you've finally realized I'm not setting these up?" Clae mocked her.

Albright scowled. "Don't try to sass me, Sinclair. I'm being civil today."

"Has someone called you out on that temper?"

"If anyone needs calling out, it's you."

"And yet *you* are the civil party here."

"Someone has to be."

Children, Laura wanted to sigh, but Clae rolled his eyes and got back to business.

"You can blame Rex for the infestations."

"Rex?" Albright's brow furrowed still further. "You think they're planting infestations in Amicae?"

"No, they're triggering the problem."

"How so?"

Clae leaned further on the counter as he replied, "You do know about their goal to reach human potential, don't you? Well, their normal forces attack other cities to prove their worth, but then they have their prized Sweeper program. That's got to prove its superiority somehow too, doesn't it? They have miniature crusades that go down south, with the intention of tracking down and destroying the hive mind itself. Every time they do, they rile that thing up and provoke it into retaliation, resulting in stronger, spreading infestations. Once they're sufficiently mauled the Rex forces will pull back, but even without them in the immediate area the hive mind can stay riled for years. That's what the increase is: we're getting more intensity because Rex is pulling that stunt again."

"How have they not been wiped out yet?" Albright grumbled. "If they mutilate their Sweeper forces, what do they have to even protect their city?"

"A hell of a lot more Sweepers. Rex's breeding program means they have the largest number of Sweepers out of any of the cities in Orien, more than enough to spare. And of course, pissing off the hive mind and making more infestations means cities with lesser Sweepers get hit hard, and if we fail, well, that means we weren't capable or worthy of reaching human potential and should be wiped out anyway." Clae looked resentful and Laura didn't blame him; if they were really the smallest Sweeper force, they were most likely to be wiped out, weren't they?

"Can you handle the increase?" asked Albright.

"You'll notice that I've worked through two of these spikes before, and that was mostly solo," Clae pointed out. His eyes flicked over to Laura. "We'll be able to handle this one too."

Laura felt stupidly proud. She fisted her hands and tried not to smile too big, though—best not let that get to his head.

Albright nodded at his certainty. She frowned at her newspaper awhile, then looked up again. "This is a bit more for my own curiosity, but you are familiar with the appearance of Rex spies two days ago?"

"Sweepers, if the descriptions were right."

"Correct. We have the two in custody now, and we've been interrogating them." She paused. "One of our men, during the questioning, brought up the idea, or threat, of having a Sweeper-to-Sweeper *chat*. No one was supposed to have mentioned the Sinclair Sweepers during the proceedings, but the minute your name was brought in they clammed up. If I didn't know better, I'd say they were afraid of you."

"So you want to know how to spook a Rexian."

"You could put it that way."

Clae leaned back now, crossing his arms and glancing up at the ceiling and the wind chime, as if this was a real bother to answer.

"I've had run-ins with them before. Once while traveling on the same train, one wilds infestation, and another when they infiltrated Amicae about . . . hell, twelve years ago?"

The newspaper crinkled under Albright's grip. "You've *what?*" she hissed.

"The train encounter was peaceful, but I told them off," Clae went on, ignoring her reaction. "During the wilds infestation we ended up working together. That's how I learned that they're all idiots, and when they took an interest. And then the last one they decided that whatever secret I was hiding, they wanted it. They snuck into Amicae and tried to break in here and I shot their leader in the kneecaps."

"You shot him in the kneecaps," Laura repeated, stunned.

"Yes."

"The *kneecaps*."

"Got the job done, didn't it?"

"Was this reported?" Albright demanded.

"I called the police after I chased them off." He shrugged. "If it wasn't noted somewhere, that's an error on your end. Of course, that last chief didn't like me much anyway. Said I had a bad attitude."

"It seems that bad attitude is fated to stay."

The only one in the room who didn't seem exasperated with Clae was Okane, who was too busy searching for something under the counter. He pulled out a necklace with shaky hands and put it on the corner to stare at.

"What did you mean by secret?"

Laura's attention returned to Albright.

"Hm?"

"You just said Rex was after some kind of secret here."

"Amicae was once the greatest Sweeper city. Even when we're almost wiped out, we keep our trade secrets," said Clae.

"If you keep them, then how does Rex know about them?" Albright challenged.

Clae fixed her with the blankest of blank stares. "Look back over that data. Think how much I've managed to get through, how young I was when I took the job. Most people wouldn't be able to get through half of that. Rex decided I must have something to carry me through it. They'd want something like that to strengthen their crusades."

"Do you have something like that?"

"No. I have a long family history of Sweepers who've left resources and knowledge, nothing other cities don't have. So maybe I'm more efficient when it comes to getting things done. That's their own fault for being second best." He muttered something like "*Human potential, my ass,*" under his breath.

Albright didn't look completely satisfied with the answer, but "trade secrets" was something she didn't seem willing to dig into. She probably wouldn't understand the details anyway. She stood, tucking the paper under her arm again, and Clae watched her progress.

"You want me to try interrogating those prisoners?"

"The one who brought that up was an idiot," Albright huffed. "I don't want those two anywhere near you, even if you do scare them. I've heard more than enough horror stories about Rexians playing dumb until their target gets close."

Clae hummed, propping up his chin with one hand. "Sounds good."

"I appreciate the information," said Albright. "Hopefully we can cooperate like this in the future." It sounded more like an order than a suggestion.

"Doubtful," Clae drawled.

Albright showed no sign of irritation at that, but no humor either. "It would benefit you, especially with the claims being filed against Sweepers. I'm far from the only one who finds you suspicious. In any case, I will look over the information again. Good day."

She left. In the short time the door was open a breeze sifted in to tug at the chimes, producing a few soft sounds before falling mute once more. Clae stared at the door, even more intensely than Okane was staring at what must've been an infected amulet.

"Something wrong?" said Laura.

Clae's pointer finger tapped against his cheek, and he replied, "Keep a sharp eye out."

"Why's that?"

"She said there were two Rex Sweepers in custody. In my experience they move in odd numbers, typically multiples of three. If she's only got two, that means number three is either dead or at large. It wouldn't surprise me if number three ran for it, but that's the smart thing to do. They've proven to be stubborn as canir in the past."

A chill shot down Laura's spine and Okane finally looked up, eyes wide.

"What do we do if we run into them?" he asked.

"There's no outrunning them," said Clae. "Stand your ground, make a hell of a lot of noise, and if you get the chance bash their head in, Egg or no Egg."

"Great," Laura murmured.

She never thought she'd ever wish death on anybody, but right then she really, really hoped that "number three" was dead. Dead or running away with his tail between his legs. That would've been wonderful.

12

KAIBUTSU

Two weeks after the "temple test," Laura woke to a noise at the door. She stirred, wondering dimly what was going on. It couldn't be later than four in the morning. Shuffling. Door opening.

"Hello?"

Aunt Morgan had answered the door. Good for her. She could take care of it. Laura buried her face in her pillow and began to drift off again. Another noise came from much closer, and she squinted to the side. Morgan leaned against the doorjamb, looking exhausted.

"Hey, Laura." The sleepy drawl slurred her words. "The office got a call for you from Mr. Sinclair. There's something going on. Says you're going to help him sometime today for something or other."

"Oh?"

"Yeah."

"Why'd he call now, though?"

Morgan shrugged. "Don't know."

"I'll ask him about it when I go to work."

"Sure."

Morgan drifted away. The door didn't close all the way behind her, but Laura was too tired to care. She closed her eyes and began to doze. She fell asleep again by the time the second noise came to the door. This knocking was much louder and more insistent, and Laura woke as soon as it began. Annoyed grumbling heralded Morgan's shuffling feet. Cheryl made a loud, unhappy noise.

Clae couldn't be expecting her to go to the shop at this hour, could he? Laura frowned at the idea and buried her head under her pillow. Maybe she could drown out the sound of the door. The next thing she knew, the pillow was yanked away. She glared at the culprit, but the look faltered as she realized that it wasn't Morgan.

"Clae?" she spluttered, instantly awake. "What are you doing here?"

"Picking you up," he replied, "like I said on the phone."

"I don't have a phone in here, you called the building phone! I didn't get the message!" Laura snapped, sitting up and pulling her blanket closer about her.

"Person who answered it said she'd go tell you."

"Well, she *didn't*."

"You know now. So get out of bed and let's go."

"Go where? It's—" She scrambled for her pocket watch on the bedside table. "It's four in the morning!"

In reality it was four forty-five, but it was in the hour of four and she resented that.

"The police are already out there, and they're expecting us to arrive before five."

"Out where?"

"The Sixth Quarter."

Laura had never physically been to the Sixth Quarter. Given the inhabitants, there were usually no amulets down there, and the few that did exist were with the military, so they were tightly regulated. No chance for infestation.

"What's going on in the Sixth Quarter?"

"Stupidity, what do you think?" Clae scoffed. "Now get dressed and ready to go. I'll be waiting outside."

He tossed the pillow back and left, shouldering past Morgan in the doorway. Her aunt sent her a frightened look but closed the door behind him. Laura stared at it for a bit, then sprang up in a burst of energy. She rushed around her room, grabbing her clothes and supplies as fast as she could. Once she was decent, she tied her hair back and left her room. The first thing she saw was Cheryl leaning out of her own room, looking tired and grumpy, but lingering out of some begrudging interest in the strangers in the living room. Morgan stood near the sofa with much the same expression though less angry, twisting the cuff of her nightgown in anxiety; she followed their guests with her eyes as if afraid they'd snatch everything up and run. Clae inspected something on the wall, ignoring her completely, while Okane hovered near the door.

"Ready," Laura called, and Morgan looked over in surprise.

"For what? What's going on?"

"Just work." Laura had to stifle a yawn.

"At this time of the morning?"

"Well, if someone wasn't so impatient—"

"Don't accuse me, go after the cops if you're so upset." Clae turned away from the wall.

"I'm sure she doesn't mean it!" Morgan squeaked. "She's just tired is all."

"No kidding," Laura muttered.

"Excuses. Come on. We're going to be late already."

Grumbling fitfully, Laura followed them out. Morgan watched as they passed.

"Good luck," she called. "Don't forget, *call* if you need anything."

Laura was about to retort that *we don't have a telephone, that's why they surprised us to begin with,* but realization dawned. She meant the police, in case these strangers tried anything funny. Clae really did give off an awful impression.

She closed the door and they walked down the hallway. Laura wove a bit but rubbed her eyes and tried to wake up faster.

"Laura?"

She looked up. Charlie stood by the stairs, a jumble of metal parts under his arms. Suspicious Morgan *and* her current nemesis? It was too early for this. What was he doing outside at nearly five in the morning?

"What are you doing out this early?" Charlie glanced at Clae and Okane, brow furrowing in suspicion.

"Going to work?"

"Now?"

"Yes. Out of the way, you're blocking the stairs," Clae grouched, using the briefcase to push him aside. Charlie gaped after him.

"Sorry. See you later." Laura hurried on Clae's heels, silently thanking him for being so rude.

But it wasn't to be. After only some hesitation Charlie followed them down, jogging to keep level with Laura and juggling his load at the same time.

"What kind of work needs a lady out at this hour?" he asked. "You understand what people might think, seeing you out with two strange men?"

Laura barked out a bitter laugh. "Sorry, but it's a little too early for me to worry about ruining my reputation."

"People talk." He glanced at Clae's back, as if torn between confrontation and fear.

"Let them. All I'm doing is working. Besides, I'm not interested in that 'perfect bride' image anyway."

"That's rather angelina of you to say."

That last line was muttered, not meant to be clearly heard, but he might as well have shouted it. Laura stopped so suddenly Okane almost ran into her. She didn't notice. She glared at Charlie, hate curling in her stomach.

"What did you just say?" she hissed.

At first he looked confused, but it clicked quickly; *Morgan Chandler, that angelina on the top floor.*

"I'm just saying that you're taking it too lightly!" he defended. "You're closing off your future. No one's going to marry a woman they think is immoral."

"So I'll end up like my aunt is what you're saying?"

"That's not what I—"

"Really? Because that's *entirely* what I heard."

"Well, she's not exactly the best role model!"

"You little rat! After all the things she's done for you, you turn around and—"

"She doesn't want you going down the same path either!"

"Oh, and I suppose you've discussed this?" He didn't immediately reply, but his expression said enough. Laura's glower darkened. "You *didn't*. I can't believe—"

"We're just worried about you," he said. "I'm serious. Keep going like you are and you won't have any options left."

"She has plenty of options," said Clae. They jumped; he had stopped to look at them, eyes narrowed. "If you think all a woman's good for is marrying, you're very behind the times."

"I think you're more out of touch with the times," Charlie retorted, bristling.

Clae ignored him and looked on at Laura. "We have more important matters right now."

"We do." Laura took three angry steps before whirling to glare again. "Don't you dare get near Morgan again. Ever since you started going to that university, you've gotten pretentious. You're not a gentleman. You're a backstabber is all you are."

"Laura!"

She ignored him, pushing past Clae in a bid for the next set of stairs. Charlie made to follow, but Okane made a jerking movement and the machine parts spilled from his arms to clang upon the floor. Charlie let out a loud exclamation and Okane mumbled something about an apology before hightailing it. He passed Laura on the stairs, but luckily Charlie didn't follow. Clae walked beside her, glancing behind them only once.

"Neighbor?" he grunted as they reached the next floor.

"Right." Laura forced her voice into calm. She was going to work. The safe zone. She didn't have to worry about nonsense like marriage or angelinas here. "We used to go to school together."

"Good. If you said 'boyfriend' I was going to throw myself off the building."

"That's drastic."

"So's settling for a moron. It'd be a damn shame if you let someone like that limit you."

They descended the stairs and made their way to the cable cars. The trolley ran at this hour, so the trek was made easier, though it was still time-consuming. Strangely enough, the police were waiting for them at the cable car station. Albright was at the head of the crowd, arms crossed and lips pursed. Laura wondered if Clae's mere presence angered her.

"What?" he demanded as he stepped off the car, apprentices in his wake.

"It's past five," Albright growled.

"We ran into complications," Clae sneered. "Now what's going on? They're not letting you in?"

Laura was mystified for a moment—who could keep the police from doing their job?—but she followed the gaze of one officer and spotted a grim-faced soldier with a rifle in his hands. Military.

"No," Albright confirmed. It was obvious in her face that she took this personally. "We got the call, but we were only the middlemen to get you here."

"What's the situation?"

"Five trainees were taken by an infestation in their barracks building. Apparently they disappeared into the dark. No bodies left, nothing—even furniture started vanishing. There was some sort of commotion. Hell if I know whether the rest made it out. Some hothead decided to lead a counterattack and asked for Sweeper backup. That's all the information we have."

"Are you expecting us to do a rescue mission?" Clae eyed her reproachfully.

"No." She returned a withering look. "You get in there and get rid of the problem. If these people know anything they'll evacuate on their own. But if you act quickly, you'll limit the damage."

"Roundabout rescue, then," Clae murmured.

"Whatever you want to call it. You!" Albright called to the lone soldier. "Here are your Sweepers. Take them over."

The soldier moved closer, watching them suspiciously, and Albright scoffed. "We're not about to make a break for it. Hurry up."

Scowling, he did as she said and moved faster. "Come with me," he told the Sweepers, and led them away.

Their destination was a military barracks building near the middle of the Quarter on the west side. The structure rose half the height of the Cynder Block and wider, a dull gray color with windows marked by dark squares on its side, set in perfect rows that only added to the stern appearance. Its strict atmosphere was the complete opposite of the rickety shacks they'd passed on the way in. A few of those shacks were visible in the distance, but the military didn't want any noncitizens (these days the thin Fifth Quarter overflowed into parts of the Sixth) getting too close to the barracks. A few sentries surveyed them suspiciously, glancing from wary noncitizens to the Sweepers being led past them. The building currently blazed with light, not from the inside but from an assembly of lanterns and electric lights dragged in from all over the Quarter. The Sweepers were asked to wait by a rickety jeep with its protruding headlights trained on the front door.

"They're going all out," Laura observed.

"The military is generally faster to act than the police and they actually retain some of the information on monsters, since they have to be able to deal with them beyond the walls," Clae responded. "It's unfortunate that they forget they can't do a goddamn thing beyond trap it." The last part was louder and directed toward the person coming toward them: a severe-looking man with a great mustache resembling a snake curling around his upper lip.

"It's about time you got here." His tone was as stiff as his posture.

"What's going on in there?" Clae demanded.

"Our trainees started going missing. The signs point to it being one of your monsters, so we called for backup."

"Yes, I've already heard that from the police. We need more details."

The man grumbled, then elaborated, "It grew hands. The shadows grew hands and dragged them in."

That definitely sounded like their sort of work.

"So you got out and set up the lights. But then you decided that charging in and antagonizing it was a good idea?"

"We were buying time for the rest of the trainees to get out, if there were any."

"Don't lie to me. Why did you really go in there?"

The man sneered. "You want the truth? Fine. It was one of the lower officers who rallied people here before anyone who *should've* been in charge arrived. There had to be at least twenty who ran in, but none of them have come out since."

Clae heaved a long sigh, rubbing at his temple. "Of course. Besides the hands, do you know if there was anything distinctive about this monster?"

"I'm told it made a strange noise."

"Was it a groaning sound? Screeching?"

"Scratching."

Clae's eyes narrowed. "What do you mean?"

"It made a scraping sound when it followed them," said the man. "It was fast, just about on the trainees' heels as they got out, and it left scores in the floor."

"It left marks?"

Clae shifted his weight, eyes pensive. Laura was confused too. On other jobs, even during an infestation there were supposedly few physical marks left by the monsters beyond what they ate. Only the tools Sweepers used should scar the area. She had no idea why or how this one was marking up the place. Unless it was like the weird ones lately? *Maverick?* she mouthed at Clae, but he was focused on the man before them.

"It did. Is that strange to you?" the man was saying.

"Indeed." Clae pondered a moment. "Where was it when it was first noticed?"

"Third floor. Midway through the hall, in one of the sleeping quarters. Took the first boy right out of his bed."

"And it followed them downstairs?"

"Took two more on the way, yes."

Clae nodded absently. "And the trainees who escaped? Where are they?"

"They've been transferred over to the southern barracks." When Clae raised an eyebrow (the southern barracks were probably a ways away), the man continued, "The surrounding buildings have been evacuated."

"Keep an eye on them. Keep an eye on anyone who was in that building."

"Do you suspect something's wrong with them?"

"This infestation's showing some unusual behavior, so best keep on the safe side. All we need is for it to develop some kind of venom or disease. God forbid it start using humans as shells instead of amulets."

Everyone, even the sentries nearby, tensed up. Any one of those outcomes could be catastrophic. Laura had never considered them before.

"You don't think that could actually happen, do you?" she whispered. The very idea made her stomach turn.

"These things have stayed the same for countless generations," muttered Clae. "Nothing does that. Animals change, develop camouflage and defenses. Humans create things like guns and walls. Just because it's been like this as long as we know doesn't mean the hive mind can't evolve."

"Can you still take it out?" the man demanded.

"Probably. We plan for this sort of thing with kin."

"When will you start?"

Clae set down his briefcase with a grunt. He opened it up and began to sort through the contents.

"Laura, Okane. Take these."

Laura knelt down and reached out her hands, and Okane did the same on his other side. Clae divided equipment between them. Laura ended up with two more Eggs, a large handful of Bijou, some wire, and a few pellets that served as flash bombs.

"If you use the Bijou, be careful. They'll roll down stairs but not up. And go slow enough that they can keep sensing the amulets in your shoes. They'll follow you," Clae told them.

"Will that make a shield against this thing?" asked Laura.

"Depending on how strong it is. Bijou can easily keep a smaller one away, but a big, moving infestation may prove difficult. And be sure to aim right with your Eggs. They won't do any good if they miss the target."

They straightened up. Laura stored her new equipment in the various bags on her belt. She was stuffing the wire in, cursing because it kept trying to unravel, as Clae announced, "We'll begin immediately. If we find any of your people we'll send them out, but they're not our first priority."

"Understood." The man nodded. "Are there any other precautions we should take?"

"Make sure no one comes in. I don't care what excuse they have, we don't want any other potential food sources available to it."

"We'll lock down the area even further. Anything else?"

"Have you got telephones in there? Of course you do. Get in contact with the police, have them get an operator to dial all the phones. It could serve as a distraction to the monster and might help locate your men. If any of them have survived, anyway. Doubtful."

"Of course." The man frowned. The military wasn't fond of the police—something about child's play in comparison to their job—so he probably wasn't looking forward to working with them. His hand circled in a wordless gesture for any more information, but when none was forthcoming, he folded his arms. "Be fast. The creature has done enough damage."

He turned away and began barking orders to the surrounding men, telling So-and-So to get those troops on the job, and So-and-So to regulate the lights and shut down any way others could get into the area. Soon only the Sweepers were left by the jeep. Clae shuffled, double-checking that his guns were still there and then checking the time on his watch, before putting a few more Bijou into his vest pocket.

"If you run out of ammunition, then get back out here if you can. There's more in the case but I don't want to bring it in there. Too bulky. Got it? Good. Let's get going."

The barracks doors were nondescript, but they opened on well-oiled hinges. Inside, the barracks were just as plain as the exterior. The walls had the same grayish color, the wooden floor polished to the point it shone dully in the light from the nearest window. Patches of light were visible down the hall, marking the places where windows were set, but for the most part darkness was overwhelming. Laura shook an Egg to get some better lighting.

"Now what?"

"We stick close and comb the place," Clae murmured, taking a step forward.

They crept down the hall. The muffled sound of shouting soldiers could be heard outside, but in here their footsteps echoed loudly. It rankled Laura to hear how much noise they made. The hallway led them right, and they did a full circuit of the first floor. This first floor was comprised of classrooms, mostly empty, with chalkboards at the front and desks and chairs scattered throughout the room. Nothing was in there, or if there was, the others didn't acknowledge it. They located a set of stairs and began to climb.

"Sir," Okane piped up as they walked.

"I thought I told you not to call me that," Clae retorted. "What is it?"

"I've noticed that --- always refer to those things as monsters, or creatures, or just things. Do they not have a name?"

"Yes and no."

Laura didn't think of it much, but she was sure at one point he'd called them something strange. "You did have a name for them, though, didn't you?"

Clae made a humming sound as he reached the landing and peered around the corner. "Sweepers sometimes call them *kaibutsu* or *bakemono*."

Laura tried to repeat the words and butchered them terribly. She frowned at that pathetic attempt. "Where do those names come from?"

"It's the native language of Orien. Same language Sweepers used to name kin, same language your name comes from," Clae replied, glancing back at Okane.

"Your name's a word?" Laura asked, baffled.

"It means 'money,'" he answered.

Silver-coin eyes. So someone else picked up on that too.

"What do those other names mean?"

"Essentially they translate into 'monster.' I'm not fluent so I don't know the details or the differences, but that's what Sweepers ended up using. The cities don't uphold those as official names, though, so they're falling out of use."

"Why wouldn't they—" Laura snapped her mouth shut and grabbed Clae's sleeve. He stopped on the stair, turning his wary gaze on her.

"What is it?"

"There's something up there." She hadn't gotten a good look at this distance, barely a glimpse out of the corner of her eye, but it was large and dark. Possibly their target. "On the floor."

"Moving?"

"No."

Maybe preparing to strike, she thought. Clae seemed to think the same. He held his arm out and motioned for them to move back. Laura descended two steps, quietly as possible. Okane leaned into the wall as if hoping to become one with it. No sound came from ahead. They stayed there, frozen, waiting for some kind of reaction. Nothing. The beam of a searchlight shone through the windows, dim and shifting slowly like the people outside were trying to observe them. It slid over the walls, just above the shape. It lit the Sweepers briefly, throwing Clae's tense features into sharp relief before leaving them and tracking up toward the next floor. It took what seemed like forever. Laura held her breath so long she felt her lungs might burst.

Finally Clae moved his hand, a light wave signaling the apprentices to stay put. Slowly, slowly, he edged out and around the corner. Despite the warning, Laura took his previous position, trying to see without exposing herself. There it was, a dark shape on the ground in the darkest corner of the hallway. It lay almost motionless, save for the slight rise and fall of its farthest portion. Clae approached as if expecting it to lash out and bite. Laura gripped her Egg tighter, calculating when to attack: before the creature moved, in case Clae couldn't make a signal fast enough? He hovered by the shape, gun raised. After a moment he relaxed.

"Not our thing." He toed it, no longer cautious.

Laura felt relief and disappointment in the same crashing wave. She relaxed her grip on the Egg, frowning at the lingering sting in her hand. How hard had she been holding it? "If it's not one of your *kaibutsu*, what is it?"

"One of the trainees."

Laura walked over to get a better look, raising the Egg to squint at the details. The boy sprawled there looked younger than she was, but he wore the trainees' brown jacket, unbuttoned and thrown on over pajamas.

"The monster didn't get him. What happened?" asked Laura.

"Hell, maybe he fainted." Clae toed the body harder. "Hey, you. Get up."

The body didn't move, so he kicked it. This time the trainee jerked violently. He curled in on himself, coughing.

"Who are you and what are you doing here?" Clae demanded.

The boy looked up at him with wide eyes. He spluttered incoherently.

"I-I-I, uh, Jonathan Harrow! I, well, maybe I ah—"

"Spit it out."

"I was running and I fell over and it was coming and I don't know!"

"From which direction?"

"W-what?"

"Which direction, I said!"

The boy pointed back over his shoulder, down the hall.

"Of course," Clae muttered. "You, get downstairs and out of this building. Get in our way and I might accidentally shoot you."

The trainee scrambled to his feet and tore off down the stairs, nearly bowling Okane over and tripping over himself on the way.

"We know it can easily go down stairs, but we're not sure about up." Clae glared after the trainee before turning his attention to them again. "If he's right and it was following him here, it might be on this floor. Keep an eye out."

He kept walking as if nothing had happened, and after a moment the other two followed.

The rooms on this floor were a mix of classrooms and sleeping quarters. All of them were the same: classrooms identical to the ones on the last floor, and all the sleeping quarters with six sets of bunk beds, three along each wall, metal frames and thin mattresses. Footlockers sat at the end of these beds, and they were unmade, but if it weren't for that, every room would've looked exactly the same: uninhabited.

"Are we sure he was telling the truth?" Laura muttered as she closed another door. "I'm not seeing or hearing anything."

"Perhaps it's moved on?" Okane guessed.

"Maybe, maybe not. Don't let your guard down," said Clae.

As the group climbed up to the third floor, Laura shook her Egg, causing it to give off more light. The renewed glow illuminated marks in the wooden stairs. They all paused to inspect them. The scratches were fairly deep, but not terribly so. It was like someone swiped at the stairs with a knife, a back-and-forth kind of movement with a larger, deeper, main gouge scribbling in the midst of the others. They ended a third of the way down the stairs, then doubled back.

"You think that's it?" asked Laura.

"Probably." Clae ran his fingertips across the scrapes, frowning.

"So it's got a fixed form, now?" Laura wasn't sure what kind of form or body could make this sort of damage, and she wasn't looking forward to seeing it.

"I don't think so. It's developed enough to eat furniture and people. If it had a fixed form it would be big enough to fit those inside. These marks were made by something fairly small. I don't think it has a fixed form at all."

"Then how's it making the marks? Or is that something completely different?"

"If we're judging by that story earlier, they're one and the same. I think this one's dragging its amulet around."

"They can do that?" said Okane.

"Usually, no. It's in their best interest to keep their roots in one place and protect them at all costs, so this one's a bit of a maverick. That could be good or bad. It drags its weakness in plain sight, but again, it moves. No way to pin it down."

"If the amulet made the marks, what's it shaped like?" said Laura.

She'd heard stories about previous occasions when infestations sucked themselves completely into an amulet to hide. She didn't want to walk right past it while it was hiding, only for the thing to pounce when she looked the other way.

"How the hell should I know?" Clae straightened up. "Whatever it is it can't be much bigger than a cat. Probably smaller."

13

TWO FOR ONE

The scuffs on the floor continued down the hallway. At some points they skittered away from the main, middle pathway. Some traces trailed up the walls too, as high as Laura's head. It made her think of a spider. She shuddered.

Okane made an odd sound, and Laura felt his shoulder bump into her back.

"What?" she whispered.

Okane stared at one of the doors, eyes wide and spooked. "Did --- hear that?"

"Hear what?"

"Listen."

Laura strained her ears but heard nothing. The only things she could detect were their own breathing and the sounds of people outside. She glanced at him again in question. Almost as soon as she did, she heard it. A quiet, scraping noise. She tensed.

"Clae. . . ."

"I heard it."

After some hesitation, Clae approached the door. The other two crept along in his wake, giving him a good head start. The door was already ajar, so Clae kicked it gently open. As he did he pulled out one of his guns. There was a split second of nothing. Laura thought maybe they were mistaken, but then came a high-pitched shriek. Clae jerked backward, but even before he did Okane moved, practically trampling Laura's feet as he scrambled back toward the window. Laura lost her balance. She stumbled, and the world was a dark blur. She could hear Clae give a pained grunt, and a sudden splintering sound. There was a smash and a crash from either side of the hall, accompanied by an awful hiss and finally a burst of light before she caught the back of Okane's vest. She blinked furiously, trying to haul herself back up and recover from that light.

"What the hell is going on?"

The hissing went off to her right and she jumped, still unable to make anything out. Soon enough the hiss ended, replaced by an odd skittering that faded quickly.

"Look," came Clae's voice, and gradually her vision cleared enough that she was able to see him again. "I get it, you don't like it. But for god's sake, don't panic and take out your coworker."

Clae happened to be glaring at Okane, who looked caught somewhere between the vestiges of fear and embarrassment. The remnants of an Egg were scattered on the ground, broken glass and kin liquid spreading along the floorboards. There was no sign of whatever had made that skitter noise, beyond a large chunk taken out of the doorway and a dent in the wall opposite. It looked like something had been launched through with enough force to rip pieces of the wall out with it. Laura gawked at it while the others squabbled.

"And you wasted an Egg. Didn't I tell you to aim?"

"--- know I hate it!" Okane hissed. "What did --- *think* I'd do, seeing one of those things?"

"Use some sense," Clae grumbled. "You were doing well with infestations in private lessons."

"That one wasn't flinging itself at my head!"

"You've got better defenses than we do, but we aren't panicking." He paused, took a deep breath. "You know what? Go outside. Wait by the briefcase."

Okane looked horrified. "What?"

"I told you to go outside. If you're going to be more hindrance than help, I don't want you in the way. The light outside will keep you out of the infestation's range."

"But—"

"But what?"

Clae glowered. Okane quailed, but choked out, "--- said I'd be a good Sweeper."

"If you're under control. *Are* you under control?" Okane didn't agree, but he didn't deny either. Clae huffed. "Stay or leave, just commit to the choice you make. Remember what I said at the temple."

He pulled down his goggles in a manner that seemed very arrogant. Laura wasn't sure how he managed it. She pulled down her own in case of more unexpected Egg explosions. She pulled up her bandana too.

"You're okay though, right?" she asked Okane. "It didn't get you?"

"Of course not," he muttered. He made a big deal of straightening his vest before sulking after Clae.

The new set of scratches led them around the floor, in and out of two bedrooms. Here beds were overturned, a few bunks warped or even missing, and the contents of footlockers strewn in a mess across the floorboards. Their quarry was nowhere to be seen, and neither were any soldiers. At the next staircase, though, they heard shuffling. Laura squinted. Between the darkness and the goggles, she couldn't spot anything up there. She held up her Egg as they began to ascend. The noise started up and stopped three different times, going from one side to the other. Laura couldn't help but think it sounded *gleeful*.

"I don't like this," she muttered.

"And you did before?" said Clae.

"No, but—"

A particularly loud, long scratch came from above. Their footsteps wavered.

"Okane? You sensing anything to go along with that?" asked Laura.

He said something quiet and unintelligible, but she got the idea. He didn't want to go up there. She walked in front of him this time; she didn't want to be knocked over again, especially on stairs. As they reached the landing they saw nothing out of the ordinary. Marks on the ground, yes, but that was no longer unusual. The three milled about at the top of the stairs.

"We definitely heard it, so where'd it go?" Laura looked around, to no avail. She wished the lights were on in here; the darkness set her on edge just as much as the noise had. She clenched her free hand a few times, trying to keep shaking to a minimum.

"It's a fast little bastard," Clae grumbled.

Another sound caused them all to whip around. Farther down the hall, in a patch of faint light from the window, sat a large wooden object. It was a disc the size of a plate, dipping in deeply. It was weirdly shaped, with protrusions on the bottom so it lay lopsided.

"Is that the amulet? It's a lot bigger than the others I've seen," said Laura.

"That's definitely the source," said Okane.

Before their eyes, the wooden object moved. It jerked to the left, then back, then up. It stood upright on its thinnest portion, revealing exactly what it was. The thing was a mask. And god, it was creepy. It had stubby little horns, bulging eyes, and strange curved carvings and marks twisting its features into an ugly grimace. Its eyes glowed rosy red in comparison to its dark brown body. The nose was huge, almost a beak. Clae swore at the sight of it.

"Two!"

"What?"

"There are two amulets! The eyes! They're amulets!"

The mask hissed, and the red sockets began to ooze blackness. That blackness grew, turning into long, thin, reedy arms that bent sharply and touched the floor like spider legs. It pushed itself forward, faster than a charging horse. The bumps on the front dragged brutally along the floor, nose gouging that deep mark from the previous tracks.

It seemed hell-bent for the wall, so Laura sprang out of the way. She nicked the Egg against her amulet and slung it down at the approaching creature. The glass cracked.

"Scatter!"

They fled as fast as they could before the inevitable happened and the

Egg detonated. It went off with a roar and a blast that sent everyone reeling. Laura was thrown completely off her feet and tumbled onto the floor. She yelped in pain as she came to a stop, but the sound was overpowered by the shrieking of the creature. The Egg blast sent it straight up in the air so it smashed into the ceiling. It dropped back to the floor with a loud crunch against the glass shards. The kin liquid and glass pieces spat angrily and leapt up, stinging the mask's sides. The creature hopped madly to avoid it. Unfortunately it was dancing toward the corner by the stairs, exactly where Okane was huddled. He stared at it like it was death approaching. Laura scrambled up at the sight, heart in her throat.

"Run!" she cried. "Get out of there, you idiot!"

But he didn't move. He just tensed up more as it got within two feet of him. That was when it realized something was there. Halfway through a hop it raised some of its arms, ready to strike.

"Move!"

Okane still didn't make to get up. Instead he drew back his legs, and in one suicidal move, he lashed out in a kick. It was a very bad idea to touch one of these monsters. They stuck to any living thing they touched, wrapped them up, and pulled them in to eat. As far as Laura knew, no one had ever gotten away from them before. Okane's feet connected with the mask with a loud retort, but instead of latching on to him the creature let out an even more piercing sound. Its hands recoiled as if burned, and with a deafening snap it tumbled away. It rolled through the glass again, shuddered violently.

"Get up!"

Clae grabbed Okane's shirt and heaved him up, shoving him away from the wall. Okane stumbled before bolting past the creature, only slowing when he passed Laura. The creature, meanwhile, began to grow. The darkness swelled, slimy body roiling and swallowing up the mask entirely. Soon it ballooned to take up the entire width of the hallway, a pulsing black mass that shone particularly slimy.

"C-Clae?" said Laura. "Clae, what now?"

"Get out of the damn way!" he yelled back, completely obscured.

Okane tugged at Laura's sleeve, shaky but getting more adamant as the infestation hit the ceiling. Its black mass uncoiled there and spread, a disarray of muddled tentacles with acrid black smoke issuing from their midst. Laura gaped at it in horror, and Okane's tugging increased.

"Laura, Laura, *Laura*—"

The ceiling tendrils began to fall, and Laura finally pedaled backward. She and Okane ran as fast as they could down the hall, and the blackness followed, crashing against the walls like a tidal wave. As she sprinted, Laura wrestled with the clasp of her belt bag, searching for more ammunition. She fished out another Egg and tapped her amulet before tossing it over her shoulder. She didn't look to see if she aimed right. They rounded the corner just in time. This explosion shook the floor, and Laura heard windows shattering. More glass shards flew across the ground, hissing and spitting, and the creature wailed horribly. Their footing was thrown off. As she stumbled, two Bijou fell out of Laura's pocket to clatter on the floor. She stopped short.

"What are --- doing?" Okane screeched.

"Lighting it!"

Laura fumbled with the wire from her bag, and once she'd wrestled it out, she flicked it. Just like before, it sparked, and she dropped it down by the fallen Bijou as she dug the rest out. The first two lit up with a bang. More of the windows nearby smashed, and the force and heat caused Laura to fall over. Screw it. She chucked the rest of the Bijou at the hissing wire, then scrambled farther away. Okane practically dragged her to her feet. With the following blasts, the entire building shuddered. They were lucky to get around the other corner before it could reach them, but the roaring, rending, and crashing behind them made Laura's heart sink.

The Bijou took out the entire wall and ceiling. A gaping hole was all that remained of that wall, and part of the floor above had fallen through, littering the hall with debris and dust. Underneath it all the Bijou popped and shrieked, throwing up sparks and causing patches of wreckage to rumble and quake. Laura doubled back, and Okane stumbled to a stop.

"Where are --- going?"

"Bijou! Don't worry, I'll be okay!"

She hopped onto a busted beam and balanced there, looking out over the damage. She couldn't see the creature, but she couldn't see Clae either. Maybe he was around the corner. Out of the way of the blast. She hoped so. The popping grew nearer and a Bijou hopped up out of the bricks. It crackled and squealed and jumped some more, probably sensing the amulets in her boots.

"Clae?" she called. "Are you there?"

Another portion of the debris shifted. For a moment she was afraid he really did get caught up in it. There was an apology on her tongue that died as another beam shifted, and the mask shot up. Its dark arms sprouted again, gooier this time, and it landed in a cloud of dust. Laura nearly tripped in her haste to get off the beam and run. Three more Bijou followed the first, rolling under the beam after her, and she forced herself to go slower so they could keep up.

"Faster, faster!" Okane hissed, gesturing madly.

"No, you get over here!" she retorted.

"No way in—"

"The Bijou, stupid! Clae said they'd help!"

Okane made a long-suffering sound and joined her. The Bijou circled them as they moved, spouting tongues of white-hot sparks. In the meantime the creature had scrambled over the beam to follow them. Laura glanced back at it and wished she had a gun. The creature gained quickly. Two of its arms reared up, aiming down at them. Laura and Okane ducked, but it didn't get within a foot of them before the Bijou spat even higher. They stung the monster, causing an acrid smell to taint the air. The creature recoiled immediately. Smoke rose from its burned limbs.

"Where's Clae?" asked Okane. "Shouldn't he be doing something?"

"I don't know! I think I might've cut him off," groaned Laura, hoping she was wrong as the Bijou assaulted the creature again. "It might take a little while for him to get over here."

"Great, that's just great," Okane hissed, and Laura glared at him.

"What have you been doing, huh? At least I'm throwing things at it!"

"And blowing up the whole floor—"

"At least I hit it!"

The creature shrieked and swiped. They jumped out of the way in time, but it caught one of the Bijou. The bead was hit so hard it flew right through the wall, causing another crash and creating a hole big enough to be a window. As a result, though, the creature lost a limb. The rest of the arms kept scuttling, gaining, but one stump simply drooped, dragging along the floor and giving off black smoke. Okane slowed just enough to kick another Bijou at it, hoping to take advantage of this weakness. It caught the creature smack in the middle of the mask, sticking in the dip between nose and forehead, and let out a noise like a train whistle. The creature stopped completely, rearing back with a wail as its arms groped at the mask, trying to dislodge the thing causing it so much agony. It swung itself from side to side, crashing into the wall and flailing madly.

"We're dead," Laura said under her breath, "we are *so* dead. . . ."

"Well, what are we supposed to do?" cried Okane.

"Get to the amulets and douse them with kin! But we can't get through that!" Laura replied, gesturing back at the creature.

As she did this, the monster decided it was impossible to get rid of the Bijou. Instead it turned on them with new vigor, blackness seething through the teeth and nostrils of the mask. It lunged, screeching a battle cry. Okane grabbed Laura by the sleeve and dragged her along, running so fast Laura could barely keep up. The infestation gave chase, thundering on uneven legs and spitting blackness to spatter the floor. They arrived at the stairs to the fifth floor. Okane took them two at a time, but while Laura did that going upstairs at home, she couldn't do it at this speed. With a yelp, she tripped and went sprawling. Her fall yanked Okane down too, and he wiped out with a howl of pain. The Bijou spat near the foot of the stairs, but they were too far away to do anything. The creature's legs grew longer, allowing it to walk right over them. Laura held up her last Egg, hoping kin light would deter the monster, but it was useless. The mask descended, and the creature shrieked with glee.

A shot rang out, and the mask jerked violently. Half of it was blown to bits in a flash of gold. The creature squealed. With half its form gone it couldn't steady itself, so it plowed into the wall and slipped down to the floor. Laura stared at it in shock, then looked up. Clae strode down the hall looking rather the worse for wear. He was battered and dusty, blood smeared on his face and favoring his left leg, but he was still on the move.

"Thank god," Laura whispered.

She scrambled over to Okane, pulling him out of his daze and onto his feet. As she did, Clae got close enough to plant one foot on the mask.

The creature reached up to attack, but his eyes promised pain. He shot at the blackness, severing more limbs and making the creature squeal loud enough to hurt their ears.

"Get that Egg over here!" he barked.

Laura jumped down the stairs. She hurried up to him, evading the flailing limbs. He used his foot to flip the mask so it faced up. Only one of the eyes remained. Sucking in a deep breath, Laura cracked the Egg open and held it over the mask. As soon as the kin made contact, it bubbled. More blackness spurted and frothed from its mouth, but it was overtaken fast by golden light. It hissed angrily. Limbs sprouted to thrash in desperation, but they didn't last any longer than the froth. An awful smell tainted the air. The kin condensed on the amulet, now cracking and spitting. It looked like it was getting cooked. The main form fizzled away into nothing, and Clae lowered his guns.

Portions of kin shone and glittered like gems, overshadowing the rest in a way Laura hadn't thought possible. It emitted sounds eerily reminiscent of the plinking of a harp. With every note it grew louder and harsher, and the mask began to quake.

"Three," Clae counted, and Laura realized what was going on.

"Okane! Cover your mouth and nose!"

Okane looked at her like she'd gone insane, but understanding dawned. "Two. One."

With an audible snap, a black cloud issued out from under the gold. It didn't get very far, but judging by the gagging behind them it still had the same potent stench. The kin now soaked into the mask without resistance.

"This one's dead. The other one should be too, seeing as how I smashed it into a million goddamn pieces," Clae seethed. He leaned to the side and spat out something dark.

"Are you okay? I didn't end up hitting you with that Egg or the Bijou, did I?" Laura fretted.

"Damn *kaibutsu* knocked me down the stairs."

"That must've hurt." Laura winced, but secretly she was glad. At least she wasn't the one to do it.

Clae gave her a look that said *no shit* and turned around.

"Stop that noise and start gathering up the pieces," he barked, gesturing at Okane and the steps. "We have to get all of those together. Leave one piece and it could end up host to a new infestation."

Okane scowled at him, eyes still watering, but dutifully began to pick up bits of mask from the stairs.

"Go help him." Clae slapped a hand against Laura's arm. "I'm going to find that telephone. It's giving me a headache."

It was only now that he mentioned it that Laura realized there *was* a phone going off. She could hear the tinny bell through one of the doors. She nodded and joined Okane by the steps. The pieces of the mask and amulet were anywhere from pea-size to chunks the length of a nail. It was hard to spot them all in the dark, and Laura pulled off her goggles to see them better. It didn't help much. On the plus side, the floor was otherwise so clean there was nothing to confuse them with. Might as well just get a broom to sweep it all up.

"Why aren't the lights on?" she muttered. "I'd think at least the military would have electricity."

"Gas lighting." Okane dropped another shard into his cupped hand.

"How do you figure?"

"The Sullivans used to have it before they remodeled their house." He nodded up at one of the light fixtures. "See that valve? That turns on the gas. Then — light it."

"We could turn it on now, couldn't we? Have you got any matches?"

"No. Besides, I'm not an expert on gas and I don't want it to explode. Come to think of it, the gas must've been shut off before we came in. Otherwise we'd probably be dead after all those explosions."

Laura frowned and tried to redirect the topic. "Not an expert, huh? Didn't you just say the Sullivans had it?"

"I wasn't very old. I couldn't even reach it at the time."

"Ah . . . Makes sense, I suppose."

Laura returned to gathering pieces. They crawled about in search of parts while Clae talked to the telephone operator in the other room. One of the things he said caught Laura's attention: the mention of the missing soldiers.

"We only came across one. We're on the fourth floor. They can't all be holed up in the top level."

Laura didn't know how many people could've been in the building, except that there must've been a lot, judging by the number of beds and the mention of a counterattack. In an ambush, any number of people could've vanished. She hoped Clae was wrong, that a bunch of soldiers lurked upstairs. Soldiers to match the scattered lives and possessions in those rooms they'd passed. In the end the missing persons would be counted, and that number would determine the death count. It wasn't like they could count bodies. Even when monsters were killed they left nothing behind. Whatever they ate was lost to the world forever.

"Laura?"

She jerked her head up to find Okane staring. "What? Did you find something?"

He shook his head. "No. --- just had a strange look on ---r face."

"It's nothing." She turned her attention back to the amulet shards and picked up a particularly small piece.

"It didn't look like nothing."

"It's not our job to think about."

She could see him frowning from the corner of her eye. "Did Clae say that?"

"Of course he did." She scowled, depositing the reddish shard into her palm. "And he's right. We've got more than enough to worry about without thinking of who died. All we need to do is figure out connections, if they're not obvious. Otherwise there's no point in lingering on the people. Then again we don't know if there's a point to connections—it's not like we can put any procedures in place to stop another accident." No point in dwelling on things unchangeable, on things that would only make them hesitate in the future.

"I don't think he believes it any more than --- do."

Laura frowned at him, but had no time to ask anything before Clae drifted back to them. He did a quick once-over of the area to make sure they hadn't missed anything, put the gathered pieces into another little box he carried in his coat.

"Good job with the equipment," he said as he sorted through them; not all of the shards fit in the box, so he picked out the wooden ones to get all the amulet to fit in there. "When it comes to infestations, particularly mavericks, overkill is better than letting it get the better of you."

"You don't think the military will be upset that their wall's been smashed?" said Laura.

"They can replace the wall, but they can't replace lives. Particularly yours. They should know that well enough. The Council sets aside funds for this sort of thing, so it shouldn't be much trouble." He picked up the other half of the mask and inspected it before glancing at Laura. "You've caught on to the Bijou very fast."

"They're straightforward." She shrugged. "Same as the amulets."

He gave a snort of disbelief. "If they were that easy, I wouldn't have lost as many apprentices as I have."

"How many were lost, exactly?" Okane piped up, looking ill.

"Eight, officially. Don't look at me like that, some of them just quit."

"You remember all their names, though. Like Hettie and Anselm," Laura pointed out.

"What does that have to do with anything?"

"Nothing at all."

No point lingering on the people. Maybe Okane was right and Clae dwelled on these things too, just didn't acknowledge it. If he couldn't properly distance himself, how could she hope to? She didn't know if this made her feel less like a failure or just more nauseous.

It was very quiet on the trek downstairs. Navigating the destruction of the hallway took a while but they managed, and from there on it was smooth sailing; physically, anyway. Clae kept looking around at the walls and ceiling, as if waiting for another monster to leap out at them.

"You're not expecting more, are you?" Laura muttered.

"No." Regardless, he cast a suspicious look at the closest doorway.

"Then what are you looking for?"

"This is the third one in two months that's scarred its surroundings. Even without letters from other cities, I can tell they're getting worse. Just wait until they work up into the spike, god knows how we'll deal with that. Damn Rex and their goddamn idiots." He continued to snarl profanities under his breath.

They exited the building without any obstacles. Outside, soldiers were armed with big lanterns. The flickering light made them look eerie, especially when they seemed ready to beat back whatever monster was in there.

"Sweeper!" The man from before strode out of the crowd. "Did you take care of the creature?"

"It's dead."

"Was it a unique specimen?"

"There were two. Two amulets, both infected, and the creatures inside acted as a single unit," Clae explained. "They were in a mask. Dragging that around created the marks on the floor."

"And they're both accounted for?"

"Broke one, purified the other. We've got all the pieces with us."

"I'm assuming the destruction of the building was part of your effort in breaking the first?"

Laura winced. She didn't look up, reluctant to see the damage she caused. Clae didn't bat an eye.

"Yes."

The man looked very unhappy. "Is it clear for us to go in?"

"Yes. Just keep in mind, by the stairs to the fourth floor there's going to be some pieces of wood from the mask. None of them are part of the amulet, I've made certain already. Beyond that, nothing."

"Right. Be sure to catalogue the amulets properly."

The man moved on, giving them no more attention as he handed out orders, and Clae glanced back.

"That'll be our cue to leave. Come on, we're heading back to the shop."

The sun hadn't risen, though the sky had brightened while they were inside. Laura would much rather go back home to sleep, but there was no time to get there before the time she'd have to get up anyway.

They passed flocks of military personnel on the way. Laura saw badges and patches that probably represented high ranks, but she didn't pay much attention. A general could be on-site and she wouldn't have known or cared. The military had always been a different world to her, so the distinctions and rankings escaped her. At the very edge of the crowd, though, stood a gaggle of people. They all wore the trainee uniform but these weren't thrown on over pajamas. These people looked like they'd been awake and doing something: some had dirt smudged on their clothes and faces, others tears in their clothes. They all looked stunned.

"What happened?" one whispered to his neighbor. "I mean, why can't we go to the barracks? Where are all the others? What's with all the noise and the lights?"

"Didn't you hear? There's a monster in there," his companion replied, and the boy reeled back.

"A monster? Like what, a canir?"

"No, *the* monster from the wilds!" the girl hissed. "It ate the people inside!"

"But monsters like that can't get in here! The wall keeps them out!"

"It's true! That's what they've been saying anyway," whispered another.

"No way." The boy looked at the lights in horror. "They're all dead?"

"A lot of them are."

"Here I thought we got the bad end of the stick. Night watch, you know, I thought we'd be the ones running into the monsters. Thought we'd be more likely to get hurt. And here they were hit at home base? But it's supposed to be safe here, right?"

The boy kept rambling, but the Sweepers passed him by and soon he was out of earshot.

14

CASTOFFS

The sun peeked over the horizon as they boarded their early-morning trolley. Laura couldn't actually see it with all the buildings, but the sky brightened to pinks and yellows against the clouds. It was a myriad of subtle brightness that belonged somewhere on a painting; Laura would think it beautiful if she weren't exhausted. In the barracks she'd been running on adrenaline and fear, but that had drained out of her system. She felt overwhelmingly tired, and she was feeling the pain from falling down. A simple glance showed she was bruising where she hit the stairs, and Okane wasn't doing much better—a bruise of his own blossomed on one cheekbone.

She wished nothing more than to sit and relax in the Sweeper shop, but traffic had decided to spite them. While normally one of the fastest routes, Nestore Street was packed with idling automobiles bound for work. A truck had been transporting equipment and been involved in an accident; the logo for Sullivan Piping had been marred so badly by the scrape it was barely legible, and some equipment had fallen out. Men heaved the dropped pipes back into place, overseen by a man who looked far less like a worker and more like an executive in his low bowler hat and nondescript coat. Another man stood just beside him, head shaved bald; it must've been a new change, because he had the wide collar of his coat popped up to hide his features in lieu of hair. Automobiles rattled past, impatient and far too close to the straining workers, but the trolley was stuck on its line and couldn't maneuver anywhere. The trolley driver grumbled and pulled the horn. The man in the bowler hat waved apologetically.

Clae's eyes narrowed and he stood. Okane started.

"What are --- doing?" he hissed.

Clae didn't reply but heaved open the window to lean out. Okane sank so low in his seat he looked ready to melt onto the floor.

"What's going on?" Clae called.

"Slight accident," the bowler hat man replied; the bald man turned away entirely. "Nothing more. We apologize for the delay. We'll be out of your way shortly."

"They're not the actual Sullivans," said Laura, tracking Okane's slouch. "They're just employees. They probably have no idea who you are."

"They do." Okane tilted his head just enough to peer out the window before ducking. "They're not employees. They're mobsters."

Seriously? Laura tried peeking out too, but Clae shifted to block the pair from view.

"Where are you going?" he said.

"Interior."

"For what?"

The bowler hat man gestured grandly at the truck. "Plumbing. The Council's approved a new line."

"Where, exactly?"

"Fifth Quarter?" The man shrugged. "Location's been changed."

The workers finally cleared the road. Traffic started moving again. The bowler hat man jammed the hat further on his head, so they couldn't make out much of his features as they passed.

"Consider switching to Sullivan yourself, sir," he cheered. "We'll flush all your problems away!"

"More likely they'll get it all stuck and back up the system," Clae muttered, closing the window again.

"Why are mobsters out doing Sullivan work?" said Laura, craning her neck to see the disappearing truck. "I thought they were trying to kill him."

"He works with them," said Okane. "Supplies them with—" He looked ill and thought better of it. "Back in June he stiffed the Mad Dogs. They didn't take kindly to it. They thought if they could catch some of the family or servants with infestations they could scare him into working with them again. But he didn't even believe in infestations. He believed in the wall."

"Did they steal his truck, then?" Laura guessed.

"I don't think so. That man in the hat is a negotiator, not a thief. They must've struck a deal."

"I don't like the sound of that," said Clae. "I'm telephoning the police as soon as we get back."

"What did Sullivan supply them with?" said Laura. "If it was only some wheels and scrap metal—"

"---'re aware of Sullivan's humanitarian campaigns?" said Okane.

Laura nodded slowly. "He's got boarding schools set up across the city, and gives college scholarships to lower-Quarter students. My neighbor qualified for one to get into university."

"They don't all make it to school. The lucky ones end up like me. The unlucky ones . . ." Okane shuddered.

Laura's brow furrowed. Even Clae looked grim, so she was hesitant as she asked, "What happens to the unlucky ones?"

"Mobs deal in infestations," said Clae. "To keep it happy and sated, you need to feed it something living."

An unpleasant thought at any time, but on the tail end of an extermination it was twice as bad.

They trekked back to Acis Road, a dark cloud over their heads until someone caught them.

"You three look like you've been through a meat grinder." Mrs. Keedler had been setting out the sign for her bakery. She looked at them all like a mother inspecting dirty children. "Where have you been? And what did you do to your face?"

Clae rubbed at his chin with the back of his hand. "Had a job. Busted lip."

"No wonder you wanted bread this morning," Mrs. Keedler muttered. "Are you sure you're all right? I can give you a discount on some pastries if you want something else to eat."

"I'll take you up on that," Laura chirped, raising her hand. "I've got some money with me. Not a lot, but what can ten argents get me?"

Argents, the money unit of Orien, consisted of silvery coins at varying sizes. The smallest unit, a one argent coin, was barely the size of a fingernail, but coins grew gradually larger in increments of tens, fifties, hundreds, until reaching the 1,000 Argent coin, which stretched almost an inch across. Laura had collected them before her collage due to the patterns on their backs—different based on the city and quarter they were first distributed in—but holding on to things with public value was difficult. It cost her ten argents for a pastry this morning.

She sat on a stool in the Sweeper shop to eat, watching lazily as Clae put away his briefcase and Okane went to linger by the back corner. The two of them tinkered with the Kin parts; Laura was a little bothered that Okane knew enough to fiddle with it that way, when all she knew to do was tighten some things if they got loose. Clae hadn't bothered teaching her any more than that. She finished her pastries but couldn't think of anything else to do. Her head fell forward a few times but jerked back up as she tried not to nod off entirely. She hoped it wasn't too obvious, but Clae noticed.

"Are you trying to sleep over there?"

"You did get me up at four in the morning," she grumbled, somewhat ashamed.

"We got up earlier."

"Well, excuse me for needing more sleep to run properly."

Laura rearranged her feet on the rungs of the stool, hoping the shuffling would wake her mind up again. It wasn't working.

"If you're still half dead, you can sleep."

Laura rolled her head about as she looked around. Stools, counter . . . where did he expect her to sleep, the floor?

"Believe me, I'd love to. There's just no place to sleep here."

"So go upstairs."

"Upstairs? As in your house, upstairs?"

"What, you afraid there are rats up there?" Clae replied, steadying a length of tubing.

"No, it's just weird." Laura made a face. "I mean, I don't know. . . ."

The idea seemed like a terrible invasion of space. She wasn't too happy with the idea of Clae in her room, but somehow this seemed worse. An uncrossable line: you could enter a church but you couldn't go into the holy of holies.

"There's a room right next to the stairs, right on the left. You'll need to pull some sheets from the closet, but it'll work. Just don't touch anything else in there."

Laura leaned toward Okane and whispered, "What room is this?"

"Unused one," he replied, just as quiet. "Old guest room or something."

"Okay. You sure?" she asked, glancing back at Clae. He was too busy tightening a screw to look at her.

"Just go. But don't take too long, we're on the clock."

When neither did anything to stop her, she slid off the stool and made for the door behind the counter.

The stairs were steep to fit in the small area behind the door. As Laura climbed she didn't look forward to going back down—she'd probably miss one of the little steps and fall and break something. Regardless, she climbed. The door at the top opened easily. There was a little entryway before the step up into the home beyond, just like in Laura's apartment. She took off her boots here before venturing farther.

From the hall beyond, she could see a change in style. A small kitchen lay to her right, with even fewer appliances than the one in her own apartment. On one side the wall was a thick screen that slid across a track in the floor and folded neatly when drawn back. It was half open, and in the open space sat a tiny table, low to the ground. The room beyond seemed to be a bedroom.

Laura wanted to snoop, but this wasn't her home and she had no right. She ripped her gaze away to search for the guest room. To her left stood a sliding door, thin but functional, and she pulled it open.

The cramped room here fit a short bed with no bedding, a rickety nightstand, a rocking chair, and what looked like a sewing basket, which Laura found strange. She never really thought of Clae as a sewer. Lots of men had housewives—little fold-up sewing kits in case of tears in clothing—but an entire sewing box? She located the closet on one wall and slid it open. It held two shelves, one at the height of her waist, the other above her head. The bottom bore a jumble of junk—kettles, broken cups, clothes racks, and the like. She looked up at the top shelf, and there she finally spotted some bedding. She pulled it down and frowned. The blanket smelled like mothballs. She fished out a pillow and slinked over to the bed.

The mattress creaked under her weight. It was uncomfortable. She found herself rolling around to find some better spot, but nowhere on the stupid floral-patterned springbag did she feel content. She realized why when she saw the label for Partch Mattresses. She used to pass that store every day on the way to school, but they shut down sometime when she was in second grade. They were cheap mattresses, low-quality.

She stared absently in front of her, cursing the mattress, and caught sight of something on the nightstand. The stand wasn't the best quality either, but on the side, ROSEMARIE had been sloppily carved into the wood. What looked like a flower was engraved below.

She'd never heard of someone called Rosemarie before. It probably wasn't anyone important.

How she managed to fall asleep, Laura had no idea. She jolted awake when she heard a tinkling sound. She sat bolt upright, looking around wildly before she was even truly awake. The tinkling came from a child's toy, a small patched-up ball with a bell inside. It rolled in from the door, wobbling erratically owing to its internal framework, and came to a halt a foot from the bed. Laura reached out to pick it up.

"Are --- awake in there?"

"Okane?"

"Right." He had to be just on the other side of the door. "It's getting toward noon, and Clae's just about done with all the forms he's filling out. Probably a good time to go down, before he realizes how long it's been."

Laura checked her pocket watch, saw it was eleven forty, and lent a new urgency to her actions. She rolled herself off the bed, wadded up the blanket, and shoved it back into the closet. After giving herself a quick pat-down to check that she looked decent, she opened the door fully. Okane leaned against the opposite wall, turning another bell toy over in his hands.

"Where did you find these?" Laura caught his attention as she held up the one that had rolled into the guest room.

"They were in my room." He gestured to another sliding door just down the hall. "It looks like it was a child's room at one point. There are some old toys in there like these."

"Toys?" Laura repeated, baffled. "It's not like he's got any kids. Shouldn't those be in storage or something?"

Okane shrugged. "They don't look like they've been used in a while. Maybe he's just too lazy to pick them up?"

"Who knows."

She handed over the ball, and Okane put them back into the other room. When they emerged into the shop space, Laura spotted Clae hunched over a stack of papers, scribbling away with a pen. Part of his hair stuck up like he'd been messing with it as he wrote. Laura skirted him and took the seat she'd been in earlier.

"How are the forms going?" she asked.

"Behold, it lives," Clae deadpanned.

"Amazing," Laura retorted, just as dryly. "But really, how long have you been at that?"

"An hour." He leaned back on his stool, using his hands on the counter for balance as he cracked his back.

"Ouch."

"When these things happen on military ground, they always end up requiring far more paperwork than should ever be needed," Clae hissed. He signed the bottom of a page with a flourish.

"You've done this before?"

"Twice. All cases of extreme stupidity. That mask this time? It was a *good-luck charm* from a trainee's girlfriend, procured from the Mad Dogs mob. Apparently she got huffy when he left for the army and was convinced he was cheating. Decided he was better off vanishing from the world, collateral damage be damned."

Laura wanted to ask how he knew this, but he looked a little too angry to hold a civil conversation. Okane rolled his eyes toward the telephone, and she got her answer anyway.

"Anything else happening today? I'm guessing no since I was able to take a nap."

"There's a package by the door. It has some things inside for the both of you." Clae jabbed his pen toward the door.

Sure enough, there was a big package wrapped in brown paper. Laura glanced at Okane in confusion, but he looked just as baffled as she felt. He went to retrieve it, and set it on the counter, just out of the way of the papers.

"What is it?" he asked.

"Open it and see for yourself."

Cautiously, Okane peeled the paper away. He took care not to rip any of it, which Laura didn't know whether to find annoying or endearing, but he got it open eventually. Laura couldn't see well, since the paper stuck up in the way, but Okane cocked his head to the side like a curious dog. He reached in and pulled up a dark green vest with subtle swirling designs in the fabric.

"I don't understand."

"That one's for Laura."

"I still don't understand."

"It's specially made fabric," Clae explained, putting the pen down. "There's only one dressmaker in Amicae who can make these kinds of clothes. They're specially treated with kin."

"I think I remember you talking about this before." Laura took the vest. She could tell right away that it had been fitted, and it was very good quality.

"It's an extra defensive measure against the monsters," Clae explained to Okane. "The fabric has been saturated with kin to the point it gives off a similar aura, which doesn't fade. With luck, they'll just register you as weak kin and try to avoid touching you."

"Hang on." It hadn't occurred to Laura before, but now it seemed painfully obvious. "Is your coat made of this sort of thing too? I mean, that one time the monster tried to hit you, but it didn't seem to do any damage."

"I prefer the coat since it covers more, but since you've both expressed your *distaste* for the style, vests seemed the better option."

"Wow," Laura muttered, running a hand over the buttons. "Thanks. Really, thank you."

"Can't have you two keeling over on me." Clae said this as if it would be a terrible inconvenience and not a tragedy.

"*Thanks.*" Laura's tone dripped with sarcasm.

Meanwhile Okane pulled out another vest, this one black with silver buttons. After examining it for a moment, he laid it over his shoulder and lifted out more vests, even shirts and sets of pants.

"Who's the special dressmaker?" Laura watched in awe as more and more expensive clothing made an appearance.

"His name is Zavodsky. He's a finicky bastard who doesn't like turning over the product until he's been over it a thousand times for error and has the complete set done." Clae plucked a dark purple vest from the pile, wordlessly claiming it along with a less flashy brown one lined with green. "He's had your vest finished for months but refused to hand it over until he had the entire batch ready to go, and then he got wind of the new Sweeper and had to hold on until he had *two* wardrobes done."

"That's nice of him," Laura grumbled.

"He's insufferable," Clae agreed.

More objects peeked out from the package paper. Okane looked busy with the wide array of clothing, so Laura picked them up. Thick ID cards, the width of her palm and shorter, to be more easily stored in pockets and coin purses. Laura had an ID card of her own tucked away on her person, but one of the new cards bore her name and information, just on yellowish background instead of white, with the addition of three small stars in the corner above her picture. *Laura Kramer,* it read, in meticulously fine print. The other two read *Okane Sinclair* and *Clae Sinclair,* with stars to match hers. Okane looked spooked in his photograph, and Laura fought a smirk at that. She recognized the backdrop in the photos. These must've been from their venture to a professional studio, a week after Okane was dragged out of the Sullivan house.

"What are these?"

Clae glanced over.

"New IDs. They're revamping public workers' cards, changing color so they're easier to spot. Stars correspond to level of importance. We may end up having to show those instead of rings soon." He gave his ring a rueful twist. "But now Okane's officially registered. Congratulations."

"I'm what?"

Okane held out one weak hand, and Laura gave him the card. She scanned the info as she did. DOB August 25, 1214. So they pegged him to be nineteen, a year younger than her. While he gaped at the card, she peered down at Clae's. April 26, 1206. That made him twenty-seven.

Clae plucked the card from her hands and frowned at it.

"What's so interesting?"

"Nothing! Just admiring that hairstyle."

He gave the card a skeptical look and declared, "I'm nothing but fashionable," before moving on. He twirled his pen and went back to the forms, ignoring them completely. Laura ignored him now too. She swapped her old vest for one of the new ones and spent the rest of the day with boosted confidence, because she knew it looked good on her.

⌘

When she arrived back at the Cynder Block and turned in her bicycle, Mrs. Haskell gave her a weird smile and said she looked nice. She also asked if Laura had a boyfriend, which was so far off Laura had to laugh. She was still giggling when she reached the apartment on the top floor. Morgan noticed her good mood even before she saw her.

"Did you have a good day?" she called as she stirred something on the stove.

"Yes and no," Laura answered. "Getting up so early was awful. I'm sorry they barged in like that."

"It was fine," Morgan chuckled, but there was some strain to it. Obviously this would not be welcome if it happened again.

"But I got to—" Mentioning a nap at a man's house was a big no-no even if it was a genuine act of goodwill; she backtracked. "To get to know Okane a little better! And Clae got me some new clothes."

"Did he?" Morgan looked back and did a double take. "Oh, my. Where did he get that?"

"A specialist." Laura patted the fabric of the vest proudly. "I'm not sure how he got my size or anything," and now that she thought about it that was a little creepy, "but it looks great, doesn't it?"

"It does."

Morgan set aside the spoon and walked over to get a better look. She made the same kind of weird smile as Mrs. Haskell had, though it wavered a little.

"How much did this cost?"

"I don't know, but it has to be a lot. Quality costs. I've got a small wardrobe in here!" She held open the bag she'd borrowed from Brecht, showing off the clothes she'd stuffed inside.

"If he's spending this kind of money on you, are you sure it's not *that* kind of present?"

Laura's smile dropped. "Morgan. We're funded by the city and this is a uniform for the job."

"I'm just saying, it seems like he went to some lengths to get you a present."

"You're crazy."

Morgan rolled her eyes. "Just be careful, okay? Sometimes things like this just get to be a slippery slope. It's okay if it's for the job, but don't make him think you owe him anything for it."

Laura took a look at Morgan's worried face and averted her gaze. The memory of Charlie resurfaced and she felt another surge of anger at him, at anyone who could see this woman and think anything bad of her. She was so much kinder and braver—strange as that thought was—than most married women Laura knew. Even if she was on Laura's back about marriage all the time, it was an attempt to help her.

"He only got it because it's a Sweeper uniform. And it's only nice because the tailor is a perfectionist. Clae got clothes for Okane and himself too. He's not targeting me for anything."

Morgan frowned and crossed her arms as she sighed. "Just keep an eye on this, okay? Get out while you can."

"Really, you don't have to worry."

With a thundering of little feet, Cheryl came running in from outside. She didn't close the door behind her and didn't bother to take off her shoes either. Morgan lunged and snatched her up off the ground.

"What are you doing?" she laughed.

"Getting money."

"For what?"

"I found a penny doll for one argent!" Cheryl kept kicking like she was running in midair. "Gotta get it quick!"

"That sounds like too good a deal to me," said Laura.

"But it's there!"

"All right," Morgan told her. "Go on then. But you're using your own allowance."

She set her down. Cheryl looked up to smile at her, but caught sight of Laura's vest.

"Ooh. That's pretty."

"Isn't it?" Laura grinned.

"If you have money for that, you have money for a penny doll, right?"

"If I had the money for this vest I'd have already spent it all, so I wouldn't have any left for the doll."

"That's an excuse."

"Didn't I say you're supposed to use your own money?" chided Morgan.

Cheryl made an unhappy sound and ran to her room. Morgan threw up her hands in surrender.

"And still with the shoes. She'll never learn," muttered Laura.

"You were the same. She'll learn soon enough."

Cheryl ran past them again, coin fisted in her hand, and Morgan caught her again, spinning her about and ordering her to spend the paper money first. Paper money had only recently come into existence, and Morgan was among the majority of people who believed it wouldn't be worth dirt in a year's time. Cheryl wasn't pleased by the delay. As she scrambled out the door, Morgan called, "Be careful!"

"I will!"

The door closed behind her.

15

GODS IN THE RABBLE

"Why do you keep working there?"

The sigh came out of nowhere, early on October first as Laura prepared for work. She'd been checking the contents of her coin purse when Morgan leaned on the counter beside her, looking sad and worn. The woman had been involved in a stressful catering job the day before, and these always sent her into a funk that had her questioning the point of everything.

"What, as a Sweeper?" Laura asked. "I told you, it's completely safe."

"Nothing is completely safe."

"So what, I should join a factory and get my fingers chopped off by machines?"

Morgan shuddered. "No! No. I just mean—why can't you be a maid or something? Work in a big house? Do laundry, or dressmaking, teach, work with the post, be a telephone operator! They're all valid, reliable positions!"

"And my Sweeper job isn't?"

Morgan made a frustrated noise, rubbed at her face, and peered between her fingers. "I just don't know. I can't even tell if you're *happy* there."

Laura fiddled with an argent. "No one's happy all the time."

"But you come home and complain. All the time. And your boss seems very abrasive. I don't want you to be stuck somewhere toxic."

"I'm not. It's kind of . . . freeing, actually. Clae's honest. That's what makes it, strange as it sounds. He doesn't have to put up with me, or anyone else. So when he does, and when he says I'm doing well, I know it's true. He sees value in what I do." *He sees value in me,* her brain continued, but she kept her mouth shut.

"I'm sure you're a valuable worker, but this isn't about him. It's about you. I want you to be happy. I don't want you to be just a tool for him to throw away."

"Clae doesn't learn the names of tools or machines."

Belatedly she realized this wasn't meant to refer to Clae's stubborn distrust of interior workers. Morgan was referring to herself: her stricken look proved it. Shame rose in a hot flush in Laura's cheeks. How could she fix that kind of mistake?

Morgan composed her face into a rigid semblance of normalcy and rested a hand on Laura's shoulder.

"Sometimes people value you in ways you misunderstand," she whispered. "You can tell you're valued, but for what? Is it because you're smart? Is it because you can hold a good conversation? Is it what they can get out of you? Are you just a pretty face? Oh, don't look at me like that, Laura, you *are* pretty. But think about it. He's a horrible person, and what is he gaining from you? Does he really think that highly of you?"

"He's not as horrible as he likes people to think," Laura defended.

"He's horrible enough. Please, just answer me truthfully. Why do you put up with this?"

Laura scrunched up her face as she tried to sort out an answer. Lots of vague thoughts swirled around her head, but forming them into something coherent proved difficult.

"I like to feel like I'm important," she settled on at last. "When I'm there, I know I am."

She knew better than most how family wasn't obligated to care—she and Morgan hadn't spoken to the rest of the family in over a decade, and Cheryl hadn't so much as seen them—but at times it still felt like Morgan raised her more out of pity. Like she was watching over a younger version of herself, or maybe some offshoot of her precious older sister. When it came to Clae, there were no opportunities for such doubts. She knew exactly where she stood in his eyes.

Morgan gave a hollow laugh and shook her head. "Is this all because of that book?"

"It's more than that."

"But that's the root."

"It's not—"

"If only we never bought it. You might be happier."

Happier? Morgan looked at her with big sad eyes, but anger coiled in her stomach. The woman might as well have scooped up all her hopes and dreams and tossed them down the stairs. "Happier," as if Sweeping were just an ugly phase that had lasted too long to be proper; something that could've been avoided entirely if only they'd taken enough care, like a disease.

"I'm going to be late for work," she said tersely.

"Laura—"

"See you later."

She hastened out the door before she could be questioned further. Laura wanted to believe Morgan honestly cared, but she kept throwing out things like this. It felt increasingly like all the value she saw in Laura was actually the value of a potential husband to drag the family into some semblance of respectability.

Using amulets is hard, but I'm really good at it. Even Clae was impressed, she thought as she left. Morgan's morose face lingered in her mind, so she kept trying to justify it all. *All that time at school feeling so tiny and useless, and people really expect me to keep going like that? People like Charlie and those teachers wanted me to believe in a version of myself I never even liked. Infestations are terrifying, but the magic, the amulets—they feel right. I feel strong. Unboxed. And I knew what I'd be getting into, knew that since I was little. If everything feels right, no one has any right to try making me leave. I'm supported. I might follow Clae's lead a lot, but I know without a doubt that if I had non-Sweeper trouble he'd be there for me. He trusts me to have his back when we're going after a monster. He trusts me to keep him alive in the future.*

The last thought startled her. She came to a stop halfway down the stairs and stared blankly at the scuffed wall.

He thinks I'm important enough that he can trust me with his life.

It took a while to wrap her head around it, but the more she thought, the more certain she was. The bravest man in all the city relied on her more than anyone else. What a horrifying conclusion. At the same time, though, it made her chest swell with pride.

"I'm worth being here," she declared.

No one was around to hear it, but it was enough assurance for her. She kept walking with a new spring in her step.

Laura arrived at the Sweeper shop to a surprise. A number of people could be seen through the large windows, black shapes flitting back and forth. With a jolt she thought some group had finally decided to go after Clae, but the movement was slow, more the milling of a crowd than a more deliberate motion. With no sound or sight of trouble, Laura opened the door and peered in. Policemen filled the room, a pack of fourteen and mostly young, who chattered and laughed at bad jokes.

Clae stood guard in front of the Kin, eyes flicking suspiciously. When a woman snooped too close he took one strong step forward, spooking her into retreat. Okane had resumed his position plastered to the back corner, motionless and silent. Neither noticed Laura's entrance through the noise.

She hauled her bike into the shop and wheeled it toward the usual wall. It took a while for some people to realize she was trying to get through, but they moved aside eventually. With the bike parked, Laura headed to the counter. The movement caught Clae's attention, so his head swiveled about and he gave her a fearsome look that made her step falter. Once he recognized her, the anger drained from his face and he deflated.

"You finally showed up."

"Don't complain," Laura grumbled, still rattled but slapping on a brave face. *He trusts me.* "I'm on time. What's going on?"

"I told you before, police of a certain rank have to follow Sweepers for a while to understand us better. Get the idea of what we do. Happens every few months. We just need to lead them around."

"All these people are here for Pit duty?" Laura looked over the unruly group, trying to imagine them all filtering through the walkways of the interior.

"All these and two more. We've got some up-and-coming politician sent over, along with a guest of his."

"A politician?"

"He's aiming to get into the City Council, so Douglas thinks he should get some education."

"Douglas" referred to Victoria Douglas, the same woman Clae had recommended to the reporter at the August infestation. Douglas reigned over the City Council, in a minor position but still one where she could push hardest for Sweeper benefits. The most Laura had seen of her was a picture in the newspaper—from that she knew Victoria Douglas was an old woman with severe wrinkles and white hair tightly curled. Laura was a little wary of dealing with her ilk.

After another five minutes the door swung open again, and two people entered. A young man came first: Laura judged him to be shortly out of university, with blond hair and strikingly blue eyes. His new brown suit fit perfectly. The tall woman beside him sported red hair, a fashionable dress, and a familiar face. It took a moment but Laura recognized her, and Clae did as well in the same moment.

"Oh, hell, it's that reporter."

The same reporter from the August infestation. She looked almost a completely different person outside of the police uniform. Her eyes roved, drinking in the room as if it were a castle instead of a shop. Her fingers twitched toward her bag and presumably her notebook. Laura was relieved to see she'd gotten away from the police, but wasn't sure if her presence would be a good thing here.

With everyone gathered, Clae tried to bring them under control.

"All right, shut up." He clapped his hands for emphasis, but, these people being unused to Clae's authority, the babble went on.

"Hey!" Laura cried. Some people looked over, but the majority remained ignorant until Clae brought his foot down with a loud thunk and a shriek.

"*Shrew! Peep!*"

Everyone jumped. Once all startled eyes were on them, Clae sneered.

"Right, first rule. When I say shut up, you shut up."

Silence. Okane sneezed and ducked down in mortification. Clae paid him no mind, but it lessened the tension in the air.

"Moving on. You're here to follow the Sweepers today. I'm Clae Sinclair, head Sweeper. That means from eight to four, I am your god. You will not defy me. Defy me and I will become tattletale to your boss, that's not below me. Feel free to imagine the outcome."

A few policemen went pale, but the suit man remained unruffled.

"These are my apprentices, Miss Kramer"—eyes turned to Laura, and she straightened up under the attention—"and Mr. Sinclair."

Laura turned to follow his gesture. Okane stared back, flabbergasted. This was the first time he'd been referred to with this surname. It sounded very strange.

"They are also gods. If you have questions and I'm busy, ask them. Otherwise don't bother them." Clae glared at the reporter, who returned a brazen smile. "What we're doing today is the same thing we do every Monday, Wednesday, and Friday. I take it you know how amulets function?"

"Um." A policewoman who looked barely sixteen raised a shaky hand. "No, not really."

That opened the proverbial floodgates, and Clae preached the functions and fallbacks of amulets. While he spoke, Laura ghosted around the counter to join Okane. Together they watched their audience's expressions, all the way up to the flicker of shock as Clae went for the jugular.

"Now, did your chief or boss tell you about how the wall propaganda's a bunch of bull?"

"Excuse me?" said the policewoman.

"*Bull.* Lies. Slander." Clae waved a hand. "You all are here because the chief or Council has hand-selected you to be one of the 'chosen.' To know the truth of our city."

"But we all know the truth," said a policeman. "The walls—"

"Walls don't do anything. Think about it. Really think about it. If Amicae, the friendly city, had actually come up with a foolproof way to prevent the spread of infestations, why wouldn't we have shared that? Why is every other city in Orien plagued by monsters? I see you looking at each other. I see you coming up with theories on why we'd possibly keep such a secret, but the truth is that there is no secret. Amicae has no defense against monsters. The walls are useless against them, just as our ancestors' castles were useless, and the natives who understood its every working were useless against it. The only thing capable of driving off an infestation is weaponized magic, which is only created by Sweepers. And yes, that's another bitter dose of reality: Sweepers have nothing to do with mobsters. We are not the MARU, and never have been. We're here to clean up the mess that the Council refuses to prevent, and minimize damage."

"But we'd know," said the policeman. "If something that big was loose in Amicae, we'd have heard about it!"

"That's where your role comes in." Clae strode forward, slow, each thud of his boots against the floor menacing with the hiss of the Kin behind him. "As the chosen, it's your job to keep this knowledge from the public. You seal off the crime scene. You escort away any and all potential witnesses, and if there are witnesses for any reason, you take care of them by any means necessary. Some witnesses comply without much force. Others are marked as terrorists and thrown in jail for attempting to make this public knowledge. Still others have to escape to the Fifth Quarter or seek asylum with the mobs. Isn't that a thorn in your side? That the mobsters do more to save your fellow citizens than you do."

He stopped in front of the reporter. Her hands had steadied over her bag and she looked back at him coolly, unflinchingly.

"As a reporter you've been recruited here, probably because you're too nosy and you'd find out about this anyway. Congratulations. You studied to find the truth and you've got it, but now you'll get to spend your days helping them keep it all hidden. Your role is camouflage. When a child has an amulet that runs out of power and an infestation takes root in it, you get to write about how the parents unwittingly disrespected a mob boss and got their just deserts. Or maybe you write how their gas system malfunctioned and the whole of the house was lost in the blaze. Write how a child ran away from home to explore other cities. It's all been done."

Finally he turned to the man in the suit, and here his eyes absolutely glittered with malice.

"And you, new blood of the Council. It's your responsibility to understand everything you perpetrate. Every decree and every lie, you must understand the death counts and damage that comes with it. This is the burden you've chosen, and this is something you can't ever ignore."

The man snorted. "I'm aware of your claims, Sweeper."

"Claims?" Okane whispered. "He didn't just—"

"Disregard my words if you want for now, but the rest of the Council will rip out your throat if you don't step lightly," said Clae. He turned back to the hushed group. "The burden's on all of you, now. You are now witnesses to the Council's great lie. You have two choices. First, to obey their every decree and go on as if nothing has happened. You will not be allowed to share this information to anyone who doesn't already know. You can't warn your family. You can't warn your friends. Your second option? You could talk. Just know that you and whoever you tell won't be long in this world. Any questions?"

Silence. The reporter raised her hand.

"How many Sweepers are there, sir?" she asked.

"You're looking at all three of them."

Eyes turned on them again, wide and horrified, and Laura couldn't blame them. The only three people capable of destroying infestations, and their combined life span probably couldn't even match the ages of some police coworkers.

"Now that you're all aware of the direness of the situation, we'll bring you out on one of our more routine operations," said Clae. "Let's get going."

The trunk sat behind the counter, out of sight of the visitors. Laura and Okane hefted it up between them. Okane lifted his side with ease, far more coordinated than the first time. He was very different from what he was, back in August; he still leaned toward the kind of clothes he wore before, dark and almost formalwear, but he'd started to wear the brighter kin-treated material, and a red bandana had taken up residence around his neck, while this hair, well groomed at one point, had gotten irreversibly tangled. While he didn't look so high-class, he did look freer. Laura felt irrationally proud to look at him; foolish, since she'd had little to do with it.

They carried the trunk outside. For once they led the march to the interior. Clae was just behind them, walking backward to address the gaggle bringing up the rear. He didn't so much as glance where he was going. Either he committed the path to memory, or he'd activated his amulets to better sense theirs.

Now he launched into an explanation of Pit duty, what it was and why they did it. He added more fluff to this explanation than the curt ones he gave the apprentices. When he finished, a policewoman near the front asked about the history of the Pits. Laura would've listened in, but the reporter went around Clae to walk alongside her.

"Hello," she said. "I'm not sure if you'll recognize me, but we met back in August. I'm Annabelle Kilborn. You can call me Bella if you want, though."

"I remember you," said Laura, quirking a small smile. "I wondered if you'd gotten away."

"My coworker had a getaway car," said Annabelle. "I dug into the Council files like you and your boss said. I guess that's why I got sent here. I didn't realize how deep this hole went until it was too late."

"I'm sorry we got you involved like this."

"Don't be. I wanted to be involved. Now I just understand why you couldn't say anything. But!" Annabelle pulled out her notebook and pad. "Now that I'm here, I'm going to work as well as I can in the box I've got. I'd say my first project is bringing attention to you anyway. Mind if I ask you for opinions on this job and some political maneuvers?"

"Sure, but I'm not sure how much you can publish."

"Feel free to be evasive. I'll edit it if there are loose ends."

"All right, but if you want to talk politics Clae would be your man. He's the one who knows all the ins and outs."

"I'll be getting his opinion too, but I want to know what *you* think. Our readers like to hear from the everyday worker, not the big man."

"So long as you're careful about what you write. Fire away."

Annabelle questioned them about some small details (How often do mobsters plant these "monsters"? Are you satisfied with the current abilities of Sweepers? Are you happy with your job benefits? How wide is your network?). Laura answered it all to the best of her ability so Okane didn't have to speak, and he seemed very happy with this arrangement. They'd almost reached the interior door when politics came up.

"What do you think of the push to eliminate the Sweeper position?"

Laura stumbled and Okane had to scramble to compensate for the movement.

"What?"

"The push to eliminate the Sweeper post," Annabelle repeated. "The idea to transfer the duties of Sweepers entirely to the police department and cut costs."

"I know that most people think we're MARU, but even they weren't under the chief's thumb. Since when did this come up?"

"Alexander Wilcox is making that part of his platform for election in the spring." She nodded back at the man in the suit, who eyed Clae like one would a growling mutt. "The Council has been questioning the wisdom of funding such a small and expensive office, but Victoria Douglas has always hounded them into keeping it. With her retirement on the horizon and new blood coming to power, there may be more indecisiveness and possible elimination. You say the Council knows the dangers, but if they did, would they really have let you dwindle to three people? What happens if this does go through?"

But they *couldn't*. There was no way the Council could allow the Sweepers to fail; if there was even consideration, wouldn't there have been signs? Budget cuts? Benefit cuts? This was her place; somewhere she could be herself with no nagging about "would Charlie approve of that" or griping about her ending up a mop mary, where someone always had her back. No one should be able to take it away.

"They wouldn't," she said. "It's impossible. The city would—"

"Miss Kramer." The strangeness of the title and the warning in Clae's tone made Laura's mouth click shut. Clae watched her, blank-faced but with narrowed eyes, and Laura ducked her head.

The interior door stood open and waiting for them, their usual man hovering in the opening.

"Morning!" he called as they approached.

"Entering the interior," Clae called. "Get into single file, don't disturb the workers."

The followers shuffled to comply, and Clae slipped between Annabelle and the apprentices. "What were you yelling about?" he asked, voice low enough that it was almost lost to the roar of the machines.

Laura looked up at him and tried to drink in everything she could. Over the time she'd been a Sweeper, she'd figured out most of his tells: his posture, the slight shifts of his eyes. Right now he was intent, expecting, complete attention on her. She doubted any other job included a boss who'd think of her this much like an equal; certainly none of the options Morgan had rattled off. Other places had people like Charlie, ones who refused to see her as a person beyond being a girl. If the Sweepers disbanded she'd lose this forever.

"That politician wants to get rid of Sweepers," she hissed.

"Not entirely," Annabelle corrected, following close behind. "The Sweepers would be absorbed into the police department."

Clae snorted. "As if that would ever work."

He seemed relaxed enough that the tension drained from Laura's shoulders.

"So you don't even see it as a possibility?" said Annabelle.

"You saw Douglas's files. Think over those again and see if any politician could overcome such arguments."

Their long line wound across the walkways, not quite single file and forcing some workers to the far side of the path. Thankfully the elevator fit them all, even if it was cramped. The Sweepers ended up next to the grilles as they rattled shut, and Laura drew back so they didn't close on her nose. The ride up was quiet, broken by some coughing and shuffling over the mechanical rattle. Laura listed so far back she practically leaned on Clae to keep a distance from the gaps in the grate. When they reached the top of the shaft and the grilles opened again, she dragged Okane and the trunk into open air.

They strode along the walkway and deposited the trunk while the crowd gathered around. Clae worked on opening the Pit. Laura watched distractedly, listening to the conversations among their followers. Annabelle murmured something to Wilcox, some policemen whispered about the interior, and a small cluster of younger policewomen giggled about Clae's looks.

"Of all the things to talk about," Laura sighed.

"The machinery?" Okane questioned, looking over at her.

"No, the girls."

Okane angled his head to hear them better. "Clae has a dip in his arm?"

"What?"

"They say he has an ugly dent."

Clae had his sleeves rolled up as he turned the handle, showing off an indented scar in his left forearm. Laura didn't know the story behind it, but the thought that these girls were gossiping about scars was a little disturbing. Laura adjusted her shirt. Her own faint battle scars were easy to hide on the worst of days, but it made her feel better to make sure.

With the Pit yawning wide, Clae straightened.

"As I've explained before, this is a Pit, one of the three functioning in Amicae. There used to be more, but those have been 'sunk' to make room for the city; they're still highly dangerous. Due to stupidity, the remaining Pits had to be modified to keep working. Broken amulets are at the bottom, the better to monitor." When some edged closer, he added, "They're far enough down you won't be able to see them, and there's no way to catch yourself if you fall. Back off." They scuttled back immediately.

Laura took the lock off the trunk and pulled it open. She and Okane lifted the large Egg out of its cushion and over to the edge. Clae hovered while Laura unscrewed the lid, set that aside, and she and Okane poured out the kin. Some people drew closer again once the kin started its little dance to watch its descent. Once all the kin was out, they pulled up the Egg and put it away.

"Is that it?" asked the young policewoman from earlier.

"Wait for it."

As Laura clicked the lock back on the trunk, she heard the sighing from the Pit.

"There. That's the sound of a destroyed infestation that took root. That's why we use the Pits."

"Seems simple," the girl murmured.

"*A simple job with far too much drain on the city funds.*" Laura looked around to see Annabelle beside her. The woman had been imitating a male voice just now, and broke into a smile. "That's what Mr. Wilcox was saying. He doesn't buy your boss's story. Thinks you're making up a hoax to get more funding. He keeps saying the police can handle it all themselves."

They doubled back and sat in the shop, so the crowd could lounge and talk as much as they wanted. They waited for anyone to come in with news about infestations or amulets to recycle. One person came in to turn in an amulet, but she left in a hurry—the amount of attention proved too much for her. Laura wished more would come in. The shop being this slow must only reinforce Wilcox's idea that their only jobs came through the police and only from mob activity. Clae didn't look bothered. He fended off people who got close to the Kin, dodging all questions on how it worked. Okane leaned against the wall by the drapes, and Laura went through the stack of papers by the door, hunting for anything that might hint at why or how long people had been cracking down on the Sweepers again. She found an article in Amicae's *Sun* newspaper: an editorial from two days ago, ARE OUR SWEEPERS NO BETTER THAN VANDALS?

The Sinclair Sweepers were recently called into the Sixth Quarter to carry out the extermination of an amulet proven to be property of the Mad Dogs. While successful, they also added to their streak of destruction. Sweepers have always been notorious for property damage, including the vandalism of private homes, businesses, and public amenities such as the Mechanics Museum of the Second Quarter. Their latest action has ruined the upper floors of a military barracks building, decimating one wall and causing over 5,000 argents' worth of damage. "They have no control," says military spokesperson Charles Goodwyn. "They have no control and they don't care what their effects are." The military isn't the only voice complaining: the Sweepers are in hot water with the City Council as well. One of their most disappointed fans is treasurer Marcus Walz, who pointed out the astronomical cost of keeping up a Sweeper department, and shared his frustration with the expectation for the Council to foot the bill for damages. "Sweepers eat up as much of the city's budget as the police, and don't have even one-third of the manpower," he explained, going on to lament the assumption that taxpayers must pay for flagrant lack of caution. With Sweepers' destruction rate climbing over the past few months, there are some fears that taxes may rise to match. Up-and-coming politician Alexander Wilcox has shared his own opinion of the situation: "The demands of Sweepers are too large to grant, and their work directly harms the lives and property of constituents. If they're truly heirs to the MARU, how is it that they never seem to leave an impact? Mob crime runs rampant and they do nothing to stop it. Is it truly wise to uphold such an inept office?" The police chief, who works closely with the Sweeper force, was unavailable for comment, but this reporter was able to contact the Head Sweeper about the case. When asked for his opinion, he simply replied, "Amicae is a city that has forgotten what the rest of the world knows." Forgetful we may be, but the city finds it hard to forget the 37 buildings Sweepers have rendered structurally unsound during this man's career.

Laura walked to the counter and set the paper, article visible, on the space next to Clae's elbow. He took in the newspaper, the headline, and looked back up at her.

"What?"

"That's all you said?"

"No, but that's all the reporter remembered. They have selective memory."

"And you're going to just let it go?"

"Reporters write what they want, and the Council already knows everything. There's nothing that can be done about it."

"Aren't you the one who's always saying we have to be a pain? There are so many routes you could've gone, but this? It just feels weak. Like the joke's on you."

"I will be a goddamn pain until I die, but they're desensitized. They don't like listening to things like this."

Laura folded her arms, frowning. "That's what you meant, then. Amicae has forgotten what the rest of the world knows."

"Of course. Look at the state of our Sweeper guild. Every other city beefs up their Sweepers because they know how vital we are. By some grim luck, Amicae came to the conclusion that there is no real threat, but why else is there a quarantine?" He gestured grandly in frustration. "Why do you think we haven't been in contact with the Old World? Why do you think any ship that goes far enough into the Beaumaris never returns?

Everyone knows that if the monsters spread and feed as they like, there will be no civilization left. Orien is a massacre waiting to happen, and Sweepers are the only things keeping that from happening. But here's Amicae, the goddamn *Sweeper city*, not even teaching people about amulets anymore, deliberately destroying Sweeper property, and deluding its citizens into thinking we're the enemy. It's almost funny; we're killing ourselves."

"Wow, that's optimistic," Laura grumbled, sitting down on the stool next to his.

Clae calmed a little, glared at empty air as if he was stewing, then looked back at her. "If the Sweepers are incorporated into the police, we won't get the equipment we need, not the same quality or quantity, and we won't be able to fight off infestations as easily as we have now. Hell, we could even be fired for the damage we've caused already. If that's the case, if the Sweeper position is gone, then you two are going to pick up and move to either Vitae or Terrae. Vitae because the Amicae Sweepers came from there; we have ties they'll uphold. Terrae because I have a good contact. Sweeper networks exist in all the cities, but those are where you'll get the most help. The Sweepers there will help get you on your feet. Whatever the case, you can't stay in Amicae."

"But—"

"But nothing. With Sweepers gone, give it a year, maybe two, and the city will be destroyed. I've gotten letters from Fatum about Rex's latest expedition, and they're going in force. The spike is going to hit soon and hit hard."

Laura gritted her teeth. She'd never left Amicae, not even gone to a satellite town. Her whole world was in these walls. The idea of leaving the job was bad enough, but abandoning the city for any reason was frightening, even when talking hypothetically.

"Us two," Okane piped up from the side, wearing an uneasy expression of his own. "What do --- mean? Where would --- be going?"

"I wouldn't." Clae crossed his arms.

"But --- just said the city would be destroyed."

"I'm a Sinclair Sweeper. My family was there in the beginning of Amicae. It'll be there at the end, too." Clae ignored their pale faces and pulled out his pocket watch. "Four o'clock," he announced to the room, and this signaled the drop of their earlier topic. "You've got another two days to follow us, but for today you're done. Scram."

The police nearest them had gone eerily quiet to listen to their conversation, and some looked just as unnerved as Laura felt. At his words, they started and moved. A few people politely thanked him for "hospitality," while the majority surged for the door. Annabelle scribbled on her notepad all the way out, following Wilcox as he made his exit. With the shop vacated, Laura breathed easier.

"Go on, you too," Clae shooed her.

Laura leaned against the counter and frowned. She wanted to keep talking about his little doom prophecy, but he'd clearly purposely derailed the topic, so she forced herself not to. "Another two days, huh?"

"Yes, two days. Then they're out of our hair."

"Are you going to try talking to Wilcox at some point?"

"Why should I? He's not going to hold up at the Council. Douglas'll whip him."

"She won't be around forever."

"What, did that reporter say something about her retiring? She's not going to retire till she's dead, and then you'll hear her roaring from the grave."

Laura smirked at the mental image.

"---'re not actually worried, then?" asked Okane.

"No."

"But --- just went on a rant."

"With Wilcox and a reporter in the room. Maybe it'll drive something home." Clae stretched leisurely, but the look in his eyes didn't fool Laura. He meant what he said, even if he pretended it was an act.

"Whatever you say," she sighed, standing again and moving toward her bike.

Okane made a funny noise of distress. "Then we're okay?"

"Yes, we're fine right now. Don't worry about it, Okane."

Laura said her usual good-bye and left, bumping her bicycle down the steps and onto Acis Road. It was only when she'd wheeled it a few feet away that she realized she'd taken the paper with her. It was an old one, so Clae wouldn't miss it. She was starting to slip it into her bag when she saw another one of the small headlines, on the same page as the Sweeper editorial: SULLIVAN WIFE FOUND DEAD.

She stopped short and stared at it, taking in only a few details. Missing for five weeks. Presumed kidnapping. Corpse floating in one of the canals.

Mind in a daze, she leaned her bike against the outside of the shop and walked back in. Okane had vanished upstairs but Clae was still there, checking over everything under the counter. He raised one eyebrow when he saw her.

"Did you forget something?"

Laura held up the newspaper. "Mary Sullivan's dead."

He didn't seem surprised. "And?"

"What happened?"

Clae glanced up at the ceiling, then gestured for her to come closer. When she did, he spoke in a lower tone, so his voice didn't carry far.

"I suspected she'd die. One way or another, she was annoying the Sullivans, so it's a miracle she survived as long as she did."

"What?" Was he saying the Sullivans did this? "But Henry Sullivan married her."

"It was a political maneuver. Those rich people in the upper Quarters, they rarely marry for love. When Henry married a lower-Quarter woman, people latched on to it as a kind of fairy-tale love story. It provided a distraction from Frank's schemes and gained public favor. Nothing more."

"Schemes like the scholarship and the Mad Dogs?"

"Exactly. She was too autonomous for their tastes in the end, and losing Okane was the final straw. She went 'missing' a few days after we got him out of there."

Laura felt stupefied. "Then . . . it's our fault she's dead?"

"Of course it's not. Sullivan is a rotten apple, always has been. Once something's outlived its usefulness, he gets rid of it, person, tool, or otherwise."

"You seem to know a lot about him."

"I've met him before, back when he had that dealing with my father. I was a lot younger then, but our whole family knew he was rotten. My father made it a point never to associate with businesses afterward, because of Sullivan and a few others. Too risky to deal with them directly. We always suspected they were linked with the mobs. Okane just confirmed it."

"But we did deal with them directly," Laura pointed out.

"Okane is safe as a result."

"But doesn't that make us, I don't know, a target?"

"He's backing Wilcox, if that means anything to you."

"He's what?"

"Paying for the campaign. If Wilcox is elected, Sullivan can use him like a puppet."

"And then he can mess with the Sweepers."

"Which is why you two would leave Amicae. But that, of course, is not going to happen. The Council may be a bunch of idiots, but they don't like the idea of big money steering politics like that. They won't take it lying down. If he gets elected, they'll impeach him."

"Because Victoria Douglas'll whip him?" Laura gave a small smile.

"Nobody messes with Victoria Douglas."

"You have a lot of faith in her."

"She's smart, and she's a pain. I approve."

Laura laughed. It was a bit strange; he kept canceling out his more foreboding words. *Be ready for this catastrophe, but it's okay, it's not actually going to happen.* She hoped that was the case.

"So you're saying we're in good hands."

"You could put it that way."

"Great."

Mind a little more at ease, Laura walked back to the door. She opened it and looked back to say good-bye again. Clae had already turned his attention away to tilt one of the glass parts of the Kin, tipping it to sit diagonally in its wire support. As he did this, something else occurred to her.

"Hey Clae? I don't want to be annoying, but—"

"Be annoying. Rowena wasn't annoying, she died."

Dead apprentice number three made an appearance.

"I was wondering about your arm. The, uh, 'dent'?"

Clae pulled up his sleeve and squinted down at the mark in question. "What about it?"

"What's it from?"

"Fell off a roof during the night infestation of 1222. Broke my arm so bad the bone stuck out."

"Ouch." Laura winced. "At least you're in one piece, though."

"The policemen weren't. Or hell, maybe they were." He stared absently at the drapes.

"What do you mean?"

"I mean that infestation decided teeth were a nice addition."

16

FALLING FEET-FIRST

"Where's Clae?"

Laura asked this as she stood at the front of the Sweeper shop, looking at Okane. Okane paused in the middle of carrying a box. He looked resigned.

"Upstairs."

"Shouldn't he be down by now?"

"Oh, he's awake. He just decided to stay up there."

"But we have a job."

"Do we?" Okane grunted, setting the box down and clapping his hands together to rid them of dust.

"I got waylaid by police on the way here." Laura made a face at the memory. At the time it had been terrifying; they'd sprung up from around a corner so fast she thought they were muggers and hit one of them over the head with her book-filled bag. "There's some sort of nest on the other side of the Quarter, residential neighborhood. They want us over there as soon as possible."

"They didn't call," said Okane. "Isn't that the standard procedure?"

"I thought so, but these looked like some of our newer police aides.

Maybe they don't know procedure yet. Do you think it's okay if I go up there and get Clae?"

"---'ve been up there before."

"That was with permission."

Okane eyed her awhile, pondering, then said slowly, "Well, if he doesn't want --- up there he'll make it pretty clear. Watch ---r step though, I suppose."

She went up the stairs to the second floor. Not much had changed up there, aside from the fact that there were some dirty dishes on the little table. But then there was Clae. The sight of him made her falter. He was doing a headstand, leaning against the wall behind him, and judging by the redness of his face he'd been doing this awhile.

"Are you okay?"

Clae's eyes snapped open. "I'm fine."

"You're upside down."

"Because I felt like it."

"Where did you get the idea to do that?" Laura craned her head to see him properly. "I mean, I don't say 'Hey, I feel like standing on my head' out of the blue!"

"That's your own choice."

"Did you eat breakfast this morning?"

"Of course I did."

"Are you sure? You get a little loopy when you skip meals."

"What are you, my—" His lips pursed tight. He squeezed his eyes shut, willing an extra flush of rage from his current tomato complexion. "What are you doing up here?"

Laura straightened with a frown. "There's an infestation we're supposed to deal with."

"How do you know before I do?"

"Because policemen are stalkers?"

Clae snorted. He took his time righting himself but didn't get up. He sat there on the floor to look at her.

"What are the details?" he asked. "Degree of damage, location?"

"They said it was in a residential neighborhood in the Third Quarter."

"That's it?"

"Yes."

"You do realize half of this city is residential?"

"Yes."

"And you didn't think to get any other details."

"In my defense, I was more under the impression that I was getting crashed by the mobs than getting a formal report."

Sighing, Clae stood up. "I'll call the police department to see where we're going. You grab Okane, make sure you're both ready to go."

She hurried down the stairs while he followed at a slower pace. Okane looked up as she came back into the shop.

"Why do you look so relieved?" she grumbled, walking over to him.

"I didn't hear any yelling," he confessed.

"He doesn't yell unless he has to, does he?"

She made to pat him on the shoulder as she said this, and he cringed. He'd gotten better since they first met, but when he wasn't panicking about life or death he was very peculiar about touching. Hated it, even. Laura didn't touch people often and she kept forgetting. She pulled her hand back immediately.

"Sorry."

"It's fine." He busied himself with the boxes again, pretending she meant something else entirely. "I know he doesn't shout so much, but it's reflex at this point. The Sullivans—well. I'm still having a bit of trouble adjusting."

"You're doing fine," said Clae, breezing past them on the way to the telephone. The hand crank rattled as he tried to reach the operator.

Clae got the information quickly, after scaring the operator and whoever answered at the police station. They were headed to a residential area near a rundown art gallery. The gallery had a prominent sign sticking up above the surrounding buildings, a big coin with cartoony features. The gallery itself was painted oddly, with colorful swirls on the walls. As such, it made a wonderful landmark. Nobody could miss it. Their destination was two blocks past it: a higher-class apartment building built of reddish brick, five stories tall. Police surrounded it, and the air was tense.

"What's going on here?" asked Laura, looking around at the dark faces. "It looks more like there's a murder than anything."

"Close," said Clae.

"Someone got eaten?"

"The infestation hasn't claimed any victims yet. It's the people with the infestation."

"Wait, you don't really mean this is a mobster hideout?" Laura finally understood why all the police looked so grim. Even the smallest of the mobster groups could put up a nasty fight.

"Are they the ones who targeted the Sullivans?" asked Okane.

"No one's bothered to tell me," Clae grumbled.

"Those were the Mad Dogs, right?" said Laura. "If there are infestations, wouldn't there be mobster Sweepers? Maybe even . . ."

The old apprentice? Clae wrinkled his nose at the idea, scanned the building.

"Considering that, this probably isn't Mad Dogs at all. This is a little too high-class for their tastes. People like them prefer places where their messes blend in. At a glance I'd say this would be the Silver Kings mob."

"But if there's a mob in there, are they still expecting us to go in? Or will they take care of the people beforehand?" said Laura. She'd never actually anticipated fighting mobsters, and didn't relish the idea.

"They don't know how bad the infestation is. We'll have to wait for Albright, or whoever's in charge."

They spent a good few minutes watching the police fanning out over the area as they picked strategic positions. It made Laura uneasy, and she shifted her weight from foot to foot.

"Sweepers."

Albright had snuck up behind them. Her voice was muted enough that it didn't scare them, but her face was unusually grim.

"What's the plan?"

"We're going to try to get in there and take down as many as we can. Of course, they're probably prepared for that by now. We're not exactly being discreet." She looked bitterly at the surrounding men, and Laura came to the conclusion that she hadn't been here to direct them at the beginning.

"We're to go in with you?" Clae frowned at the idea.

"And risk you getting shot? Not a chance."

"Why are we here, then?"

"The infestations are mobile. If they can carry them to their targets, they can carry them out of the building. We're putting you on both sides of the building, so if they try to use those amulets you're there to take care of it."

Sounded plausible. Laura glanced up at Clae to see his opinion. He didn't seem too bothered.

"You'll have police covering us, though," he checked, and she nodded.

"Of course. Don't do anything reckless, but if you see something suspicious, go for it."

He looked over at Laura and Okane and ordered, "You two take the other side of the building. I can handle this side myself. But be careful. I don't care if there's some runaway mobster with amulets. If he's got a gun, don't attack him. You're *not* the MARU. You come in after police have taken care of everything."

Albright nodded her approval but said nothing, gesturing some officers over instead.

"All right, boys, I want you to take these two around the back. Keep them safe but don't get in their way."

"Yes, ma'am," they affirmed in unison, saluting.

"Cut that out," she grumbled. "Just do your job."

"Yes, ma'am."

Laura allowed herself to be led away, Okane on her heels. The policemen took them through a narrow alley on the side of the building. Windows were there despite the lack of space or light. Laura ducked down, hoping that whatever mobsters were inside weren't paying attention. The policemen didn't seem to expect anything to happen, but she felt like a sitting duck. They skirted trash cans, jogged a little ways, and they were out of the alley. The back side of the building matched the front: same red brick, same design elements, but there was the addition of a fire escape built in. The back faced another, wider alley, with laundry lines spanning the gap above them. Another group of officers lingered here.

"If you could stay back, even as far as the other side of the alley, that would be appreciated," said one of the officers.

The pair went to the shadow of the opposite building, and Laura squinted up at their target. The strung-up laundry blocked part of her view. Okane stood next to her, looking antsy. He kept shifting how he held himself, and his eyes were fixed on the building ahead.

"You okay?"

"Fine." He shifted his weight to the left foot now. "It's just—Mobsters actually use those things as weapons? The amount of times --- insist the city's wrong, it seems almost strange for mobsters to be behind it for once."

"It is rare. The mobster Sweepers take care of most of them, but every once in a while Clae and I get stuck with a few that have been used for assassination. Mobsters plant them in houses and such, out of the way so no one notices them and the monster can grow until it starts reaching out and feeding. They don't know how long it'll take, and figure we work just as well as a cleanup crew."

"Are all their targets like the Sullivans?" He sounded like he was searching for some redeeming quality to it. Laura frowned at the thought, shoving her hands into her pockets.

"The Sullivans were definitely the least likable we've met. With the others, I guess mobsters wanted to threaten them or shut them up. There was this man who owned a toy store—he was in the wrong place at the wrong time and heard about something shady. He was going to go to the police, but the people he'd run in on decided to get rid of him first."

Okane frowned just as deeply. "But they can't control monsters any better than we can."

"No one can. So a lot of the time, their target isn't the only one who gets hurt. Toy store man? His whole family got eaten."

A distant sound made Laura straighten again. She wasn't sure what it was, but it appeared to be a signal. Police swarmed in on the back door. One kicked it open and led a group inside, while three more stayed back to watch the windows. Shouting erupted from inside. The raid had begun. The sound of a gunshot made Laura flinch back.

"They're going all out, aren't they?" she muttered, unnerved.

They watched as jumbled forms passed by windows and more guns went off. It went on awhile, and Laura was almost sure they wouldn't be needed, when a window on the third floor opened. A man stuck his leg out, trying to climb through, but he caught the attention of the police left behind.

"Stop right there!" cried one, lifting her gun to point at him.

At the shout he hopped awkwardly back inside. Another man came to the window, aiming a gun of his own. The policewoman dodged to the side. The bullet hit the ground where she'd been. The other two police started shooting up at the window.

Laura plastered herself against the wall. "This is exactly what we weren't supposed to be caught up in!"

She watched the proceedings frantically, hoping she'd be able to see it if a bullet ended up going toward her, get some warning of when to move. It got harder when two more windows opened up with shooters to man them. The police scattered further for cover, and Laura felt exposed. Why weren't there trash cans to hide behind over here?

Up on the third floor, the man from earlier made another bid for escape. He hopped out onto the fire escape while the others covered him. As he charged for the stairs, Laura realized he was carrying a leather luggage bag with gold clasps.

"He's got the amulets!" She pointed.

One of the men in the windows turned to aim at her, and with a yelp she darted toward the alley of the building behind her. She reached its relative safety without injury, and huddled in the shadow of the wall for five seconds before realizing Okane was missing. She scrambled back and looked around the corner, hoping he hadn't been shot. There was no one in the area where they'd been standing, so that was a relief—at least he wasn't dead—but she had to scan the wider area before she saw him. Okane was dashing toward the building. He took a running jump and caught the bottom rung of the fire escape ladder. With an almighty clatter it came loose, the bottom half rattling down toward the ground before clanging to a halt at its farthest point. Even before the frame stopped moving Okane swung himself up and scaled the ladder. He started sprinting up the fire escape.

"What are you doing?" Laura shouted, but either he didn't hear her or he wasn't paying attention.

Meanwhile the man with the bag had reached the top of the fire escape. He jumped onto the roof and glanced down to make sure the police were occupied. He spotted Okane and panicked. He looked around wildly before hurrying to the right. Laura saw him scuttle across a board that had been left to span the distance between this building and the next. He kicked the board so it toppled into the alleyway.

"Hey!" Laura called, trying to get one of the police officers' attention. "He's getting away!"

The officers were too preoccupied with the guns in the windows, and really, Laura didn't blame them. Okane somehow managed to get past the third floor. Laura wasn't sure how—she looked down at the officers for only a few seconds before looking up again, and somehow he'd managed to magic himself up to the fourth level and clamber onto the roof. He looked around, located the man, and started running after him. When he came to the edge of the roof there was a loud crack. He went sailing through the air, landing on the other roof with ease to continue his pursuit. That gap hadn't been impossibly wide, but it was still something too much for Laura to have attempted. His amulets must've been activated. She gaped before realization sank in. She was being left behind.

She ran down the alley in the direction they went. They couldn't pass across the wider street in front, so had to go either straight or risk jumping the alley above her head. Judging by the cracking noises, they chose straight. She couldn't see them from her position, though, and the cracking was getting farther ahead. Cursing, she touched the amulet at her hip, and the two in her shoes kicked into gear.

A shout rang out up ahead. She gained on it fast and drifted to the far right of the alley, craning her neck to see what was going on. She couldn't make it out through the clotheslines, but it seemed like Okane caught up. He did it in record time, jumping four buildings. He and the man were moving around up there, and she could hear unintelligible talking, but couldn't figure out what was going on. She glanced around for a way to get up there. The only way she could see was this building's fire escape. She backed up and glared at the ladder, trying to calculate how high she needed to jump to reach it, how much energy to pull out of the amulets since there was only so far they could go.

Before she could do anything, someone yowled. The luggage bag crash-landed in front of her with a shattering sound, like it had been filled with fragile pottery. Laura glanced up to see the shapes of the two people still moving, then down at the bag before she grabbed the clasps and ripped it open.

She reeled back just in time. A black tendril burst out and swiped.

It missed her by a foot and hit the pavement hard enough to break the surface. Belatedly it realized there was sunlight out here, and yanked itself back into the bag. Its sides heaved closed.

"Oh no you don't," Laura hissed, pulling out an Egg.

She kicked the side of the bag and jumped back. The infestation reared out again, purling unhappily. It barely had time to brandish its feelers at her before an armed Egg descended into it. The infestation jerked back into the bag, but it didn't have time to fumble before the Egg detonated. Light seared through the bag's sides, and the seams strained; three different pitches of screams came from it. Laura kicked it once more. While the clasps sagged open, all that came out was smoke. She ripped it all the way open and cracked another Egg over it. The smoke fizzled out fast, and she squinted in. Ten amulets of varying styles were there, all glittering with kin and all making popping sounds. Within moments they issued their final dark cloud.

A loud noise came from the top of the building. This one was a panicked yelp, and it was definitely Okane's. Laura sprang up, trying to see through the clotheslines, and she spotted something falling. As it got closer, she realized it was a some*one*.

"Okane!" she shrieked.

Her mind raced as she tried to think of what she could possibly do to help. She couldn't just try to catch him; he was falling five stories, and even if she managed to catch him, he'd flatten her. She had no clue what to do with the amulets that could help, either. As he passed the clotheslines, he flipped. Okane twisted like a cat in midair and landed on his feet. As his feet touched ground another loud snap rent the air, echoed by a series of smaller ones. Part of the alley beneath him buckled with a crunch, sending cracks into the hard surface. His fingertips brushed down as his knees bent, and then he shot up straight before losing balance and stumbling back. Shocked and clueless as to anything else to do, Laura reached out and steadied him. He reeled, but looked back at her in surprise.

"Are you okay?" Laura gasped.

"I don't know." He sounded normal enough. He looked down at himself, then back up. "I think I am. How did that just happen?"

"I don't know! Are you sure you didn't break your legs?"

"--- can't stand on broken legs, can ---?"

"I don't know! You're the one who just fell five stories!"

He stared, then started to pat himself down, searching for anything broken. Laura looked back up at the roof but couldn't see any sign of the other man.

"I'm good," Okane sighed.

How he could possibly be, Laura had no idea, but she wasn't going to question it too much.

"What happened up there?"

"I caught him." His eyes were distracted, flitting to follow something invisible and ignoring Laura's presence. "Managed to get the bag away . . . dropped it . . . then he pushed me over the side. And I landed." He looked pointedly at what was now plainly an indentation in the concrete, and gave Laura an expression that clearly showed he was questioning his sanity. "And I didn't die."

"If it helps at all, I'm very glad you didn't die."

"That helps everything." That was probably meant as sarcastic, but he was so out of it, it sounded genuine and weak.

"How about we go back to find Clae? Thanks to you we've got the amulets, and it might be nice to have police help right now."

Laura clipped the bag closed and picked it up. She began walking back the way they'd come, slowing down because Okane seemed unsteady on his feet. She held out her free arm, silently asking if he needed help, but he shook his head and kept walking. As he passed, Laura caught a strong whiff of vanilla, and her nose wrinkled. It brought a sharp pang of something like jealousy, and it took her a moment to realize why. The few times she'd been close to the drapes in the shop, she'd picked up on a faint smell of vanilla. She'd connected the two subconsciously. *How stupid*, she thought, and crushed that down. She was happy he was alive at all.

The more they walked the stronger his steps became, though he still weaved a little by the time they reached the original building. One police officer remained in the backyard, but there was no gunfight and not much noise from the building. The officer ran over as soon as she saw them.

"Where did you run off to?" she demanded. "You were supposed to have a police escort!"

"I tried to tell you we were leaving, but you were busy getting shot at," said Laura.

"You did?" She frowned, looked over her shoulder, and shouted, "Danny! You said you had this!"

A blond policeman looked at them from the first-floor window and gave an exaggerated shrug. The woman heaved a resigned sigh.

"And you, what were you thinking?" She glared at Okane.

"I wasn't."

"Obviously."

"We got the amulets, though!" Laura butted in, lifting the bag. "The man carrying them got away, but this is important, right?"

"Sure is."

"Did you get the mobsters?" Laura leaned to look at all the police moving around inside.

"The raid was for the most part successful. There was a safe full of amulets too. Your boss is taking care of that now."

"I'm done," called Clae's voice from the third floor. He leaned out one of the windows, peering down at them like a hawk. "What are you doing out there?"

Laura held the bag above her head. "Ten amulets purified! They looked barely formed, so they didn't have the power or smarts to do damage yet."

"Good job. I'll be right down." He hopped out onto the fire escape.

"Beyond that, we think we've got the majority of the mobsters in custody," the policewoman told them. "If they've got any more amulet stores, we'll go after those later. Once we get the locations out of the prisoners."

"Will you ask us to go with you on those raids, too?"

"It didn't look like we needed you this time, but we'll transport it all to you as soon as possible."

Clae dropped from the ladder with a thump and walked over to them. "How many Eggs did you use?"

"Two. It's packed, so they were all caught in the attacks." Laura undid the clips and held the bag open for him to look in. He glared at the contents, eyes flicking back and forth.

"With ten amulets, we don't know how much an Egg can properly purify. We'll unload them all at the shop and examine them thoroughly.

We've got to bring the safe-load with us too and transport it all to the Amuletory eventually, anyway." He caught a glimpse of Okane out of the corner of his eye and straightened up to regard him. "What happened to you?"

"Fell off a building," Okane admitted.

"How high?"

"I think she said five stories?" Okane muttered, glancing at Laura. "I'm fine, though. Nothing's broken or anything."

"Five goddamn stories," Clae hissed.

He pulled off his old coat and tossed it over Okane's head. Okane jumped, pushing the fabric out of his face to stare.

"I'm sorry, what is this?" he mumbled.

"Security blanket."

"That's not a blanket," said Laura.

"I can see that," Clae growled. "But he fell five goddamn stories. Security blanket. Coat works just as well."

"I don't—"

"Remember what I said about fight-or-flight? How it can go *seriously and completely wrong*? The last thing we need is you going into shock."

"Really, I'm fine," Okane insisted, trying to pull off the coat, but Clae gave him a look and he froze.

"Please just do this. If it has any effect, you'll need it. *Anselm*."

"Anselm. Right. Calm." Somewhat paler than before, Okane wrapped himself up in the coat. It looked far too small on him.

Clae rubbed his shoulders, but turned back to the building and shouted, "Hey! Hurry up in there!"

"Yes, sir!" came a hurried response.

After a minute the blond policeman came out, carrying another large bag. Clae took it from him.

"I've been ordered to remind you that there's some paperwork to go along with all this. You need to have it signed and turned in to the station by the weekend so it's not delayed too long. We need it all taken care of as soon as—"

"I know the drill," Clae snapped, hefting the bag into his arms.

"Just what I was ordered to say, that's all."

17

THE GIN CYCLE

Okane wore the coat all the way back to Acis Road. Every time he acted like he'd remove it, Clae turned to look at him. It wasn't like he was giving the stink eye or anything, just a blank look, but considering Okane's reaction he might as well have been; he pulled the coat tighter every time. They walked back to the shop in relative silence, but as they passed the Keedlers' bakery Clae spoke.

"I want you to work this weekend."

Laura pulled a face. "Are you planning to follow along on the next raid?"

"No. You're my apprentice and you should know how this works." He stepped up to the shop door.

Her reluctance faded in favor of curiosity. "How what works?"

"We're going to another city."

That didn't shed much light on things. Nevertheless, Laura perked up at the idea. The wilds outside the walls were dangerous and transport was expensive, so few people traveled on a whim.

They entered the shop. Clae deposited the briefcase and the amulet bag to lock the door behind them. Okane began to fidget.

"Clae?" Laura couldn't remember a time when Clae had locked the door during business hours. "What do you mean, we're going to a different city? What does that have to do with Sweeping?"

Her unease grew as Clae went to the windows. She'd never noticed blinds there but they were obviously present, as Clae pulled them down to block out the light. Laura and Okane shared an uneasy look.

"We're going to Puer for a trade," Clae explained. "It's supposedly an act of goodwill between cities, but more importantly it's a Sweeper gathering."

"Sweepers have gatherings?" said Okane.

"Once a year we travel to specifically chosen locations to exchange Gin."

Laura's brow furrowed. "Gin? We exchange our amulets?"

"Not quite."

Clae pushed aside the black drapes and walked behind them. Laura immediately brightened—was she finally going to see what was back there, what he was so protective of? The drapes wavered at his passing, and there was a shuffling sound before he came back out, carrying a rock. The sight made Laura's shoulders slump again. Really, a rock? He might as well have been keeping a collection of marbles. The object in question was a big, strangely shaped, light gray rock at least the size of a baby. The light from the Kin caught it and caused its surface to shimmer.

He set it down on a stool and beckoned them over. Laura approached cautiously. There was something strange and *warm* about this thing, and she couldn't help but relax as she got close. Light winked across it, and she swore she could faintly hear a child giggling. She glanced at Okane to see his reaction. He was entranced; this must've been completely different from what he'd been shown back there.

"This is Gin." Clae's voice snapped Laura back to attention. "I've told you before that Gin is a magic source. Amulets made from it never need to be refilled. That's because Gin is an individual strain of magic. It *is* the thing that regenerates other amulets."

"So that's the rock that's way under Amicae?" Laura remembered her father and how he talked about his work. *We have to be careful not to disrupt this silver rock. The chimneys and the silver, you don't go near those if you can help it.*

"This one is actually from under Vitae." Clae rested one hand on it. "Almost all of the cities are built on top of a Gin strain. It leaches energy into the earth around it, and people back then decided it had to be blessed or hallowed ground. Thought it was good luck to build homes on it."

"It winds through the earth like a snake," Okane whispered. "I remember it."

"You probably lived in the caves alongside it."

"--- know where that is?" Okane peeled his gaze away from the rock to peer up at him.

"Gin strains are found all over the main islands. You'd need an expert to locate a specific one."

"But you know where this one comes from." Laura didn't quite follow where this was going.

"The ones owned by Sweepers are registered and kept track of very closely. Part of the trading."

"Are you giving this back to Vitae, then?"

"We have a system going. Each city has two Gin stones like this. One is the Gin from under our city or region, and the other is rotated throughout the cities. Every year, Sweepers carry their foreign Gin to its next destination. Last year this one was in Avis. This year, Amicae. For the next year it'll be in Puer. There's a Gin stone from Amicae floating around somewhere in Ruhaile."

"So this is like a ceremony? A holiday?"

"Not the kind of ceremony you're thinking of, just part of the job. And networking. Some experts found subtle differences in the magic of each region and got scared that the monsters we hunt might be able to become immune to specific strains. The rotation is so the monsters won't be exposed to the same thing long enough to develop immunity. Stupid, but they're convinced."

"Stupid?"

"Gin is pure magic. Unfiltered magic like that wards off any monsters; it's instant death to them. You're not about to get immune if the essence of death comes down on your head. That's that."

"It's true. The Silverstone caves were always the safest place," Okane agreed.

Laura wasn't sure what he was talking about. Had he really lived underground?

"But it's also networking?" she pondered. "So you *are* in contact with a bunch of other Sweepers?"

"Haven't you seen all the letters going in and out? We talk about techniques and equipment mostly. Exchange of ideas."

Laura liked the sound of it. She wondered if the other Sweepers could give her tips. Maybe they gathered and talked about their experiences; that would be fascinating. Were the other places set up like Coronae, the way it had been presented in that old book?

"That takes place this weekend?"

"Yes. We'll be taking a train."

"We'll have to pack, then!" Laura turned her giddy smile on Okane.

"Oh, not you," Clae amended, and for a moment she was baffled.

"I'm not going?" asked Okane.

"What? Why not? You're an apprentice too!" Laura protested.

"He's not going because someone has to stay and watch the shop."

"Can't you get Brecht to do that? Or just keep it locked up?"

"We'll be gone several days and the Pits still need to be maintained. Besides, I'm not leaving that crone all access to this place."

"But—"

"Laura. We have a permanent Gin here. It's the key to making kin, and without it we're sunk. Look at this." He clapped his hand on the rock again. "Imagine what would happen if someone found out about this. How many amulets could be made from this stone? How much would even one of those little amulets go for in an auction?"

Just one Gin amulet had a massive price tag, and it would only need to be the size of a marble. She gave a low whistle. Even if Gin wasn't the big bad mystery of the drapes, Laura could see why he was so protective of them now.

"Exactly." Clae nodded at her understanding. "I've had wannabe thieves try to get in here before. I'm not risking this being unprotected."

"--- can't really think I can protect them," said Okane. "I'm just one person, and if the Sullivans—"

"The Sullivans aren't going to set foot on this street."

"What makes you think that?"

"I'm not the only one here they'd have to look out for, and I've made

it very clear to my *esteemed* neighbors that they have free rein over anything suspicious. Mr. Keedler is an ex-military man with a collection of
guns, and the pawnshop owner is very handy with baseball bats. They'll
take care of the outside. You just have to make this place look inhabited."

Okane still looked dubious but nodded. Clae eyed them both, strummed
his fingers on the rock again, and went to pick it up.

"Clae?" Laura piped up.

"What?"

"I'm more experienced with how things work here. Are you sure I
shouldn't be the one staying?" She glanced at Okane as she spoke. A little
demon in her gut railed at her to *shut up, this is the kind of big job you've
wanted,* but she tried to quash it. She wanted to be an amazing Sweeper,
be significant, but at what cost? She didn't like the idea of him being left
alone, especially not when Sullivan might be waiting to catch him again.
To her he still seemed woefully inept, in need of guidance.

"I'll be fine," said Okane. He didn't look terribly confident, but sent
her a small smile. "I know I look like a goldbrick, but I've been learning
a few things. I won't let the place burn down if ---'re gone a few days."

"But—"

"He's right. What he said at the temple. I need to pull my own weight.
Stop pulling --- down."

"It's because you're more experienced that you need to go," said Clae,
pushing past the drapes again. "It's part of the requirement to become an
actual Sweeper instead of apprentice."

"I'm moving up?" She stared at the cloth, baffled.

"You've been functioning like a regular Sweeper for a while now. The
trip will just make it official. We'll be gone at least four days. Two traveling, two or more in the city. Make sure you're ready to go."

∞∞∞

When she went home, Laura was excited to share the news. Morgan
would probably dread her leaving, but both she and Cheryl would be excited at the same time. It was late notice, but still. Maybe if she dug out
her savings Laura could buy them a souvenir.

"I'm back," she called as she came in.

"Great timing," said Morgan. "Could you grab the pepper?"

Laura did so without question. Morgan was busy putting diced chicken and soup into a pan, and shook the offered pepper in without even pausing to measure. The kitchen was already full of rich and wonderful smells, and dishes like fish croquettes, creamed potatoes, and steamed apples were set on the table. Cheryl hovered by the door in a very Okane-esque way, eyes set on the apples.

"Looks like a tasting night," said Laura. "Are we your testers, or have you invited people over?"

"We'll be eating with some coworkers," said Morgan. "The boss wants a new menu ready by spring, so he's given us a bit of extra budget to experiment with. If I can get some of the other workers on my side, I might be able to contribute."

Laura laughed. "You're still trying to get into the yearly cookbook, aren't you?"

Morgan smiled. "It's only a matter of time. Much as they don't want to admit it, I'm a perfectly good cook."

"Well, if I have anything to say about it, this is the year." Laura sniffed at the air. "What are you making now?"

"Chicken soufflé."

"I thought soufflé was dessert," said Cheryl.

"This one will taste so good, it may as well be. It's a shame my coworkers could only work today into their schedules, or I might've been able to share all this with your parents."

Laura stiffened. "My parents?"

"Of course." Morgan switched over to a new bowl and a veritable army of eggs. "Remember? They're on leave starting this weekend."

Laura hadn't remembered. Her father worked underground in Amicae's interior or satellite towns, mining for coal and expensive rock; her mother tended the farmland outside Amicae. Both worked long shifts, but always made sure their breaks lined up with each other's. A perfect opportunity for family bonding, one would think, but it wasn't. They were still stuck somewhere in the honeymoon stages of romance and had eyes only for each other. Laura had always felt like a mistaken by-product of their marriage more than a thought-out decision; obligation for the situation more than family.

"I won't be here this weekend."

Morgan cracked an egg a little too hard and clicked her tongue as both yolk and whites slipped into the bowl. "What do you mean? Where will you be instead?"

"A business trip." Laura pushed herself away from the counter and toward the front hallway and its closet to put away her coat.

"I didn't know you had those. Where will it be? I hear the First Quarter has some luxurious lodgings."

Laura opened the closet door. "It's in Puer."

All the sound in the kitchen paused. "But that's a whole different city."

"I know."

"Why would you be in a different city?"

"Meeting with other Sweepers." Laura shrugged. "They exist."

There was a mirror on the inside of the closet door; she caught her reflection as she hung up her coat and paused to look at it. She looked different. Her face wasn't so round, freckles dotted across her nose, her ashy blond hair in a tangle and her eyes altered in a way she couldn't pinpoint. She looked older than she had even when she'd joined up as a Sweeper. But she knew that her parents wouldn't notice any change if they looked at her. No, she thought, tracing a small scar on her forehead—an unfortunate reminder of one of her first infestations—they'd probably ask her how class was going, despite her having graduated years ago.

When she turned back to the rest of the apartment, Morgan had looked away from her cooking.

"Are you sure that's a good idea? There are monsters out there."

"I'm traveling with a man who preys on them for a living. Trust me. I'll be back, unharmed, before you can miss me."

"That's hard to do. I miss you all the time."

"Blegh," said Cheryl.

Morgan's lips pulled in a smile and she swooped down to hug her daughter, despite the indignant squeal. "And I miss you too, every day that you're at school!"

Laura rolled her eyes and went back to the kitchen to sit in front of the steamed apples. Cheryl escaped shortly, and thundered in to hide under the table. Morgan went back to her cooking but brandished a spoon at Laura.

"It's not like I can stop you, but let us know that you got there safely, all right? Give us a telephone call or something."

"That would cost a fortune," Laura laughed. "How about a letter? It wouldn't be fast, but it's worth a try."

Cheryl peeked out, eyes wide in excitement. "Send me stamps!"

"I can't remember you ever wanting those before."

"It's her newest interest," said Morgan. "She might rival your collage someday."

"Then I'll be sure to send some. And if you want, I'll ask Clae about his mail. He gets letters from other Sweepers all the time, and it's not like he can use those stamps again."

Cheryl looked as if Underyear had come early.

"Will you be sending anything to the lovebirds?" said Morgan.

Laura's smile faded again. "No. It's not like they'll notice either way."

Morgan gave a sad hum, but didn't deny it. "I'm sorry they're like this."

"It's not your fault. Besides, with this perfectly timed trip, I don't have to deal with them at all."

"If they do start asking, I'll cover for you," said Morgan. "I have a long list of flaws with my sister, so if she tries nagging you about anything, I have more than enough blackmail to shut her mouth."

"But weren't you going to nag Laura tonight?" said Cheryl.

Laura was thrown off for a moment, then narrowed her eyes. "Those coworkers of yours, are they the ones from that last matchmaking scheme?"

"No they are not! One of them *may* be an eligible bachelor, but I won't throw him at you while you're dealing with bigger issues. Just relax and enjoy our company-sponsored feast. Actually, start on those apples. By the time I'm done with this they'll be cold."

Laura laughed as she and Cheryl each took one.

"Thanks," she said.

"For what?" said Morgan, already turned back to the soufflé. "Cooking is my hobby."

18

AIREDALE

Three days later, November first, Laura stood in the cable car station of the Sixth Quarter. It was nearly 4:00 A.M. The sky above was strewn with bright stars, a faint ribbon of blue and purple winding through like a wake in muddy water. The chill in the air made Laura shiver and shrink further into her coat. Beside her, Clae popped up his collar.

"It's almost winter," he observed. "They say it'll be a cold one. Maybe it'll even snow."

Laura muttered darkly, stuffing her hands into her pockets. He watched her, unimpressed, as the cable car retreated up the line. The policemen accompanying them averted their gazes.

"What are you waiting for, then?" Clae asked, looking at them. "Take us to the train."

"Of course, sir," the first replied. He had freckles all across his face, and his name tag read A. COLLINS. "If you'll come this way."

The train station was relatively close to the cable car stop. There weren't many shacks or military buildings nearby, just tracks, idling train cars, and the Union Depot rising like a behemoth over it all. They didn't go to the depot, though. They detoured over more rails, to a set of cars all hooked up and ready to go. The steam engine loomed in front, more black against the dark sky. The shape showed it was a steamer, but the silver-rimmed wheels revealed amulet assistance; this would move much faster than the usual train.

"This is the one," Collins pointed out. "You can put your luggage in the storage cars. We've got you a compartment in the second passenger car."

Clae squinted at the cars. "Is that a sleeper?"

"I'm afraid not. We had some trouble with the train system. The one you were supposed to be in still hasn't left Gaudium, so we had to scramble."

"It was either get you in second class on this one or have you resort to hobo travel," added the other policeman.

"Hobo travel might be interesting," said Laura.

"They throw hobos off in the middle of the wilds," said Clae.

"Spoilsport."

"How's the security on this one? Do we have the Rails Sweepers or the ERA troops?"

Railway companies hired Sweepers and regular fighters to protect trains on their way through the wilds. ERA (Eastern Rail Alliance) was a group of fighters who focused on the more common obstacle: animals that ran out of the wilds to attack trains. Felin sometimes charged slow trains and smashed through the windows, so ERA troops were there to gun them down before passengers could be injured. ERA Sweepers cleared any infestations on the tracks.

The policemen looked uncomfortable. "No. You were supposed to have a large ERA guard, but again, their train is in Gaudium."

"Then what's our replacement?" Silence answered him, and he raised a disbelieving brow. "Are you trying to tell me that you're sending more than half of your Sweeper department into the wilds without an escort?"

"We tried to reallocate ERA workers from other details, but they're refusing to help. It sounds like the company's willing to fire anyone who sets foot out of line, so it doesn't matter to them how important this is. We don't have the leverage to make them do anything without the railway companies' approval, and we can't get those people to agree on anything."

"*Lovely*," Clae sneered.

"The train is scheduled to depart very soon." Collins glanced at the depot's giant clock. "I'd advise you get on now."

He knocked on the door of one of the cars, and the side rattled open. A light inside illuminated stacks of crates and bags, and a shabbily dressed man. The man leaned out and grumbled, "You took your time."

"Unfortunately," said Collins.

The shabby man rolled his eyes and held out his hands. "Let's have it, then."

The police watched Clae suspiciously, like they thought he wouldn't comply. He certainly didn't look happy.

"Mr. Sinclair, regulations state—"

"I know the regulations, and they're ridiculous." Nonetheless he hefted up one of the bags he was carrying, enough so the man could catch hold of it, but didn't let go. "You are going to take care of this like it's worth more than your life. As far as I'm concerned, it is. If I find that this has been opened, damaged, lost, or changed in any way I will find you and make you wish you'd never been born."

"Scary," the man deadpanned.

Clae's eyes narrowed, but he relinquished his grip. Laura watched this with a furrowed brow.

"Come on, let's get you seated so the train can go."

"Sounds good to me," she grumbled. "It's warmer on the train, right?"

There were two passenger cars closer to the engine. The first looked a little fancier, so that was probably the first-class sleeping car Clae mentioned. The second wasn't quite so elaborate. Up by the front of this second car, some steps led up onto a little railed-in balcony and door. Collins led them up and opened the door to bring them inside, into a narrow hallway with thin mauve carpeting. He walked halfway down the hall and slid open the door on his right.

"Here's your compartment. An attendant will be checking in on you, and breakfast should be brought in around six thirty. Other meals will also be provided. If everything goes smoothly, you should arrive in Puer somewhere a little after midnight."

"Are we expecting bumps?" asked Laura, walking up beside him.

"You always should," Clae muttered darkly.

"Do you need anything else?" asked Collins, ignoring Clae's pessimism.

"Go tell the conductor to get moving already. If we're out of the depot we can't be waiting for any more people."

"Of course. If you do end up needing anything, ask the attendant. Safe travels, sir."

The policemen inclined their heads before leaving. Laura sighed.

"I suppose that's it, then. We're on the road."

"Not until this train gets moving, we're not," said Clae, sweeping into the compartment.

It was small, enough to fit two benches facing each other with a decent amount of legroom between them. Four people could squeeze onto each of those benches. Shelves loomed overhead with thick netting to keep luggage in place, and the far wall was a window from waist height to four inches from the ceiling. The plain electric light on the ceiling made it hard to discern anything in the dark beyond the window. Even with that dark, Clae walked over and drew the curtain.

"Sit there." He gestured to the seat on his left. "It's easier to go forward than backward. I don't want you getting sick on me."

"How thoughtful."

They put their luggage in the racks above and Laura sat with a heavy sigh. The cushions of the bench were worn but not uncomfortable.

"Hey Clae?"

"What?" he grunted, fussing over the placement of his bag.

"Why did you give away the Gin?"

"I didn't."

"What?"

"The police seem to think Gin can be transported the same way you transport regular goods, and they seem to think that *baggage handlers* are sufficient protection. Lies. Gin has been stolen in transit before today, even with ERA on the lookout. I'm not taking any chances here."

"If you didn't give them the Gin, what did you give them?"

"Eggs. That was our backup bag." He patted the side of the luggage in the rack. "This one is Gin. The police would've had a fit if I tried withholding it, so I 'confused' the bags. We poor, overworked Sweepers can only be expected to remember so much."

"Ha! Nice." Laura felt both relief and wariness. She was glad the Gin was nearby and safe, but . . . "What will they think if they open the other up and see Eggs?"

"They aren't supposed to peek in the first place. Part of some ridiculous treaty the cities signed, same one that states Gin be carried in the luggage car. It's a load of bull."

Clae gravitated to the light switch. Laura had thought it was a simple switch, but instead he twisted it and the light dimmed.

"What are you doing?"

"Turning it down so I can sleep."

"But it's a train."

Trains were new. Trains were exciting. Laura didn't want to miss anything.

"Trains are to sit and sleep in," Clae grouched. "Should've been on the sleeper car."

"But we can see the wilds from here!" Laura gestured at the window.

"Not at this hour." He pulled something down from the rack and tossed it at her. She caught it before realizing it was a blanket. "We have a long way to go and I'm not getting to Puer without sleep."

The light was just barely on now. He sat down opposite her, wrapping a blanket of his own over his coat as he closed his eyes. Laura scowled, but it wasn't bright enough for him to see it even if his eyes were open. She scooted closer to the window and pushed the curtain to peer out. She could make out the faint shapes of other cars on nearby tracks. There were winking lights and the faint glow of the depot, but other than that, not much.

She kept looking until a whistle shattered the quiet. She jumped and almost smacked her head on the glass. There was a shudder and a jolt, a screech, and she realized they were moving. It took a while but the train gained speed, the lights outside going faster and faster past them. The dull, rattling roar stayed with them as the wheels moved, and Laura waited with bated breath for them to reach the wall.

There weren't many openings in the main wall of Amicae, and what few existed were usually barred shut. Farmland might surround the city, but beyond that stretched the wilds and their monsters; beyond that, more cities. Cities like Rex could be worse than the monsters. Thus the wall, the doors, and the military standing by, alert for any sign of assault. Laura had never seen the doors but her mind conjured up the doors of a castle, grand and ominous and beautiful.

She didn't see them.

The doors must've been open, because the train entered a tunnel. All light outside was eclipsed, the noise of the train amplified. It lasted ten seconds before abruptly returning to normal. There was no light now, but they had to be out of the doorway.

Laura couldn't see anything no matter how long she stared. She fell asleep at some point. She wasn't sure when or how but she came around, coherent enough to know that leaning her face against the wall was really uncomfortable. She slid down to lie on the bench, pulled the blanket tighter, and nodded off again.

The next time she woke up, it was to the sound of knocking. She blinked her eyes open and looked at Clae, expecting him to answer it, but he was so far gone he was actually snoring. There came another knock and a muffled voice.

"Pardon me, but I have your breakfast."

The mere mention made her stomach growl. She glanced at the window, still dark, and forced herself up to get the door. On the other side was a thin-faced man dressed in a red and gold uniform. He smiled nervously.

"Good morning, miss. Am I correct in thinking there are two people in this compartment?"

"That's right." Laura rubbed her face to wake herself up more. "He's sleeping like a log, though."

"Wonderful. If I may?"

Laura stepped back, and he wheeled in a metal cart covered in a white cloth. He parked it between the benches and pulled off the lid, revealing silver plates full of food. The spread looked like the dishes served at the Sullivans' house, much of the same recipes with a different flair.

"Please enjoy your meal. I'll return later to clean up."

The man smiled again and backed out, shutting the door behind him. Laura nudged Clae.

"We have food. Wake up." Clae didn't stir, so she swatted his shoulder a little harder. "Hey. Come on, eat."

His eyes cracked open to glare at her, and she judged that good enough. She gestured grandly at the food and went back to her seat. She dug into the skillet closest to her.

"This is really good," she mumbled through a mouthful, impressed.

"*Professional chefs,*" Clae growled.

He took a piece of toast but otherwise tried to go back to sleep. Since he drifted off, Laura felt no remorse in picking at the best bits of his food as well. Twenty minutes later the attendant returned. He smiled at her yet again as he retrieved the cart and left. Door closed once more, Laura settled in to sleep.

She woke a third time with light streaming through the curtains. When she saw it she jolted up and yanked the curtains open. Clae made a disgruntled noise but she didn't notice.

Outside the window the sun had risen and the sky was pale blue, not a cloud in sight. It was paler toward the horizon, but the land below wasn't flat or covered in farm fields. The ground rose up, jagged and towering into the sky, completely covered in dense trees. Shadows marked the clumps and maybe individual plants, but the ground itself couldn't be seen for the abundance of them. Smaller heights jutted up along the sides of the larger, casting more shadows and making it all the more breathtaking.

"Are those *mountains*?" she whispered, awed.

"Why are you so excited? You can see mountains from Amicae," Clae grumbled.

"But those are just little bumps in the distance. Look! There are little ones too! And look at all the trees!"

"You said you didn't like trees."

"I never said that, you're just obsessed with your own tree."

"You can still see them from Amicae."

"Because a blue shadow is so interesting. You can only see them on a good day anyway. Everything you can see clearly is crops. Crops, crops, and more crops. I'm sick of looking at crops and walls."

"So become a Ranger. What are you doing working as a Sweeper if you're sick of walls?" Clae scoffed.

"You hired me."

"You asked for the job."

This was true. Laura dropped the topic. "If this is an annual meeting, you must've been on trains before. Is it all like this outside the cities?"

"In the area around Amicae it typically is. Go further and there are flat areas, valleys, and cliffs. They need somewhere to record their films."

"I never thought of that. Some are filmed in the wilds, aren't they?"

"They have high security for those, but yes."

"Have you ever seen any? Are they visible from the train?"

"No."

"Then how—"

"It's common sense."

"What's it like around Puer, then?"

"Flat."

"That's helpful."

"If you want to know about the damn landscape, go out and stand on the back of the car, look all you want. Just let me sleep already."

"Fine. Go ahead and waste the experience," Laura grouched as she drew the curtains again.

"Family business," he called after her.

Laura shut the compartment door behind her. She found it hard to balance on this train now that she thought about it. It shook enough to make her unsteady, but she stumbled down the mauve aisle to the back door. She could see a little of the outside through a round window, but it wasn't enough. She hesitated, but set her hand on the handle. It took a moment to work up the nerve, but she opened the door. The balcony on the back of the car provided enough room for her to step out. She set her hands on the railing and leaned out to look at the mountains. The air was fresh. It didn't smell like baking bread, or the inside of the city, or anything else she could think of. It was kind of wonderful.

"It would be interesting to live out here," she mumbled to herself.

"Not particularly."

The voice made her jump. The attendant from earlier stood in the open doorway, looking apologetic.

"Didn't mean to scare you, miss. Just saw the door open and thought I'd check. I don't want anyone falling off the train."

"People have fallen off?"

"Mostly drunk ones," the attendant admitted. "They try to jump off, claim they're off to conquer the wilds. We catch them, though."

"I just came out to get a better look at the view."

"Did you? Well, watch your step anyway. The railing's there for a reason, but it's not foolproof."

The attendant made to go inside and shut the door, but paused halfway through. After some hesitation he asked, "I don't mean to be a bother, but how did you get to traveling with that airedale?"

"Airedale?"

It took a moment, but he realized she had no idea what he was talking about. "Oh, sorry. Hobo term. It means 'extreme loner.' Guy who doesn't travel with anyone else. In all the time I've worked here, whenever I see him he's always been alone."

Family business rang in Laura's head again, and she asked, "How long have you been working here?"

"Ten years."

"Oh. Well, I work with him. This is sort of a business trip. He only hired me a few months ago."

"That makes sense." The attendant nodded. "If nothing else, he's more tolerable with company. If you don't mind me saying so. Have a nice ride, miss."

He shut the door.

After a while, Laura left. The mountains continued to be amazing, but there was only so long she could look at something that, while varying, tended to stay pretty similar. Tree-covered mountains looked beautiful but got repetitive. She went back to the compartment in time to catch the attendant when he brought lunch (another grand spread she had to wake Clae for), and ended up falling asleep again. The train was like an uncomfortably rocking cradle. She woke a few times, peeked out the window, and dropped off again. There wasn't anything to do beyond look or sleep.

Eventually the land outside melted flatter as they went through dips and channels between mountains. Over the day Laura saw many plants and animals, including several canir in a pack, deerlike creatures with broad white stripes down their sides and black tufts of fur at the eyes that scattered across a valley as the train approached, and dark shadows of wheeling birds. The ruins of a city long abandoned could be glimpsed through a gap between mountains, and Clae informed her the place was called Thrax. Laura had heard of Thrax in her history books, so actually seeing it was exciting.

Thrax was once a thriving city, but it was host to a lot of native refugees and welcomed their influence. The surrounding cities weren't fond of their policies or their plainly Immortalist leanings, so no one was motivated to help when Rex swooped in to attack them. Everyone thought they'd fight Rex off and life would go on as usual, but Thrax was razed and its people slaughtered. That sent the rest of Orien into an uproar and paved the way for the current alliances. The cities weren't irrevocably bound to each other, but there were conditions now so if any city was attacked, others would come to its aid. They already had monsters to worry about; they didn't need the threat of extermination via neighbors hanging over their heads too.

"Clae?" she muttered, still staring out the window at the ruins of Thrax. "What kind of ceremony is it that we have to do in Puer?"

Clae shuffled under his blanket, scowling. "We exchange Gin. That's the most ceremonial part of the deal. It's a delicate matter and only the head Sweepers can do it properly, but it doesn't take very long."

"And the part about my promotion?"

"That's not so much a ceremony as it is a formality? Or maybe not even formality. It's not even an official rule for the cities. It's just a rule among Sweepers. Before an apprentice can move up to a regular Sweeper position, they have to be recognized by the wider community. They're presented at another city, to another group, by their head Sweeper. So I'll introduce you to them, and they'll get the message that you're important and pass it on to other cities themselves. You might not know it, but Sweepers are horrible gossips."

"Why do I have to be presented at another city? Why not just Amicae?"

"Because I could introduce anyone in Amicae. I could introduce a Sweeper to the Keedlers if I wanted to, but that doesn't mean anything to them. I could introduce a baby, but that doesn't make them recognize it as a Sweeper. You have to go out of your way for it. If you aren't presented to them properly they won't accept your status when you're promoted. Amicae could make you head Sweeper, but that doesn't mean any other Sweepers will listen to you if they think you weren't presented right or not worthy of the position. Appease them if you want to succeed, because once you're introduced they'll start networking with you too, and the more friends you have in other cities the more help you'll get if you find yourself in trouble. So, you're being presented. You don't have to do anything, so long as you're there and they learn your name."

"That's it?"

"That's it. It's worth it in the long run, believe me."

"But you seriously network with other cities? Seems kind of out of character for you."

"How else am I getting news on Rex and infestation movements?" he retorted, sour. "There, I talked."

"But—"

"I refuse to face that woman unless I am completely alert. Now let me be."

"That woman"? He must've made enemies out of some of his contacts after all.

Laura turned back to the window while he rolled over. The train took a turn and the wreckage of Thrax vanished behind a small mountain.

The sun reached its zenith and descended, more and more until the sky bled pinkish orange and it vanished entirely. With the gathering darkness it grew easier to sleep undisturbed.

19

DERAILING

Laura lazed about until it was very dark. During one of her light dozes, Clae's eyes snapped open again. He stared straight forward.

"Something's wrong."

"Huh?" Laura mumbled intelligently.

Clae stood, shucking off the blanket as he did. He put a hand to the amulet on his belt and frowned.

"Something's happening back in the storage cars."

A moment of hesitation, then he pulled the Gin back down, making for the door.

"What do you mean? How do you know that?" Laura tottered after him.

Clae opened the door and stalked down the hallway. "There's very little spell work that can actually be practiced, and I used one on the Eggs. Sends a signal to my amulets if something's wrong."

"Something like what?" Laura woke quickly. She'd had more than enough time to sleep.

"Like an infestation, or if it senses it's going into the wrong hands. I placed it in case any thieves did try to pull something. We can catch them.

Probably Rex, the bastards. Gaudium isn't far from Amicae, but it's still southerly and they range far. Maybe the Amicae invasion was just a distraction for a larger operation."

"But how can Eggs tell any of that? They don't have a brain or hive mind to think with."

"Eggs take on the will of their parent Gin. Gin is somewhat sentient, not on the level of a person or an animal, but enough to know it likes something and enough to sense danger."

"So this 'will of the Gin' is sending you an SOS right now."

"That's right."

"Hang on, if it's really Rex causing trouble, shouldn't we be staying away? They won't be getting the Gin anyway, and the police were really adamant about keeping us away from them."

"They'll check the bag before they leave the train, obviously. We'll get the drop on them before they come looking for us."

"But the police—"

"They don't want to lose us, but Rex knows my reputation. Idiots or not, they'll retreat if they don't have proper backup. Besides, I've got a gun. It may be for kin, but if I aim right I can kill the bastards."

He opened the car door. Outside it was pitch black, but a lamp on the back of this car and another on the front of the one connected gave enough illumination for them to cross over the gap without trouble. Smoke filtered back from the engine—Laura nearly choked on it. The door to the storage car opened easily and they walked in. It looked much the same as the other one they'd seen, crates and bags of supplies bound for the north, with faint lights on the ceiling. No one visible.

"Did you see where that man put it?" Laura looked around at the cargo. None looked like the supply bag.

"Two more cars back. I can track it with the amulets."

They crossed into the next car, and were barely through the door when somebody ran smack into them. It was the man they'd met earlier, the one who took the bag. Another baggage handler came just behind him. Clae caught him by the jacket.

"Where do you think you're going?"

"The hell out of here!" The man tried to wrestle free.

"Didn't I say that bag was more important than your life? What are you running from?"

"The monster, obviously!" the man spat.

"A monster?" Laura echoed. "What kind?"

"It was black," said the other handler, terrified. "It was big and black and it was everywhere and gaining on us—"

"Did it have a shape?"

"You mean beyond *slimy*?"

"So it's just an infestation," Clae growled, letting go.

"Infestation. We can deal with that." Laura gave a shuddering sigh of relief.

"And of course it has the backups. Did you bring equipment?"

"I've got two Eggs and a couple Bijou."

"So you've taken that lesson to heart." Clae sounded pleased. "That makes three Eggs between us, a stock of Bijou, and a few rounds of bullets. I've dealt with worse."

From what Laura remembered, that kind of ammunition could take out a smaller infestation easily. Of course, if this was a *big* infestation and they had no cover, they might be screwed. If Okane had come along he would've sensed the monster and they wouldn't have to deal with this at all.

"You're going to fight it?" cried the man, incredulous. "You're not ERA Sweepers!"

"It's our job, regardless of location. Stay back here." Clae pulled out one of his guns with his free hand. He paused, a muscle jumping in his cheek, and set down the Gin bag. He gave the handlers the meanest glare Laura had seen him make. "Don't touch that bag. If I get back to find you sifting through my drawers, I will not hesitate to shoot you. If I'm out of bullets, I'll gouge your eyes out." He brandished the gun, and the men drew back in fear.

Laura followed him over to the next balcony, but they hesitated by the door. Clae glanced through the window and let out a frustrated noise.

"It's all over the cargo."

"So it's a big one."

"It must've been festering in some of the luggage. They loaded it on without realizing what was in there. Like those mobsters earlier."

"So this is just coincidence?"

"Gin only travels once a year, so I'm not believing in coincidence. Might still be Rex after all, using an infestation to do their dirty work and waiting to pick up the spoils at the next stop."

"You did say they were after our Sweeper secrets." Laura took a steadying breath. "So what's our plan?"

Clae looked all around, back to the door, and after a moment of consideration, slammed his elbow into the window. The glass smashed and he pulled out an Egg, nicking it against his amulet before lobbing it through the hole. Laura heard it clatter against the floor and ducked down to the side of the platform. There was a pause, and then it blew. The explosion made the entire car buck. Wood burst up and out from the back of the car, twenty feet into the air before raining down. Two sets of screeching rent the air, one the monster cry Laura was used to, the other more metallic. She leaned out, looking down the side of their car, to see that the back end was completely mutilated. The force of the blast had snapped the connection between the train cars. The one behind theirs actually reared up into the air. It twisted, creating that metallic shriek as the rest of the cars derailed. The cacophony fell behind quickly, out of earshot and out of sight.

"Holy crap," Laura breathed. "Did that—did we blow up the backups just then?"

"Stop staring and start attacking!"

The door had burst open too, and they slipped in quickly. Starting halfway down the car, the ceiling and walls were missing. Much of the cargo had been blown off too, though one of the remaining bags was ripped open and leaking letters. The creature itself remained, clinging to a pile of crates just out of the way of the blast area.

Clae lifted his arm and shot. The creature pulled out of the line of fire just in time, and the bullet buried itself into a crate with a flash and a crash of splintering wood. The monster scuttled on a multitude of legs that stretched just enough to reach the ground, its body twisting long like a millipede.

"Ugh, that's nasty."

"It's not moving far." Clae's eyes tracked its movement. "The source is in that pile."

The creature bunched together. It grew larger on one side, then the other, a spiraling kind of movement that made Laura think of swirling batter in a frying pan. Its top surface began to bubble.

"Get out your Eggs."

Laura reached back to the bag on her belt to grab them, but all her fingers found was the soft cloth of the bag. Horror dawned as she searched more desperately, craning her head around to look as she sifted through. The Eggs weren't in her bag. All that was left was a pair of Bijou.

"They're gone! I had them just a second ago!" She checked all her other pockets and dug into the bag again to no avail. "I think one of those people pickpocketed me!"

She expected Clae to be very unhappy with this, but didn't expect him to grab her arm and heave her to the other side of the car. As it turned out, that was a good thing. The creature's bubbling had burst into a black smokescreen. All its many legs split apart and surged along the car, ripping up the wood floor and sending the luggage crashing down. They narrowly avoided one of these legs, only for it to curl and heave the planking up behind them. The sudden hole showed off the welded framework of the car and the ground flashing below; Laura leapt to avoid it. The rest of the legs wreaked havoc. She heard what was left of the side door wrench away, almost deafening her to Clae's shout.

"Get back to the other car!"

"Don't have to tell me twice!"

They dashed out the open door and leapt across the gap into the forward car again. There was a shout. They ducked down just in time for something to sail over their heads. Inside the car they ran into the baggage handlers again.

"Did you see that?" cried the younger, ecstatic. "I told you I had great aim!"

Confused, Laura looked back. There was shattered glass by the doorway of the other car, with gold liquid pooled on the ground with it. *The Eggs.* They hadn't been armed properly. The creature stopped short by the mess, skirting the edges before realizing that the fragments were harmless and plowing straight over them.

"You stole those?" Laura demanded, glaring at the handler.

His smile faltered. "Yes? But look, I helped out—"

Laura stared at him in incredulity for a moment, then punched him in the face. Almost immediately she regretted it, because that *hurt*. He reeled in surprise and his friend stepped up, furious. Clae caught him.

"Let go of me! You can't attack railroad personnel!"

"Considering it was obvious theft, I don't think the railroad will be taking your side on this one."

"It's life or death, there's a monster on board!" the man roared.

"And you chose death," Clae retorted. "You realize you went and destroyed valuable, irreplaceable equipment here."

"But that's how Sweepers use them!" defended the younger, hand up to cup his reddening cheek.

"Are you a Sweeper? I don't think so," Clae scoffed.

"They were by the depot in Avis, I saw how it worked! I'd make a better Sweeper than either of you two if that equipment wasn't faulty!"

Laura made a strangled noise and cracked the knuckles of her other hand. The young man's eyes widened and he backpedaled. So much for being a better, braver Sweeper.

"Look. Due to your actions, it's likely that this infestation will take over the entirety of this train." When the younger opened his mouth to protest, Clae cut him off. "You stole highly specialized weapons without knowing how they work and broke them. We don't have backups available to fix what you've done—our other Eggs are either destroyed or miles behind us by now. I have bullets that can delay it, but we can't destroy the infestation without them."

"So what, we jump off the train?" asked Laura.

"We're not abandoning the train."

"But we have to," said the man.

"You said there were Sweepers in Avis. Did they send something in this train?" asked Clae.

"What do you mean?"

"I mean did they load something meant for another Sweeper gathering?"

"They were working," the younger muttered sullenly.

"But did they send anything?"

The man hesitated. "They had us load a crate. Why?"

"If we're lucky, they sent some equipment. Maybe an Egg."

"That's what can kill that thing?"

"Yes."

Clae let go, and the man moved off toward a pile of crates.

"It's over here. Come on, brat, help me get it out."

A horrible shriek caught Laura's attention. The creature had heaved its body to the door, but there it caught the light of the lantern. Even if they had no ERA guard, the train must've been wired to prevent infestations; the lantern on that car guttered brighter, bluer, and the infestation smoked as if burned. It retreated again, but continued lashing out. Thirty ropelike limbs swung through the door, crashing and rending the balcony area. Wood panels splintered. The rail bent easily as fabric under a single blow. The light flickered. The rest of the world was still horribly dark, stars covered by clouds now; once it disabled the lamps it would move fast.

The baggage handlers were by the luggage, trying to move crates. Clae helped them unearth a large crate with PUER SWEEPERS GUILD emblazoned in red lettering on the top and sides. The man dug out a couple of crowbars and they set to work ripping off the lid. It didn't take much time. The lid came off with a groan, revealing checkered blankets inside. Clae reached in and rummaged around, flipping the blanket away.

"This looks too big for Eggs," said Laura.

"It's not Eggs at all." Clae leaned back and looked at her. "It's a gun."

Laura moved closer and peered in. That *was* a gun. A machine gun. Laura had seen some in films but never in reality. For all she knew, not even the Amicae military had one.

"You can't be serious."

Clae pulled out a few papers from the side of the box and looked over them quickly.

"It's a prototype kin weapon. Works like my guns, just longer range, more power, faster."

"Do you know how to work it?"

"What do I look like, a soldier?"

"I've got this," the man butted in. "I was in the army back home."

"You used a machine gun?" asked Laura.

"Not officially, but my buddy showed me how. I can make it work."

"Good." Clae looked at the door. "Here's the plan. This gun shoots kin bullets . . ." ("Whatever the hell that is," the younger man grumbled.) ". . . so it'll drive the infestation back. Force it as far as you can. Laura, you and I are going forward."

"To get the attendant?"

"To get to the infestation. We're going to use the Gin like an Egg."

Laura had no idea how that was supposed to work, but the baggage handlers had heaved the gun out of the box and were setting it up.

"Come on, we're going onto the back. And you, shoot through the doorway, not at us."

"Got it."

Clae picked up the discarded carpetbag. This in hand, they went back onto the platform and stayed as far from the door as possible. The monster was barely feet from them, still railing at a doorway too mauled to be recognizable. Its next swipe wrenched a chunk of the frame back with it, and the light went out. For a split second Laura's heart stopped and she was sure it was loose, but there was a crack to her left and the lamps of their own car flared to life. The infestation's limbs had crossed half the distance. At the light it stopped short, squealed, and pulled itself back to shelter. Laura forced herself to breathe.

"How long do you think these lights can hold it back?"

Clae was more preoccupied with squinting at the darkness beyond the train, clutching the bag with a white-knuckled grip. He clicked his tongue and looked forward again. "Long enough."

20

BONE POLISHER

The machine gun rattled to life. The sound was harsh and sudden, and Laura ducked down when the noise reached her ears. The bullets hit with a pinging sound and brief flashes of gold, and the impact actually made dents. Dents that soon smoothed over as the infestation panicked. Amid the onslaught it teetered precariously, dark smoke billowing up from it, and beat a hasty retreat. From her position Laura couldn't see any more, but the bullets kept going for half a minute more before the noise died with a grinding clack.

"That's all we've got!" the man called.

Clae didn't reply, vaulting over onto the next car. Laura scrambled after him. The car was empty, save for what was left of the luggage. Laura looked around quickly before pointing at the hole from before.

"There!"

Blackness surged up from the undercarriage with a swirl of arms and high-pitched shrilling. Clae shot at the nearest sections to drive them away and held out the bag.

"Laura, take this!"

Laura took it quickly and almost stumbled. It was as heavy as the Pit Egg.

"The source of the infestation is in that pile!" The only pile untouched, the only one the infestation hadn't rent apart. "Get right next to it and put your amulet on the Gin. It'll release a wave of magic. Enough to kill that monster."

"But won't that be enough to kill me too?" squeaked Laura.

"It won't kill you."

"What makes you so sure?"

"Because it'll recognize you as alive! Just go and get the damn thing, and when I say stop, you pull the amulet off *immediately*, do you hear me?"

What being alive had to do with it Laura couldn't even begin to guess. Clae started shooting again. He had the infestation's full attention, and it kept on spinning across the floor, dyeing the boards black in its wake and swirling its arms over his head. Now that it was on the attack and focused, it had left its trail obvious. Laura raced to the luggage pile and threw the bag down next to the line of darkness. She unzipped the case with one sharp jerk and pulled aside the blanket they'd been using as a cushion. But just because its main focus was Clae didn't mean it couldn't go in multiple directions. The trail bubbled and out of it came the eye. She was too busy unclipping the amulet from her belt to notice beyond a glimpse of white and red where it shouldn't be, and that kept her from being paralyzed. But the eye wasn't the only thing building. More limbs reached out, but these weren't the sloppy clawed things infestations usually sprouted. These were long, thin, actual human fingers dripping in black and rushing for her head. Hoping desperately that this would work, she set the amulet on the Gin with a loud clack, giving it the only order she could think of: Wake up.

True Gin didn't have the kitten feeling of Niveus or the loyal-dog feeling of her little amulet. When she felt it stir she felt it hugely, a tremble of power and awareness; like realizing the hill she'd stood on was now an uncoiling dragon. A heavy impression probed her mind.

Wake up.

What?

Wake.

Wake?

Up?

WAKE.

A sensation of understanding hit her so hard she felt as if she'd been physically tackled.

The Gin shimmered, getting brighter and brighter until it was almost blinding, and then came the rush. It was like the dark wave infestations gave out as they died, but this was kin-gold. It surged out in multiple waves, accompanied by a roaring sound. Where it hit her skin Laura got an itchy, prickly feeling, and it filled her nose with the overwhelming scent of vanilla. It made her cough and sneeze. The black arms of the infestation bent backward, shredding and swirling to smoke. The eye winked into hiding quickly, but it couldn't escape. The trail sparked with light, and within seconds the luggage burst into golden flame. The resulting scream rang in her ears. Popping and snapping issued from the fire, before the scream reached an impossible pitch and black smoke bubbled to mix with it. But the Gin didn't stop. It kept shining, kept spewing gold and vanilla, and Laura couldn't breathe.

The gold near her swirled as Clae knelt down next to her. "Remove it! God damn it, I said *stop!*"

He grabbed her wrist and yanked the amulet away. Immediately the Gin's luster dimmed, and the gold slowly faded out. The awful sensation left her mind, and Laura sucked in a breath of clean air. Clae let out a rattling sigh, gaze jumping around the ruined car. He didn't relax.

"What was that?" Laura choked. "Was it magic?"

"In its purest form. It's good in small doses, but you get too much and it's overwhelming."

"I-I couldn't breathe."

"That's the worst Gin can do to people."

She closed her eyes, held a shaky hand to her head. Breathe. Fresh air was good. "Didn't you say it wouldn't hurt me because I'm alive?"

Clae grumbled as he zipped up the Gin bag. "What I meant is that it recognized you as a strain."

"A what?"

"Strain." He sounded irritated, rushed. "All living things have magic in them. You can't access it because it's a small amount and it tends to focus on you. Nothing else. You see Okane, his people, Magi, have a larger, easily manipulated magic pool, but it stays focused on him. He can't breathe fire but he can land on his feet. Everyone alive has their own unique magic, and therefore are strains. The Gin saw you were a strain, and didn't hurt you. Or couldn't. Either or."

"I have magic?" she repeated, baffled.

"It tends to keep you alive, yes." He paused, jerking to face the front as if he'd heard something, and the color drained from his face. "Laura, take the Gin. Get back up to the front car, keep running until you hit the engine."

"What?"

"Now!"

He pulled her to her feet and shoved the bag into her arms before pushing her toward the door.

"Get down!" came a shout from the next car, and, swearing, Clae heaved her out onto the platform.

"Go!"

Angry and confused, she hopped onto the next platform, but as she did, she caught sight of something glowing. She'd barely made it through the door when the object let out a roar and smashed into the train. The corner of the first cargo car was rent apart as it jumped, its huge spiked body crashing into the damaged car. The wall there gave way and part of the ceiling crashed down. Laura watched in horror as the creature rose above the debris, eyes like blazing coals and multicolored spikes shining along its massive shape. It was a felin, an unholy hybrid of lion and dragon standing twice the height of a horse. It raised its ugly muzzle and opened its jaws, letting out another roar.

"Disconnect!" Clae shouted from out of sight.

Immediately the baggage handler ran over, leaning down on the platform to grab at the couplings connecting the cars. The younger one wailed at some contraption on the wall that looked like a one-way telephone; even as he spoke the train gained speed.

"It's a straight line for miles," the man grunted. He tugged at a lever, which failed to work, and cussed as he leaned farther to make a grab for the pin, which he ripped out and dropped; it clattered onto the wooden slats of the tracks and fell behind in the blink of an eye. The couplers groaned but the knuckles stayed, barely, together. "We'll speed up and leave the beastie behind us!"

Laura stood frozen for a moment before casting the bag aside and jumping back to the other car. The man let out a startled cry but she ignored him. The felin was rooting around in the rubble, floor creaking ominously beneath its weight as it sought its prey. Clae scrambled out from beneath a portion of fallen roof and the felin looked up at the movement, baring its fangs.

"I told you to take the Gin and get out!" Clae snarled.

"And let you get lost in the wilds?"

"It's after the Gin!"

Oh. Well, shit. Laura took a step back as she asked, "What do we do, then?"

"Get this thing off the train and get out of the area as soon as—" The felin turned to eye Laura; her stomach flip-flopped, and Clae started to shout. "Get out of here, now!"

The felin changed direction at the noise, but before Laura could turn tail, a squeal rang out farther up the train and the engine jolted forward, whizzing down the tracks at breakneck speed. The coupler's knuckles unfastened completely. The forward car rocketed faster, but was jerked sharply as the safety chains pulled taut with a loud crack. With the resulting lurch everyone lost their balance: the felin toppled with a howl, Laura and Clae sprawled on the debris, and the baggage handler nearly fell off. Clae clambered to his feet again, made a furious gesture for Laura to move, then aimed and shot at the felin. One of the kin bullets hit home in the felin's eye and burst with a flash of light and spatter of blackish blood. The felin bellowed and thrashed, its spiked tail swooping overhead to smash more of the walls down. Laura ducked and covered her head. With a snarl the felin hauled itself up properly and scrabbled forward. Clae dodged its jaws and rolled to the side, but his movement wasn't as fast as it should've been. Cussing, Laura dug the Bijou and some wire from her bag. The Bijou lit up with a blinding flash and spat angrily, drawing the animal's attention. Laura blinked back at the door, saw the man gesturing madly, and yelled, "Clae! They're ready to ditch it! Come on!"

The felin thrust its snout through the sparks of the Bijou, teeth gnashing, and Laura toppled over with a shriek of surprise. The animal kept snapping as she tried to get out of the way, but she found herself moving slower than usual. It took too much energy just to move. She struggled, clawing at the scarred floorboards as panic rose in her chest. The more she floundered the worse she felt, like an awful weight was crushing all the air from her body. She tried to call for help but could only wheeze. A piece of sideboard came crashing down on the felin's nose, and it jerked back; almost immediately the weight was gone and she could breathe again. Clae threw the wood after it and urged her up once more.

"*Bijou?*" he hissed. "You thought *Bijou* would hurt it?"

"It was worth a try!"

The felin shook its head, dislodging wood chunks and sparks before lunging for them again. The pair scuttled back onto the platform, and the baggage handler reached out to help them over.

"Only one more chain," he explained quickly, "we break that and the car's lost. We just need to make sure it doesn't follow us here."

"I'll take care of that," Clae growled.

As the felin rushed the door, he raised his gun and fired again. Two more bullets ricocheted off the animal's hard face before one sank into its good eye, stopping its charge and resulting in another pained yowl. With that, he turned and fired at the last safety chain. It snapped under the strain, and their car began to fall behind. Laura took a running jump and caught the outside rail of the opposite platform. Clae followed shortly, though he had to activate his amulets to cover the growing distance. Gripping the bars one-handed, he turned and aimed his gun at the car behind them. He pulled the trigger, but the gun simply clicked—he was out of bullets. Fortunately the felin was too preoccupied with its lack of sight. It clamored about the ruined car, wailing to high heaven and smashing what little remained of the structure. They could see it illuminated by the flickering of the Bijou, growing more and more distant. With no idea how far or fast a felin could run, Laura didn't relax for a long while. Eventually Clae tossed his gun into the car and reached out to pat her shoulder.

"Go on. Get up."

Did that mean they were safe? She exhaled slowly and allowed the man to help her onto the platform. She staggered into the car and only paused once she was past the machine gun. Her hands hurt with how hard she'd clutched the railing, and she had the feeling her bruises wouldn't be pleasant tomorrow. Clae set his hand on her shoulder again. If she didn't know better, she'd think he was reassuring himself that she was still there.

"Good job," he breathed. "And . . . thanks for going back. But if you ever do something that idiotic again I'm going to fire you."

"I thought you hired me so I could help you," she grumbled.

"Not if it gets you killed in the process."

The baggage handler followed them, a relieved grin on his face. "Well done," he said. "Well done!"

"That was amazing!" said the younger man.

Clae caught his wrist and stared him down. "Don't think I'm not still going to turn you in."

"But—"

"Theft is theft and you endangered everyone on this train." He let go and turned to the other handler, while the younger looked on in shock. "Put that gun back in the crate. There's nothing special about it without the bullets, but it still needs to go to the Sweepers."

"Right, we'll handle it."

"Good. We're going back to our compartment."

The man nodded, still smiling with victory despite his coworker's predicament. Clae gathered up his gun and bag, and they left. Almost as soon as they were in the passenger car, they were hailed by the attendant.

"I'm sorry, but do you know what's going on back there? There was so much noise, and one of the workers was shouting about felin," he fretted.

"There was a felin on board, along with an infestation. We've already taken care of it, though the back end of the train is gone."

"G-gone?" the attendant squeaked.

"It should be on the tracks a ways back. The felin was still in the last car when it separated. You'll want to call that in as soon as possible."

"Y-y-yes!"

He panicked for a moment, then turned around to go back up the train, but Clae caught him. "Oh, before I forget. You've got two baggage handlers in that back car. The younger one's a thief."

"Huh?"

"He took equipment we needed to kill the infestation. I hope the appropriate punishment will be given?"

"O-of course."

The attendant hovered, waiting for any more information, and when it was obvious there wouldn't be, he sprinted back toward the engine. Clae slid open the door to their compartment and they sat down. Laura leaned her head back and allowed herself to relax. No more felin. They were safe. She never wanted to run into those again. Just the memory of that weight made her queasy.

"Why didn't the Bijou work?" she wondered aloud.

"Because Sweeper weapons use magic, remember?" Clae replied. "Felin survive on magic. It's what they eat. That's also why it was a bad idea to use Gin in the wilds: they sensed a lot of food and came running. If anything, Sweeper weapons are only snacks for them." He clutched the Gin bag in his lap, as if letting go would allow it to run off.

Laura opened her eyes to squint at him. "What did you mean, when you said people have magic?"

"Exactly what I said."

"Elaborate?"

He huffed. "Magic is your life. Or your soul. Look, no one really knows what magic is, beyond it being some kind of energy that's tied to life. Felin were created by some batty alchemist with magic, so they feed on it. Studies show that being in the area of a felin for an extended period, direct contact or not, causes lethargy and illness. Why? It absorbs your magic, your energy. Some people say that a felin doing that will take years off your life, since your magic is your life. But they also say that magic is your soul, and your soul is what makes an individual, so eating or using your magic would fracture your self, correct? So a felin eats part of your soul, then? Are we a soul-powered society? Does that mean Gin has a soul?"

"You're waxing philosophical," Laura pointed out dully.

"Because no one understands it. The only thing we know is that it's linked to living creatures and Gin. Few people have bothered to define or research it beyond what it can be utilized for."

"What do you think it is?"

He pondered awhile before replying, slowly, "I believe magic is created by the soul. A product, not the same thing, that nurtures the body and keeps one alive. There are flaws to the theory, of course. You may as well be arguing about religion."

When they arrived at Puer it was still dark and somewhere in the early morning. Laura would've checked her watch, but in the limited light she wouldn't be able to read it anyway. She didn't see them go through the gate, only registering when they stopped. Clae stood immediately and pulled down his luggage. Laura followed his lead. They got off the train as soon as the attendant opened the door.

The Puer depot was empty at this hour. The big room with its soaring ceiling, pillars, and empty benches must've been some kind of gathering place in the daytime, but right then it looked like a ghost town. Their footsteps echoed as they strode across the space and out the large doors. Lights glinted from nearby windows, but Laura couldn't make out much beyond that. But there in the glow of the depot waited a horse-drawn carriage, decorated with gaudy colors that identified it as a pleasure ride or entertaining taxi. The driver shifted, leaning over to inspect them.

"Are you from Amicae? The Sweepers?"

"We are."

"I'm here to take you to your quarters. If you'll come aboard, the sooner we can get going, the sooner I can go home and sleep."

Laura wanted to sleep too, so she wasn't going to argue with that logic. Clae just grunted, and they climbed up into the carriage. It was cramped but the seats were much more comfortable than the ones on the train, and when they began to bounce and rattle across cobblestone Laura wasn't bothered.

"So, Puer," she drawled. "The flat place."

"You're going to start talking again." Clae had his eyes closed, face tilted toward the ceiling.

"Something tells me the driver won't be happy if we nod off in here. Besides, I can't see much out the windows. Do they not have streetlights?"

"They have streetlights in Puer."

"Glad that's covered. What else do they have here? Five Quarters instead of six, I know that much, but the most I know is that they have a big tower with lights all the way up it. No one talks much about other cities in Amicae. They like to think Amicae's the center of the world."

Clae opened one eye. "I remember that one. You pulled that picture off a Second Quarter theater."

Laura chuckled. "I didn't even see the film. Most of what I know about cities, I learn from scraps of posters and the films we get from them. Or the semi-legal books on Paglia Road. So I know what a city like Carmen or Coronae looks like, basically. I know one's big on mobs and cheese, and the other has royalty. I kind of know what the accent and the fashion is. But Puer?"

"Puer prides itself on technological advancements." Clae pulled out his pocket watch and dangled it in front of her. "Take this, for example. They couldn't do the art, but they're the first ones to bring in a moving clock face. They like taking things apart, seeing how they work, and making it run in the smoothest way. They don't focus on the human form like people do in other cities, claim it restricts them. But they can go into ridiculous detail, and they always cover up the workings on their projects. Man-made magic, they like to call it. You may as well think things are amulet-powered. You won't see the technology just walking the streets, but it's everywhere. They're pretty modest when it comes to that, possibly so no other cities decide to snoop on their secrets. Of course, they brag about anything else. Their social structure and fiscal policies are different, so they're wealthier than Amicae with a much stronger emphasis on upkeep in all levels of the city. Amicae focuses on the top two Quarters, but Puer divides evenly all the way down. Most cities get stratified badly, so Puer gets a big head about it. Someone's probably going to say they're much better than you if they get wind you're from another city. Long-winded bluffers is what they are, just ignore them."

"The flat land of rich, machine-building braggarts. Anything else I should know?"

"They make this egg dish." He gestured vaguely. "Don't eat it."

They drove a long way. It seemed like it took an hour. They went uphill a few times, so Laura wasn't sure what to make of it until the carriage stopped.

"Here you go. Sweeper quarters," the driver announced.

They were on what looked like a street of businesses, this one well lit by ornate streetlamps. The buildings all looked well maintained, even rich, and the one they stood directly in front of was freshly painted white. If the Sweeper shop in Amicae looked like a candy shop, then this looked like a multilevel candy emporium. The letters on the main window to the right of the door read, in flowery writing, *Puer Sweepers Guild*.

"You okay from here?" asked the driver. "Looks like they're closed at this hour."

"I've got a key," Clae assured her. "I've been here before."

"Have a nice night. Day. Whichever."

The carriage drove away, leaving them alone in the lamplight.

"So we're staying here?" Laura looked up at the shop, trying to figure out if the second level was a home like the one in Amicae.

"Next door, actually."

Next to the shop was another door, but the building it belonged to, squished between other buildings to the point where there was no separation, was thin. If Clae hadn't said something, she would've thought it to be part of the other shop. He went up to the door and pulled a key from under the stairs. He turned this over in his hand, hesitating—he seemed to be hesitating a lot after that felin attack—before unlocking the door.

"It's a guesthouse, but it's not very big. You can take the top floor. I'll take the second."

As predicted, the inside was tiny, maybe half the width of Laura's bedroom and a little longer. This first floor housed a rudimentary kitchen area with a covered basket on the table and no windows. A small door stood ajar on the far side, through which Laura could glimpse a bathroom. The light came from a naked electric bulb on the ceiling. A ladder protruded from the wall on the opposite side, leading up through a hole in the ceiling.

"We'll get some rest for now, but be ready to meet with the Sweepers in the morning."

"Don't worry about me. I got plenty of sleep on the train, if nothing else. Good night."

Laura adjusted her satchel, then climbed her way up the ladder. The next floor was a bedroom, equally cramped, but plain. At least it looked like there were clean sheets on the bed. Another ladder on the other side of the room led into the third floor: a bedroom almost identical to the one below, just arranged the opposite way, with no other ladder. She set down her bag near the nightstand and changed into a nightgown before crawling into bed. It was nowhere near as uncomfortable as that Partch mattress, and she found herself smiling. She was looking forward to the meeting tomorrow.

21

GOSSIPMONGERS

Laura didn't sleep well. Having slept so long on the train meant she was restless, so while she napped a bit, she mostly lay awake, staring at the ceiling as the sun rose to shine through the window. She got dressed and brushed her hair once she convinced herself it was late enough and sat on her bed. The old Coronae book lay open on her lap, simultaneously worn and pristine. There was no counting the number of times she'd flipped through these pages, reverent. The man with the sun in his hand was there the same as he'd been when she was five. *None put terror into the fiends of Orien like the Sweepers. While small in numbers they are the bravest men in Coronae.* She ran her fingers over the image. This book had given her direction, and she didn't regret it for a moment. Sinclair Sweepers weren't what she'd pictured, but the work was better than she'd dreamed. Were other Sweeper guilds like the one she'd glimpsed in this book? Surely they were, with proper backing. It was foolish to think that this armored man would greet her in the Sweeper shop, but armor hardly made a person. The confidence, though, the importance—surely she'd find it here.

She stayed like that until she heard movement from below, and listened until that movement descended to the first floor before putting the book away and following. Clae was dressed and moving around the kitchen.

"Good morning." Laura hopped off the last ladder rung.

"Morning." He pulled the cover off of the basket on the table to reveal a large pile of pastries.

"That looks good," Laura observed. "A lot for two people, though."

"I told them I was bringing an apprentice, and some Sweepers take multiple apprentices on these trips. They were probably playing it safe."

"That's nice of them." Laura took one and sat down.

Clae sat opposite her and took a pastry of his own. He inspected it like he thought it might be poisoned. "There are a lot more Sweepers in Puer, lots of incoming apprentices. Their city promotes them a lot better, and their public isn't being misled. Might be a little overwhelming."

"I'm looking forward to it! I've always wondered how other Sweepers work."

"I suppose you'll find out, then," muttered Clae, taking a sullen bite of his pastry.

"What are the Sweepers here like? Unless you came when you were really little, then they may have changed."

"There are three main Sweepers I know of. Melody Dearborn, Joseph Blair, and his wife. Helen." He paused, as if the last name left a bad taste in his mouth. "Melody doesn't talk much, but she's strong and she's capable. Very levelheaded. She's the one I'm usually in contact with. Joseph *does* talk—too much. He's an antsy person who goes over everything too many times. As for Helen? I don't know much about her anymore. What little I do I don't like. Be wary around her."

Clae had made quick judgments like this before, so Laura wasn't surprised.

"Do we have a time set up to meet them?"

"It's about seven thirty now. We can go over after we're done eating."

They ate quickly. Or at least, Laura did. Clae didn't eat much. Eventually they gathered up the Gin and left the guesthouse. Cars rumbled up and down the road outside, and people strolled the sidewalk to window-shop. Judging by their rich clothing and the sheer abundance of automobiles, Laura guessed this was somewhere in the Second or First Quarters.

But despite being in an upper Quarter, she was startled to see that the clouds looked much farther away. In Amicae it almost seemed like the tallest buildings of the First Quarter could brush the clouds, but here they looked miles away. The two of them walked over to the next door. A sign in the window declared the building closed until eight, but Clae knocked anyway.

Almost immediately the door swung inward. A tall, thin woman stood there. Her skin was dark, her short hair tightly curled. Gold hoops dangled from her ears to accentuate the thin strands of gold in her clothing. She looked at them with a stony glare that made Laura uneasy.

"Clae Sinclair," she rumbled.

"Melody," he replied. "It's been a while."

"With the letters it doesn't seem so long. Come inside."

They walked past her, into the shop. It was immaculately clean inside, with wooden chairs along the walls and a long counter on the opposite side. It was a similar setup to the Amicae one, just with more chairs and no Kin sprawling all over the place.

"When did you arrive?" Melody drifted past.

"Early morning. Must've been two or three." Clae followed her movement. "Where's the cavalry?"

"The other Sweepers will be gathering once the store opens. We'll exchange Gin once they're assembled."

"Right."

He sat in one of the chairs, setting the carpetbag with their Gin by his feet while Melody walked to the counter. Laura hovered in the middle, intimidated but still vaguely annoyed. She'd been ignored, not even subtly.

"It's like dealing with another you," she mumbled, sitting next to Clae, and he snorted.

At exactly 8:15, a crowd walked in. At least twenty people filtered through that door, of all different ages. Elderly ladies, middle-aged men, teenagers and two children. A tall, reedy man with a gaunt face led the pack, and spotted them immediately.

"Ah, hello, hello, welcome to Puer," he greeted, approaching them. "I hope the guesthouse was satisfactory?"

"It was fine." Clae's tone was clipped, but in a lesser degree of rude than Laura had heard before.

"Good." The man smiled before turning back to look at the others. "Everyone, this is the head Sweeper of Amicae, Clae Sinclair. And your apprentice?"

"Laura Kramer," Clae supplied.

"Lovely to meet you, miss." The man nodded at her.

Laura decided she liked him. He seemed almost timid in his happiness, and it reminded her of Okane.

"I'm Joseph Blair, the head Sweeper here. This is my team." He gestured with pride at the gathered people. "I think you've met Melody already, but this is my wife, Helen—"

Helen, a dark-haired woman, had an expression of blankness that somehow managed to be hostile at the same time. Something about the shape of her face made Laura think of Clae. Maybe she was a distant relative?

"My son, Leo, he's an apprentice—"

That one was a dark-haired boy, maybe thirteen years old, and far too arrogant-looking for his own good.

"Mr. and Mrs. Idstrom here work on our Kin, Miss Moran constructs equipment. . . ."

He went on to introduce them all, but Laura only remembered the first few. She thought this was a ridiculous number of apprentices, and was a little baffled that there were people hired here who didn't even go on exterminations. She hoped no one would quiz her on any names. Clae had been right, in a way: when regular workers were presented in their home city, they didn't make much of an impression in the mass. Laura doubted she'd remember to pass word along about any of them when she got home. Her own introduction had been short and sweet, so she hoped they'd remember her well. When he finished at long last, Joseph looked back at Melody.

"Would you please retrieve the Gin?"

She nodded and disappeared behind a door. For a moment Laura thought this door was like the Puer version of the drapes, but realized that if Melody went in there it wasn't secret, and she didn't take any great measures to shield its contents from them. Before long she returned, carrying another Gin stone in her arms. This one was smoother than theirs and a little differently shaped, but beyond that they were identical. She brought it over to Joseph, and he took it from her.

"All right, then . . . Shall we?"

Clae stood and pulled their Gin out of the bag. Balancing this in his arms, he brought it forward and stood in front of Joseph. He looked a foot shorter than the other man.

"Are you familiar with the process?" asked Joseph.

"I know what I'm doing."

Curious, Laura inched her way out of her seat and closer to the proceedings. As she watched, both of them balanced the Gin on one arm, setting the other hand on top. There was silence for a moment; then Clae sighed. Under his fingers the Gin activated with a gentle hum. It shimmered faintly and emitted gold magic-fog again. It wasn't near as bad as when it activated on the train, though. As if in reaction, the other Gin piece lit up. Now there was a set of humming. The gold fanned out, still faint, and Laura felt like it was reaching out, searching. She shuddered, half expecting that heavy presence to start prodding at her mind again, but it never came. Eventually the humming hit a higher pitch. Clae shifted his grip on the Gin, and the two exchanged them. The gold wavered and the humming dropped in pitch again, but after a while it returned to that earlier sound. Clae made another soft noise, which probably only Laura and possibly Joseph could hear, and ran his hand over the smooth surface of their new Gin. It hummed a bit stronger, then faded out. The other Gin did the same.

"The Gin have accepted the transfer," said Joseph. "I have to say, I've never seen someone do that with such ease, Mr. Sinclair."

"I *have* had practice."

"Of course. Last time I saw you, you were so young. I forget."

Clae ignored Joseph's abashed chucking, turning to offer the Gin to Laura. "Put this in the bag."

"Yes, sir."

Despite its smooth surface, Laura got a prickly feeling where she touched the new stone. Unnerved, she hurried to put it away. Meanwhile Joseph had handed off his own Gin and shook hands with Clae.

"It's truly an honor to have you here. I've heard some great things since last we met. You've really become a well-known name in Terual. Even our contacts in Zyra and Ruhaile marvel at your progress."

Clae grunted.

"Well, in any case, let's talk. You all can go back to your schedules." Joseph glanced back at his group.

Most of that group split up. They gossiped quietly as they left the shop, but the Blairs and three others stayed behind. Joseph gestured for Clae to go toward the door at the back.

"If you'd like, miss, you can stay out here and mingle. I'm sure the others are eager to get to know you."

"Oh. All right," mumbled Laura.

She was nervous about being separated, but this was what she'd been waiting for. This was the chance to connect with other Sweepers. While the pair disappeared into another room, she walked up to the other five.

"It's nice to meet you," she greeted, speaking more quietly than normal, but she was anxious.

"Nice to meet you, too," replied another young woman, who didn't look much older than her. "It's troublesome traveling with cargo like that, so it's a relief you made it."

"There was a little bump in the road, but we managed." Laura tried to remember this woman's name and failed miserably.

"Well, you're here now." The woman smiled.

Laura felt embarrassment and shame bubbling in her chest. She had no idea how to start a Sweeper conversation. In her experience it was Clae barking at her or explaining something to Okane, not trying to dig things out of people. She didn't want to just ask "how's work," because that would just sound stupid.

"So that was Sinclair, then." The woman glanced back at the door with a gleeful look.

"You've heard of him?"

"Oh, we've heard *things*," the woman giggled.

"What kind of things?"

The woman leaned closer to the elderly woman beside her and made a tittering sound.

"Oh, she hasn't heard," she whispered, too loudly for it to be real.

"I suppose he must not talk about it, then!"

"Talk about what?" demanded Laura.

"Oh, nothing." That teasing grin on the woman's face was really annoying.

"If it's really nothing, why are you talking about it?"

The woman looked a little put out, but continued. "It's that sordid family affair of theirs. All the deaths and such."

Laura knew Clae's father had died on the job, but she made it sound as if they were *all* gone. And what was "affair" supposed to mean?

"I've never heard of that. I mean, he said something about the risks of the job being the breakdown of the family business, but—"

"Is *that* what he told you?" The woman looked delighted again, and Laura had the feeling she was going to hate this gossipy woman in the future. "This really is sordid!"

"Sordid Sinclairs, sure. You want to elaborate?"

"Oh honey, you're kind of blunt, aren't you?" The woman frowned. "The boys don't like that in a girl."

So they preferred squeaky gossipers instead? Idle talking was one thing, but these women were the mean kind of gossips. Laura wouldn't be surprised if they talked about scars, too.

"Elaborate? Please?"

"Fine." The woman rolled her eyes. "How do I break this to you?"

"Give it to her straight," cackled the old lady.

"How straight?" She giggled again.

Laura looked over at Melody, hoping for assistance from someone a little less silly, but Melody simply watched like a hawk from the counter. Helen stood by her, fussing over Leo and paying them no attention. The other women twittered between themselves some more, then turned back to her.

"There were five Sinclairs, once upon a time. Three of them died, one ran off, and the last one was a twisted little monster child. Guess which one you got landed with?"

Laura felt a lot of things about that. First off she was stunned, because she hadn't thought about how much death was involved in that family. Secondly, she was offended because of that obvious insult about Clae. Third, she didn't know what to think about all of that happening to him as a *child*.

"I'm sorry?" That was all she could think of to say.

"Unthinkable, right? *Scandalous*, right? I know. He didn't tell you anything, did he? Of course, I hear he's still twisted. I don't know how you work with him."

"You hear," Laura retorted grumpily. "He's obnoxious, not twisted."

"Oh?" chirped the woman, and Laura realized she'd just opened a new door for gossip. Just not a door she liked.

"What about you, you've got to have some eccentric Sweepers here too, right?"

"Not really," the woman said dismissively. "How crazy is he?"

"Not a lot. Why are there multiple floors here? Do people live up there?"

"Nobody lives up there. Come on, Sinclairs!"

"It's obvious she doesn't want to talk about that. Drop it," ordered Melody.

The women fell dead silent at her words. After a long while the old woman murmured, "You know, I think we could do some fine-tuning upstairs. Come along, dearie."

The two of them went up the stairs in the corner, leaving the others behind. Laura drifted over to the counter. Melody watched but said nothing. Leo, on the other hand, seemed very interested.

"Hey." He grinned at her. "You're from Amicae, aren't you?"

He mispronounced it. Well, he said it the proper way, like "ahmeekay." Only foreigners pronounced it like that.

"I am," she replied anyway.

"Does your city really lie to everyone about walls protecting them from *kaibutsu*?"

It wasn't as if Laura had any hand in setting that up, but she still flushed with shame. The expression was enough of an answer, because he laughed.

"And your city actually believes it? That's hilarious!"

"We'd change it if we could, but we're not too keen on being thrown in jail," Laura said shortly. Was this standard? Did Sweepers actively mock each other's cities at these events and then expect some kind of camaraderie? She glanced at Helen, but the woman made no attempt to correct his behavior.

"I'd change it anyway," said Leo. "I'm not scared of things like *that*."

"Right," Laura drawled, unimpressed. "So, you're a Sweeper apprentice too? What kind of things do you do here?"

"Mostly clean," he groaned. "I get to clean and put things away. I never get to do anything fun like the others."

"No infestations for you, then?" She was only mildly surprised. There were a lot of apprentices—taking them all on a job would be dangerous and difficult.

"No. Do you get to do that?"

"Clae's been bringing me along since day one."

At Clae's name, Helen's face darkened. Leo didn't notice.

"Lucky!" he moaned. "My dad's not letting me on missions until I've been here three years."

"I'm sure he's just worried about you."

"*Worried.*" He rolled his eyes. "He shouldn't be. I can take care of myself. If other Sweepers can—"

"In his defense, Clae didn't have much of a choice. At the time I was the only other Sweeper. He needed some help."

Leo looked a little put out.

"Why did you take the job?" Helen's voice was sharp, and Laura was taken aback by the question.

"Because I wanted to be a Sweeper. I wanted to help protect Amicae. Why else would anyone take the job?"

"You shouldn't have. There's a reason he can't be trusted with an apprentice."

"Well, he's got two of us now and we've been doing just fine."

"You should've left him alone," Helen muttered darkly. "Let the mobster Sweepers take over. They'd do a better job."

Laura looked at Melody for some kind of explanation, but the blank expression didn't help at all. This woman was worse than Clae.

"Is that Sinclair really crazy?" asked Leo, looking at his mother, and she replied, "Sinclairs can't be counted on for anything. His father proved that well enough."

He took this as a yes and laughed, "You work with a crazy man?"

"He is not!" Laura retorted, fed up and glaring. "How do you have any right to judge what kind of person he is? You don't know him. As far as I can tell, you're all hapless gossips here! Except you, you don't talk much." The last sentence was deadpanned to Melody, who didn't react at all.

"I'm not a gossip!" Leo objected angrily.

"I've known him.," said Helen. "And I know you're an idiot for getting involved. You too"—she turned her nose up at Melody—"but at least you had the sense to leave it. There's something *wrong* with them. The whole lot of them."

"You don't know *shit*," Laura hissed.

"Whoa," Leo snickered. "Don't bite our heads off."

"Maybe if you had any semblance of manners I wouldn't have to!"

Leo's laughter stopped. "Hey, just because you're overprotective—"

"You're insulting her coworker. It's entirely within her right to be angry," Melody butted in.

"We're not insulting," said Leo. "We're just talking."

"Oh yeah? How about I call your dad a batty little ingrate?" said Laura.

"You can't just—"

"Is there a problem here?"

Clae's voice cut the air like a knife. All the fight went out of Laura in a whoosh. She felt ashamed. She'd been thinking about how great this would be, but she ended up blowing up at a bunch of idiots like a testy child. She stared at the ground as two sets of footsteps grew nearer.

"We heard some raised voices out here. Is something wrong?" asked Joseph.

"Your family is being offensive again," Melody informed him.

"She's yelling at us!" Leo whined.

"Leo." Joseph's voice sounded so sad, so disappointed, that Laura felt guilty too.

Leo fell silent and shuffled his feet. Joseph walked past and up to Helen. He took her hand and said, in that same sad, sad tone, "Helen. I thought we were going to be nice and civil. They're our guests and they deserve our respect."

Helen just looked at him. Completely unapologetic.

"Laura?"

Laura glanced up. Clae stood right next to her. He gave her a look, but not one of his usual, critical looks. More like an *it's okay, I kind of approve* type of look. It made her feel a little better.

"I hope we will all get along now," Joseph wheedled. "No more arguing. Just mutual respect. Everyone in this room is an excellent Sweeper of outstanding merit, and we should all be treated as such."

"Okay, Dad," Leo muttered.

"Good." He patted the boy on the shoulder and turned to Laura and Clae. "I apologize for this. We're normally very professional."

"It's okay." Laura could tell that he at least respected Clae and expected others to do the same. She wasn't going to think badly of him as she did his family.

The two head Sweepers stayed in the main room. They sat in some of the chairs and talked about Sweeper things, mostly the effectiveness of various weapons against the monsters. They talked about the size and shape of grenades to use (apparently Eggs were only a variation: the same bomb could come in the shape of plain circles, cones, cylinders, even squares, and had different names depending on shape), how that affected their potency, change in colors, the whole shebang. It was more information than Laura had ever heard before. She sat near Melody to listen in and paid rapt attention. They talked about grenades practically the entire day. Joseph mentioned this apprentice or that apprentice and this helper or that one in his stories, but Clae never mentioned names. Laura found that strange, especially when he kept bringing up dead apprentices with her, but then these people already thought he was incapable of having an apprentice. Best not encourage them. While they kept talking, Helen and Leo entertained themselves with books and notes. Melody sat and stared, seemingly not listening to anything, and Laura decided she was kind of creepy.

They were going on about kin-filled bullets when a delivery team brought in a familiar wooden crate. Joseph was intrigued by, if uneasy about, the machine gun and its use, while Clae explained how it had worked on the train. At the mention of that infestation and felin, Helen's lip curled, like she couldn't believe they'd been so stupid that they had to face danger getting here. Laura glared at her as darkly as she could manage. Clae, on the other hand, spared the audience only infrequent glances, and always his eyes avoided Helen, as if he pretended that she didn't exist if he couldn't see her. At long last they wrapped up their talk.

"It was a pleasure talking with you today, sir. I'm glad to get your insight on this. We've been having some errors with our equipment, so we'll see if we can adapt some of your style."

"It might not work the same way with your Gin combination."

"You've made it work astonishingly well for the past few years. Perhaps we'll get some of your luck."

"Perhaps."

"Indeed. Well, good night then. I look forward to seeing you in the morning."

Clae and Laura left. It was dark outside and the streetlamps were lit again. The dim lights of an automobile cruised past as they entered the guesthouse. Almost as soon as the door shut, Laura spoke.

"I see why you don't like Helen."

"Oh?"

"She's so rude! And she's got no control over that child and she's got to be a gossip, and she won't apologize for anything! Just looking at her face makes me angry."

"Some say her face looks like mine."

"It's not. I mean, I guess there's something in there, but they're not the same."

He snorted as if the idea was hilarious. Laura watched him move around the little kitchen for a while.

"How did you two know each other?"

"It's been a long time."

"Still."

"That woman blames me for what happened to her."

"What happened to her?"

"The reason she left home. She needed an excuse, and I turned out to be the perfect scapegoat."

There was bitterness in his tone. Laura's opinion of this woman dropped even further.

"Do I have to talk to her at all anymore? I don't think I'd be able to without snapping. She just makes my blood boil."

"You don't have to talk to anyone if you don't want to. Melody's like that, they like her."

"Right, Melody. She's a little creepy. How'd you meet her?"

"I came to Puer shortly after becoming head Sweeper. She was the only reason Helen didn't throw me out, made sure I got listened to. She's unconventional, but not unkind."

Laura had sensed no great kindness from her apart from blunt statements, so only shrugged in response. "Will tomorrow be like today?"

"For the most part. There's some sort of dinner planned, though. Big social gathering."

"So all those apprentices are going to get gathered up again?"

"The apprentices and some of the more important people in Puer. Politicians and the like. Our arrival is an excuse to throw a rich party."

Clae turned on the stove to heat up the kettle. One hand remained in his pocket, resulting in the now-familiar click of a pocket watch in restless fingers.

22

THE FAMILY BUSINESS

The next day they arrived later at the shop: more around nine than seven thirty. That was partly due to the fact they had to find breakfast, and also because they were putting it off as long as possible. Joseph welcomed them in and brought Clae over to the chairs once more while Laura took a seat by Melody. Helen and Leo weren't there, but there was a girl cleaning the place. Laura tried to say hello, but the girl kept her head down and went on sweeping. There wasn't much talking apart from that between the two bosses. This time they talked about Gin combinations and kin-treatment of clothing. Sometime around three, Joseph announced they were leaving.

That was how Laura found herself in what had to be the First Quarter. They were at a big party location. There was a huge dance floor with branching paths and gazebos, with railings along the sides draped in amulet-powered twinkling lights. A long banquet table on the side of the dance floor stood laden with rich food. The partygoers looked like something out of a film, all decked out and bobbing along to the sound of a band in the corner. All of this was right on top of a big pool of water. They had a lake for their entertainment. To reach the dance floor Laura and the others had to be ferried by little boats, and now that she was here she didn't like it. She looked like a sewer rat compared to the ladies in their fashionable dresses and makeup. The food was good, though, if nothing else.

Joseph had ushered Clae away to introduce him to various bigwigs, leaving Laura stranded. She wandered the dance floor and picked at the dinner buffet, but ultimately arrived on one of the branching paths, leaning against the railing. She didn't know anyone and this wasn't an atmosphere she felt comfortable in. She watched the dancers across the water as they broke into a fox-trot. She half wondered what it would be like to be one of those girls, laughing as they swirled in their partners' arms. She tried to imagine one of those dresses, her hand clasped in another, but the face that came to mind was Charlie's. She balked at the idea, and the whole dream seemed tainted again. If she ever did a fox-trot, she decided, she'd have to make sure to have a proper partner. Clae fit the description, but substituting him in the dream made her snort. Okane would probably work, if he ever got over his dislike of touching.

"Having fun?"

Apparently Clae had escaped, because he was striding toward her. Only took him two hours.

"Not really," she sighed, tossing a chicken bone into the water. A large spotted fish darted forth to nibble on it, but finding it not to be fish food, swam away again. "How was the meet and greet?"

"I don't remember any of their names and I don't care to."

"As always." She rolled her eyes.

"It matters even less here. It's not like I'll be running into them again."

"There are always other Gin trades, aren't there?"

"Not here there's not."

"I thought you came here before to trade Gin, when you met Melody."

"That was a completely different situation; there wasn't Gin involved. As far as it's been planned, there are no Gin trades between us and Puer for another twenty years."

"Then what were you doing in Puer?"

"Chasing a vain hope." He glanced back at the main platform. "Didn't appreciate the dancing?"

"Nah, I can't dance worth anything. I don't understand why people like it either."

"And of course, there are no posters to vandalize."

"I only go after the old ones," Laura defended, glaring at him.

"Hey, it's the bat and his sidekick."

Laura gave a frustrated sigh as she saw Leo coming up the path. She wasn't in a particularly good mood, and didn't want to deal with his taunting about Amicae's problems or insulting Clae. If he was brave enough to do that to Clae's face anyway. Leo stopped alongside them.

"I figured out where I heard of you," he announced, looking at Clae. "People talk about you sometimes, but it's usually just that you're a nutcase."

"And you've come to tell me this why?"

"Because you're the one who killed his brother, aren't you?"

Laura froze. Not only was that blunt, it was unbelievable. Clae's expression didn't change, but his eyes hardened and his hands slipped into his pockets, presumably for the watch. When neither said anything to the contrary, Leo grinned wider.

"I heard that when you were six, you dragged your little brother out and slaughtered him. Fed his body to an infestation to cover it up. After that the rest of your family started dropping like flies. I bet you got rid of them too, didn't you? At the very least you did the fratricide."

All of that had to be lies. Those gossipy women at the Sweeper shop filled his brain with fiction so Helen's dislike could be justified. But even while Laura knew that, memories of Clae's home came to mind. Specifically the children's toys, left out and untouched for years.

"What kind of proof do you have for any of that?" Clae leaned back against the railing.

"Everybody knows."

"And everybody knows that pigs can fly."

"Doesn't change facts."

"You seriously think I'm bent on fratricide?"

"I bet you enjoyed it, too. You really are twisted, aren't you?" Leo sneered.

That was a really idiotic thing to say to a would-be murderer, Laura thought. Or at least, that was the thought in the back of her mind. Most of it was preoccupied with stalking toward him, growling, "You little brat! How dare you go accusing people of things like that?"

Leo's smile faltered and he backed up. Smart, because Laura seriously considered pushing him into the lake.

"If that story was true," Clae began, and Laura stopped, "then I'd watch myself if I were you. It just so happens that my deadbeat mother is the same as yours."

Leo's face went pale, then angry red. "Don't talk about my mom like that, she's got nothing to do with—"

"Helen Sinclair abandoned us. She decided she didn't want to deal with reality and ran off to crawl into another man's bed, and you're the result. What was that you were saying about fratricide, *brother*?"

Leo spluttered indignantly.

"You really are crazy!" he hissed. "We'll see how well my dad treats you when he hears how you talked about her!"

"Go ahead. He already knows."

"Freak!" Leo blurted. Laura took a menacing step forward and he ran off, shrieking, "You're both freaks!"

In the following silence, a few fish thrashed in the water.

"You do a good impression of a guard dog," Clae mused, watching Leo's retreating form.

Laura's shoulders slumped. Her head was in a whirl, and she didn't quite know what to think. She'd heard that vague story of the Sinclairs, but she hadn't connected them to actual people. Now those characters were suddenly breathing, the people suddenly coming out of the woodwork. But really, Helen? Leo? Could that be true?

"Was that true?"

"Hm?"

"That Helen's your mother?"

"She used to be. But as I said, she ran off."

Seriously? She felt weirdly betrayed, but it made too much sense. *Some say her face looks like mine*? Of course it did, it was family resemblance!

This was probably a bad idea, but . . . "Why is that?"

Clae sighed.

"To begin with, my brother did die. I didn't kill him, though. When we were nine, we decided we wanted to be Sweepers when we grew up, like our father. I'm sure I mentioned it before, but he was head Sweeper at the time." He paused a moment, staring off into the gathering darkness for a while before continuing, "We tracked down an infestation, but we weren't prepared. It got him and I couldn't do anything about it. So I was the only one who came home. Between that and the fact I was the older one, never mind that it was only by *ten damn minutes,* Helen decided I had to be responsible. She shoved all her troubles on me, and never let me forget it. When my father died a year later on the job, she decided she couldn't stand me anymore and left in the night. No warning. No note. We had no idea where she'd gone. So it was just me and Rosemarie for a while."

The nightstand with the carved ROSEMARIE came to mind again.

"Who's Rosemarie?"

"Great-grandmother on father's side. She died too. Old age with her, though. That's how the family business fell apart. Happy?"

"That's not exactly a happy story," Laura muttered. "And that time you came to Puer and met Melody . . . that was when you heard about Helen being here?"

"The Sweeper who came to visit us that year told us. Once Rosemarie died, I decided I had nothing to lose. Thought I could try to get my mother back. Didn't work, obviously."

The story filled in a lot of gaps. The amount of space in that home above the Sweeper shop, the carving in the nightstand, the toys . . . and everyone here in Puer only heard Helen's side of the story. *There's something wrong with them. The whole lot of them.* How could she say something like that about her own family? Her own child? Laura looked back over at the other partygoers and felt sick.

"Do you want to leave?" she asked.

"What do you mean?"

"I mean I didn't like this party in the first place, and knowing about Helen . . . I don't want to be with these people anymore."

"We can't get a trolley back. Not for free, anyway."

"We can walk though, right? I haven't seen much of Puer yet."

Clae regarded her for a moment. "There is one area where Puer is superior to Amicae. They have posted town maps." With that he leaned over the railing and waved, calling, "You in the boat! Bring us back to shore."

The boat was paddled over, and they clambered over the railing into the vessel. After being rowed back to land, they got out and began wandering.

It was early in the night, and with this being a secure Quarter they weren't afraid of muggers. The buildings in this part of town were big and ornamental, with statues and carvings and electric lights to illuminate them. Laura was quietly impressed by it all. Maybe Amicae's First Quarter was similar, but in the Quarters she frequented the buildings had always seemed worn or faded in some way; here they shone as if newly built, though some plaques on walls indicated that a few of these locations had been around for almost a century. The whole city seemed clean and aglow, almost like a film. Like something divorced from reality. They bantered about some décor and meandered through the thin crowds. There were small, freestanding pillars with maps of the city wrapped around them, and Clae used these to guide them in the general direction of the Sweeper shop. They took their time, though. It wasn't like they were in any rush.

"So you kept in contact with Melody. For gratitude or for business?" Laura asked, as they passed a lit pub topped with a mechanical horse; the metal creature trotted smoothly along a circular track above the door, gliding so naturally it might as well have been real. The sound of singing inside rang in her ears.

"I told you before, I keep in contact with a lot of Sweepers through mail."

"Are they all lovely young ladies?" she teased.

"They tend to be, yes."

Laura stumbled on the cobblestone. "Wait . . . seriously? And you're saying Melody is, uh, lovely?"

Laura had never heard him mention anything nearing the realm of romance before. For a while she'd thought him incapable of it. Romantically stunted.

"She is," Clae agreed, echoed a moment later by the click of that goddamn pocket watch.

"And you . . . get along."

"I'd say so."

"So are you, um, *interested*?"

"We 'courted' at one point." He actually pulled out the watch to observe the time with a bored expression.

"And it didn't work out?"

"For being curious, you're also being very hesitant. I thought I got it through your skull already. Be a pain."

"Fine! So you dated. How long and who dumped who?"

"Six months, mutual dumping. Neither of us are particularly amiable, and she found someone better."

"Ouch."

"If we built a home, it would be rather bleak." He showed no sign of bruised ego or regret. "Besides, seeing her new partner, I don't blame her. That woman's a beauty."

"She's dating a woman now?"

"Name's Priscilla. Good woman, though her bust's outrageous."

"My god, you do have a libido."

He gave her a pointed glare. "What's that supposed to mean?"

"I don't know, it's just, I always thought you seemed to have all the romantic capability of a brick."

"A brick?" He mulled on it for a while. "Bricks can be a pain. I can live with that."

"You're really hung up on that, aren't you?"

"It's what you need to survive in the world."

Laura pondered this for a while before deciding to act on it again. "So why aren't you being a pain to Helen?"

Clae blinked, expression twitching toward some mix of surprise and revulsion. The watch clicked again. "What is that supposed to mean?"

"I mean I think that if she ran out on you when you needed her, she deserves some rudeness from you. She was trash-talking you before, why don't you trash-talk back? You do it all the time back in Amicae! But here you just . . . you just don't look at her. Does it have something to do with the networking, is that why you don't do anything?"

"Riddle me this," he snapped. "What's the point? What do I gain by doing that?"

"She deserves it!"

"But what does it do for me?"

"What does being a pain ever do for you?"

"When you're a pain, it means people will pay attention to you. No one forgets a thorn in their side for very long, and the more you kick at them the more they'll have to take you seriously to get you out of their hair. If I weren't a pain when it came to Amicae, the Sweeper guild would've been looked over and abandoned already. I demand recognition."

"But not from her."

"What do I need recognition from her for? You think I need *her* to take me seriously? Forget it. I've taken enough shit from her, I don't need any more. She could die for all I care. That—" He shut his mouth, warring with his thoughts as he brought his bitterness under control. The watch clicked incessantly. Eventually he gave her a spiteful look from the corner of his eye and said, "What about you? Don't think I don't know about your own mother. She left you. Why aren't you a pain to her?"

"That's different."

"How so?"

"My parents never cared enough for me to even feel abandoned."

She pointedly avoided looking at him. She'd had years to get over the feeling of not being worth the air she breathed, and it wasn't as if her parents were the only ones enforcing those thoughts. She was in a different city now, a Sweeper, and a good one at that. Everyone in Amicae could eat crow.

Clae didn't seem to know how to reply to that, and simply grumbled "Left" when they reached an intersection. Laura waited for him to say something more, but when it became clear he wouldn't, she went ahead.

"What about your father? How did he offend her, if you were the scapegoat? Stand by you?" She hoped he had; Clae seemed attached to the memory of his father, so thinking that had been ripped away too . . .

"He didn't give her any warning, I suppose." The watch clicked. "He told her why I was able to get away, and she didn't take it well."

That sounded like he'd thrown his brother to the lions. "How did you escape?"

"I'm a Magi."

Laura gave him an incredulous look. "A Magi? Like Okane?" But they looked nothing alike. Besides, Clae very clearly pronounced his "you," there was no getting around that.

"My blood's too diluted to show any of the usual signs," he acknowledged. "The true Magi was Rosemarie. She came out of the wilds to snoop on the regular cities, and in the process she came across the Sweepers. My great-grandfather fell head over heels for her. She thought he was amusing, so she stayed around. My grandfather, even my father had some difficulties with the 'you' thing. They were able to use their magic on the job. I ended up with some weak instinct, but that's it. I have no ability like Okane's. Any *kaibutsu* has to be huge for me to notice it. But useful as the abilities can be, they make us a target. I told you before that people hunted Magi, thought they were witches or demons. Helen thinks something like that. Or maybe she thinks Magi is more like a disease. Magi are very secretive, they have to be. My father never shared that secret with her until after the death. She never forgave him for it. Never looked at any of us the same way again."

"Stupid," Laura muttered. "Magi, or whatever. Why should it matter so much?"

"People always pick at little things. Sometimes it seems that's all they're good for."

"It's stupid."

"Most people are."

He tugged on her sleeve to steer her left again. She followed without thinking, but stopped short. The conversation flew out of her mind. They were on the edge of a wide plaza lined with small decorative trees. From the middle rose a massive tower, soaring from bulky arches at the bottom to an elaborate clock face and spires at the top; the clock glowed like a second moon while glittering lights shone on the lattices of its many windows and trailed up its corners. She'd seen it before but never expected it to have this kind of presence.

"It's the tower from the poster," she whispered.

"They call it Gustave's Moon, after the architect," said Clae. "It used to be prominent in Puer's films, but there are bigger, newer buildings they've latched on to."

"But it's—You—Why didn't you tell me we were going here?"

"It was a whim. I saw it on the map."

"It's fantastic!" She craned her neck to make out the top spires. It looked like it belonged in her Coronae book. No, better. "Is that an observation deck? Can we go up?"

"We can try."

She made an embarrassingly excited noise and rushed for the open door. The bottom floor housed a small café and gift shop. Laura was immediately drawn in by a display of illustrated postcards of the tower and other Puer landmarks. After a moment she realized she was alone. Clae had stopped outside, looking up at the clock with a pensive expression.

"Is something wrong?" she called, going out to join him.

"Nine o'clock," he said, pointing. "Gustave's Moon chimes different songs every year."

Above them, the minute hand ticked into place. A song rang through the air, simple but somehow familiar. A fragment of a lullaby.

"Thank you," said Clae.

Laura sent him a puzzled look. "For what? You're the one who brought me here."

"Not this," he grumbled. "I'm aware that I'm not easy to work with. I'm abrasive. I'm bitter. I'm secretive. It's not a good combination."

Laura frowned, unsure what he was getting at. Clae looked intensely frustrated, but at least he was aiming that scowl at the tower.

"You didn't have to put up with that, or with the amount of danger we go through on the job. But you still do, and you're still . . . *bright* at the end of it. Hardworking despite the laws of Amicae, still supportive of Magi even though you recognize we're not normal, still . . ." He breathed in deep. "Still going back for other people."

"I'm fairly certain those should be normal," said Laura. "Besides, it's not like I take all that happily. My aunt will gladly tell you that I complain all the time."

"I don't blame you for it. Our situation is terrible."

"And yet you're thanking me for it?"

"I'm thanking you for a lot of abstract things."

He looked down at her now. When they'd first met he'd seemed nearly extinguished, but here his eyes shone with the tower's light and he was sharp, present, hyperreal. For a moment Laura forgot to breathe. She was dazzled.

"So yes. Thank you, Laura Kramer."

"Thank *you*," she murmured.

The lullaby ended.

———∞———

The next morning they returned to the Sweeper shop the same time they had yesterday. It was the same crowd as was there the first day, with the addition of two more apprentices, who sat near Helen and Leo. Despite the Blairs' sour expressions, these two looked attentive and excited to be here.

Joseph began by asking where Clae ran off to at the party. By the sound of it Leo hadn't told him anything, and he'd come to the conclusion that there were just so many guests Clae got lost in the mix. He apologized profusely for abandoning his guest in the midst of strangers, but was elated when he heard they'd discovered Puer's tourist spots.

He and Clae went back to talking, this time about the various abilities and mutations of monsters they'd come across. When Helen and Leo looked up, Laura glared at them. Helen was normally quiet in the first place, but Leo kept his lips sealed. On this day Clae spared Helen no glance at all, as if she truly weren't in the room, but Laura couldn't help but keep looking back at her. The more she stared the more she could see familial resemblance, age concealed by cosmetics. Every time the woman looked at Clae, infrequent as it was, she would turn to Leo, smoothing his hair, whispering to him, gesturing at something, and Laura felt angry, like she was doing it to rub facts in Clae's face—*This is my son, this is the one I wanted.* Laura felt almost sick with anger.

Tension was high in the room, so when the telephone rang many of them jumped.

"Ah, Melody, could you get that?" asked Joseph.

Melody nodded and walked over to answer it. "This is the Puer Sweepers Guild. How may we assist you?"

Joseph turned back to Clae. "Where were we?"

"The china doll," Clae prompted.

"Oh, yes, of course."

Melody's brow furrowed and she turned back to them. "It's the operator. She says she's patching through a call from Amicae."

"From Amicae?" repeated Joseph, amazed. "But that must cost a fortune! How are they even managing it?"

"I'm not sure, but they're looking for the Sinclair Sweepers."

"Laura, you can get it," said Clae.

"You're sure?"

"You're better dealing with operators."

She took the earpiece from Melody and moved in front of the mouthpiece. "Hello?"

"Hello, who is this?" asked a shaky, female voice.

"I'm the apprentice with Sinclair Sweepers. My boss is a little busy right now."

"I'm sure you'll do. I'll put the call through. It may be a bit distorted, we're not good with long distance."

"That's all right."

"Right. Patching it through now."

Crackling noises followed. The first was loud, but it died down so it sounded like crinkling paper in the background. There was no voice, even when she waited half a minute.

"Hello?" She heard a distorted echo of her voice on the line, and it was a moment before there was an answer.

"Laura?"

The crinkling increased along with the voice, but Laura recognized it immediately.

"Okane? Hey, what's wrong?"

"Laura, I don't have a lot of time on this line." Even with the crackle she could tell he was panicked. "But --- have to get back here. I said I could handle it, but I've got no idea how to fix this. Something's really, really wrong."

"What do you mean, what's wrong?"

"I don't know, something just is. I can't pinpoint it, but the whole city feels wrong!"

"Calm down. What do you mean, it—"

"It's like I'm sensing an infestation. It's far away, but it's close, and no matter where I go I can feel it. It changes even when I'm standing still! This thing is big and it's nasty and I don't know where it is but it's there."

"You mean like on the jobs we've done, you're sensing it like that?"

"It's worse than all of those put together. I haven't been able to *sleep*. I'm scared, Laura. Everything here is just horribly, horribly wrong and I don't know what to do."

"Hang on a second, okay? I'm getting Clae." She turned around. Clae and Joseph were still talking, but Clae was looking at her. "Sorry, Mr. Blair, but I have to steal Clae for a moment."

"What's wrong?" Clae stood up.

"It's Okane," Laura said as he grew closer. "He says he's sensing infestations everywhere, and he wants us to come back. Keeps saying something's gone really wrong."

"Ask if there's any one place he senses it more strongly."

Laura relayed that over, to which Okane replied, "No, it's all bad. What should I do?"

Clae thought for a moment. "We're going back. Tell him to keep doing the rounds, monitoring Pits and taking note of any signs. We'll figure this out."

Laura repeated this into the telephone.

"Hurry," Okane replied. "I don't think I can stand this much longer."

"We'll be there as soon as we can. But you have to sleep, okay? Do the rounds, but make sure you rest."

"But it'll get me in my sleep."

"Sleep, or you won't be able to function properly and it'll get you when you're awake too."

Okane grumbled uneasily.

"We'll see you as soon as we get there."

"Please make it fast. The infestations aren't the only ones on the move." The line went dead.

"I'm sorry, what's going on?" asked Joseph.

"My other apprentice is in trouble back in Amicae. He thinks he's found multiple infestations. We have to go back and fix it."

"That sounds grave," Joseph fretted, getting to his feet.

"Unfortunately, it seems so. Thank you for your hospitality, but we should leave as soon as possible."

"I'll ring the depot for you, then. Make sure there's a train for you," Joseph offered.

"That would be appreciated."

"Good luck to you." Joseph shook his hand. "It really has been a pleasure."

"Likewise," Clae replied.

Joseph walked to the telephone. Clae and Laura headed toward the exit, but as they passed the other Blairs there was a whispered "*Fratricide.*"

Clae stopped short. He eyed them with subdued malice. Joseph was too busy cranking the telephone to notice. Leo ducked his head after a while but Helen stared back, accusing. Clenching her teeth, Laura grabbed Clae's sleeve and tugged him away. They kept glaring at each other until the shop door closed again.

23

SICKNESS IN THE EARTH

The train to Amicae left around five in the afternoon, and they arrived in Amicae at three the next day. Clae spent the time with their new Gin either on his lap or directly next to him as he dozed. Laura tried to sleep and was half asleep when they reached the city. The roar of the train didn't change, but Clae did.

Immediately he sat bolt upright, eyes wide, clutching the Gin bag. His normal neutral expression dropped, and Laura could see that he was downright shocked.

"What's wrong?"

"No wonder he called us back," Clae hissed. "How can you not feel that?"

"Feel what?"

"The sickness in the earth."

"Waxing poetic, are we? Seriously, what's going on?"

"There's something below us. Like an infestation, only bigger. A *lot* bigger."

"Below us? How is that possible? You don't think there's an infestation in the sewers, do you?"

"God only knows. Wherever it is, it's big, active, and moving. We have to figure out what's going on."

His default expression settled back into place, but if he was really anything like Okane he was ready to panic on the inside.

This time the train carried mainly passengers, not cargo, so they disembarked inside the depot. The building was full of people. Wealthy travelers and shabbier businessmen pushed through loud peddlers and vending stands. Railroad workers bustled about the trains or tried to direct the crowd, shouting over the already deafening chatter. Okane hovered between a snack stand and a pillar, and hurried over as soon as he spotted them.

"---'re here, thank god."

"We caught the first train we could. Are you doing okay?" Laura asked, because while the circles under his eyes weren't terrible, he was shaking.

"Just stressed."

"Do you have any other information on the situation?" asked Clae. "I can tell it's there, but where exactly and how are a good start."

"I don't know any specifics," Okane admitted. "But I did the Pit round today, and when I opened it, smoke came out."

"What kind of smoke?"

"Thick. Black. Smelled awful." Okane shuddered. "I also saw someone suspicious."

"Who's that?"

"He had a number on his face." The mention stunned Clae into silence, so he hurriedly continued, "Do --- remember that morning, on the way back from the barracks? There was a Sullivan truck blocking the way, and --- spoke to the man in the hat? There was a bald man with him. It was him. That was the Rexian."

"The Rexian Sweeper was working with the mobs?"

Okane shook his head hopelessly. "I don't know for sure. They were arguing about which Sullivan said what, and they didn't seem happy with each other. The Rexian was very intent on finding a bulwark and breaking it."

Clae was quiet for a minute, then walked purposefully toward the door. The other two trotted in his wake, trying not to lose him in the crowd.

"Do you know what's going on?" said Laura.

"I have an idea, but I need to be sure. Keep close and keep an eye out. It sounds like the Rexians are finally making good on their Sweeper attack."

Laura understood where they were going when they took the cable car to the Fifth Quarter. Clae only frequented two places in this Quarter, and as far as she knew, he didn't need to check in with the Amuletory. He didn't have reason to check the tree either, but he never did. She was prepared for another long spell of sitting on roots, but that thought died when they arrived.

The tree's leaves were now a beautiful, vivid red with undertones of orange. While some still clung to the branches, most were on the ground, probably scattered by passing feet. But it wasn't surprising those were on the ground. The tree was on the ground too. It looked as if someone tried to rip it up out of the earth and failed, so hacked through the roots. The trunk lay horizontal a foot from its mauled stump, branches broken by the fall and its magnificent crown of leaves strewn like a pool of blood from a crime scene.

And it was a crime scene. A symbol had been painted before it, hurried but distinct: a kingshound with its jaws open and legs stretched in full gallop. Laura had grown up with this picture in films and textbooks, as familiar as the mobster circle, all accompanied by blood. It was Rex's calling card. Some leaves still stuck in the paint; it was fresh.

Clae looked over it in silence. He didn't bother to come near the leaves. It hardly even looked like he was breathing.

"What happened?" Laura whispered.

"Sabotage."

"Who sabotages a tree? Why would Rex—"

"It was vital. I don't know if that ex-apprentice opened his mouth, or if that Rexian figured it out on his own. Either way this is bad. We're going to the police."

Laura was completely lost, but she could tell by Clae's tone that they were in deep trouble.

The police station was in the Third Quarter. There were smaller stations in multiple locations all over the city, but this was the main office and probably where Chief Albright was. They barged through the door and to the front desk. The elderly man there looked up through glasses that magnified his eyes to the point where he looked like a bug.

"May I help you, sir?"

"I need to talk to the chief of police, now," Clae demanded.

"The chief? I'm afraid I'll have to direct you to a lower level first. I'm sure they'll be able to help you just fine."

"Look, old man, I am the head Sweeper and I need to see the chief of police. This is an emergency."

The old man squinted at him before recognition dawned.

"Sweeper? Ah, MARU business! Right." He turned around in his chair and called, "Somebody get the chief! Sweeper needs to talk to her!"

"She's working on some papers. Just send him back to her office," someone called back.

"There you have it, sir," the old man sighed. "She's at the end of the hallway, can't miss her."

They strode down the hall, ignoring the windows into other offices, and arrived at the end door. Clae pushed it open without so much as a knock. Albright sat behind a large desk laden with paperwork. There were pictures and some wanted posters on her walls, along with a nicely sized window. Albright herself hunched over her desk, pen in one hand, other hand massaging the bridge of her nose where her glasses usually rested.

"Did you need something, Sinclair?" she asked, sounding tense but exhausted.

"We have a problem."

"'We'?" She glanced at a small calendar. "You're not due back for another day at least. Why are you even in the city?"

"I was called. As I said, we have a huge problem. We have to evacuate."

The word made Laura's heart skip a beat. What could possibly warrant an evacuation? Albright obviously felt the same.

"What are you talking about?"

"Look," Clae hissed.

He snatched her pen and turned over one of the papers to draw on the blank side. He made a simple sketch of Amicae and drew three vertical lines down the center and below the last level.

"These are the Pits." He pointed at the three lines. "You know what they're for. Drop any broken amulets down them, wash the contents once a week to keep out infestation. The bottom of the Pits used to rest on top of the magic strains underground, but due to excessive mining, most of the magic and its buffer are gone. To replace that, we put a tree here"—he circled a point on the Fifth Quarter line, then sketched branching lines downward and toward the Pit lines—"which, being a living creature *and* an inanimate object, acted as a living amulet. The roots were guided around the Pits to be that magical buffer, and as long as it lived, it would have magic running in those roots. It killed infestations, kept any that existed from getting out. That same tree happens to have been *cut down*. The buffer is destroyed. If those roots die off, they're as good as empty amulets."

"Infestations could begin in the roots?" Albright rose from her chair.

"It'll take a while after the chopping for the roots to be habitable, and that tree only just came down from what I can see. We're safe for a little longer. But once the roots are breached, that's not the only place these things will go. They can get through the buffer, into the mining area. And from there?"

He scribbled a thick line, right up through the core of the city.

"Access to the interior. To the workers, to the utilities, to the pipes. We won't be able to stop the spread."

"Damage control," said Albright quickly. "What can we do to stop them from getting out?"

"I would flush the Pits well and put charged amulets around the bottom until we get a permanent solution. But that isn't going to solve the problem. There's more."

"How can there possibly be more?"

"Okane took care of the southwest Pit this morning and reported black smoke coming out of it. That means there's a multitude of maturing infestations down there, maybe months old, all festering. The weekly magic dose isn't killing them. It can't *reach* them. The Pit has been compromised. Can you think of anything in the past few months that could've damaged it?"

"No, there can't have—" Albright realized something, and her face became enraged. "Sullivan," she hissed. "He was complaining to us about the Pits and how he wanted the space for his sewage pipes! We told him it wasn't acceptable but he must've gone ahead and done it. I'll kill that little bastard, I'll kill him!"

"If he damaged the Pit, infestations may already be in the interior. Have people been going missing yet?"

"They told me it was a mining accident." Albright curled her hands into fists. "We lost a number of people in the lowest levels."

"Get everyone out of there and evacuate the city."

"Where are we supposed to be sending people, into the wilds?"

"At least there your guns will work on the enemy."

"Can you take care of this?"

"The existing infestations?"

"Yes."

"We can damn well try. I'll need to investigate the area to find them, though."

"Good. I'll send out the evacuation order."

"When you're done with that, telegraph the other cities. Send out an SOS. Ask for assistance and shelter, but most of all call in the other Sweepers. Three of us may not be able to handle everything."

"I'll have some officers take you to the place soon. They'll pick you up from your shop once we've got the evacuation on the road. In the meantime, get ready."

She stalked out the door. Down the hall they could hear her barking orders.

"All right, men, we've got an emergency on our hands. We need the entire city evacuated, ASAP. I want the telephone operators calling everyone. I want police overseeing the evacuation, make sure everything stays orderly. I want the military leading out, fully armed, and I want every single person who isn't necessary to our operations outside the walls by sundown. Normally the Council would be making this order but I'm overriding them. We don't have time for the official decision; god knows some of them would fight it. The walls are breached. We have a massive infestation in the interior and it's spreading as we speak. I don't care if you have to tell people that it's an infestation, or that the mobs have decided to burn the city to the ground, whatever it takes to get people out of here. We take too much time, and we are all dead. Get going."

The time was now 4:45 P.M., and the evacuation order traveled fast. Laura had heard it broadcast on the pawnshop radio as they passed.

They currently sat in the Sweeper shop, waiting to be picked up. Laura had as much equipment as she could comfortably fit in her bag and pockets, and was very glad she wore kin-treated clothing today. She kept patting at the bag, tapping at the glass of Eggs every few minutes to reassure herself that she hadn't forgotten them. The nervous habit seemed right at home in this atmosphere. Clae flitted between his briefcase and the drapes, restless. Every once in a while he deposited more equipment on the surfaces next to them without a word, not even pausing before continuing his pacing; Laura had long run out of room and simply pretended to pack them even as she stowed it all under the counter. Okane sat on his stool, still quivering. If the presence of one infestation could scare him, the group of them must've had him terrified.

Outside the windows people rushed to evacuate. Shop owners passed with what wares they could carry, but others were smart enough to bring shelter and protection from the cold instead. A few went by with sticks and blankets to furnish tents, pillows, and winter clothing.

Mr. Brecht was not one of them. He tried to walk off with a teetering stack of books, but Mrs. Keedler caught him and scolded; she dumped an extra comforter on his load and kept him close to her and her husband. Laura watched until they were out of sight, trying to ignore the tugging feeling in her chest. How many people were uprooted now? Would every last person escape the city, or would there be a skeptical or wary few staying in familiar surroundings? With a jolt, she wondered if she knew one of those people; many times Morgan refused to acknowledge when situations went wrong. During the pregnancy debacle she'd acted like everything was fine, kept reaching out to family or to Cheryl's father even when they shouted or threatened her. Would she be in the apartment now with that placid, fake smile, convincing herself and Cheryl that nothing was wrong? The idea made Laura's stomach turn. She sprang to her feet so fast Clae stopped his pacing to stare.

"Can I make a call? Just a quick one. It's important, I swear."

"If the operator will put it through," he grumbled, pushing back through the drapes.

Oh, she'd *make* them put her through. Laura cranked the telephone so hard the entire setup rattled on the wall. Someone picked up right away.

"Did you have a question about the evacuation?" asked the operator.

"No, sorry. Is it possible to put me through to the Cynder Block?"

"My apologies, but I have to tell you to get out of the city. There's an evacuation order."

"I know, but I can't leave. I'm a Sweeper, so I get to deal with the problem." The operator was silent, so she hurried to explain. "Don't worry! I just need to get through to my family. I have to make sure my aunt gets out."

"It'll have to be fast. The switchboards are busy here."

She connected the call. It took a while to be picked up, and Laura was surprised when Morgan answered.

"Hello? This is the Cynder Block. You don't have to worry, we're on our way out!"

Laura let out a shuddering breath. "Morgan? It's me."

There was a laugh, both despairing and relieved. "Oh my god, Laura. Are you okay?"

"I'm fine. I never sent you that letter you asked for, but I wanted you to know I got to Puer and back in one piece."

"When did you get back? Are you still inside the city? Oh, of course you're in the city, you're on the telephone."

A weak smile tugged at Laura's lips. "I'm at the Sweeper office. Just needed to check if you were evacuating. How's Cheryl taking it?"

"Not well!" The shrill tone told Laura that Morgan wasn't thrilled either; it sounded like she was working herself into a tizzy. "Not well at all, but at least she's got her doll. Don't worry, we're all getting out. Do you want us to meet you somewhere?"

"No, just go ahead."

"But how are we going to find each other? I mean—"

"Sorry, Morgan, but I'm staying here. It's the kind of monster we're supposed to be hunting, so we get to take care of this one too."

"But we're being evacuated! They can't really be expecting you to fix all this! I mean, you only work in inventory! What if you get hurt? Or—or killed?" She ended with a horrified squawk.

Laura had never felt more horrible about that lie. She hesitated a moment, considering telling the truth, but clenched her teeth instead. She couldn't do that. Not now. She bit back her loathing and threw on a fake smile, willing her façade back into place. Just keep up the act. "Don't worry, I'll be fine."

Okane slowly turned and gave Laura a disbelieving stare.

"I don't believe that," Morgan whispered.

Okane's eyes felt like an accusation. Laura avoided them and hunched toward the phone, but she could still feel them boring into her back. "I promise, I'll be fine. Just get out of here and I'll find you later."

"You better make good on that promise."

"I will."

"Y-you promise. You promise . . ." Morgan's voice tapered off into a wavering hiss of distress, and Laura felt a wave of guilt as she realized the woman was starting to cry.

"I promise," she whispered. "See you, Morgan."

"See you, Laura."

The earpiece clicked easily into its hook. Laura stood there awhile, eyes fixed on the bells and hand not quite willing to drop.

"That was a lie," said Okane.

"Just a little one," Laura growled, crossing her arms.

"Look alive, you two. Our ride is here," Clae barked, walking past.

There was a car parked outside the shop, a long, boxy black wagon with white wheels and AMICAE POLICE DEPARTMENT emblazoned on the two doors. The driver greeted them as they emerged.

"Hop in, we're going to the interior." He held the door open. "There's a squad over there already to assist you."

Okane and Laura clambered into the back. Clae and his briefcase claimed the passenger seat. Their car didn't move fast—too many people clogged the street and they didn't dare risk hitting anyone—but they reached the door to Amicae's core eventually. It was one of the doors they used for Pit monitoring, the one that should've been visited today. The sight was familiar, though the people outside were not. Workers filtered quickly out the door between lines of policemen. The car pulled up just out of the way, and the engine died with a gurgle. The Sweepers climbed out and Clae called, "What's the situation?"

The police looked around, but they weren't the first to step up. The one who rushed forward was the bearded man who always opened the door for them.

"There ya are, son!" he cried. "You the one who ordered evacuation?"

"What of it?"

"Ya were damn right to do it! Every man workin' under the Fifth Quarter's gone! Completely gone! Elevator came up empty!"

Laura's stomach dropped. She had to remind herself that winter months were almost an off-season for mining, that so close to his break her father wouldn't be in the mines but would be writing reports in a satellite town.

"Fifth down, you say?" Clae's brow furrowed.

"That's the last of them!" announced the policeman nearest the door.

The line of men had ended. They hurried down the road while the police gathered closer together.

"What's your plan, sir?" Their driver hovered by Clae's shoulder; now that he was close, Laura realized it was Collins. "We'll help you as best we can."

"We need to investigate the situation, so we need to get in there."

"If that's what you need."

"I can help," offered the bearded man.

Collins shot him down. "No. Civilians need to leave the city."

"But I know how everythin' works in there," the man argued.

"We may need the elevator, at least," said Clae. "Let him come."

Collins looked dubious but relented. "How should we proceed?"

"You all stay near the exit." Clae gestured at the policemen. "You don't have the weapons to fight infestations, so your best defense is the sunlight out here. It won't last long but it may last long enough. Now that people aren't swarming down there, the monsters might be looking around up here to hunt. If something comes at you, run. And you"—he glanced at the bearded man—"stay close to us."

"Sounds good."

"Let's begin, then."

They followed him through the door.

The center of the city was quiet now. There was no hum of machinery in the factory areas, no booming of the miners. No voices. The boilers still spat, but more quietly, and the smoke had thinned significantly, simply trailing up in thin wispy clouds. No one was there, and it made Laura uncomfortable. It had always been busy before.

Clae handed his briefcase to Okane and shucked off his coat. This he put around Laura's shoulders. She jumped and gave him a suspicious look.

"What's this? Security blanket?"

"Okane and I have more of an advantage when it comes to defense. Keep that on and don't get killed."

He talked big, but he looked pale.

"Are you sure? I have kin-treated clothes now. I should be fine."

She made to take it off but he set a hand on her shoulder and grumbled, "We covered this before. I'm not bringing you along so you can get killed. You wear the coat or you get to wait outside."

Laura wrinkled her nose but pulled it on properly. It was too big for her, shoulders too wide, sleeves reaching halfway down her hand. Clae muttered something to Okane, then stepped out onto the bridge. The others were half a step behind him.

This empty core was eerie, and it made Laura shudder. There seemed to be nothing here. Abandoned machinery, sure, but no sign of life or amulets. Looking down over the railing gave a nearly unobstructed view of the lower levels, but Laura could only count the lights of one. Everything below was dark. When she said this aloud, Clae replied, "The infestation has been there in force. Broke the lights for its convenience."

"So we know it's limited to down there."

"Not necessarily. That's just where it's mainly concentrated. For all we know, some have crawled up."

"That's reassuring," Laura muttered, pulling the coat tighter.

"Look." Clae pointed up and to their backs.

Turning, Laura followed his gaze. There was a long black pipe, several feet wide, running straight down; on this level it floated alone in space, and in the next-highest level it was flush against the wall.

"Is that the Pit?" wondered Okane.

"That's the one that was damaged. Can't see where, though."

Clae squinted up above and then down below, looking for a breach.

"The Sullivan pipe project was being built between the Fifth and Sixth Quarters," said Collins.

"Then that's more than likely where it is. I'm going down in the elevator."

"To do what?"

"Confirm that this is the broken Pit and locate the damage. Likely as it is that Sullivan pipes are to blame, we have no hard evidence for it. Besides, I want a better look at the infestations. Depending on their maturity, this could be more difficult than expected."

"I can get the elevator ta work," the bearded man assured them. "Hang on just a minute."

He hurried to the control panel.

"I don't think it's a good idea to go down there." Laura looked uneasily over the edge again. The dark felt menacing. Just looking at it made her stomach lurch.

"We've got no other way to check it out."

"I could go down," Okane suggested.

"What?"

"I can repel them a lot better than --- can. They might leave me alone." Brave words, but he was still shaky.

"You think I'm going to send my apprentice down there?" Clae's voice was acidic.

"It's the smarter move. They might attack --- if --- go down there. Just . . . just don't, okay?"

"I'm not putting either of you in any more danger than I have to."

"That's not much better if—"

"You are not going down there."

Okane backed down, but he obviously wasn't happy.

"Here." Collins held out a large box with dials and a speaker like a radio. "It's a radio transmitter; one of the university students came up with it. We've got the receiver being brought in. This way you can report the situation as you go without yelling. We probably wouldn't be able to understand you, and besides, from what I remember you don't like to be too loud around those monsters."

"Not bad," Clae murmured, turning the cumbersome box over in his hand.

"We hoped so, sir. The military carried all their radio equipment out with them, so it's a good thing the students were willing to help. Otherwise all we have for communication are the call boxes. Needless to say, those wouldn't work too well."

"I've got this all ready ta work," called the bearded man.

Clae pointed at Laura and Okane with the transmitter. "If the infestation attacks, get out of here. One or two you might be able to fend off, but if you end up with an entire swarm on the move there's no way you'll make it. If that happens, run. Run fast, seal the door, get somewhere with light."

"We're not sealing the door if you're still stuck in here," said Laura.

"Yes you will. Okane, I know you can run, you can tell when it's stupid to stay. If she tries to play hero or something, drag her out too."

Okane nodded, and Laura glared.

"But what about you?"

"I'm resourceful." Clae shrugged.

"You're batty," she grumbled.

"Better a pain, remember?" he hummed, walking off to the elevator.

He climbed in and the grille closed behind him. After some conversation with the bearded man, he dug out an Egg and shook it. The elevator descended, slower than usual. The Egg's glow dipped lower and lower into the dark.

It was a while before a noise prompted Laura to turn around. The policemen had brought in a large box with many dials and meters and another, larger speaker. This one filled the carrier's arms, and she deposited it on the grated floor with a grunt. The needles jumped as Clae's voice issued from it.

"I can see the break. That's Sullivan piping all right, got the name stamped on it and everything. Looks like they tried to redirect the Pit, but they did a bad job of it. No wonder kin isn't getting to the amulets."

"I'd like to see the look on old man Sullivan's face when the chief gets ahold of him," mumbled Collins, and the other policemen chuckled.

There was another, longer bout of silence before Clae continued. When he did, his voice was quieter.

"The infestation has filled out. I can't see amulets. I can't even see the floor. They occupy all the space from halfway down the Fifth Level. They're calm, though. Slight movements. More searching than threatening. I think at this stage they're still small enough where they only register things that move and breathe as food. Takes a while for them to graduate from that. But there's a hell of a lot of them, to cover this much space."

There was a pregnant pause, and when he spoke again, it was with a deadly calm that chilled Laura's insides.

"Bring me up."

The policemen looked up at each other in surprise.

"Bring me up," Clae repeated. "I have a *kaibutsu* staring me in the face."

Laura remembered the bloody eye she'd seen however long ago and sprang to her feet. "Come on, get him back up here!"

"On it!" The bearded man did something with the control panel, and the elevator reversed.

"Faster!" Clae's voice hissed. "And get out! It's following me up and the others aren't far behind!"

The bearded man pulled a lever, and the cables squealed in protest.

"That's fast as it can go, but if ya really want us out I won't be able ta stop it for ya!" he shouted over the side.

"Then get out!" Clae's voice roared from the receiver. Strange noises issued from it, like the transmitter was being cracked against something; the garbled sound of the grille made Laura realize he'd forced the elevator open.

The police made a mad scramble for the door, bearded man among them. Before Laura realized what was happening, Okane grabbed her hand and gave a sharp tug.

"It's coming up! Keep to the right!" he cried, eyes wide in panic.

They took a few steps after the police, keeping to the right-side railing as the elevator shot up. Clae jumped out. His amulets must've been active, because he landed on the platform far too easily. He was sent tumbling forward as a surge of blackness roared up from below. It clipped the edge of the platform and caused it to snap forward, sending him sprawling onto the bridge. The blackness split, surged, twined together into a skeletal hand, far too many fingers and far too sharp. The fingers sliced through bridges and smoke before catching the elevator with a horrific crunch and yanking down. The entire shaft broke. Cables came free and the part of the shaft not bolted to the wall came crashing down. A metal beam plunged through the air not two feet from them, trailing sparking wires and loose pieces as it careened into the wall and fractured further. Debris landed and smashed upon the bridge, causing the surface to shake violently, while more of the structure groaned and snapped overhead. Laura almost lost her footing. Beyond the wreckage Clae stumbled to his feet.

"Clae!" Laura shouted. "Get over here!"

"What are you waiting for? Start running!" he yelled back.

"That's a good idea," said Okane.

"But Clae is—"

"Is going to kill me if we don't get out of here now!"

Clae scaled the debris and sprinted toward them, gesturing furiously for them to *move*. Laura finally got her feet going and they ran for the door. A strange sound like that of the boilers went through the air, followed by a crescendo of hissing, squealing infestation. There was an echoing gunshot and flash behind them, and Laura looked over her shoulder.

Clae was still running, gun in hand. Parts of the infestation swept onto the bridge to block him, roiling and bubbling like water through the grates, mutated hands cresting every wave. He fired at them so they recoiled and fell away again. As he concentrated on that, he didn't notice the enemy at his back. A dark tendril lashed out, wrapping around his ankle and yanking him off his feet. His face smacked hard against the metal grating, but he recovered fast. He pointed the gun down at the creature and shot. It squealed but didn't relent. If anything, it got angry. It split again, clawed at him the way the one on the train had clawed at the doors. Kin bullets only made it scream louder. Light could be glimpsed in the mess, and the amulet on his belt matched the luster, shrilling almost as loud as the monster, but kicking was doing no good. The rest of the infestation bubbled in the grate near his head, and this portion of the bridge jerked, groaned. Clae ran out of bullets. He chucked the gun and grabbed for the second one in its holster, but the creatures pulled harder. The bridge section twisted sideways and he had to cling to keep from falling off completely. The loaded gun skidded over the grating and plummeted into the interior.

Laura skidded to a stop and turned to go back, but Okane grabbed her arm. She threw him off once, twice, before he went to physically block her path.

"Get out of the way!"

"No! Laura, please, we have to get out now!" He looked completely terrified, snapping and popping issuing from him, but Laura was too upset to care.

"I'm not leaving him behind!"

"What are you, an idiot?" Clae shouted. "Get out of here before it catches you!"

Laura tried to get around Okane again, to no avail. The bridge wavered, Clae just barely clinging on. His face was furious but his eyes were wide and alight in a way she'd never seen them. Wild. Afraid.

"Run!" he screamed. "Now!"

The structure shuddered again, and his fingers slipped. He tumbled over the side. Laura lurched forward, but Okane caught her and this time he didn't let go.

"I'm sorry, I'm sorry, I'm sorry," he hissed, pushing her back. "But *please*, he said to run!"

Cackling. The infestations that had harassed Clae bubbled and turned now. They moved through the grating like a many-armed shadow, grasping with flat claws, wriggling madly over and under debris and closing in fast. Laura forced herself to turn and run. The pair sprinted for the door and safety. All the while Laura could hear gleeful hissing on her heels. She almost didn't think they'd make it, but then, maybe five feet from the door, an unearthly howl rose up from the bowels of the city. The bridge rattled and snapped as the howl grew louder, and something illuminated the walls in a cast of eerie light. The monsters stopped their pursuit and milled in confusion as the near-nonexistent airflow became a strong wind.

They got out of the door and it slammed behind them. The gears at the top ground furiously and policemen rushed to jam them so the door couldn't open again. The others yelled for some reason or another: how could this happen, get the chief, we need a plan of action, abandon the city.

Laura and Okane stood rigidly in the middle of it all. Laura watched them rushing, heard the noises, but it seemed muffled somehow. A weird calm settled over her mind. All she could think about was how she felt like she was swimming in a coat that was impossibly big, and she could never fit the shoulders that seemed so wide now.

24

ANSELM

The street outside the Sweeper shop was lit. With every house emptied, the police diverted energy to the streetlamps: they blazed like miniature suns to ward off any monsters.

Laura and Okane had been sent back to the shop under the pretense of regrouping or forming some plan or getting equipment. Laura didn't really know which. It was more because they looked on the verge of a breakdown and no one knew what to do with them. They probably thought familiar surroundings would help, but the shop looked alien.

Laura stopped in the doorway and stared. Suddenly she couldn't comprehend what was once a safe haven. It occurred to her that the drapes had no more protector, so she could go in if she pleased. The thought was more sickening than satisfying. She'd rather never know what was back there if it meant Clae would come back. Okane flipped on the light and walked farther into the room. He paused near a stool and studied it like he couldn't figure out if he wanted to sit or not. Laura's eyes burned. She clenched her jaw and looked at the ceiling until the feeling lessened.

"Why didn't we help him?"

Okane looked up with a wounded expression. "He didn't want us to help. He wanted us to escape."

"But we could've brought him with us. I mean, he was right there! We should've done something!"

"Something like what?" Okane demanded, eyes narrowing.

"We could've used Eggs, or Bijou, I don't know!" At the time it hadn't even occurred to her to use equipment. Now it seemed painfully obvious.

"Eggs and Bijou wouldn't work against that many. It just wouldn't have worked."

"You don't know that."

"I know it's a bad idea. And I know it was impossible."

"Well, why didn't we just charge in? I have this coat on and you've got some anti-monster aura, why—"

"*That wouldn't work!* --- talk about that, but it didn't do Clae any good. Those monsters didn't care about his active amulets. Even if we repel them naturally, we're too small. They could easily overpower us."

"Okane, I don't think you understand," she hissed, clenching her hands and catching part of the coat's sleeves in her fists. This just made it worse. She didn't need a reminder that he was gone, that this didn't fit at all. "What the hell are we supposed to do without him? We need him! Clae was our linchpin! He's the best! He's the only one who knew what he was doing! He's the only one who cared and he's gone and we're all going to die! The city's sunk! He's the only reason anyone ever listened to us! And that—he's what I wanted to be! I wanted to be that person everyone has to take seriously, because I'm not just some stupid girl, I'm here and I have talent and I'm worth something more than this stupid little body, because Clae wouldn't waste time on something pointless! He's the only one who saw me clearly, he's the only one who had faith in—But it doesn't matter anymore! Who cares if I had any talent, because it didn't do him any good!" *So yes—* "He was scared! He trusted me to have his back and I let him die!" *Thank you, Laura Kramer.* "He thanked me, he counted on me, but I couldn't do a thing! Not a stinking thing! We're useless! Why didn't you just let me try?"

She didn't register the fact that her voice was rising, but Okane yelled back.

"---'re not the only one he helped, --- know! Stop making me out to be the villain!"

"I'm not! But we didn't even do anything, and you keep saying—"

"Because if we stayed we all would've died!"

"But—"

Okane yanked up his sleeve and held his forearm in front of her face. Another thing Laura had noticed in the past was how Okane always wore long sleeves. It was getting into the colder months, so it made sense, but other people rolled up their sleeves sometimes when working; Okane never had. She saw now this was because of the multitude of old scars carved into his skin. They were scattered, thin and reddish or white and nearly healed, all about the same size and same shape: a capital "A" with an extra line going through. The symbol for argents. The symbol for money.

"The Sullivans carved me up since I was a child," he hissed. "Clae Sinclair pulled me out of there, so don't act like ---'re the only person he's saved. Don't act like ---'re the only one who hates that he's gone!"

He tugged the sleeve roughly down again and turned away. He went to the middle counter and slid his back down it so he sat on the floor, legs splayed out in front of him.

Laura lingered for a minute, trying to gather her wits. Argent symbols winked before her eyes. Was her mind playing tricks on her? There was no reason why anyone would have argent symbols on them. She wanted to think drawings, maybe tattoos, as rare as those were, but ink didn't look like that. Carved me up. *Carved me up.* Scars?

They took him in as a child, fed him, clothed him—

Abused him. Did you think it wasn't obvious?

She felt a wave of disgust and sorrow. She opened her mouth, couldn't figure out what to possibly say—"That's horrible"? "I'm sorry"? both obvious and too weak for the situation—and closed it again. She took a few unsteady steps and opened her mouth again, but there was nothing. She thought better of it. She sank down beside him instead, close enough that their shoulders almost touched. They stared out at the glare beyond the store windows. The silence was unbroken save for the popping and rushing of the Kin above their heads until Okane spoke again.

"My mother brought me out of the caves."

Laura wasn't sure what this had to do with the scars, with Clae, but kept her mouth shut. His voice sounded hollow, and the look in his eyes was hardly better.

"I was three, maybe. Really little. I don't remember the caves well. What little I do is . . . dark. The caves are still there. The people aren't. Monsters got in. I can remember the panic and the screaming. I had friends there once, but they were eaten. I think . . . I think I saw some of them disappear. I don't remember what their faces looked like anymore, but the sound of it? That's something I'd never forget. My mother took me into the Silverstone caves to escape. We were among the few who did. She said the others went to other havens, but she wanted to find my father. He'd been sent to see how things had changed in the cities. He never came back. Mama said we had to find him, to make sure he didn't go back to a monster nest. She said once he saw us he'd be happy, that he'd make that home we needed. We wandered in the wilds for a long time before we reached Amicae. They let us live in the Fifth Quarter, gave us food and shelter. We'd been there a month before Mr. Sullivan came through on one of his 'humanitarian efforts' and saw us. He hired Mama. She was so excited, because we'd get better food and she'd have better means to ask around about Papa. But when we moved into the big house, they gave her the worst jobs and kept her away from me. Mr. Sullivan only hired her because he saw my eyes and decided I must be some kind of moneymaking luck charm. Funny, huh?" He tilted his head, a bitter smile on his features. "The Fifth Quarter child raking in money? But he said my eyes were money. He knew I could be lucky, but he didn't know it only helped *me*, not others. So he'd go to me when he wanted more money, and somewhere along the line he decided carving money symbols into me was the way to invoke the luck."

Laura felt something nasty creeping up her throat. The scars burned in the back of her mind. She hated herself for ever comparing his eyes to silver coins.

"He told Mama that no one would believe her if she went for help, because she was only Fifth Quarter trash. She didn't know any better. She got sick one winter, horribly sick, and he didn't get her any medicine. He just let her die, because she was an *annoyance*. He could get rid of people easily. If --- resisted him, he'd get rid of ---. So no one so much as questioned him, and I stopped fighting. But then --- and Clae showed up, and he hauled me out of there and I was free. Clae may have been mean at times and all-around strange, but he rescued me and gave me a place to go where no one could find me and drag me back to that house. He was protection, and I *told* him not to go down there! I should've gone. Maybe the infestations would've ignored me longer. I didn't want him to take that elevator. But he did, and he's gone like the haven, and I don't know what to do anymore."

He hung his head and his hair fell like a curtain, cutting off his face.

"It's so much worse when I think it's Sullivan who caused it. Got rid of the annoyances, just like he always did."

Laura reached out, hesitated, then took his hand. She did so gingerly, since he hated being touched and now she knew the reason. When he didn't object, she gripped tighter.

"I'm sorry," she whispered. "I wasn't thinking about anything besides Clae being—" Dead, but she couldn't say it. "I wasn't thinking. I'm just . . . I'm just angry, and sad. It's not your fault. Don't act like it is."

"But ---'re right. We should've done more."

"Didn't I just say I wasn't thinking? Forget everything I've said up to now."

Okane gave a mirthless snort. Laura frowned.

"Look, I didn't know anything about you beyond where we met you and what Clae told me about Magi. When you came into the picture I was scared and . . . jealous, really. I'm sorry for that. I don't hate you, and I don't want you to think I do. You're my friend, I guess. So I don't want to see you blaming yourself. We're going to get through this, okay?"

Okane murmured something in agreement, and Laura turned her head back to the windows. The streetlamps were so bright they hurt her eyes.

After a while, Okane spoke again. "I think I can help a little with the jealousy bit. --- should probably know what's behind the drapes."

"That's where he keeps the Gin."

"That's not all there is. Here, I'll show ---."

He straightened up, slow enough for Laura to get up too without letting go of his hand. He led her over to the drapes and pulled them aside.

The room behind the drapes extended twelve feet to the left and wide enough to fit four people shoulder-to-shoulder. Shelves lined the walls, supporting a multitude of empty Eggs ready to be filled, though a ratty journal peeked out from the glassy shapes. At the far end sat a large clear tub. Tubing ran over the side and into the floorboards; Laura recognized it as part of the Kin setup. The tubes probably traveled under the floor and came back up behind the counter in the main room.

Inside the tub were the two Gin stones, submerged in water. The left-hand one was the familiar, smooth one they'd gotten in Puer, while the right-hand one must've been the stone from under Amicae. It wasn't so smooth, with sharper angles that made it look like a giant's arrowhead. Between them was something Laura had never seen before.

It looked like a child curled in on itself, made out of yellow crystal that turned dark gold at its densest points. It was roughly hewn, but Laura could still make out the details of hands, fingernails, the folds in clothes and the laces of shoes. The statue threw off a light similar to the shimmering Gin beside it.

"What is that?" she whispered, stepping closer. Okane trailed behind, hesitant to get closer but not quite willing to be left behind.

"This is Anselm," he answered. "Anselm Sinclair."

"Sinclair" made something click in Laura's mind. "Are you saying that's Clae's little brother? But . . . he died. How did he end up like this?"

"It happens sometimes with Magi. It turns out their great-grandmother was one of us." Of course, Clae had said that back in Puer. "That's how they got the roots of that tree around the Pits. She'd whisper to it and ask it to grow whatever way. She told Clae about everything. She said that sometimes when we get too stressed, then we can delve too deep into our magic and actually convert ourselves into it. Anselm was about to be killed by an infestation. Between the presence of that infestation and his own fear, his magic reacted. His magical strain consumed him."

Laura remembered Clae saying that all living things were strains, and felt uneasy. "That can happen to people?"

"Only Magi. Normal people can't convert because their magic isn't large or abstract enough."

"So Anselm changed into this." Laura tilted her head. Anselm's hands nearly covered his face, but she could see that his eyes were closed, his face screwed up like he was crying. "And Helen blamed Clae for it."

"Helen?"

"Their mother."

"She's alive?"

"Yes, and she's awful. She's in Puer."

"Clae never mentioned that."

"Trust me, you never want to meet her. But why is Anselm in here? I mean, I understand that Clae might want to keep him safe and close, but why is he with the Gin? Why not upstairs? If Clae didn't want anyone to find him, there would be less likelihood of people stumbling in on him if he were upstairs."

"It's . . . kind of bad," Okane admitted. "Anselm became a strain of individual magic a lot like Gin, but different. Their father decided to use him like Gin."

"They use him like a tool?"

"Combining his brand of magic with the Gin gives it a major boost. Other Sweepers have to use a lot of Eggs to kill an infestation. The ones with Anselm are potent enough to only need two or so Eggs if they're used right."

"But that—It's his brother's *body*! Why would he ever agree to do that?"

"The reason Clae showed me this is because he wanted to see if I knew how to reverse it."

"Can you?"

"I was three when I left the Magi, remember? And Mama wasn't in a position to teach me much before she died. If there is a way I never learned about it. So he stays here, like this." Okane pointed with his free hand at the tubes. "I'll tell --- how the Kin works, too. When the Gin's activated, it gives off a gold kind of fog. Usually that goes into the air, but here it all leaches into the water and mixes together. Then it goes to the setup outside. It's not so much distillation as it is purifying? The system burns out everything but the magical mixture, and the more the magic mixes and the longer and hotter it burns, the more potent it gets. Once it's finished it gets put into Eggs."

"The more magic, but—" She looked at Anselm again, shuddered.

"I know. It's hard to look at."

No wonder he wanted to keep his distance from it. They stared at the tub for a while. Laura wondered what had been happening when Anselm had changed. Where it had happened, when, whether Clae had been right next to him or farther away.

A ring broke the silence, so loud it made them jump.

"Telephone?" squeaked Okane.

"I thought all the operators evacuated," said Laura. She walked back into the main room and picked up the earpiece. "Hello?"

"Laura Kramer?"

Albright. Laura recognized her voice immediately.

"Yes?"

"We've been doing some recovery operations for material in the interior, and we found something. We need you two on-site as soon as possible."

Back on-site. Back with that nest of infestations. If Clae couldn't—no. She dropped that thought immediately.

"Where are you?"

"Second Quarter, same side as the Sweeper building. We've got people waiting at the cable car for you."

"We'll be there as soon as possible."

∞

It had to be half an hour before they arrived at the meeting place. They ran through the streets but the cable car took forever. Police were waiting by the door to the interior, with two of the nearby buildings fully lit. A multitude of cars hauled supplies away, probably down to the people outside. They'd need supplies. It was cold enough for Laura to appreciate the big dusty coat.

Albright stood near the edge of the crowd and held up a hand to get their attention.

"Sorry," Laura apologized as they reached her. "We got here as soon as we could."

"I know. You two doing all right?"

"Given the circumstances."

Albright nodded and led them into the crowd, avoiding a car that bounced past with a load of lanterns and tents.

"I know you're both apprentices, so I'm sorry it turned out like this. Ideally we'd have a backup, but Amicae's policies don't exactly encourage recruit of Sweepers. There's no point in having benefits if no one even knows the office exists."

"Did you send out that call for help?" asked Laura.

"We've had confirmation from Terrae, but they won't be here until noon tomorrow at the earliest. We've yet to get a response from other cities. We've even tried contacting the mobs to get their Sweepers on the job, but we can't reach them. We suspect they fled the city with the rest of the civilians, like rats off a sinking ship."

Albright stopped by a police vehicle. This one was a truck with a covered back, probably used to transport prisoners. Albright turned to them.

"I don't know what's all going on here. Basic amulets and monsters are all I've had to deal with, so this has got me stumped. I'm hoping you have some sort of explanation."

She gestured at the back of the car, and after some hesitation Laura climbed in. There was a small bench on either wall, but lying there on the floor was Clae. He looked like Anselm, gold crystal and all. He seemed frozen as if halfway through a fall, and his expression was enraged, not terrified. Laura knelt and rested a shaky hand on his arm. The crystal was warm, but it was solid and dead. She recoiled, cradling her hand to her chest. Of course he was *dead*. She knew that already, didn't she? But seeing him here like this, expression frozen in crystal, made her insides squirm and her tongue turn to ash.

She distantly heard Okane explaining to Albright. "This has happened before. He's turned himself into that to keep from being eaten. It's magic, but he's not going to change back. He . . . he's gone forever."

Clae's eyes were blank, staring off into empty space. They were nothing like the eyes she'd seen under Gustave's Moon. Laura shuddered and turned her own gaze to the people outside. Albright rubbed her eyes under her glasses.

"That's how it is, then," she muttered. "I don't want to put you on the spot, but do you know what we can do to contain this? Something to keep it down until the other Sweepers arrive? Or was he our only defense?"

Okane shrugged helplessly.

Albright's fingers pressed against her eyelids for a full minute. She exhaled slowly, then peered around at the police nearby. They kept on running, shouting orders, as if movement alone could stave off the disaster.

"So we die, then. Amicae falls."

Laura clenched her teeth and turned away. She couldn't stand to see the resignation in Albright's posture, the people outside she'd failed. Now was the time to do as Clae had ordered: run away to Vitae or Terrae and hope the Sweepers there would accept them. The rest of the city wouldn't be so lucky. Amicae was one of the few cities that allowed refugees. Cities like Puer rejected even small groups. An entire city's worth of people? Even satellite towns would refuse them, if they got that far. Felin weren't the only monsters of the wilds. Infestations, canir, *Rex* awaited them outside the walls. Amicae's people would be decimated even before they set foot on the Terulian Plains. Another Thrax, ridiculed and spoken of as if it belonged to some far-off time that no one could possibly have done anything about. The thought made her feel sick. A lucky few might make it. If the Sweeper guilds would accept Laura and Okane, she could probably smuggle Morgan and Cheryl in with her. They'd be lost, miserable, but at least they'd be alive. She blinked back tears, trying to focus, but the only thing to see here was Clae's ugly statue. What an awful way to go, she thought, but she was almost jealous; he didn't have to face any of this anymore. He ended up just like—

"Kin."

"What?" Albright frowned at her.

"Kin!" Laura repeated, louder. The gears in her mind were turning, clicking into place and moving faster, faster. *Just like Anselm.* Just like another strain of powerful magic. "We can make kin and dump it down the middle of the city, like a giant Pit!"

"We don't have near the amount for that." Okane frowned.

"No, listen." She scrambled back to hang out of the truck. She held the door with a white-knuckled grip and she almost shook, but met his gaze and held it. "Okane, we have four strains now. I know this is bad, it's horrible, but with that combo, couldn't we take out a monster with a *single Egg?*"

"I suppose, but it would take forever to make enough kin," said Okane, slow and dubious.

"What if we used a bunch of amulets to do the work instead of the machine?"

"What do you mean?"

"We put the strains in water, activate them, and get a ton of amulets in the water too, to mix and burn it quickly. It could give us a huge amount of kin in a short time, wouldn't it?"

"But there's water to think about, too."

"How would we get it all down there? Bucket by bucket won't do any good," Albright interrupted. Her voice was dubious but she was straightening, defeat sliding off her shoulders, and Laura's confidence grew at the sight.

"Amicae has a sprinkler system. They installed it in case something inside caught fire."

"Since when do we have that?"

"Since the city was built. My neighbor asked me to look over an essay he wrote on it last semester." She hadn't understood all of Charlie's technical gibberish, but she knew it existed and at this point that was all that mattered. "It was part of a unit in one of his classes: an example of bad design because it poured water but couldn't do it the right way or something. I don't know how it works, but he does."

"You think that'll work on an infestation?" Albright asked skeptically.

"When you dump kin down a Pit, it moves." Laura tried to mime the motion with her arms and failed. "It's *alive,* and it seeks out monsters. If we can get it down there, it'll do the job."

"And this person can figure out the sprinklers? This could work?"

"There's a chance."

"Then we'll try it." Albright's brow furrowed in new determination. "We'll get the amulets and we'll get the man. Describe him. We'll have officers bring him up."

Laura described Charlie as best she could. Inside, she was beginning to get a grip. She could control this situation. This would work.

25

A LIGHT IN THE DARK

"Who is Charlie, again?"

Laura and Okane leaned against the truck with Clae in it, waiting while the police tracked down Charlie. Laura blinked as the question sank in.

"He's one of my neighbors. Remember that time we had to get up at four in the morning to go to the barracks?"

It took a moment before recognition dawned, and suddenly Okane was uncomfortable again; his feet shuffled and his shoulders hunched. "Oh! That person. I remember him. I didn't think he was a friend. --- didn't react well."

"He really isn't."

"Then why did --- help with his classes?"

"We used to be friends." She rubbed the cuff of the coat between her thumb and forefinger, fidgeting and hoping to gain some confidence from the material. "Back when we were Cheryl's age we were almost inseparable. But when people grow up, things change. People grow apart, and that's what we did. What I did, anyway. I don't think he notices much beyond his robots and his own ego. I don't understand robots or machines, and that's all he talks about. It's a real bore having conversations with him. They're not really conversations, more like he's just talking at you to make himself feel smart. *That's* how I got stuck knowing about the class."

"Oh."

"I try to avoid him most of the time now. At first it was just because I didn't like talking to him, but after that time, and the things he said about Morgan?" She shifted into a deeper sulk. "My whole view shifted. He's not that boy I knew anymore, and he's not the ignorant neighbor either. Morgan keeps trying to push us together, but that just makes it worse. And it hurts because she thinks so highly of him." She looked over at him. "How can you say something like that about someone who's cared about you your whole life? How can you break that trust so easily?"

Okane shook his head. "I don't know. I don't have much experience in it." He paused a moment, then said, "--- didn't have to suggest him. --- could've mentioned that it was the class, not specifically him. Surely they'd have retrieved anyone."

"Charlie is my source. If we want this to run smoothly, then we have to make sure there's no communication breakdown. He's our best bet. Don't worry, I can deal with him. I promise I can be professional."

"But if he makes --- uncomfortable, I don't want --- to have to deal with him."

"It's okay." She smiled, but it did little to ease his worry.

A police car rattled back onto the scene, bumping across the cobblestones of their Second Quarter meeting place and coming to a stop just out of the way. A familiar young man with an irregular haircut clambered out.

"That's him," Laura muttered, straightening up. A wash of doubt swept over her mind. The memory of their last exchange resurfaced, mingled with a different memory, of an empty classroom, a teacher with severe eyes. *You're not worth*—She turned quickly to face Okane. "Do you believe in me?"

He blinked at her in surprise, but his face settled into determination. "Of course."

I am worth being here, she told herself as she faced forward again.

I am capable. I can handle this. If Clae believed it, and if Okane believes it, surely I can, too.

Baxter led Charlie over to them, and Albright approached from one of the buildings.

"I'm sorry, but the officer earlier wasn't very clear. Why am I here?" asked Charlie, looking warily around at the proceedings. He had trouble meeting Laura's eye.

"Do you remember talking about Amicae's sprinkler system?" said Laura, crossing her arms.

"I guess, but what does that have to do with anything?"

"Trust me, it's relevant. How does the system work?"

Charlie looked at Baxter, who motioned for him to answer. "Well, it pumps water from the canals up to a central point in the First Quarter, and from there it goes down. Of course, this is the worst of all possible designs. It won't put out a fire, but it'll flood the mines. It only works if you want a big waterfall."

A big waterfall. For a moment Laura could only blink at him. A snort escaped her, and she doubled over laughing. There was uneasy silence from the others. Okane gave her a light pat on the back and mumbled, "Are --- sure ---'re all right?"

She forced herself back up and beamed at his nonplussed expression. "Amicae's a Pit! It wasn't an insult, Clae was being literal! The city was built to be a Pit! This is going to work!"

"Work for what? What's going on?" Charlie sounded terribly confused.

"We can kill the infestation with it," Laura explained. "We'll just pump the magic down."

Charlie looked skeptical, and Albright admitted, "This is the only plausible idea we have. Do you know how the system works, how to get it going?"

"I think I do. If I can get to the central part of the system, I can follow it back and figure it out," said Charlie. "But are you sure that you want to—"

"We're positive," said Laura.

"Is there anything you'd need? Equipment, manpower, anything?" asked Albright.

Charlie shrugged helplessly. "I won't really know until I see it."

"Then we'll get you there right away. You said the sprinkler system was central?"

"Probably right in the middle."

"You two Sweepers come with me. Baxter, take this kid up to the First Quarter and find that sprinkler. Vardy, go down to the evacuation site and fetch the Amuletory staff. We need them and their amulets on hand for this," ordered Albright.

"Yes, ma'am," cried Baxter, snapping to attention.

While the police began to move, Charlie took a step toward Laura. Immediately Okane moved closer, angled enough between them that Charlie stopped short. Laura gave a terse smile.

"Don't you need to follow that officer?"

"I'm sorry," said Charlie. "I know last time we talked, there was a misunderstanding. I mentioned your aunt, and you thought I was saying something different from what I really meant. You got really upset over it, but you had the wrong idea."

"It was what you thought."

His brow furrowed, and his hands fisted. "It wasn't what I thought. You took it out of context and ran with it. I understand you're protective over family, but you can't lash out at other people for things they didn't—"

"Are you really trying to get me to apologize to you, when you're the one who was insulting in the first place?"

His head jerked back in surprise. "I was not—"

Laura held up a hand. "You have every right to say what you think. But at the same time, I have the right to walk away. I have bigger things to worry about than what you think of me. I don't know what Morgan may have said to you, but I am in no way interested in marriage, especially to you. Stop trying to enforce a hold you don't have."

"That's not fair."

"I'm my own person. Emphasis on the *person*. Please respect it, and keep your nose out of my family's business. You've lost that right. Even when you're 'sorry,' your whole demeanor is trying to force me to accept that I'm wrong, and I'm not. This isn't an apology. It's not even a good pretend-apology. I've been reading my boss's tells for a year. Yours are embarrassingly easy to read. Okane, don't we have somewhere to be?"

She turned away completely and focused on Okane's nose as Baxter herded a flabbergasted Charlie back toward the waiting police car. Okane watched them go.

"Are --- okay?"

"Of course I am. Thank you, though." She couldn't exactly word why, but she was grateful. "Just—Thanks."

Albright had climbed into the covered truck and gestured for the two to get in the back. "We're going to pick up the supplies needed from your shop. Make sure that cargo doesn't rattle around too much."

"Cargo"? The word felt wrong, but Laura kept her mouth firmly shut as they clambered in and the engine started. Laura sat on the bench, and Okane sat across from her. As the truck got going and turned sharply, Clae scraped across the floor. Laura and Okane both dove, throwing out hands to keep him in place. Laura glanced out the back to check if anyone saw this, but the door was high enough that people couldn't see the floor.

They arrived at the shop in little time and jumped out to get their supplies. Loading Gin was probably a lot more discreet normally, but with no one around they paraded it out to the car. Laura and Okane moved the actual Gin with relative ease. Albright carried Anselm out with a look of sorrow and disgust. After some shuffling to fit them all in the back, Laura wasn't able to lower her feet to the floor for fear of stepping on one.

Albright drove them to the First Quarter. The streetlights there caught the statues and décor strangely, turning them into ghostly shapes that made the hair on the back of Laura's neck stand on end. A sculpture of Queen Terual XXIII loomed particularly dark, her severe features thrown into sharp contrast. They drove around, seemingly aimlessly, until Albright located the very middle.

The center of the First Quarter was a square with a tall fountain in the middle. Water cascaded for three levels before hitting a wide basin; the pool rose in the center of a sprawling five-pointed star made of glittering white tile, surrounded by a patterned circle. Raised pieces of metal filled in the spaces between star points, overlapping the shapes and completely at odds with the design.

Albright climbed out of the car. She stomped on one of the metal pieces, and it made a low, hollow sound.

"This must be the place," she announced. "Not sure how a fountain is a sprinkler, but this is the only central location that focuses on water."

More cars arrived after them, carrying Charlie and a load of policemen. Not far behind came another officer with the pair from the Amuletory. Baxter led Charlie to the covered truck; both were flushed, as if they'd been running.

"We've located the operating system," Baxter wheezed.

"Then you know how to get it working?" said Laura.

"We do," said Charlie. He didn't look like he wanted to go on, but with two policemen staring him down he couldn't stay quiet. "The system will pump water from our canal system. There are five operation points we'll have to monitor, but even if they're old they seem in good condition. There shouldn't be a problem with the water source. Your problem is the distribution method. See the star design? The metal is covering up holes to the interior. The fountain itself is held up by the piping, which goes through the points of the star. Water goes through and into the fountain bowl. That's when any cleverness in the design dies out. The water overflows the bowl and spills wherever it wants. Technically it should go through the holes, but it could just as easily just go on the tile. There's no pressure, no direction. What gets through the holes just falls through the middle of the interior."

"Once it's kin, it'll move the way we need it," said Laura.

"Take however many men you need to get the system running—we have to get started as soon as possible," said Albright.

Charlie pursed his lips but stepped back. He spoke quietly to Baxter, who relayed these orders to the surrounding officers. Albright got back into the truck and reversed up to the fountain. One tire dipped down onto a metal slab with a banging sound, but the cover held.

Laura and Okane unloaded the Gin and crystal. They kept the strains wrapped in blankets to keep people from seeing what they were. The last thing they needed was someone getting greedy and stealing Gin, or alerting someone who would. Besides, how many people here would recognize Clae? That was one conversation Laura wanted to avoid at all costs. She carried in the Amicae Gin, stooped to place it gently in the water. It was deep enough to cover the rock completely and soak into the blanket. As she drew away again, she felt a prickling feeling.

Laura.

She froze. The water near her knees sloshed faster for no reason, and something strange, something heavy, descended on her with an almost physical weight.

"Gin," she whispered.

The sensation wavered. Pleased.

Laura. See you. See you. What this?

It wasn't words so much as feeling. Images and fragmented emotion flickered through her mind: the shop, humming, water, wrong water, a missing hand a missing friend but that was all right because she was a friend too, wasn't she? Gold fog. It pulled back, prodded more gently.

What this? What this?

Laura hesitated. She pulled the blanket back, ran her hand over the stone, and thought as hard as she could about the situation: about Clae's death, about the infestation below them, about her plan. The Gin seemed to mull over this, but its presence withdrew. Laura waited for some kind of response, but nothing happened.

"Laura, I think ---'re right." On the other side of the fountain, Okane had leaned in to inspect the side of the basin. "There are indents. I think our Sweeper amulets are supposed to fit here."

"Really?" She sloshed over to get a better look. "How many?"

"Five, seven . . . looks like sixteen spots."

"We don't have enough Gin amulets to fill that."

Okane glanced at the group outside the fountain. "Hopefully we have enough from the Amuletory to make up for it."

Albright got the truck out of the way, and police moved in to inspect the metal covers. Unlike Pit covers, they'd been bolted down permanently. Efforts to pry them up ended in failure until someone had the bright idea to call in robots again. Laura still wasn't fond of these things. She slouched in the fountain as the robots trundled in and ripped the covers up out of the ground. Five triangular holes were left in their wake, leading down into darkness. The cleaning bots carted off the scrap metal.

With them out of the way, Freda Ashford came up. She crossed the point of the star as if it were a thick tightrope and set her bag on the edge of the fountain.

"Amulets, as requested," she declared, sounding bored. "I don't know what you want them for, since it's not like you use amulets anyway. Where's Mr. Sinclair?"

Currently wrapped up in the checkered blanket next to Laura's left foot, but she wasn't about to advertise that. Of all people who could know about him, Freda was the absolute last on the list. Laura shifted, putting herself between Freda and the checkered shape.

"He'll be here soon enough," she lied.

"He better be. He's the only good thing there is about Sweepers."

Laura bit her tongue and said nothing. Marshall followed shortly after with another bag, which he deposited with Freda's.

"We've got more amulets in the car if you need them," he said. "I don't know what you're planning to do exactly, but if there's any way we can help, we'll do it."

Freda rolled her eyes and scanned the area for signs of Clae again.

"I think all we need are the amulets," Okane mumbled, keeping his head down. "Thank ---, though."

"Are they full amulets?" Laura pulled a flower-shaped brooch out of the bag to inspect.

"We brought up all the ones ready to sell. They won't run out on you anytime soon."

"Glad to hear it." Laura looked back at Okane. "What do we do with them, again? I'm guessing they'll need more direction than 'mix and burn.'"

"I'll take care of it."

Okane took amulets out of the bags and distributed them in the pool, muttering orders to them that Laura couldn't quite catch. She watched his progress, noting where all the amulets landed. There must've been forty amulets plunked into the water.

Okane patted his hands against his pants once he was done. "---'ll want to get out of the water. It's going to get hot."

"You're staying in?"

"I need to get the strains active. It should only take a minute."

Laura climbed out onto the star. She felt discontent with the gaping holes on either side—they were easily wider than she was tall—but there was enough surface area for her to move easily. It helped that Marshall and Freda had moved back to help with the pumps. On the downside, that time in the fountain meant the bottom of the long coat soaked up water, so Laura felt like she was dragging a weight.

Okane rolled up his sleeves and waded through the pool. He went to the Amicae Gin first, lifting the blanket just enough to touch the stone. Laura half expected something to happen, but despite its "conversation" earlier, the stone didn't act any different, and Okane moved on. In his wake the stone glowed and the water around it became tainted gold. He did this with the other Gin, then the Sinclairs. He hesitated over Clae, and only held contact with Anselm long enough to activate before wading quickly away. By the time he hopped out, the water barely looked like water anymore. He stomped on the ground to shake off any droplets he could.

Before their eyes, steam began to rise from the water's surface. The liquid seemed to be moving clockwise.

"Have you got it ready?" Albright called.

"It's going! I don't know exactly what it's doing, but it's doing something!" Laura shouted back.

"Get those pumps going! We need more water up here!" Albright ordered.

Movement flickered along the edge of the square, and gurgling sounded beneath their feet. The movement of water was interrupted near the bottommost fountain bowl as a fresh supply bubbled up. The movement of the rest of the water grew faster. The steam thickened, creating a fog over the fountain, but Laura could still see the water as it began to froth.

It was only a matter of time before liquid spilled over the side. It started sloppily, just splashing over and falling without a sound. As water began to overflow freely, another gurgle went bubbling through and the pseudo-kin turned deeper gold. Where it slipped over the side it caught the light like Gin, flashing shimmering white.

Before anyone could get their hopes up, there was a low rumble from below them. The ground trembled. Laura caught sight of movement down one of the holes, and the breath froze in her lungs. The infestations were moving, glinting reddish even in the light from the kin water; they were spiraling straight up, toward the fountain.

"Run!" she cried, dashing off of the star. Okane gave a yelp of his own as he sensed the incoming monsters, and fled just as fast.

They were barely off the patterned tile when the infestations hit, slamming into the bottom of the star and flooding around it. Slimy black forms careened through the holes and around the fountain. The black mass formed hands again and tried to grab hold of the fountain, but a single touch prompted the release of black smoke and a series of high-pitched squeals. Unable to grasp that, they wound around the spokes of the star pattern and began to pull. They were trying to destroy it, to stop the kin from being completed and used. Laura pulled out one Egg but didn't arm it. Suddenly she was horrified. What if she broke the support with the explosion? If that star fell, Clae and the Gin would be lost for good.

A curse behind her made her whirl around. Collins stood there, face twisted in a grimace. He turned back to look at (presumably) one of the pumps and shouted, "Chief! The monster's trying to bring it down!"

"Fight it off!" came a strained, distant reply.

Laura didn't know exactly where Albright was but added her own voice to the shouting. "Our equipment might bring it down anyway!"

A few moments of silence passed, and then: "The east door! Get them down there!"

"The what?"

"The east door," Collins repeated, standing still for a second before lurching into action. "Come on, this way!"

"But what is the east door?" Laura demanded, even as she and Okane jogged behind him.

"It's a door to the interior," he explained, climbing into his police car and starting it up. "It'll take you around the inside wall and down to the Second Quarter level, then you can distract the monsters long enough for that fountain to work right."

Okane stopped short, horrified. "We're going back in there?"

Collins paused to stare at him with guilt and apprehension. Laura sucked in a deep breath and grabbed Okane's hand. He jumped and looked at her.

"We can do this," she said firmly. Even if she didn't really believe it, she tried to pretend she did. "Come on. We said we were going to do more. Right?"

He could see right through that act, but while he shook, she gripped his hand a little tighter and he gave a jerky nod.

"Look, I'm sorry we have to send you down there, but you're all we've got," Collins pleaded from the car, trying to get them to hurry up but trying to be polite about it.

"I know," Laura said as she and Okane climbed into the car. They hadn't even sat down before it started moving.

Soon the squealing of the infestation at the fountain fell behind them. As the car sped across the pavement, whipping around corners and charging down streets with a mechanic whirring to rival the squeal in pitch, the passengers slid around in the back. Laura wished there were something to keep her in place, because she was afraid she'd fall out. Automobiles shouldn't go this fast, but Collins was a speed demon. They got to the wall in what must have been record time; the car skidded to a stop near it. It went several feet even after he'd hit the brakes. Laura almost fell out of her seat and onto the floor.

"There!" Collins leaned out to point at a door in the wall, also made of metal but much smaller than the usual doors to the interior. No gears at the top. There was a lock on it, and Laura's heart plummeted at the sight. "Don't worry. I've got this."

Without even turning off the car, Collins jumped out and ran for the door. As she ran after him, Laura checked her equipment. She hadn't discarded anything over the past few hours, so she was still as prepared as she could be—that gave her a little more courage. Collins fiddled with the lock, creating a clacking sound, but soon there was a louder click and he drew back, lock in hand.

"Being from the Fifth Quarter isn't completely useless."

He'd picked it open.

"Thank god," Laura laughed.

He pulled the door open and stood aside, looking at them expectantly. "Good luck down there."

The door opened to a small boxy area a foot and a half wide; to the left, the stairs began. The steps were cast in shadow, going steeply down without so much as a railing.

"This goes down to the Second level?"

"It probably takes a while to walk there. You might want to hurry."

Laura took the first step onto the stairs. With no light ahead, she pulled out an Egg and shook it. Its glow showed blank cramped walls and stairs curving gently into what looked like an abyss. She hated the dark but didn't say anything about it—Collins was right, they didn't have time—and started walking. She went as fast as she could while still feeling safe. Okane stepped lightly behind her. The Egg light traveled over the walls, revealing some wear and tear but otherwise nothing new. After a few minutes she heard metal groaning, a rattling and shifting as the infestations moved. She hadn't heard a crash yet. The star must still be intact.

Finally the light alerted them to a change. Instead of smooth hard wall, the ceiling and left side changed to metallic latticework, the side of one of the familiar caged-in stairs of the interior. With more visibility, Laura could squint and see the infestations. They wound in a twisted black pillar through the middle of the interior, hooked on the star at the top and squirming and shrieking. More pseudo-kin spilled over the mass and they wriggled away from it. The liquid wasn't burning them, but it was enough repellent that they hadn't pulled it down yet. Laura jogged down the stairs, faster now because if she could see them, they could probably sense her. The landing came up, now in view, but a whooshing sound came from below and Okane started to shout.

"*Go, go, go!*"

Laura hurled herself at the landing, skipping stairs and stumbling onto flat ground. She didn't see the infestations until they'd hit. Five different limbs speared through the walkway, hard enough that the grating smashed apart. The closest point had come through barely a foot from Laura. It splattered into the wall and spread up like a crashing wave, looping to cover the ceiling of the latticed stairway. Here it changed direction, transforming from liquid to solid again and wrenching the latticework in its wake. Laura dodged just in time. The infestation split again, drilling five new points into the structure where she'd been, and the lattice came on its back like a spiny hide. Okane managed to evade it, and they both ducked as it flicked; the broken lattice soared just over their heads and crashed into the wall. They bumped shoulders as they straightened.

"We go for the big pillar, right?" Laura breathed.

"We need to draw its attention, but with this one after us I don't know how easy that'll be. --- want to split up, or—"

"No, they'd pick us off easily then."

"True enough."

After only a moment's hesitation they charged across the walkway. The infestation made a piercing sound like laughter and gave chase. More spears shot through the path in front of them, so they had to evade while smoke rose through the grating to curl around their feet. As she ran, Laura replaced the Egg, pulled a length of wire from her bag, tied a knot at the end of it, and threaded Bijou along it. She dropped that end as they reached a branching path and veered right, unraveling the wire as they moved closer to the main problem. The infestation screeched on their heels. Tendrils of black wove through the railing on either side. More hands grew to slide down onto the bridge and grasp the grating. They morphed into jagged teeth, misplaced fingers, caught on the metal and pulled. A low groan rose as the metal warped beneath them.

"Okane! Hang on!" Laura stopped short. Okane halted a few steps ahead of her as she flicked the end of the wire in her grip.

The monster gurgled with glee. Its darkness wrapped to encircle them, dripping all over the bridge and forming a mess of teeth overhead. Okane backed up beside Laura. She could hear, again, snaps and crackles issuing from him as the monster descended. Still louder was the roar that erupted behind them.

The Bijou ignited one after the other down the laid line, ripping the monster away from its source. The first weapon was close, and the shower of light and sparks stung enough for Laura to drop the wire. The darkness around them melted, accompanied by an earsplitting wail.

"Laura! Are --- okay?"

"Fine!" she snapped, pulling on her goggles with smarting hands. "Come on!"

The two closest Bijou registered their amulets quickly and pursued them as the two ran again. Despite Laura's fears that they would fall through the grating, these zigzagged on the metal to avoid the warped gaps. One rolled in front of Okane like a tiny vanguard while the second spat angrily at Laura's feet. The multitude left behind popped, spun, and shrieked on their wire, which glowed red with heat and energy as they slid along it. Their sparks went right through the grating to shower infestations below. More smoke rose beneath them, and a shudder went through the main pillar.

Laura and Okane reached a middle walkway. They weren't quite in the center, the pulsing "pillar" still a ways away, but this was as close as they were going to get.

"Can you hit it from here?" asked Laura, because she certainly couldn't.

"I'm lucky. I can do it," he replied, pulling out an Egg. He tapped it against his amulet and drew his arm back. He let it fly with a loud crack. His momentum almost sent him tumbling over the railing, but Laura caught him.

The Egg sailed through the air, smacking into the dark mass just a foot above their level to detonate on impact. The Sweepers staggered back into the opposite railing at the light and rush of heat. An unholy scream rent the air. Laura blinked furiously. Even with the goggles, looking directly into an Egg explosion stung.

"Okane, put on your goggles!"

"A little late for that!" he growled, but pulled his green-tinted goggles over closed eyes. "Did it work?"

The pillar had fractured. The Egg had pulverized the side, so a section ten feet across was missing. How deep it was Laura couldn't guess, owing to the excessive smoke pouring from the hole. Even as she watched, infestations twirled and slid to cover it. Portions of the side, lower down, shrieked and withdrew toward the lower levels. Still more of the creatures released the star and curled down to investigate.

"It worked," she said. "Can you still see?"

"I'm fine."

"Good." Keeping a hand on his arm to steady him if needed, Laura straightened up and bellowed, "Hey, you! Yeah, you, ugly! We're right here!"

Okane gave a whimpering groan.

The new seeking limbs liquefied. They plunged through the air like viscous rain. They twined back together just under the bridge. A single blow sent a section of grating skyward. The creature surged through the opening like a mess of snakes, but was quickly beaten off by the Bijou. Okane pulled more Bijou from his own bag and tossed them through the sparks, which did a good job of lighting them up; they erupted in midair. Squalling and incensed, the creature retreated. It coiled above and below the bridge, hissing when sparks touched it and roiling as it planned its next attack. Laura pulled out an Egg again, this one still glowing from earlier, and armed it before chucking it at the cloud above them. The Sweepers ducked down, arms over their heads as this one detonated too. The glass didn't fall on them, instead scattering to sear the monster it had burst upon. This creature wailed too, and from the corner of her eye, Laura saw more peeling away from the star.

"We've definitely got their attention."

"We just have to keep it." Okane scowled, tossing another Egg at the oncoming reinforcement.

Another explosion and a loud hiss, and Laura felt a tug at her ankle. She looked down, only to find slimy, toothy blackness slithering around her foot. After a moment of disbelief, she gave a shriek of her own and tried to jump away, but the creature held fast. Her foot was stuck. She was stuck. There was no way it would let her go. She clacked another Egg against her amulet and held it overhead, prepared to throw it at her own feet. It could easily hurt her, even take off her legs, but all she could think of was getting rid of the monster before it ate her. Lose a leg, keep a life.

"What are --- doing?" Okane wrenched the Egg away and threw it, to where Laura didn't know; she was more preoccupied with the infestation writhing its way up her calf.

"Trying to get free!" she screeched at him.

Finally he realized what the problem was and dropped down to grab her knee. "Just give me a second—"

A growling, rumbling sound started behind them. Over by the other walkway, darkness moved. A great wall of it crashed like a wave along the bridge, causing the metal structure to shudder and buckle under the force, and eclipsing all in its path. The Bijou there winked out like vanishing stars, and all the while it approached, *fast*.

"Forget it, just go," she hissed, grabbing Okane's shoulder.

"What?"

"Go! Bijou won't hold that off!"

"But—"

"*I'm stuck, just go!*"

Okane snarled and another loud crack split the air. For a moment she thought he'd broken her ankle, but he leapt back up and dragged her with him along the bridge. Somehow she'd been freed.

"How did you do that?" she panted as they ran.

"Don't really know," he shot back.

"Well, remember it for later!"

The clamor underfoot changed from clanging to thumping as they reached a large platform along the wall. It was even wider than the shop space, so they had more than enough room to run, now without the grating that had lost them a few Bijou. A total of six remained: these circled at high speed, spouting sparks higher than their heads. Laura and Okane both scrambled for Eggs and threw them at the incoming wave, but the Eggs vanished right into the mass. The attack was nearly upon them when they finally blew. Heat rushed over them, mixed with a swirl of dark smoke that made Laura cough. Glass clattered onto the floor, and soon the darkness burned away in the light of the Bijou. The wave had dissolved entirely. It wasn't as strong as it seemed: it had picked up the wire-strung Bijou and been eaten away by them as it progressed. Those Bijou sparked near the edge of the platform.

The liquid spilling downward from the fountain shimmered, but it still seemed useless against the infestations. Laura let out a shaky sigh at the sight.

"Are we sure the fountain is set up right?" she asked as she pulled out another Egg. She didn't have many left at this point. She missed Clae and his briefcase.

"As far as I know," Okane rasped. He tugged his bandana over his face, glancing up at the thinner pillar. "Like I said before, it'll probably take forever to make."

Laura squinted up, running the plan over in her head again. The fountain was the glass tub, the amulets were the Kin. . . . Realization hit like cold water.

"Okane," she said, too evenly. "How long is the water staying in the fountain?"

"I don't know. It's constantly overflowing."

"So we might be pumping in too much water for the process to keep up?"

Kin had to stay in its glass-and-tubing system for an extended period to properly burn out water and other particles. It needed to be isolated after the water stages. She'd been so determined to find an answer that she'd skipped entire steps, and now the whole operation was useless. Comprehension dawned on Okane's face, switching fast to fear and then to tense resolve.

"The amulets are still powering up," he said. "The water's getting darker the longer they go."

"What if this is as far as its power goes? What if it's too diluted?"

"We gave those amulets the order to burn, not boil. If --- give them clear enough orders, they don't fail. They might have a power surge, and some of them might go completely dry, but they'll do it."

Laura took a deep breath, tried to inhale whatever confidence he'd found, and forced a smile. "I saw a few Niveus amulets go in. I suppose we've got that working in our favor; they'll streamline the rest."

"It'll work."

"Then we just have to keep holding the monsters here." She gripped the Egg tighter as the infestations before them roiled, sifted toward them like a black ocean tipping its axis. "What should we do when our supplies run out?"

His breathing was fast. "Rely on the Bijou?"

"How long is that going to work?"

"Can we just focus on staying alive, please?"

"I'm trying to figure out *how* to stay alive!"

A chorus of shrill sounds started up. The lighted levels flickered as a sea of creatures boiled up, clawed hands and tendrils squirming up the walls. The lights on the Fourth Quarter level popped and smashed, demolished by the onslaught as monsters clawed through them. Jutting buildings, wheels, elevator shafts, and machines bent and snapped under the force, sending up their own clouds of wreckage and the groaning and wailing of mutilated metal.

Were they going after the Sweepers or the star?

Laura swore under her breath as she sprinted to the edge of the platform and slung another Egg. It burst on the mass below but didn't slow it. The majority surged up, though some broke away; they arched over Laura's head like myriad skeletal arms twisting in and around each other. She scrambled for another Egg, but this monster moved much faster. The sounds of Okane's footsteps and the hiss of Bijou were cut off as it swooped around her back, swelling to a solid, slimy wall and curving to isolate her. It had almost completely closed around her when something whistled past Laura's nose. She squeaked and clapped her free hand to her face before casting around for the culprit: a stick embedded in the monster to her right, thin, perfectly straight, and colored like bronze, the end decorated with creamy white feathers. She barely had time to wonder what it was before the blackness around it bulged. Like a rash, bubbles spread across its surface, accompanied by muffled gurgling. The creature squirmed, then burst apart. Out of the bubbles ripped a hail of pale yellow sparks, whose lights sang as they leapt out to infect the rest of the creature. The remnant of the monster slid to the ground, ignoring Laura as it squirmed across the platform in a vain attempt to rid itself of what she finally recognized as an arrow. Where had that come from?

She looked up to the left, scanning for whatever shot it, and spotted movement in one of the enclosed stairways. Another arrow peeked through the latticework, and after a moment, Melody Dearborn shot this one into the fray.

26

THUNDER UNDERGROUND

Okane grabbed Laura and heaved her away as another roaring wave of infestation crashed onto the platform, seething over the place she'd just been.

"Thanks," she breathed. She glanced back at the stairway and saw more movement reaching the walkways. "I think the cavalry is here."

"The what?" Okane sounded baffled as they backed up to avoid the writhing mess in front of them.

"More Sweepers!"

"But—"

He stopped short as the monsters consolidated and grew tendrils to lash at them. Most of these were deflected by the Bijou, but they still had to duck under a flailing limb. Okane spoke again as he armed an Egg and scuttled back.

"But we don't have more Sweepers!"

"The SOS must've gotten to someone!"

The Egg went off at the same time as the second arrow, though the arrow struck an infestation off to the side. The Egg blast chased this one off the platform, sending it and the first sparking arrow into the depths of the interior. The Sweepers on the other side scattered, some going straight on the warped walkways, others taking a more roundabout way by the walls, and within a minute more grenades were glowing and being dropped. Colors in varying shades of yellow and even green-tinged erupted on the mass of monsters. They halted their advance to mill in confusion.

"Helen, Michael, get on those bridges! Joan, cover Melody! Diana, Seamus, with me!" For such a reedy man Joseph Blair had a loud voice, directing the Sweepers behind him, gesturing with a hand that already held a gun; his tone left no doubt that he was the one in charge. More groups split up, spreading the damage.

"Who are these people?" said Okane.

"Puer Sweepers Guild," Laura replied.

The fastest of the other Sweepers reached them: a young woman with short black hair and blue eyes who dashed across the damaged bridges with a staff bumping against her back. All the way over she strung a wire of her own along the railing, and when she stopped she jerked it. The wire came to life with a rattle and glowed gold.

"You doing okay?" she panted, swinging the staff off her back and into her hands.

"I think?"

"You're not dead, that's what counts." The woman bared her teeth in a grin.

A middle-aged man ran up and past them. He breathed hard as he knelt and took a machine off of his own back, hands flying to set it up. He didn't bother to acknowledge them, but Joseph did when he arrived. He shot at the pillar as he passed it but otherwise conserved his ammunition.

"There you are. You had us worried!" There wasn't much time to say anything else, but he added, "I got worried when Mr. Sinclair mentioned multiple infestations, so I gathered a crew and took the train after yours. These two are Diana Kimball and Seamus Benham. They're with the Terrae Sweepers; we ran into them on the way here."

"Where is Sinclair, anyway?" asked Diana, looking around.

"He died a couple of hours ago," said Okane, and she froze.

"Diana," Seamus growled. "You want to mourn, do it later. I don't want to be mourning you, too."

"Right, no time," Joseph agreed. "You two, Laura and—I'm sorry, Money?"

"Okane." He looked offended, and Laura didn't blame him for it.

"Can you circle around to that side? There's another platform like this if I saw correctly. Let's hit it from all directions."

"Sounds good to me." Laura nodded, and Okane copied her motion.

"Let's show this *kaibutsu* why they called this place the Sweeper city." Joseph gave them an encouraging smile, then turned and ran back onto the bridge, into shooting range.

"Here." The next thing Laura knew, Diana was pressing another length of wire into her hands. "This repels the monsters. Run it along the railing so they don't destroy the bridges entirely."

"Okay."

"Go for it." Diana grinned again, though this time it didn't have the same feral quality. "I know Clae didn't teach any pushovers."

She knew Clae, then? Laura smiled back at her before Seamus's machine—a grenade launcher—fired a green-tinted cylinder at the monster pillar. It let out a sharp retort as it did, cutting the conversation short.

"Get going!" he snarled, and Laura didn't need telling twice. She and Okane tore off toward the next walkway.

Greenish grenade light spilled across the bridge as Laura started to lay the wire. It stuck to the railing easily, so she could run without worrying about it falling off. While she concentrated on that, Okane threw another Egg at an incoming monster. Between that Egg and the five Bijou following them, they made it across two bridges and onto the platform Joseph had pointed out. The wire wasn't long enough to reach the whole way, so Laura got it going and left it behind.

By this time the infestation was balking.

The various weapons had agitated the monsters. The bulk swirled fast, churning about in a kind of inky whirlpool with the pillar at the center. They dipped down unexpectedly, sinking two, three levels deeper to simmer and gurgle. But this respite didn't last long. They surged again like a sharpened geyser, ripping what infrastructure had escaped their last assault. The wires on the rails glowed brighter and gave off an electric hum, crackling and casting eerie light that burned away any infestation that grew near, but the infestation didn't seem to care. It swarmed onto unprotected platforms in a massive black swell. Its waves were topped with everything it knew could strike fear into them: bones, warped claws, spidery limbs, cascading tarry skulls with jagged teeth that turned completely inside out. The noise was everything bloodcurdling, a perfect blend of dying animal and fast-incoming footfalls and nails on a chalkboard. Two Sweepers vanished under the assault, and those were just the ones Laura glimpsed. She and Okane used more Eggs to drive off the waves charging for them, and similar flashes could be sighted at other Sweeper locations. Arrows and grenades were still being launched at the pillar.

"Where's Clae's gun when --- need it?" Okane puffed, kicking a Bijou at a slimy black arm—it evaporated almost immediately and the Bijou whistled victoriously. "We're close enough. A gun could hit it."

"Probably on the Third level, still," Laura replied, dodging behind a Bijou's stream of light. "You want to try another Egg?"

Okane scanned the area and shook his head. "There's no railing, and I'm almost out."

"Me too."

Laura hadn't been counting how many Eggs he used, but she knew all she had was one Egg, some more Bijou, and a handful of flash-bomb pellets. She rolled a pellet between her fingers, then decided she might as well try it. They typically went off upon hitting the ground, but she was going to throw them at the monsters and wasn't sure if their sliminess was firm enough. She copied Okane's actions and tossed one through the Bijou's sparks. The pellet caught fire and fell soundlessly until five feet below the platform, and then it went off. These flashes made no noise, but the whiteness could be blinding. Laura didn't get a direct look, but the light danced across the forms of the infestation and prompted alarmed screeching.

"Nice," Okane chuckled, pulling pellets out of his own bag.

They took turns flicking flash bombs over the side. These did absolutely nothing to harm the creatures, not being kin-based, but they did startle and get some attention. Laura threw another bomb, free hand digging in the pockets of the big coat to check if Clae had left any equipment. More Bijou, more wire, packs of bullets. . . . Her fingers closed on something oddly shaped and she pulled it out. The object in her hand looked like a tiny Egg, as long as her thumb and colored pale blue instead of gold inside.

"What's that?" Okane glanced over, more preoccupied with the bombs and the quickly angering infestations near them.

"I don't know. It's *blue*." Laura rolled it between her fingers, but whatever this object was it stayed just as strange. "Should we use it like an Egg?"

"Will it blow up as soon as it touches an amulet?"

"You think I know?"

"It would be a big drawback."

"I don't think it would be in the pocket if it did. I mean, that's kind of close to the amulet and you wouldn't want that happening by accident, right?" Laura eyed it some more, then held it out. "You can throw farther than I can. See if you can hit the pillar."

"I just told ---, no railing!"

"I can tie you down?"

He rolled his eyes and took the blue object. After checking the distance, he ran forward, smacking it against his amulet, and hurled it into the air. Laura lurched forward and grabbed him by the vest. He teetered on the edge of the platform for a moment, but she managed to haul him back, and he stumbled into her with a delayed squeak of terror.

The blue liquid glowed as its container flipped through the air. It rose in an arch, but halfway through its progress it dropped as if pulled by a magnet, and plummeted down into the black.

"Well, that did a lot of good," said Okane.

"It was worth a shot, right?"

Okane stiffened, then threw his left arm around her and pulled her alongside as he scrambled backward, arming another Egg and slinging it down. While they were distracted another monster had scaled the side of the platform to attack. The Egg blew its outstretched arms away easily.

"I'm out of Eggs," he hissed.

"We should've asked them for some more weapons."

For now they could keep going with the flash bombs. Laura dug through her equipment to find them again, but something caught her attention. The middle of the infestation swarm rose abruptly and fell again like a strange, slow hiccup. Faint blue light flickered in the gap. The swarm began to settle, but jerked up again. And again. And *again*. It seethed uncontrollably.

Crack!

Crack-crack-crack!

Portions were thrown free of the swarm, infestations shrieking and vanishing into acrid smoke as more and more blue flashes crackled and the sounds of something shattering became increasingly louder. The infestations at the platforms lost their shape, too startled to focus on frightening them.

"Hell, I think that actually did something," said Laura.

The creatures floundered. Even if they weren't particularly smart, the idea of attack from above and below sparked a new desperation. More tendrils reached up to grab at the star. Arrows, guns, and that grenade launcher slowed this movement but couldn't stop it. Creature after creature curled around the points of the star pattern and clung, issuing smoke as they eclipsed the light and movement of pseudo-kin. The structure creaked as the pillar thinned, then thickened, and a dull moan came from the lower levels. The level of the infestations rose again, but this time they weren't attacking. They were moving. They were using the star as a handhold to heave the base away from the snapping blue lights. They were moving the root amulets; the entire group had become a maverick. But could that star hold up under all the weight? Laura didn't know how much a monster itself weighed, but could it bear a Pit's worth of amulets?

Cursing, Laura slipped out from Okane's grip and pulled out her last Egg. When Bijou crossed her path she kicked them over the side of the platform. The base was coming up fast. She threw the Egg down into it in the vain hope that it would do something to break the monsters apart, lessen the load. It burst but did nothing to slow them. All it did was rattle the platform.

There was another mumbled cuss beside her as Okane stopped to stare. The last two active Bijou skittered behind them. It wasn't as if those could protect them. Laura bit her lip as she dug through her bag and the pockets again, searching for some kind of deus ex machina, but nothing was there. She could see Okane shaking like a leaf, and Clae's instructions to run came to mind. He wasn't running, but then again, where would he run? It was too late, for them, for the city. Everyone else would be forced into the wilds permanently. Morgan's visage wavered in her mind, but she closed her eyes against it. Morgan had lived without her for a long time, and would do so again. This way she had one less drain on the family resources. The Chandlers would survive just fine after she died here.

For a moment, everything went quiet. The infestations were silent. There was no smashing of Sweeper weapons, no screech of twisting platforms or bridges. Above them the pillar shuddered. Eyes opened all along its length. Red irises swirled. The spell was broken as a spot six feet from the fountain burst apart. Pieces of infestation went flying, fizzing away into nothing as whatever was inside blossomed like a great golden firework. A rattling hiss accompanied this as the golden display rained outward and down. With the top clear, Laura could see as the kin in the fountain came to life, roaring, surging over the edge and striking down like a lightning bolt. Wave after wave hurled itself down, sparkling and crackling, and Laura almost swore there *was* lightning spanning the space between droplets.

The first strikes obliterated the pillar entirely. This kin spread out in streaks of blazing gold, smashing and crackling along bridges and walls like a lightning storm. It was deeper yellow than any kin Laura had seen before, and while the liquid they dumped down the Pits made a laughing sound, this was starkly different. With every motion this substance ripped out a scream of outrage, roaring, wild and vicious, so loud it reverberated in Laura's ears and clutched, rattling, at her insides.

With the pillar went the main mass. Even as they squirmed out for the walls, the infestations shrieked in pain and alarm; soon there was so much black smoke it was impossible to see what was going on beyond blazing gold and distorted shadows. Black hands and legs crawled the sides to seek escape. More kin crackled from the top level, moving along the walls and slicing through the creeping infestations like a scythe.

Laura covered her ears and backed away from the edge of the platform. The Bijou hopped and spun erratically, unable to determine whether to follow her amulets or the greater source of magic. Her elbow bumped into Okane, who'd turned his back on the light and cupped his hands over his own ears. They staggered back on the trembling platform, trying to get away from the wild kin. They stopped a foot from the wall and crouched there, facing away from the light as they waited for it to do its job. A few infestations bubbled up with a halfhearted attempt to eat them, but more blazing gold swiped down the wall to smash them away; each time it did, the air burned. Laura glanced back and felt like this view was being seared into her brain. If she lived through this, she'd never forget the sight of that kin. The fountain glowed so bright it must've been a beacon for miles around. It was two in the morning by now, but she didn't think anyone could sleep through the storm inside the city.

Everything shook. The platform quaked so badly she wouldn't be surprised if it fell, and her senses felt overloaded. Too much noise, too much light. She turned her head back around, closed her eyes, and leaned into Okane, because he seemed like the only thing solid in the world.

Somewhere around three, the wailing of the monsters stopped. It had tapered before, but now it was gone completely. The bellowing and booming of the kin grew quieter and vanished as well. Laura stared at the wall, counting seconds as she waited for a sign that it wasn't over. Sixty seconds passed. Sixty-three. Seventy. She stood up, slow and unsteady, and looked around. The kin knew what was going on even if they didn't. Its luster had dimmed, and it didn't change its path anymore. It flowed gently down with a sound more like soft chattering than the previous roar. Dark smoke still twisted through the interior, but there was no more blinding light. Laura hesitantly slid off her goggles.

"Is that it?" she asked.

Her voice sounded strange to her abused ears. Okane heaved a sigh and looked up. He'd had his face buried in his folded arms, and he blinked bemusedly.

"I think so."

"You're not sensing any infestations?"

"No. Seems like it's all gone."

"We made it." Laura laughed. She felt giddy, even though everything sounded like it was underwater. Maybe she was still running on adrenaline, or maybe just realizing it was over.

"We did." Okane stood up. He was shaky, but it was a far cry from the nervous wreck he'd been earlier. "I thought for a moment that we wouldn't."

"You did cut it close." Another man approached them, jamming a bowler hat further down on his head. "That was impressive, Sinclair Sweepers."

Bowler hat. The same one they'd seen with the Sullivan truck, with the bald man; the Mad Dogs negotiator.

"Thanks," Laura said slowly, edging in front of Okane. The man had come alone, but a group of other people in civilian dress were gathered on the bridges behind him; they seemed to be heading toward the staircases, a little too fast to be normal. "You're not Puer Sweepers."

"Just another interested party."

Laura's eyes narrowed. "You're mob Sweepers. The Mad Dogs."

"Guilty," he chuckled. "You can't blame us for avoiding police contact. They'd arrest us as soon as the infestation was taken care of."

"When did you get here?"

"A little after your foreign friends. Puer? Don't worry, we won't get them involved in anything strange. We're going back underground for now. We just wanted to check in and make sure you weren't dead. I trust you're not having difficulty breathing? No itchiness?"

"My ears will need some recovery," Laura grumbled, rubbing at her right ear. "Beyond that, we're in good condition. Why do you care?"

The man's smile was the only thing she could make out under the hat's rim. "By the looks of things, you two got the brunt of the damage from the kin. There's evidence of effects from unprimed kin, smaller weaponized doses . . . but this goes beyond our experiences. Marvelous formula you concocted there. I don't suppose you'd share how that worked?"

"The same as regular kin," Okane said shortly.

"You're a rude one," the man snickered.

"---'re a mobster."

"True. I should get going before your foreign friends get suspicious."

"Wait," said Laura, as he was turning away. "Are you the ex-apprentice? The one from our Sweeper department?"

"Right mob, wrong man. Don't worry, I'm sure you'll make the boss's acquaintance very soon."

He took off at a run, just in time. Diana arrived on the other side of the platform, her staff in hand and ready to swing. She tracked his dash before turning to them.

384 ∽ MIRAH BOLENDER

"Are you all right? He didn't hurt you?"

"Not at all," said Laura. "Did you know who he was?"

"Mobster. I may not have been in Amicae much, but I at least know that. Careful, or they'll cut your Achilles and leave you for dead." Diana closed her eyes and forced herself calm. "By the looks of things, the main issue's resolved. We'll head down and start gathering up the amulets. We can't let those get lost or broken any more, or things could start back up and get even worse. Blair's going to go with you topside, so you can get in contact with whoever's doing all this." She gestured at the falling kin. "Get them to stop it. We don't want your mines flooding too badly, if they aren't already crushed under all that debris."

"You might need boats to fish out all those amulets," said Laura.

"Seamus has always said he wanted to go fishing." Diana spotted movement and waved at it. "There they are. Get going; we've got this."

The people she waved at were the Blairs, both Joseph and Helen. Joseph was putting away his gun, and Helen held another staff. Laura felt a flicker of animosity toward the woman, but Helen did come to help them, so she crushed it as best she could. Now wasn't the time to start a fight.

"Thank you," she said, as sincerely as she could manage, and Diana smiled.

"It's not a problem."

Laura and Okane walked over to the Blairs, and Joseph beamed at them.

"Well done," he said. "Very well done. You're pretty good in a pinch! I don't think half my apprentices could've handled this near as well as you did."

Helen didn't compliment them but she didn't look so stormy as the last time Laura had seen her. She subtly glanced around, and Laura wondered if maybe she was looking for Clae. She shoved her hands into the pockets of Clae's coat and bit her tongue to keep from saying anything.

"We had a good teacher," Okane mumbled, and Joseph's smile grew a little sad.

"Yes. A shame. Really, a shame." Helen frowned at him in confusion but he avoided her eyes. "Well, I'm sure we'll need to talk with whoever's in charge. Where do we find them?"

"First Quarter." Laura pointed up. "The police chief is working on the pumps."

"Of course, police. What's the fastest way to them?"

They located the closest stairway and climbed up, back to the First Quarter. The mobster Sweepers had already been through here; while Laura saw no other sign of them, the door at the top was wide open. The main roads of the First Quarter led inward to the central point, and all they had to do was follow. On the way they met a supply truck, and the driver was happy to speed them back to the main square. A block from the fountain they passed a group of police officers, and Laura recognized Albright in the mix.

"That's her! Stop!" she cried, and the driver hit the brakes.

Albright looked around at the noise and strode briskly toward them. "Are those the Sweepers? Kramer and Sinclair?"

Helen gave a noticeable start but Laura ignored her, calling, "It's us!" and waving from the truck bed. Albright stopped before them, squinting through tired eyes.

"Hello!" Joseph held out one hand while Helen leaned farther back. "I'm Joseph Blair, and this is my wife, Helen. We're Sweepers from Puer. We heard about the problem and came as soon as we could."

"I was told you'd arrived." Albright shook his hand. "Thank you for coming on such short notice, especially from so far."

"We couldn't let our fellow city stand alone."

"The infestation is gone," Okane piped up.

"Then we can stop the water. Baxter! Shut down the pumps, it's over!"

Baxter leaned around a corner to gesture that he'd heard, then vanished again, off to find the pumps and alert the people working.

"I'll go with you to get your supplies," said Albright, climbing into the truck. "We don't want them unattended for long."

They settled in again and the truck drove on. Joseph talked with Albright about the measures they needed to take to recover the amulets and ensure that this wasn't about to happen again. Albright explained the situation with the broken Pit and damaged tree. While the policewoman wasn't an expert on that system, Helen began to chime in with her own experience. Apparently she knew Amicae's system like the back of her hand. While they talked, Laura rubbed at her eyes. She'd been running out of energy since they got out of the interior.

"I'm going to take a really long nap," she mumbled.

"I think I'll do the same," Okane agreed, and she saw he was only in slightly better shape. He yawned. "I wonder how long they'll keep us."

"Not long, I hope."

By the time they arrived, the water in the fountain had stopped refilling. The steam started to fade away, and the glowing of the strains dissipated too. Laura got up and peered over the strains. Yes, all four were present and accounted for. The breeze tugged steam toward them in a slow roll. Okane flinched and stepped away, but Laura stayed put and closed her eyes. It was almost nice to feel a wave of heat, as if it were still August. Still simple. With it came a fainter impression.

It is gone.

See you friend.

Joseph kept talking to Albright about security measures and plans for the next few days. Helen wasn't inclined to talk to anyone, and Okane decided now was a wonderful time to imitate a statue—he only moved when he jerked to keep himself from nodding off. Laura stifled more yawns.

Once the water had significantly cooled, Laura and Okane moved in on the fountain. The fog was completely gone, and while the water eddied, that was from the normal cascading, not the churning of pseudo-kin.

There was a flicker, not like the movement of the water, but different. *See you friend.* Could it be? Had the quilt moved? Laura's heart leapt into her throat. She plunged her hand into the water and lifted the quilt. Clae's crystal winked gold in the glow of the streetlamps. It was still frozen in the same position, the same angry expression. Laura's shoulders slumped. He hadn't moved. It must've been a trick of the light. She squeezed her eyes shut, trying to force down disappointment. Of course he hadn't moved. She should've known that already. She exhaled long, tucked the blanket carefully back over him, and murmured, "You really are a pain."

She turned back and almost jumped out of her skin. Someone was right behind her. Helen stood there, staring down at the fountain and the covered strains. Her wide eyes were fixed on the bundled quilt, color visibly draining from her face. She'd seen him. Laura shifted into a more defensive position. Anselm had gone the same way, so Helen must know what was going on. She could stir up a ruckus, try to steal Clae away and use him in Puer the way his father had used Anselm. *Not this time,* Laura thought fiercely. *Not this one. You have no right.*

"Okane?" she called, not taking her eyes off of the woman. "Could you help me over here?"

Okane stepped around Helen to fuss over Clae's quilt, pulling it tighter to make sure no one else could see. Albright reversed the covered truck up to the fountain again, at a distance now, and climbed out to help load.

"Help me with him first," said Laura.

Okane nodded and grabbed one end, and they heaved Clae up with a grunt. Helen took a step after them but stopped. She watched as they carried first one twin, then the other into the police truck. As they loaded the two Gin as well, Marshall and Freda came to gather their amulets. Marshall made a sound of surprise, reaching down to pluck a fragment from the water.

"Broken," he observed, disappointed and awed.

Laura guiltily shuffled back over. "We ended up putting a lot more strain on them than I'd thought. Are any of them salvageable?"

Marshall climbed into the basin and waded through in search of more. After a while he replied, "Only one variety broke. It's all the Niveus amulets. Strange. Niveus are usually the more hardy, reliable ones. What do you make of it?"

He looked up at Helen, who remained stunned and unblinking.

"You got screwed, Marshall," said Freda. "They must've lied about the material."

"No, they were definitely Niveus. I checked them myself."

A hand tapped Laura's shoulder.

"Albright says we're to go back to the shop," Okane told her. "The other Sweepers will take care of things for now."

"I thought they'd want us on the job."

"You've done more than enough for tonight. Better get some rest now," said Albright. "We'll call you if we run into any trouble, but you removed the main threat. We'll be fine."

Albright gave her officers some more orders, then drove away, leaving the cleanup for the stragglers. She dropped Laura and Okane off at the shop, assisted in unloading the strains again, and advised them to stay near the phone in case she needed them later.

After some awkward conversation, they put all of the strains, Clae included, in the room behind the drapes and went upstairs to sleep. Okane headed to his own room, and Laura went to the one she'd slept in before. It was a grandmother's room, she reflected as she stood in the doorway. Rocking chair, sewing box, old handmade furniture. She wondered why she hadn't guessed it before. She pulled out the bedding from the closet and flopped down on the awful Partch mattress. She couldn't see it in the dark, but if she turned her head she knew she was looking at the carved name in the nightstand. For some reason she found that a comfort, and fell asleep easily.

Five hours later there was a loud noise from downstairs. Laura jolted awake. She was disoriented at first, casting around for the source. It happened again, and her addled mind translated it as the telephone ringing.

Cursing incoherently, she rolled out of bed and shoved the door open. She stumbled down the stairs and into the shop, miraculously not injuring herself. It wasn't the telephone ringing, though. She stared blankly at it before the noise occurred again, and she realized it was someone banging on the door. She must've missed a call from Albright, and the chief had turned up in person. She rushed to unlock and open the door. There was an apology on her tongue, but it never made it out.

Morgan was on the other side. She looked like she hadn't slept at all, and her expression was caught somewhere between fear and relief.

"Laura!" she choked, and she grabbed Laura in a hug that made her wheeze.

"Whoa! Hey, Morgan."

"Thank god you're okay!" Morgan had her head buried so hard in Laura's shoulder she was almost unintelligible. "All the noise, and the light—I was so afraid you were in the middle of it. That you wouldn't make it out."

"Well, I did make it out. Look, I'm in one piece and everything," Laura joked, rubbing her back, and Morgan snorted.

"We came back as soon as they opened the doors again. We've been searching for you all morning."

"You found me. Really, I'm okay," said Laura, holding her tighter.

Over Morgan's shoulder she could see Cheryl standing just outside, clutching her penny doll. The girl seemed baffled by all the fuss, and her eyes darted toward the place where Okane had tottered downstairs. He stood in the doorway behind the counter, wearing a nightshirt and an out-of-it look that was even more confused than Cheryl's.

27

IN THE WAKE

Frank Sullivan was arrested.

A cartoon accompanied the article in the Amicae *Sun,* showing him in handcuffs being carted off to jail, saying something about "all for the humanitarian cause," while three caricatures of schools wept and a grubby Fifth Quarter child cheered. The article itself (coincidentally written by one Annabelle Kilborn) went on about who he was, why he was important, and went into detail to say how it was completely his fault that Amicae had been in danger. He claimed he'd had nothing to do with it, that a mold for his business logo had gone missing months ago, but that hardly mattered. The story of his defeat took up the entire front page.

It was the big news floating around the city: the fall of a prominent businessman. Laura was sure that, at some point before the sensation died down, people would start to speak out about how badly he'd treated people, the fates of those he'd led into the Mad Dogs' hands. Maybe they'd dig up what really happened to Mary. Okane might come forward, but he didn't seem willing to talk about those scars anymore, so probably not. In any case the man was incarcerated, his son and company publicly disgraced.

The rest of the paper gave mention to the police and a certain student of the university, who heroically assisted the Sweepers in destroying monsters with "the wrath of god," a term many people had come to call the veritable lightning storm of kin. More and more articles abounded with talk of the cause and damage of the monsters. The more details came to light, the more people panicked. It was clear from the articles that this wasn't a mob-planted mishap. No, this was a natural event, and the walls hadn't prevented it. The Council tried to argue by radio and by paper, but between Annabelle's interviews of the foreign Sweepers and prodding at old reports, and another paper—*The Dead Ringer*, suspected to be a front of the mobs—publishing graphic evidence from those same reports, their credibility was ruined. Police raids were staged. There was an actual shoot-out between police and mobsters outside the *Sun*'s offices. Both peaceful and armed rallies erupted all over Amicae, demanding the truth. After seven days of absolute chaos, the Council relented. Victoria Douglas took to the radio. The police commissioned a large ad in every paper, warning people about improper use of amulets and the dangers of infestations.

Somewhere in that paper was a long list of people claimed by the infestation. Laura didn't read all the way through it—she didn't want to think about all those lost people she never even knew—but she read enough to see Clae Sinclair listed at the top. In all honesty that was the main reason she'd put it down. A week and a half later, Clae was still lying next to Anselm in that room beyond the drapes. Laura and Okane weren't sure what to do with him, or even if anything could be done. If nothing Clae ever tried managed to revert Anselm, they were out of luck when it came to either of the brothers. They seemed to be doomed to eternity as living stones.

Laura was having some trouble after the fact, thinking of how they essentially exploited some corpses to flush out the infestation. She didn't like the idea of incorporating Clae into the kin production, no matter how much stronger his strain made it. He didn't belong there. He wasn't a tool. It was wrong.

The few infestations that had escaped the interior were hunted down by the Puer and Terrae Sweepers. These were the only ones who got to Amicae to help, but they weren't lacking in numbers. The head Sweeper of Terrae herself arrived a day late, bringing some of her best workers with her. Laura's short encounter with them left her with a much more favorable impression than the extras in Puer. On the downside, the Terrae Sweepers were very businesslike and eager to get this done with. They mostly stuck around the police, harassing Albright for more orders until they got the all clear and left. That was kind of a blessing too, though: they hadn't asked about that "wrath of god" at all. The Puer Sweepers lingered longer. Joseph Blair took a large part in the Sweeper efforts. Other Sweepers came to the shop, but they seemed to be there less for conversation and much more for protection. At that point the riots were still in full swing, and people were clamoring at the door with questions that Laura wasn't yet sure how to answer. What would the Council's decision be? Would talking now endanger her family? Was it all right to talk? Were these people even rational enough to listen? She'd rather have run home to hide in her apartment, but that wasn't an option. She couldn't leave Okane to deal with it on his own—he looked like he'd have a heart attack every time someone opened the door—and someone had to make sure the drapes were secure. She wasn't as good a guard as Clae, but she could do something.

During that time Melody was their main guard, standing by the door to monitor who came in and out. She talked to them in a slow, deep voice about how her bow and arrows worked, the grenade launcher, other assorted equipment, all while people outside kept shouting and shadows wavered beyond the closed blinds.

Strangely, Helen was the one who came to their rescue. She'd arrived on the day after the *Sun* shoot-out to report something. For a moment she'd stood on the doorstep, looking into the shop with a blank face as the crowd wailed outside.

"Come in or leave," said Melody. "I can't defend an open door so easily."

Helen had turned, stepped into the crowd, and brought her staff down on the pavement with a deafening crack and flare of yellow magic.

"My name is Helen Blair." Her voice cut sharply through the din. "I was once a Sweeper of Amicae. Now I'm a citizen of Puer, and your Council cannot touch me!"

She answered the questions Laura had been afraid to. Laura crept over to peer through the blinds, and Melody watched through the panes in the door.

"I never really expected her to help," Laura admitted.

"Helen is a complex mixture of duty and spite," said Melody. "Duty usually takes precedence. I think she's the best person to address this, having the perspective she does. She'll break it to them, but it won't be gently."

Laura gave a sad smile. "Clae would've killed to be able to do this."

A pause, and Melody chuckled. "He took after her that way, I suppose. By the way, the message she came to deliver was good. It seems your tree is sprouting again. Your barrier system will continue to hold."

Diana and Seamus turned up after the crowds, but they were only inside for five minutes before Diana claimed she had something to do and hurried out, hand to her mouth, while Seamus muttered something about not getting so attached to other Sweepers.

Otherwise, the city was settling. Not into normalcy; their idea of normalcy and safety had fled and would never return. This was a new Amicae, the same core as the old but wrapped in something terrifyingly new. Newspapers called it an age of truth. Personally Laura thought it was an age of confusion. People were still looking over their shoulders, but they were getting back to business. Shops and restaurants reopened. Workers swarmed in to repair the interior. Laura and Okane took care of Pit rounds. The routine was picking up again, but Laura didn't think it would ever be so natural as it was before. She felt like she'd lost something integral. It helped that Okane was connected and struggling through the same loss. Still, it was strange to enter the shop and not see Clae fussing over something. Half the time Laura expected him to emerge from behind the drapes as if nothing had happened, but of course he never did. The very thought made her feel hollow and small. Morgan had been very supportive in her grieving. More than that, though, she'd found herself feeling a little better when reading that ratty journal she found in the room with the Gin. It had originally belonged to Clae's father, and was passed down to him when the man died. It was more of a diary than anything, and the entries could be short and abrupt, but old man Sinclair liked to complain about his children, and Clae's personality was very present in the latter parts. It helped a bit, but it still hurt. It had taken up a permanent residence beside her Coronae book and postcard of Gustave's Moon.

Laura had these in her bag now, a week and a half later, on the way to the Averills' restaurant. There was a gathering tonight in honor of Clae. They wouldn't be having a funeral; with infestations involved there wasn't supposed to be a body, so there was nothing to send off for cremation. Coffins and funerals were out of the question. Instead they were throwing a kind of memorial potluck.

Laura arrived at the restaurant at four with Morgan and Cheryl. As they walked through the door, Laura held it open so Morgan could get through: she'd brought her newest version of chicken soufflé.

The restaurant was crowded, all the people inside being friends or acquaintances of Clae's. Dan Averill laughed at Brecht, who hunched over a glass of alcohol and slurred badly. Peggy and the Keedlers fussed over the tables that had been pushed together for the various foods; despite other contributions, pasta dishes from the restaurant took up the majority. Freda sat in a corner, smoking like a chimney and looking at the paintings on the ceiling, while Marshall debated with a one-eared woman the proper way to use amulets. A short man wandered around with a fizzy drink, making snide comments about everyone's clothing until he came across Okane and approved of his vest ("I made it, of course it's top quality"). The only other Sweepers left at this point were Joseph and Diana. Joseph was nursing a drink of his own as he surveyed the room, while Diana had fallen into that mourning Seamus had been so worried about. Her eyes were red-rimmed, and she looked around with a watery smile that fooled very few people. A lot of others Laura didn't recognize at all, but they acted as if they were right at home here.

"That boss of yours had a lot of friends, didn't he?" said Morgan.

"I never knew this many people could stand him."

"Surprising man, I suppose."

"You're finally here!" Mrs. Keedler descended on them. "How are you doing, Laura?"

"I'm okay, I suppose. It's been hard to adapt with the city as it is, but I'll learn to live with it. Oh, this is my aunt, Morgan. Morgan, this is Mrs. Keedler. She runs the bakery."

Both women began to blurt things at each other ("You're Laura's family? It's so good to meet you at last, you've raised a wonderful girl—" "Laura's talked about you! Thank you for looking after her, and you are such a talented baker—") but it sounded like positive things and Laura was sure they'd get along. Mrs. Keedler insisted on helping Morgan carry the soufflé over to the tables, Cheryl trailing behind in hope of cookies.

"It's a bit lackluster," Joseph chuckled, from a few feet away. "Then again, Clae Sinclair wasn't exactly a lustrous person."

He was now, but as far as Laura could tell Helen was keeping her lips sealed about that. Speaking of which . . . "Is Helen here?"

"No! No. She's been . . . well. It's been very difficult for her. She's lost both of them now, and she and Clae weren't on very good terms to begin with. She said something about feeling like she would be intruding. Like he wouldn't want her here anyway." He fidgeted with his glass.

"I suppose," Laura mumbled.

She didn't think resentment had leaked into her tone, but Joseph grew flustered and rushed to his wife's defense. "I—Well, you do know about their background, I assume. At the least you get the basic idea, anyway. She's not a bad woman, Helen. She never meant to hurt Clae that way. She didn't even intend to leave, it just happened. Not to say I'm condoning what she did at all, but she was in a very fragile state, very afraid, and wasn't in her right mind. By the time she realized what she'd done, the damage was dealt and she was too afraid to reach out to him again, so it kept getting worse and worse over time." He took a loud sip of his drink and fidgeted some more. "She was always so afraid of this, you know. One of the reasons she was scared enough to leave was because she couldn't stand to see her other son die."

Helen's stunned expression at the sight of Clae's crystal flickered to mind, and Laura felt a stab of guilt.

"She went back on the train this morning, with Melody. Neither of them were comfortable saying good-bye like this, among strangers. They wish you well, even if they couldn't say so themselves. I'll be leaving myself, tomorrow. Can't leave Puer without a head Sweeper for long."

"What do you think we should be doing here?" Laura asked, seizing on the change in subject. "How do we get a new head Sweeper?"

"I've talked with your council about it. Told them all about how well you two did in the middle of that infestation. They seemed very pleased . . . pleased enough for me to convince them that you don't need that 'apprentice' title. You're both fully fledged Sweepers now, and you, Ms. Kramer, will be promoted to the head Sweeper position. It's not exactly in line with city requirements since you haven't been around for a full year yet, but you have definite talent. That requirement is really in place to be sure that the candidate has experience and skill, and you have that. You showed it well enough during this disaster. I'm sure Mr. Sinclair would've wanted it this way. Besides." His mouth quirked in bashful humor. "It's not like they have a lot of other options clamoring at the door! But I don't want you to feel overwhelmed by this title! If you run into any trouble please feel free to contact us in Puer and we'll be happy to give you advice. I actually petitioned to send one of our Sweepers over to join you. Lessen the load, as it were. If we get the Council's approval for that, she'll be bringing a load of new equipment for you as well. Things to carry your equipment, weapons, et cetera. I don't know how Mr. Sinclair managed with a briefcase of all things, but I think we'll make it a little easier on you."

"I—Me? I mean, that would be wonderful! That's really, really generous, thank you."

"Don't thank me! Just keep up the good work. You're doing marvelously for only having worked this long."

Laura beamed. Someone shuffled between them to inspect the food, and Joseph was soon distracted. Laura rounded Diana's table and walked up to Okane. He was intent on the drink he was holding, so she tried to make her presence known in the least startling tone she could.

"So, how have you been holding up?"

Okane looked up from his glass and blinked as if he'd only just now noticed she'd walked in. "Oh . . . I'm doing all right. It's very quiet when ---'re not in the shop, though."

"Maybe you can ask Mr. Brecht if you can borrow his phonograph."

Okane's lips twitched toward a smile, but he hid it by taking a sip of his drink. "I've heard enough of his records to last a lifetime. Maybe I'll buy a radio."

"Hey, Laura!"

Laura looked around at the shout. Peggy stood on her tiptoes and waved to be seen over the other people.

"What do you want to drink?"

"Cocoal, please!" Laura called back.

Peggy gave her the thumbs-up and disappeared.

"She's very intent on serving drinks," said Okane.

Peggy fought her way through the crowd and presented Laura with a large glass of the sweet drink. Laura took it, careful not to spill any as it was dangerously full. Once she had a good hold on it, Peggy turned to the crowd and raised her own glass.

"Okay, everyone!" she cried, and they all turned to look. "Here's to Clae Sinclair, Sweeper extraordinaire! The man who should've just eaten our lasagna!"

There was a smattering of laughter, during which Laura snorted ungracefully, and the others raised their glasses before taking a drink.

That seemed the cue for everyone to go get dinner from the tables. The crowd filtered into a line and moved from dish to dish, filling their plates with whatever caught their eye. As Laura went through with her own plate, she saw pictures spaced between the dishes, along the wall so as not to get damaged. There were photographs of two identical children with a dark-haired old woman, a disgruntled Clae in his teenaged years, a blurry one where Clae seemed to be trying to avoid the camera altogether, and another that Laura actually recognized. That last one was taken maybe a week after Okane was brought in, and it was of the three of them in a photography studio with a dark backdrop. Laura remembered sitting for that photograph and being immensely annoyed with the photographer's perfectionist approach to lighting and exposure. The memory made her smile.

She went back to the place she'd been standing with Okane. He joined her once he got his food, Cheryl on his heels. They took a seat at a nearby table to eat.

"Are those all cookies?" Laura eyed Cheryl's plate.

"I got carrots, too." Cheryl lifted the cookies to reveal some carrots from a stew. Just the carrots.

"At least have something with the carrots." Laura scowled.

She picked up a spoonful of her own food and moved to dump it on her plate, but Cheryl quickly pulled it away. Laura rolled her eyes. Okane watched this exchange with guarded interest. Once Cheryl busied herself with the cookies, he looked up at Laura.

"How much do --- think will change?"

"Beyond everything?" Laura chewed slowly as she contemplated an answer. "I get to be head Sweeper now."

"I figured as much."

"You sound confident."

"Don't I?" He blinked owlishly at her. "It's not supposed to be bad. I think ---'ll do good. It's just—Can I still stay in the house?"

"Of course! What do you think I am, heartless? I'm not about to kick you out on the street! Besides, I'm sure Clae willed the place to you. The building was his, after all. But maybe you can keep the . . . uh . . . *you know* in the house. Joseph is trying to send us some backup and I don't think they'll go over well with any new employees."

Crystallized people probably wouldn't go over well with *anyone*, which was why just the two of them and Albright were privy to the secret.

"I can be your new employee," Cheryl mumbled through a mouthful of cookies.

"Keep dreaming," Laura scoffed.

"Excuse me."

They looked up. Diana stood there, holding her own plate of food. She'd regained some of the feral aspect she had before, but still seemed fragile. She dug in the pocket of her bag and pulled out an envelope. She held this out to Laura. "Here. Before I forget."

Confused, Laura took it. The envelope was thick but old. Its material had started to discolor and the surface was soft with wear. On the front was a series of names, all crossed out. Only the initials "L.K." remained unblemished. The envelope was sealed.

"It's something Clae entrusted to me," said Diana. "He said if something were to happen to him, then I had to get this to the right person. It's been a while since we last talked, but your name was the last one he gave me for it."

Laura's mind blanked. He'd left her something? She thought he trusted her, but seeing proof like this . . . She turned the envelope over again in shaky hands, squeezing the paper in hopes that would reveal what was inside. As far as she could tell there was a small object, nothing else. She frowned at Diana in confusion, to which the woman shrugged.

"I never knew what was in it."

"Open it," Cheryl squeaked.

"You're sure?"

"Go ahead." Diana gestured for her to go on.

After a moment more of hesitation, Laura fit her finger under the flap and tore the envelope open. She dug around, then pulled out the object. It was a strangely shaped thing, the size of a large key but with a stubby handle. One end jutted out only to wrap itself back in a sharply angled swirl, the other end decorated with a small tassel. Laura squinted at it, then held it up, wordlessly asking for an explanation. Diana was just as perplexed as she was.

"What is that?"

Okane leaned forward, reaching out one tentative hand. Laura let him take it and watched as he tilted the object so the tassel swayed.

"I don't know. Clae never said anything to you about it?"

Diana shook her head. "No, he just gave me the envelope and said it absolutely had to go to the right person, and never to lose it. I wasn't even thinking I was bringing it to you. I was coming to Amicae to return it to him. That . . . well, that obviously didn't happen."

Okane held the object in one hand, eyed it with furrowed brows, then announced, "It's a key."

"A key?" Laura couldn't see how that could possibly function as a key.

"I've seen one like this before. It was a lot bigger, though. And red. Something from my childhood," he mused, before returning it.

"How does it work?"

"I don't know. I just know it was called a key."

"But what does it go to? Where's the lock?"

He shrugged.

"Well, you have it," said Diana. "That's all I had. I'm just going to . . . you know . . . go eat."

"Right. Thank you," Laura replied, though as soon as the first word was out of her mouth, Diana began to leave. "I don't think she's very comfortable around us."

"Maybe we're finally succeeding in being pains?"

"It's better to be a pain than a comfort?" Laura sniggered. "I wonder how Puer Sweepers would react to that motto?"

They chuckled while Cheryl took the key and examined it with an exaggerated pout.

"Whoever joins us, we'll manage," Okane mumbled, nodding to himself.

"We'll just stick together, right?" Laura beamed.

Okane appeared uncomfortable looking at her smile, and glanced off to the side as he grumbled something in the affirmative.

The chatter and clinking of silverware went on, echoing through the room. It seemed the restaurant was overflowing with noise and people, save for one empty table. Here Clae's coat had been thrown over the back of a chair, while the metal briefcase rested by its legs. A single glass of water sat on the table before them, as if waiting for their owner to storm through the door as he had countless times in the past. No one acknowledged it.